Virginia Andrews is a worldwide bestselling author. Her much-loved novels include SECRETS OF THE MORNING, TWILIGHT'S CHILD, DARKEST HOUR and DAWN. Virginia Andrews' novels have sold more than eighty million copies and have been translated into twenty-two foreign languages.

Virginia Andrews® Books

VIRGINIA®
ANDREWS

Twilight's Child

POCKET
BOOKS

LONDON · SYDNEY · NEW YORK · TOKYO · SINGAPORE · TORONTO

First published in Great Britain by Simon and Schuster UK Ltd, 1992
This edition published by Pocket Books, 2002
An imprint of Simon & Schuster UK Ltd
A Viacom Company

3 5 7 9 10 8 6 4 2

Simon & Schuster UK Ltd
Africa House
64–78 Kingsway
London WC2B 6AH

www.simonsays.co.uk

Simon & Schuster Australia
Sydney

A CIP catalogue record for this book is available from the
British Library

ISBN 0-7434-4025-0

Printed and bound in Great Britain by
Bookmarque Ltd, Croydon, Surrey

Twilight's Child

Part One

The Battle for Christie

The Virginia countryside flew by as Jimmy and I drove toward Saddle Creek, a suburb of Richmond. My heart was pounding in anticipation because the road signs announced that we were drawing closer and closer to our destination. Soon I would be holding my baby in my arms. I had barely had a chance to look at Christie when I gave birth to her at The Meadows, for soon after she was born she was taken away from me. It was the last in a series of horrible things Grandmother Cutler had done to me before she had died, bitter and broken, hating me right up until the end for reasons I didn't come to understand until the reading of the wills.

"It won't be much longer now," Jimmy said, smiling at me. He was almost as excited about my retrieving Christie as I was. I was so happy that Jimmy was willing to consider Christie his own.

While Jimmy had been in the army and away in Europe I had fallen in love with Michael Sutton, my vocal teacher at the Sarah Bernhardt School of Performing Arts. But rather than being disappointed in me for not waiting for his return, Jimmy had told me he understood how I had fallen under Michael's spell. As soon as he had learned that I had become pregnant and that Michael had deserted me, Jimmy came searching for me and rescued me from the clutches of horrid Emily Booth, Grandmother Cutler's older sister. He was truly my hero, whisking me out of that strange plantation house where I had been sent to have my baby in secret. Jimmy arrived shortly after Christie had been born. And when we found out what Grandmother Cutler had arranged – the immediate giving away of my child – we both vowed that we wouldn't rest until I had her back in my arms again.

But joyful anticipation wasn't the only thing that made my heart pitter-patter so fast it made me dizzy. I couldn't help but be overwhelmed by the quick sequence of events that had literally changed my life and determined my future. Two wills had been read after Grandmother Cutler's death: hers and a secret letter and will left by the man I had once thought to be my grandfather and now knew had been my father. To repent for what he had considered the sin of my birth, he left me a majority interest in the family hotel. For all practical purposes, I was suddenly the true owner of Cutler's Cove.

But did I want to be, and perhaps even more importantly, could I be? I could still hear my half-sister Clara Sue screaming at me just before we set out to retrieve Christie. Her shock and envy had been fueled by the jealousy she had always held against me.

"You couldn't fill Grandmother's shoes!" she cried, twisting her mouth, her hands on her hips. "You'll be the laughingstock of the Virginia shore. If Grandmother was alive, she would die laughing."

Clara Sue's words taunted me. It was almost as if the stern, vicious old woman were speaking through Clara Sue and smirking skeptically. I felt the challenge,

4

but I also feared what inheriting the hotel and all the responsibility would do to my dreams of becoming a singer. Then again, I thought, perhaps all those dreams had died the day Michael deserted me. Maybe I wasn't meant to dwell in the show business world after all. Maybe everything that had happened had happened for the best.

Jimmy seemed to think so. All during our trip today he had been making plans and promises.

"As soon as I'm discharged from the army, we'll get married," he pledged.

"And live at the hotel with my crazy family?" I asked.

"They don't bother me. Besides, you're the real boss now, Dawn. I'll become the maintenance manager. I've learned a lot about motors and electricity and engines . . ."

"I don't know if I can do it, Jimmy. It frightens me thinking about it," I confessed.

"Nonsense. Mr. Updike, the family attorney, said he would help you, and Mr. Dorfman, the hotel's comptroller, promised to do everything he could, too. No one expects you to bear all that responsibility immediately. Cutler's Cove will become your new school," he said, laughing. "And as soon as I'm discharged I'll be there at your side, always," he promised, and he squeezed my hand.

I believed him. He was at my side now, when I needed him the most, wasn't he? And I was tired of the lies and the deceit and the pain. I wanted my life with Jimmy and Christie to begin on a happy note, and the prospect of holding Christie in my arms promised to bring just that: music of joy, blissful, sweet, hopeful.

5

But promises, like rainbows, usually come only after storms, and this was to be no different.

When Grandmother Cutler had died unexpectedly, we feared we might never find Christie. However, Mr. Updike had been involved and knew of her whereabouts. Before we had left Cutler's Cove he had told us the couple who had Christie, Sanford and Patricia Compton, were expecting us and were fully aware of the situation. However, we found a different reality when we went calling on them.

Saddle Creek was a prim and proper suburb of Richmond where the homes looked like dollhouses, everything perfect – the lawns fresh and green, the magnolias, roses and petunias bright and colorful. The bright late-summer day, with its fluffy white clouds pasted here and there on the soft blue sky, made it seem as if we had entered a make-believe world. Everything was clean and freshly painted. For a moment I remember thinking that maybe Christie was better off here after all. It was certainly a happier world than the one to which I would bring her.

But then I recalled how painful it had been for me to learn about my real family. Nothing – not even wealth and high position – was worth more than the truth when it came to who you were and where you belonged. That was a lesson I had to learn at the end of a trail of pain and suffering. I was determined that my daughter would never face such a fate.

A kind policeman sitting in a patrol car on a corner gave us exact directions to the Comptons' house. Sanford Compton owned and operated the biggest business in the area, a linen factory. The Comptons' home was one of the prettiest and largest houses on the street: a two-story, red-brick colonial with a set of triple windows on each side of the first floor front.

After we parked we got out and walked in between two square white posts crowned with brass balls and then started up a slate walkway. On both sides were waist-high hedges. There were fountains with cupids in them and fountains with marble birds, the water streaming out of their beaks. Everywhere we looked we saw beds of roses: yellow, red, pink and white. I had never seen such perfect lawns and hedges.

"Is this a home or a museum?" Jimmy wondered aloud.

"A home like the one I hope we will live in one day," I said wistfully.

"Home? I thought we decided we're going to live in the hotel," Jimmy reminded me.

"Yes, but someday we'll build a house like this and live off the hotel grounds," I promised. "Wouldn't you rather we did that?"

"Sure. Why not?" Jimmy said, smiling, his dark eyes twinkling with mischief. "I'll start building it myself."

We both laughed. We couldn't have been in better spirits. In moments I would have Christie again.

The door chimes seemed to go on forever and ever, playing what sounded like the Nutcracker Suite.

"That beats any old ding-dong," Jimmy said. Finally the tall, light-oak door was opened by a butler, a thin black man.

"My name is Dawn Cutler," I said. "And this is Jimmy Longchamp. We're here to see Mr. or Mrs. Compton."

7

"That's all right, Frazer," we heard a deep male voice say. "I'll handle this."

The butler stepped back, his eyes wide with surprise, as a tall man with short carrot-red hair appeared from behind. His face was speckled with freckles, and he looked out at us with ice-blue eyes. His nose was quite thin and a bit too long, which caused his eyes to look as if they sank deeper. Although he was easily over six feet two or three, his shoulders turned in and downward, making him appear shorter.

He seized the door handle to pull it open farther with an abruptness that made Jimmy and I look quickly at each other.

"You're Lillian Cutler's grandchild?" he snapped at me.

"Yes, I am," I said.

He stared at me for a moment and nodded softly. "Well, come in, and we'll make this fast," he said, stepping back with a show of reluctance.

A ripple of apprehension shot down my spine. I reached for Jimmy's hand, and we walked into the marble-floor entryway. The house had a perfumed, flowery scent, redolent of dozens and dozens of roses. We looked down the corridor and saw a slightly curved stairway with paintings all along the wall going up. Just about all the paintings were of children – some simply portraits, while others were pictures of children at play or children reading. The steps of the stairway were covered with a soft-looking blue velvet carpet.

"Into the sitting room, please," Mr. Compton said in a tone of command, and he gestured toward the doorway on the right. Jimmy and I moved quickly to it.

At first neither of us saw Patricia Compton sitting

8

there. She was perfectly still and wore a white cotton dress that matched the silk drapes over the window behind her so that she blended into the room. All of the furniture was done in light-colored silk. To our right was a curio case at least eight feet tall containing dozens of precious figurines: glass figures of animals, hand-painted Chinese men and women, and hand-painted figures of children with mothers or with animals.

Because the room looked so immaculate and so unused, both Jimmy and I hesitated to step in. It was like entering a pretty painting. Then I saw Patricia sitting there on the sofa, her dark eyes wide, her long, thin mouth drooping at the corners. She looked like a sad clown at the circus.

"Go on in and sit down," Sanford Compton ordered as he walked in past us and took a seat in one of the wing-back chairs, crossing his long legs. Jimmy and I moved toward the settee. "This is my wife Patricia," Sanford said, barely nodding toward her. A tiny smile came and went on pale lips that seemed to have forgotten how to smile. She said nothing, not even mouthing a hello.

"Hello," I said, and I smiled. Mrs. Compton did not take her eyes off us, eyes that resembled dark pools in a forest, deep, melancholy eyes, wells for tears. Her entire face looked like a nest for sadness. She was very slim, fragile and delicate-looking. I saw that she had long, lean fingers. She kept her hands clasped tightly together in her lap and sat with her back so straight it seemed she was on an invisible hanger. She swallowed nervously, her gaze glued on us.

She had very light blond hair, so light it was

nearly white, I thought, and it was pinned up softly.

"We've come for my daughter Christie," I said quickly. I came right to the point in order to break the ice. The moment I mentioned "my daughter," Mrs. Compton moaned, her right hand lifting and fluttering to the base of her neck.

"Easy," Sanford Compton said without turning to her. His eyes were fixed firmly on Jimmy and me.

"This is quite outrageous," he finally said.

"Pardon?" I looked at Jimmy, who sat up firmly, his shoulders back in military posture. "Mr. Updike spoke to you, didn't he?"

"We received a phone call from your grandmother's attorney, yes," Sanford Compton replied. "Why didn't your grandmother call us herself?" he demanded.

"My grandmother passed away. Unexpectedly," I added.

"Oh, dear," Mrs. Compton said. With her left hand she brought a lace handkerchief to her eyes. She had been clutching it so tightly in her hands, I hadn't seen it before.

"Don't start," Sanford Compton snapped under his breath. Patricia Compton stifled her sob by pressing her lips in and holding her breath. Her fragile shoulders lifted and fell, but she kept her back straight, her small bosom barely outlined in the bodice of her dress.

"Now, then," Sanford continued, "we went through all the legal procedures. We signed papers, and signed papers were given to us. We did nothing wrong; everything we did was on the up and up."

"I understand that, sir," I said. My heart had begun to thump against my chest, shortening my

10

breath. "But Mr. Updike must have explained the circumstances."

"We understood the baby was born out of wedlock," he quickly responded, a clear tone of accusation in his voice. "And it was an embarrassment to the Cutler family."

"She wasn't an embarrassment to me," I shot back. "Only to my grandmother."

"What's the difference?" Jimmy piped up. "It's her baby," he added, his hands out, palms turned up.

"Whose baby it is remains to be seen," Sanford Compton replied.

"What?" My mouth gaped open, and I sat forward. "You mean you don't have Christie ready for us to take home?"

"Christie's name has been changed to Violet. She's been named after my mother, and Violet," he said, punctuating the name sharply, "*is* home."

"Oh, no," I cried, turning to Jimmy. This couldn't be happening! I couldn't lose Christie. Not again! Especially not after finally finding her!

"Wait a minute," Jimmy said in a controlled voice. "Are you telling us that you won't give Dawn her baby back?"

"We did what we were supposed to do legally. Babies are not toys," Sanford Compton lectured. "They're not things you give and take back, things you exchange lightly. Violet has a home here now, a home in which she is loved and cherished, a home in which she will grow happily and have all the best things life has to offer. You can't cast her off one day and reel her in the next like some fish you throw back into the water."

"But I didn't throw her back into the water!" I

11

exclaimed. "My grandmother stole my baby and forged my signature on documents. Didn't Mr. Updike make that clear?" I cried out in dismay.

"All Mr. Updike said was minds have changed; you want the baby back. I have been in contact with my lawyers, and they have advised me I have a legal position. I intend to enforce it."

His words sent shivers down my spine. I felt as if someone had thrown a pail of ice water over me – a legal battle? For my own baby? Grandmother Cutler's revenge continued even after her death. She was still controlling my life and happiness, even from her grave.

"Look," Jimmy said, still trying to quiet his temper, "you're making a big mistake here. Maybe you don't understand what happened. Dawn never agreed to – "

"We were offered an infant that a mother didn't want," Sanford interrupted. "My wife and I have been trying to have our own child for years now. While we want a child desperately, other people," he said, spitting his words in my direction, "have them in a very cavalier manner and then want to get rid of them. Well, we didn't question all the details; we accepted the conditions, signed papers and were given the child.

"Now you come here and want to undo all that has been done. Some time has passed. We love Violet, and, as unlikely as it might seem to you, Violet has taken to us, especially to my wife. You can't play with people like you play with dolls."

"That's not fair, Mr. Compton!" I exclaimed.

"That's stupid," Jimmy snapped back.

"Jimmy!"

"No, he has no right to talk to us this way. He doesn't know anything," Jimmy sneered.

"I know we're not turning the baby over to you," Sanford Compton said, standing up abruptly, "and I know I would like you two to leave my house immediately."

"You can't keep her baby!" Jimmy shouted, rising to his feet.

"I told you," Sanford Compton said calmly, "it's not her baby anymore. Violet is our baby."

"Like hell she is," Jimmy flared. "Come on, Dawn. We'll go to the police. These people are stealing your baby."

"Oh, dear," Mrs. Compton said, and this time she could not hold back her sobs.

"Now look what you've done – you've upset my wife. I must insist you leave, or I will be the one to call the police."

"Don't worry about it," Jimmy said, reaching for my hand. "We'll see the police, and we'll be back. All you're doing is making unnecessary trouble for everyone."

The butler appeared in the doorway as if Sanford Compton had pushed an invisible button calling for him.

"Frazer, see these people out, please."

I looked at Mrs. Compton before leaving.

"I'm sorry," I said to her, "but I never agreed to the giving away of my baby. It's not my fault. I didn't intend for this to happen."

Patricia Compton began to sob harder.

"Please leave," Sanford commanded.

Jimmy and I walked out. The butler stepped back

and then moved forward to open the front door for us.

"Damn stupid people," Jimmy muttered loud enough for them to hear.

We stepped back into the sunlight, only to me the day had turned pale gray. It might as well be raining, I thought. Would nothing be easy for me, ever? Mistakes haunted me like ghosts. I had begun to believe that because I was a child born from evil I would be cursed forever. The sins of the fathers do rest on the heads of their children. I couldn't keep my own tears back, and before we had left the portico I was sobbing hysterically. Jimmy embraced me quickly and kissed my cheek.

"Hey, don't cry. Don't worry. This isn't going to be hard," he promised.

"Oh, Jimmy, don't you see that everything's going to be hard? I don't know why you would want to marry me. You're only going to suffer along with me. I'm cursed, cursed!"

"Come on, Dawn. Take it easy. It's not you; it's what that evil old lady did. Well, we'll just see it undone. That guy's stupid and asking for trouble."

"I can't blame these people, Jimmy. He wasn't all wrong. And did you see the expression on that woman's face? She finally got a baby she could call her own, and we're here to take it away," I moaned.

"But you want to, don't you? You want Christie back?" Jimmy asked.

"Yes, of course I do. I just can't stand all this pain and suffering. Why was one old woman given so much power to hurt other people?" I cried.

"I don't know. She did it, and it's over with. Now

14

we've got to make it right. I guess we'll go to the police first," he said.

"No, we had better check into a hotel someplace close by and call Mr. Updike. The police can't help us. Sanford Compton is right – it's going to be a legal battle."

I looked back at the house once, trying to imagine which room Christie was in. I was sure they had bought her the finest crib and the most expensive baby clothes. Just a baby, she didn't know where she was or what had happened to her. She was probably as content as she could possibly be. In a short while I would disturb that contentment; but I had to believe that even an infant as young as Christie would sense her own mother when she was finally placed in my arms, and that would give her a deeper, more complete sense of security and love. Armed with that faith, I hurried off with Jimmy to begin our battle for custody of my own child.

We checked into a small hotel just outside of Richmond. It was a restored old mansion, and the rooms were quiet, large and comfortable, but we were not able to enjoy anything. Our time here was to be filled with waiting for phone calls and preparation for a hearing.

When I phoned Mr. Updike I was surprised at his reaction.

"Maybe it would be wiser just to leave things be," he suggested. "The baby's in a very good home and will be very well taken care of. Sanford Compton is wealthy and powerful i n his community."

"I don't care how wealthy he is, Mr. Updike. Christie is my baby, and I want her back," I said sharply. "I

15

thought you had explained it all to the Comptons," I continued, not disguising my annoyance. If he intended to continue as the family's attorney, he would have to satisfy me now that I was the majority owner of the hotel and property.

"I didn't get into the nitty-gritty details with them," he confessed. "I was just trying to protect the Cutler name. You can imagine what a field day the newspaper people would have with such a story, and that might very well reflect on the hotel."

"Mr. Updike," I said, speaking through clenched teeth, "if I don't get Christie back and get her back soon, I will feed the story to the newspapers myself!" I flared.

"I see," he said. "I just want you to understand what will be exposed – your affair with this older man, your pregnancy out of wedlock, your – "

"I know what I've done, and I know what has happened, Mr. Updike. My baby is more important to me than any of that. If you can't help me and help me quickly, I will see another attorney," I said, no longer veiling any threat or anger.

He cleared his throat.

"Oh, I'll help you. I just wanted you to understand all the aspects of this," he quickly explained.

"What do we do next?" I demanded.

"Well, I know some people there. I'll get right on it. Maybe we can settle this in a closed hearing in front of a judge with just the attorneys and parties present. I'll work toward that, and hopefully – "

"Then Jimmy and I will remain here and await your making the arrangements quickly," I emphasized.

"Okay. I'll call you. Where are you?"

I gave him the place and the number and repeated my

desire to have the problem solved as quickly as possible. He promised to get right on it.

The day after I had first phoned Mr. Updike he finally called to say he had managed to get the Comptons and their attorney to agree to a hearing in front of a supreme court judge, Judge Powell, who was both a friend of the Comptons and an acquaintance of Mr. Updike.

"If Mr. Compton is so powerful around here and this judge is his friend, will he be fair?" I asked with concern.

"Well, this is sort of an off-the-record hearing, a favor the judge is doing for both of us," Mr. Updike explained. "We can always turn to formal legal remedies afterward if we're not satisfied with the outcome. The Comptons aren't happy about the prospect of a public hearing either."

He gave me the address and time to be at the judge's chambers and told us he would meet us there an hour earlier. It was an afternoon meeting. I was so nervous about it, I couldn't eat a thing for lunch.

"It's going to be okay," Jimmy continued to assure me. "Once everyone understands the truth of what happened, it will be settled simply and quickly."

"Oh, Jimmy, I'm not as confident as you are. Mr. Updike keeps emphasizing just how powerful Sanford Compton is, a man of great influence with politicians and lawyers alike, and he's forever reminding me about the sordid details of my background."

"I don't care about any of that," Jimmy insisted. "The truth is the truth, and Christie is your baby," he said with a firmness that helped me to revive some of my own confidence.

"I'm so glad you're with me, Jimmy. I couldn't do any

of this without you," I told him. He reached across the table in the restaurant where we were having our lunch and put his hand over mine.

"I wouldn't want to be anywhere else but at your side, Dawn. Now and forever."

I wanted to kiss him there and then, but we were surrounded by people, all well-dressed and sophisticated-looking. It was a fancy restaurant, too, and I was sensitive about doing anything that might attract attention and gossip. Jimmy said events were making me paranoid, but I couldn't help it. He laughed but made me promise to kiss him twice as much when we were alone.

The afternoon of the hearing was gray and even a bit chilly. Fall was creeping in like a wolf on the prowl around a chicken coop. It cast its shadow first. Birds seemed more restless around us, their biological clocks ticking closer and closer to that hour when they would be nudged to go off and seek warmer climates. Clouds looked darker and more ominous, and the wind was stronger. Leaves weakened by age snapped off branches and began their slow singsong descents to the ground, while other leaves had begun to take on tints of orange and yellow and brown.

Mr. Updike met us in the lobby. Although he was an elderly man, easily in his early seventies, he carried himself with an air of strength and authority characteristic of men much younger. His cap of white hair still had a slight wave in front, and he stood firm with broad shoulders and a bit of a barrel chest. The sight of him and the sound of his deep, resonant voice restored some faith and confidence in me. He shook hands with Jimmy firmly

18

and described quickly how he wanted to conduct the meeting.

"Just let me do all the talking until Judge Powell asks you questions."

I nodded. Just then we saw Sanford and Patricia Compton enter the building with their attorney. Mr. Compton was holding Mrs. Compton at the elbow as if she had to be guided along. She had her lace handkerchief closed in her small left fist. I saw the terror and fear in her face when she glanced our way. It sent shivers of ice through my heart.

The Comptons' attorney was a shorter man with a much slimmer build but a surprisingly beautiful speaking voice. As a musician and singer, I couldn't help but notice. His name was Felix Humbrick, and the moment he began to talk I knew we were in for a time of it.

We all gathered in the judge's chambers, a large office on the second floor. It had marble floors, and both walls were lined with shelves containing volumes and volumes of law books. On the wall behind the judge's large, dark oak desk were framed pictures of Judge Powell shaking hands with politicians, even one showing him with the president. All of it gave the office a magisterial air of authenticity and officialdom. There was a feeling we should whisper when we spoke.

The Comptons and their attorney took one side of the room, and we took the other, with both attorneys sitting in the leather chairs closest to the desk. Mr. Compton refused to look our way, but every once in a while Patricia Compton gazed at me, her eyes glassy.

Judge Powell was an intense man, focusing sharply on whoever spoke as if he could see into the speaker's

19

face, behind his words. Of course, I studied his face for some hint as to what he was feeling, but when he began to conduct the hearing his face became a mask – his lips unmoving, his eyes simply reflecting what he saw and not reacting. Not even his eyebrows lifted. He was as still as the statue of Justice herself.

"I would like it understood at the start," the judge began, "that this is an informal hearing requested and agreed to by both sides concerned, and therefore I have not asked for a stenographer to take down any notes or record the proceedings. Also, any recommendations I might make at the conclusion of this informal hearing are not binding on either party, nor can they be used as evidence or testimony in any formal hearing that might result. Is that clear?"

"Yes, Your Honor," Mr. Updike said quickly.

"Quite clear, Your Honor," Felix Humbrick said.

"As agreed to beforehand, then, we will begin with Mr. Humbrick," the judge said, and he turned his swivel chair slightly so that he was looking directly at Felix Humbrick. Jimmy took my hand and squeezed it gently.

"Thank you, Your Honor. As you know, my clients, Sanford and Patricia Compton, were interested in adopting a newborn infant. Naturally, they were concerned about the child's background and were very happy to learn from a friend of theirs that the birth of a baby whose background was clearly known was imminent. This friend, who has asked that his name not be brought into the matter unless absolutely necessary, was a close friend of Lillian Cutler, the owner and operator of Cutler's Cove Hotel.

"Mrs. Cutler had passed on the information that her

20

granddaughter had had an illicit affair. In short, she was seduced by an older man while she was away at school in New York City. As a result she became pregnant.

"Mrs. Cutler and her granddaughter, for obvious reasons, wanted the matter kept confidential, so Mrs. Cutler arranged for her granddaughter to leave school and reside at Mrs. Cutler's sister's home until such time as the baby was born. Mrs. Cutler's sister is an experienced midwife.

"Faced with the prospect of having a child at such a young age, and a child out of wedlock at that, and hoping to continue her own musical career, Mrs. Cutler's granddaughter agreed to have her child placed for adoption. She signed documents to this effect, willingly giving her child to Mr. and Mrs. Compton immediately after the baby's birth.

"The events followed suit as outlined. The Comptons accepted the infant in their home, proceeded to take all necessary medical steps to insure the baby's well-being and quickly developed an emotional tie to the infant. They have even named the baby after Mr. Compton's deceased mother.

"Now, as you know, Mrs. Cutler's granddaughter wishes the child to be returned. We feel her request is unreasonable, arbitrary, a violation of a contract entered into in good faith. In point of fact, the contract was drawn up by the Cutler family counsel himself, and none of the covenants were challenged. One of these covenants reads, 'Mr. and Mrs. Sanford Compton of 12 Hardy Drive accept full responsibility for the health and welfare of said infant from the date of delivery and agree not to make any additional demands on the Cutler family concerning the said infant, to wit the life and limb

21

of said infant will from this day forward remain their sole responsibility.'

"I emphasize 'sole responsibility,' Your Honor, a stipulation to which they wholeheartedly agreed and which they undertook, for which Dawn Cutler and the Cutler family then agreed to make no other demands or inquiries concerning the said infant.

"This is all signed, sealed and delivered," he concluded, sliding the document onto the judge's desk. Judge Powell looked at it quickly, turning to the page for signatures, and then nodded without expression. He swung his swivel chair in our direction.

"Mr. Updike, your presentation?"

"We don't contest the contract, Your Honor. We are here today, however, to present some new facts, the main fact being that Dawn Cutler did not agree to this, nor was she aware of it."

"Not aware of it?"

"No, Your Honor," Mr. Updike said. I couldn't see the expression on his face, but I could feel his embarrassment.

"You drew this up without speaking with the mother?"

"I . . . yes. I had been assured by my client that the mother agreed to all of it. Dawn was some distance away, living under the circumstances described. Mrs. Cutler assured me that the decision to give up the infant was one she, Dawn's mother and father, and Dawn herself thought best for all concerned."

"And the signature on this document?" the judge asked.

Mr. Updike seemed uncomfortable in his seat now. He shifted, cleared his throat and spoke.

22

"Apparently it is forged."

"Forged?" The judge finally reacted to something. His eyebrows lifted slightly. "You didn't bother to compare it with samples, I assume?"

"I had no reason to be suspicious, Your Honor. I have been the Cutler family's attorney for quite a number of years now, and my experience has always been that Mrs. Cutler, especially, conducted her affairs with the utmost honesty and business acumen."

"Your Honor?" Felix Humbrick interrupted.

"Yes?"

"We have other samples of Dawn Cutler's signature here, and they match perfectly. It is our contention that it is not forged." He submitted the documents. The judge looked at them.

"Mr. Updike, I'm not a handwriting expert, but these do look quite similar." He handed the documents to our lawyer. Mr. Updike gazed at them and then took off his glasses, folded them and placed them in his upper pocket.

"Your Honor, I don't know how the forgery was committed, but I have no doubt that it was," he said.

"I see," Judge Powell replied. "Can you share your reasoning with us?"

Mr. Updike turned to look my way. He saw in my face that I wanted him to go on and do and say whatever was necessary for me to get Christie back.

"Your Honor, Mrs. Cutler recently passed away, at which time wills and other documents were unsealed. It was learned – painfully learned – that Dawn Cutler is not Mrs. Cutler's granddaughter."

Patricia Compton, who had been staring down

throughout all this, lifted her head sharply and looked across the office at me with new interest.

"I see. Go on," Judge Powell said.

"Apparently Dawn Cutler was Lillian Cutler's husband's child."

"You mean she is her daughter?"

"No, Your Honor."

"I see," Judge Powell said quickly. "You don't have to go into those details any further."

"I don't understand," Sanford Compton said angrily. "What does this base behavior have to do with anything?"

"Mr. Updike is suggesting another possible motive for the actions Mrs. Cutler took. There is a clear history of subterfuge and deception here. Miss Cutler," the judge said, turning to me. The moment he did, I felt my heart jump and the heat rise in my neck and face. "Do you deny signing this contract?"

"Yes, sir."

"What did you intend to do when your baby was born?" he asked softly.

"I don't know, Your Honor. I wanted my baby very much and was shocked to discover she had been given away."

"Mrs. Cutler didn't threaten you or advise you of the difficulties that lay ahead and as a result convince you to sign this document?"

"No, sir. I never saw Grandmother Cutler after I left New York to go to The Meadows."

"The Meadows?" He looked at Mr. Updike.

"Mrs. Cutler's sister's home."

"I see. So until you returned you had no knowledge of Mr. and Mrs. Compton?"

24

"That's correct, Your Honor."

"Why did you agree to have your baby in secret if you had no intention of giving her away?" the judge asked.

"Your Honor, I wasn't in any position to disagree with anything Grandmother Cutler demanded or suggested at the time, but I never knew what her full intentions were. Of course, now I understand why she hated me and why she wouldn't have wanted any child of mine in her presence."

"I see." Judge Powell turned away and sat back a moment. Then he lifted his eyes toward the Comptons.

"Mr. and Mrs. Compton, the information Mr. Updike has presented does create some definite gray areas. While it is true you do have an apparently legal contract, there is some reason for it to be challenged. Any formal court hearing will obviously bring all this new information to bear, and I suspect that Mr. Updike has only scratched the surface of it here today.

"In short, unfortunate as it might be for you, you should take into consideration the ugly atmosphere in which this case will be argued. It doesn't bode well for the future of the child even if your position should prevail." He leaned forward. "It could very well become a media circus."

Mrs. Compton began to sob. Sanford Compton nodded and then embraced her.

"We had no idea about all these other circumstances," he said angrily.

"Of course not," the judge said in a soothing voice. He sat back. "Mr. Humbrick, I recommend – informally recommend – that you advise your clients to return the infant to its mother forthwith."

"We will take your advice under serious consideration, Your Honor," Felix Humbrick replied. "Sanford," he said softly.

"Thank you, Judge," Sanford Compton said. He helped his wife to her feet, and they started out of the judge's chambers, Mrs. Compton's sobbing growing harder. Felix Humbrick rose and turned to Mr. Updike.

"Are you staying anywhere in town?"

"I wasn't intending on it. Why don't I phone your office? How long do you want?"

"Give me two hours," Mr. Humbrick replied. They shook hands, and he followed the Comptons out.

The judge stood up and gazed down at Jimmy and me. My legs felt so weak and wobbly, I was afraid to stand.

"Well," Judge Powell said, "something like this is very unpleasant. You have a great deal to overcome, young lady, some of it not your fault, but some of the blame rests with you."

"I know, Your Honor."

"Apparently you have found a champion to stand at your side," he said, his eyes twinkling at Jimmy. "I can only wish you good luck from now on."

"Thank you," I said. Jimmy and I stood up.

"I'll be right out," Mr. Updike said. We left him with the judge and retreated to the lobby. We could see Sanford Compton speaking heatedly with Mr. Humbrick outside. Patricia had apparently already gone to their car. A few moments later they left, too.

Mr. Updike decided we should return to our hotel. I was so nervous and frightened, I could barely walk or speak. My heart felt as if it were filled with tiny moths all flapping their paper-thin wings at once. Mr. Updike kept telling us how sorry he was all this had happened, how Grandmother Cutler's actions had been so out of character for her. I understood he had great respect for her, and when he described her in her early days I almost wished I had been alive then to see her in a different light.

Two hours later Mr. Updike called Felix Humbriek and learned the Comptons had agreed to give up the fight. I broke into a flood of hysterical tears of happiness. Even Jimmy had tears in his eyes as he embraced me.

"Sanford Compton has asked that you stop by as soon as possible to get the baby. He doesn't want their pain and agony to last a moment longer than necessary," Mr. Updike told us.

"Of course," Jimmy said. "We'll go right over."

"Thank you, Mr. Updike," I said. "I know how difficult this was for you."

I had a suspicion Judge Powell had chastised him for not being more assured that I had been a party to the agreement. He didn't strike me as the kind of man who made such mistakes. But in a real sense, he had been violated by Grandmother Cutler, too. He was just unwilling to face up to that, for reasons I had yet to understand.

Some of the shadows and the skeletons in the closets of the Cutler family had been exposed and revealed, but deep in my heart I knew there were closet doors yet to be opened.

Sanford Compton was a different man when Jimmy and I arrived at the house to get Christie this time. He allowed Frazer to show us in, and he greeted us in the

27

hallway standing beside a box, which, he explained, contained things he had bought for Christie.

"Some baby clothing, diapers, crib toys and the formula our pediatrician recommended. Even though I am sure you have your own doctor who might recommend something different, it will tide you over," he said. He gazed behind him at the stairway. "Patricia will be along any moment with the baby."

"I'll just get this out to the car," Jimmy said, picking up the carton. "Thank you."

"I am sorry how all this worked out," Sanford said when he and I were alone for a moment. "It was never our intention to add to anyone's suffering."

"No, no. It wasn't your fault. You weren't told the truth," I said.

"If I had been, you can be damn sure it wouldn't have gone this far," he replied, his eyes icy blue again. "Your grandmother, or the woman who called herself that, must have been some piece of work."

I couldn't help but laugh at his description, but my joviality was short-lived, for when I lifted my gaze toward the stairway I saw Patricia Compton coming down slowly, baby Christie in her arms. My heart began to pitter-patter, both in anticipation and in anxiety, because Patricia walked as if she were under a spell. To me it appeared she could fold up at any moment and topple down the staircase, dropping the baby out of her embrace.

"I wanted to do all of this," Sanford whispered, "but she insisted."

I stepped forward quickly to greet her at the base of the stairway. She stopped two steps from the bottom and stared at me. Christie was wrapped in a pink blanket, her tiny nose and chin barely visible. Patricia continued to gaze at me silently. Her sad eyes and trembling lips kept me from simply reaching out to seize Christie.

"She's just been fed, and she's dozing," Patricia finally said. "She always drops right off after a feeding. Sometimes" – Patricia smiled – "sometimes she falls asleep with the nipple of the bottle still in her lips. She just stops suckling and closes her eyes and drifts off, contented. She's a wonderful baby."

Her eyes shifted to Sanford. Jimmy returned and approached slowly.

"Give Miss Cutler her child now, Patricia," Sanford said firmly but softly.

"What? Oh, yes, yes." She lifted the baby toward me, and I stepped forward quickly to take Christie in my arms. When I looked down into her little face I finally felt the shadow lift from my heart, filling with sunshine and joy. I had forgotten how blond her hair was. It looked like a crown of gold.

"Thank you," I said, turning back to Patricia. "I am truly sorry for the pain you are suffering now."

Patricia's lips trembled harder. Her chin began to wrinkle, and her shoulders started to shake.

"Patricia. You promised," Sanford reminded her.

She took a deep breath and pressed her small fists into her bosom as if to hold her sorrow inside.

"I'm sorry," she whispered.

"We'd better be going, Dawn," Jimmy said. "We have a long ride back."

"Yes. Thank you for the baby's things," I told Sanford. He nodded, but I could see he, too, was holding back a flood of tears. Jimmy and I started out of the house. Just as Frazer closed the door behind us we heard Patricia Compton's wail. It was a loud, shrill scream, the moan any mother would express if her child were being taken away.

The heavy front door was closed rapidly, and it mercifully entrapped the wail within. Even so, Jimmy and I hurried down the walkway, driven along by the horror of Patricia Compton's agony. Neither of us spoke until Jimmy had started the engine and driven off. I couldn't help but gaze back once more at the house and grounds that might have been Christie's home. Then I closed my eyes and drove the image back into the deepest closets of my memory. When I opened my eyes again I gazed down at my baby, her tiny pink face just waiting for my kisses.

Back at
Cutler's Cove

Before Jimmy and I had left for Saddle Creek I had asked Mrs. Boston to prepare the room across from Grandmother Cutler's suite. It had two big windows looking out over the hotel grounds, and I liked the light blue wallpaper. There was a room that had served as a nursery for Philip, me and Clara Sue, but it was from that room that my abduction had been arranged. I didn't ever want to put Christie there.

Mrs. Boston helped me get Christie's things organized. Jimmy brought up the carton of clothes and other items Sanford Compton had given us, and Mrs. Boston unpacked it all and put it away.

"It's a good thing to have a newborn child here now," Mrs. Boston said. "The birth of a child washes away the shadows Death leaves behind when he visits a house. And she's a beautiful baby, too," she admitted.

I thanked her. I had half expected Mother might come in to see Christie, but she kept her suite door shut tight and didn't even acknowledge our arrival.

After Mrs. Boston left and I had Christie sleeping comfortably in her crib, I felt someone's eyes on me and turned to see Clara Sue leaning against the doorjamb. She had her arms folded under her bosom, and the corner of her lip twisted up in a smirk.

31

"Aren't you embarrassed bringing her back here?" she asked in a haughty tone. "After all, she is a bastard, just like you."

"Of course not," I said. "What happened doesn't make her any less beautiful or wonderful. And don't you ever let me hear you call her a bastard again!"

"What are you going to tell her when she grows up and asks who her real father is?" she shot back, trying to stab me with her hateful question.

"When she's old enough to understand, I'll tell her the truth," I said. "She's not going to be brought up in a world of lies like I was."

"It's disgusting and disgraceful, and Grandmother would never have permitted it. It hurts the hotel's reputation," she insisted.

I turned on her, my hands clenched into fists, and walked toward her slowly, my eyes fixed on her so firmly that the hateful smile evaporated quickly from her face and was instantly replaced by a look of fear. With every step I took forward, she took one backward.

"I'm going to say this once and only once, so make sure you listen. Don't you ever, *ever* say anything to make Christie seem like something evil. If there is anything that is disgusting and disgraceful in this hotel, it's you. Keep away from Christie. I don't want you anywhere near her!" I cried. "And if I hear about you spreading any nasty stories, I'll beat those extra pounds out of your face and body myself," I added, raising a fist. Clara Sue shot me one last dark look before she fled.

In the days that followed, little of this changed. I really began to feel like an orphan. I already knew that Randolph, who had always been distracted by his busywork, had become very melancholy after

Grandmother Cutler's death. Once a man with one of the most charming smiles and the most suave, sophisticated Southern demeanor, Randolph moped about the hotel and grounds speaking to people only when it was necessary. His eyes became shadowed, and when he spoke, it was barely above a whisper.

I had met very few men who were as concerned and as fastidious about their appearance as Randolph had been, but now he was taking even less care of his clothing, wearing wrinkled shirts and pants, creased and stained ties and scuffed shoes. I knew Mother had to have noticed all this herself, but she chose to ignore it. I was positive that if anyone did bring it up to her, she would complain about the stress, paste her palm against her forehead and declare the entire subject one of those "unmentionables."

With Clara Sue off in a sulk most of the time, and Philip brooding because I wouldn't spend any of my free time with him, the atmosphere in the hotel became a heavy, dreary one that the guests soon felt and began to complain about. All of them missed Grandmother Cutler, who, say what I would about her, had created a charming and elegant atmosphere for her clientele. Now everyone was anxious for the summer and the high season to come to an end.

A little more than a week after we had returned with Christie, Jimmy had to go. His leave was finished, and he had to report for duty. He had been at my side during so much of the turmoil and agony I had experienced over the past weeks that I couldn't help being frightened and depressed about his departure. Once again I felt like someone being deserted. Our parting was very sad for both of us. We said our final good-byes in the privacy of his car in front of the hotel.

It was a gray day, overcast with clouds that looked so heavy, I thought they were made out of iron. They loomed over the ocean, which had turned a dull gray itself and looked like a field of cement. Across the grounds, leaves blown by a severe wind rained down and were then scattered everywhere. They seemed to hop madly over the lawns and driveway.

"Don't look so sad," Jimmy cajoled. "I'll call you every chance I get, and I'll be back as soon as I get my next leave."

"I can't help the way I feel, Jimmy. This is a big hotel with many people in it, but no one's there for me," I said. I couldn't keep the tears from burning under my lids.

Jimmy's dark eyes gleamed.

"I just knew you were going to be this way when I left. I just knew it. And so," he said, stretching, "I had to move up my plans."

"Move up your plans?" I smiled through my emerging tears. "I don't understand." Like a Cheshire cat he sat there grinning at me. "Are you going to explain?"

"Uh-huh," Jimmy said, and he dug into his uniform jacket and came up with something in his closed fist. I waited as he brought his hand to me and then opened his fist. Glittering there in his palm was the prettiest diamond engagement ring I had ever seen, and big, too! My breath caught and held and for a moment, I couldn't speak.

"Jimmy, when did you get this? How did you get something so expensive?" I finally cried, practically bouncing on the seat. He laughed and slipped it on my finger.

"I got it in Europe," he confessed, "when I took a short hop over to Amsterdam. That's where the real bargains in diamonds are, you know," he added, proud of the worldly knowledge he had acquired during his travels. "Of course, my buddies made fun of me saving every nickel and dime I could, but" – he took my hand into his and gazed into my eyes – "it was worth it just to see the look on your face and to be able to wipe some sadness out of your eyes."

I shook my head. My heart beat with such excitement, it took my breath away. In fact, I felt a little dizzy, and for a moment the car seemed to spin.

"You all right?" Jimmy asked when I gasped.

"Yes. I suppose I'm just . . . so surprised. Oh, Jimmy," I said, and I threw my arms around him. Then we kissed as we had never kissed before, both of us clinging lovingly to each other. I held on to him as long as I could, and then we pulled away from each other, and he wiped the tears from my cheeks gently with his handkerchief.

"Just think," he said, his dark eyes twinkling with that impish brightness I had learned to love, "someday soon I'll be making you Dawn Longchamp again."

"That's right. Oh, Jimmy, isn't that funny? I can't wait."

We kissed again, and then he said he really had to be going.

"They don't take kindly to us being. late. It's not like getting assigned detention at Emerson Peabody," he said with a smile. "Well, take care of yourself and little Christie," he said.

I hated getting out of the car, but I had to let him go. He rolled down his window, and we kissed good-bye one last time. Then he started the engine and drove off. I waved until his car disappeared around the bend in the driveway.

The cold winds of autumn lifted my hair and made it dance over my forehead. I embraced myself and turned to go back into the hotel, the sight of the diamond engagement ring on my finger filling me with warmth and hope.

The combination of the excitement and the sadness in saying good-bye to Jimmy left me very tired and eager to go upstairs and take a nap alongside Christie. I walked up the stairs slowly, not thinking of anything at all, my eyes half closed. When I entered the room I went directly to Christie's crib. I wanted to place her beside me on the bed and sleep with her cradled in my arms. But when I leaned over to get her, I found she wasn't there.

For a moment it didn't register in my mind. It was as if my eyes were playing practical jokes on me. I actually smiled in disbelief, closed my eyes and opened them. That didn't help. Christie was gone!

Mrs. Boston must have taken her somewhere, I thought. My heart began to pound. No, it did more than pound; it thumped sharply, as if it were trying to break out of my chest. I lost my breath, and for a few seconds I stood there gasping. Then I caught hold of myself, forced myself to stay calm and left the room to go down to find Mrs. Boston. I didn't find her in her room. I finally found her in the kitchen talking to Nussbaum, the chef. They both turned as I came walking briskly toward them. I was sure my face was terribly flushed. I felt as if my skin were on fire. I could barely speak.

"What is it, Dawn?" Mrs. Boston asked, seeing the wild look in my eyes. She didn't have Christie in her arms and wouldn't have brought her in here anyway.

"Christie . . ." I had to swallow before I could continue. "Christie's missing," I said, and my tears burst forth, charging out of my eyes like water crashing through a weakened dam.

"Vot are you sayin'?" Nussbaum asked.

"Missing?" Mrs. Boston said. She shook her head. "There must be some mistake."

"No, no mistake. She's not in her crib," I cried.

"Here, here," Nussbaum said, embracing me. "I'm sure she's all right." He shifted his eyes quickly to Mrs. Boston, whose face now registered some deep concern.

"Let's go up," she said sharply. I followed her out, and we hurried through the corridor and up the stairs. Once again I confronted an empty crib. Mrs. Boston shook her head.

"I don't understand," she said. "I left her not twenty minutes ago. She was sleeping so soundly."

"Oh, no," I said, no longer able to stay in control. Christie was gone. She was really gone! "*Oh, no!*" I screamed. I screamed so loud and so shrilly, it brought Mother out of her suite.

"What is it?" she demanded, giving me an annoyed look.

"It's the baby," Mrs. Boston said. "She's gone. Someone's taken the baby."

Those words turned my mother's face into a mask of horror. Her mouth contorted, and her eyes seemed to sink deeper into her skull even as they grew larger and larger, her pupils dilating with fear. She had heard those words before, of course, when I had been taken, only then she had had to pretend. It was as if she had been thrown back through time and made to relive it. She shook her head and backed away.

"No," she said. "It must be . . . must be a mistake. This can't be happening. Not again. I can't deal with this. Why can there never be any happiness in this cursed place?" she muttered, and she ran from the room.

"Let's get help," Mrs. Boston said.

I couldn't keep myself from shaking. Jimmy had just left me, just when I needed him the most, I thought. Oh, please, please, God, don't let Christie be gone. Not again. Not to have the same fate I had. Could my mother be right? Was this place cursed? It seemed like a cruel joke fate wanted to pull over and over. I smothered my tears and followed Mrs. Boston out of the room. We charged down the stairs to the lobby, where she gathered the staff around us.

"Someone's taken Christie from her crib," she announced. "We need everyone in the hotel lookin'."

Everyone was equally shocked and concerned. The bellhops fanned out. The receptionists joined the search. Dining room staff members who were relaxing in the lobby took the outside and circled the hotel. As more and more people found out what was happening, the search party enlarged until it involved almost everyone in the hotel.

Philip, who had been in the card room playing poker with some of the dining room staff, came running.

"The baby's actually missing?" he asked. I could only nod. I sat on a soft chair and embraced myself, feeling that if I let go, I would literally fall apart. My stomach felt as if it were ready to empty itself at any minute, I felt so nauseous. My throat was choked so tightly, I couldn't swallow. Every once in a while I had to close my eyes and struggle for a breath. Chambermaids, receptionists, Mrs. Boston, everyone tried to comfort me.

Finally we heard someone shouting from the far end of the lobby. It was one of the chambermaids.

"*The baby's been found*," she cried.

"Christie. *Christie*," I called, and somehow I found the strength to stand. It was as if I were floating over the lobby floor as I walked forward. Moments later Millie Francis, the lady in charge of the laundry, came walking out of the corridor carrying Christie cradled in her arms.

"Is she all right?" I cried.

"Just fine," Millie said. She handed my baby over to me gently. Christie's eyes were open wide in surprise. Her face was filled with curiosity as I held her tightly, not wanting to think of what I would have done if we hadn't found her.

"Where was she?" I demanded.

"I almost missed her. She's such a good baby. She was lying there so quietly."

"Lying where?" I asked quickly.

"In the laundry room, in a bin, on top of a pile of towels," she said.

Everyone looked at one another in astonishment.

"How could she get down there, and who would put her in a laundry bin?" asked Mrs. Bradly, one of our older receptionists.

"Sick joke, if someone did that," one of the bell-hops said.

"Thank you," I said, turning to them all. "Thank you all for helping."

"She don't look the worse for it," Mrs. Boston assured me. We took Christie up to my room immediately and there inspected her more closely. There wasn't a mark on her body, and she looked very alert and happy now.

"Who would do such a thing?" Mrs. Boston wondered aloud.

Moments later Clara Sue appeared in my doorway.

"What happened?" she asked, a wide smile on her face. "Did I miss some excitement?"

"Where have you been?" Mrs. Boston asked, her eyes narrowing with suspicion.

"I fell asleep listening to records," Clara Sue answered nonchalantly.

"I didn't hear no records playin'," Mrs. Boston said.

"Well, who says your hearing's so good?" Clara Sue snapped before smiling again. Then she turned to look at me, and her eyes gleamed. "I had them playing during Christie's nap, and it didn't bother her at all. She is such a good baby, isn't she, Dawn?" With that she left.

Mrs. Boston and I looked at each other, Mrs. Boston's face screwed tightly in anger.

"From this day on, Mrs. Boston, I don't ever want her in my room, and never near Christie," I said in a sharp tone.

"Amen to that," Mrs. Boston said.

Christie slept in my bed with me that night. The events of the evening had left me so frightened, it took hours for me to stop shaking. Every once in a while I had to reassure myself that Christie was all right, and when I did fall asleep, I woke up with a start every few hours and checked her again and again. Finally, just when the morning light was breaking over the horizon, I fell into a deep sleep. As if she knew how much I needed it, Christie didn't cry to be fed, and it was Mrs. Boston who woke me the following morning.

I shook the sleep out of my body the best I could and got up to go prepare Christie's formula, but Mrs. Boston was right there at the door with it.

"I thought it was about time," she said.

"That's so nice of you, Mrs. Boston. Thank you," I said, and I lifted Christie into my arms. Then I sat in the rocker and fed her. I thought to myself that she had Michael's eyes, but my nose and mouth. She clutched her tiny pink fingers into little fists and opened her eyes wide to gaze into mine. I thought her mouth formed a silent "Oh," and that made me laugh. When she drank she focused on my face and didn't shift her eyes the whole time.

It seemed so long ago, truly in another life, when Momma Longchamp had given birth to Fern, and I had to take care of her because Momma was so weak and sick; but once I began to take care of Christie, all that I knew and had learned about babies returned.

I was so entranced with Christie and had been concentrating so hard that I didn't hear Mother come to the room, nor had I realized that Mrs. Boston had left.

"My God," she moaned, "what was all that commotion about last night? Was it a dream?"

"It was no dream, Mother. I'm afraid Clara Sue pulled a sick prank. She took Christie and left her in the laundry bin downstairs. Of course, she denies it, but I'm sure she did it."

Mother shook her head as if the words confused her. She looked drugged on sleep. I couldn't believe how Mother had let herself go. Her good looks had always been so important to her, even when she was supposedly in the throes of some terrible ailment. I never saw her in or out of bed without her makeup on her face and her hair brushed and styled. And she always wore some jewelry.

Here she was in one of her older and more ragged-looking robes, her hair unbrushed and straggly, wearing no jewelry and no makeup, her face as pale as it could be. Even her lips had lost color. She shook her head and walked farther into the room. Then she grimaced.

"Don't you feel ridiculous?" she asked.

"Ridiculous? Why should I feel ridiculous, Mother?" I replied.

"Sitting there with a baby in your arms, unmarried and with so much responsibility now in your life." She sighed deeply. "I wish you had listened to me when I spoke to you just before you left to get her back.

"Her real father deserted you both, and you're so young yet," she lectured. "Despite the manner in which Grandmother Cutler carried out her plans, she made the right decision for you at the time. The baby was with an excellent family. Now you're weighed down with a major burden."

"It's just like you to say something like that, Mother," I replied coldly, my eyes fixed on her so that she couldn't look away. "Christie is not a burden. She is my daughter, and I love her with all my heart. She is what matters most to me, and there is nothing I wouldn't

42

do for her. How easy it was for you to agree to giving away your baby without thought of the consequences. You think it's the same for everyone. You were so selfish and still are. You, You, You! All you've ever thought about is yourself! Well, I consider Christie a blessing, and if anyone is a burden, it's you," I said, spitting the words at her.

She stared at me, and then she blinked her eyes and smiled in that childish manner she had so perfected.

"I won't be drawn into an ugly spat with you, Dawn. Not now, not ever. Think and do as you wish. I'm only giving you the best advice I can. If you don't want to follow it, then don't."

Despite herself, she gazed at Christie.

"The most horrible thing about all this," she mumbled, "is you've turned me into a grandmother before my time. Well," she said, stepping back and folding her arms firmly under her small bosom, "you can be sure I won't permit anyone to refer to me as Grandmother Cutler."

"Suit yourself," I said. "Believe me, you will be the one who will be missing out."

"Missing out?" She released a short, high laugh. "On what, feeding an infant that burps and fills its diapers? I had enough of that, thank you," she said.

"Oh, Mother, you never had any of it. You either had a mother's helper, a nurse or . . . or gave away your child," I said pointedly.

"Go on, hurt me," she said, her chin quivering, "pound the nails into my coffin. It gives you pleasure, doesn't it? You'll never forgive me for what I've done, no matter how many times I apologize. I haven't suffered enough to suit you, I suppose. No

43

one realizes the sacrifices I've made and continue to make."

"Mother, you don't realize how silly that sounds," I said. I put Christie back into her cradle after burping her. Mother looked surprised at my expertise. She wiped the two tears from her cheeks. Suddenly her face lit up.

"What's that?" she asked, pointing at me.

"That?" I really didn't know what she was pointing at . . . something on my face, my clothing. . . I had forgotten for the moment that I was wearing the ring.

"That ring. It looks like an engagement ring."

"That's because it is an engagement ring, Mother. Jimmy and I are now formally engaged," I said proudly.

"Oh, no." She brought her hand to her forehead and ran her palm over her hair slowly as she shook her head. "You are a fool after all. You're actually going to marry that boy, a soldier without a penny to his name and a name that bears no great honor, no position? When are you going to start listening to me?"

"Jimmy and I love each other, Mother. We've been through a great deal together, and we – "

"Love." She threw her head back and cackled. "That's such a ridiculous word. A romantic notion drummed up in novels, but not something for real life. Love someone who can give you what you need and deserve. All love really is, anyway, is fulfilling a need. Believe me," she said, nodding, "I speak from experience."

"Not my experience, Mother. Your experience," I said sharply.

"What's wrong with you?" she asked, her hands out.

"You're now the owner of Cutler's Cove. Overnight you have been given position, power and money. Why, decent, respectable suitors will be lining the driveway. You'll be courted by the richest and most important young men, just like the ones who used to court me. You can keep them all on a string. They will all shower you with expensive gifts and make endless, impossible promises. And then, when you finally have to choose, you can choose from the cream of the crop," she promised.

"That's not what I want, Mother. I told you – Jimmy and I love each other. All the rest – position, power, wealth – that's not important to us as long as we have each other. I'm sorry you don't understand how important that is. I think that's why you're so unhappy. You have no one to love but yourself, and I don't think you like yourself very much these days, do you, Mother?"

"You're a very cruel child, Dawn." Her eyes narrowed. "You don't know how much of your real father you've inherited."

"How much have I inherited, Mother? Tell me," I pursued. I wanted her to talk about him and what had happened. I needed to know. But she waved me off.

"I'm tired and disgusted," she said. "Do what you want," she muttered. "Do whatever you want."

She returned to her room, shutting the doors tightly again and withdrawing to continue to feel sorry for herself. All I had done, apparently, was give her more reason.

Just after Philip returned to college and Clara Sue returned to high school I began my education, too.

Shortly after Grandmother Cutler's death and the reading of the wills, Mr. Updike and Mr. Dorfman, the hotel's comptroller, came up with a plan to continue the running of the hotel as smoothly as possible during the time Mr. Updike called "the interim period." I knew that meant the time it would take for me to grow knowledgeable and mature enough to take on really significant responsibilities.

Mr. Dorfman was a small, bald man with eyeglasses as thick as beer mugs. Although he was quite a competent comptroller, he was very uncomfortable talking to people. I found him to be a shy man who didn't like to look directly or even indirectly at the people with whom he was holding a conversation. He would look down at his desk or at some papers in his hand. It was almost as if I had just wandered in and was listening to a conversation between him and someone invisible.

"Well, I don't have the best news for you, I'm afraid," he began when we first met. "I've done a complete evaluation of the hotel's assets and liabilities. You know, of course, that the hotel is heavily mortgaged, and that most years Mrs. Cutler has managed only to pay the interest?"

I shook my head with an obvious look of confusion on my face. But rather than becoming impatient with me, Mr. Dorfman appeared to enjoy the fact that I knew little about such matters. He then proceeded to explain what mortgages were, what interest involved and what significance all this had for the hotel.

"So we're really no better than paupers," I concluded with surprise.

"No, no," he said, smiling for the first time, if that twitch at the corners of his mouth could be described as a smile. "All major property owners carry big mortgages. It doesn't mean they're paupers. Quite the contrary. Your enterprise here employs many, many people, and the property value is very high, very high. Some years, as you will see, the hotel made a considerable profit, and some years – the last three, to be precise – it just about broke even. Maybe a small profit," he added, as if to make me feel better.

"But if we paid our mortgage principal, we would have no profit," I declared.

"You don't have to pay the principal. The bank's very content collecting the interest, which is considerable. They have no desire to become operators of a hotel, believe me."

"It's still all very confusing to me," I cried.

"In time you will understand this as well as I do. I've taken the liberty of preparing a number of papers for you to study. Read everything carefully, especially what it costs to run each aspect of the hotel, and then you and I will talk again. It's not all that complicated," he promised, and he handed me a thick packet of papers that included studies that went back twenty years. This really was going to be like attending school, I thought.

"What does Randolph think of all this?" I asked, sitting back. Maybe it was better for me to become a silent partner and let Randolph take over most of the responsibility after all. Mr. Dorfman's short, bushy eyebrows lifted.

"Oh, I thought Mr. Updike had already explained . . . that is, I assumed . . ."

"Explained what?" I demanded.

Mr. Dorfman fidgeted for a few moments and then

47

looked firmly and directly at me for the first time since I had arrived.

"Mr. Randolph," he said calmly, "is quite incapable of any real responsibility and has been for some time, even before Mrs. Cutler's passing. Why, you already know much more than he does about the hotel," he added, astounding me.

"What? I know he behaves strangely sometimes, doing things that don't seem very important, but surely . . ."

"Mrs. Cutler never gave her son any real responsibilities, Dawn. Why . . . he never so much as made a bank deposit," Mr. Dorfman revealed, and then he started flipping through a folder.

I sat back and shook my head. I had been hoping to depend on Randolph and really let him do most of the running of the hotel while I concentrated on caring for Christie. The packet of papers in my lap suddenly took on more weight. I couldn't do this. My inheritance wasn't a blessing; it was a burden. I would feel just terrible if I somehow messed things up and all these people working here lost their jobs.

"Mr. Dorfman, I . . ."

"I can tell you that you have some very fine, very qualified people working for you, Dawn," Mr. Dorfman said quickly. "Everyone's very efficient. Mrs. Cutler did run a tight ship in that respect. If she didn't make a big profit one year, it was because of the economy, and not because of her business practices or the practices of her subordinates. It was a waste not, want not philosophy. My job is to help you keep to it," he concluded. And then, as if to add a challenge, he sat back and said, "Why, when Mrs. Cutler married Mr. Cutler and became an executive in this hotel, she wasn't much older than you are."

"Yes, but she had Mr. Cutler," I fired back. He shook his head and twisted his fingers around his pen nervously.

"I don't think I'm speaking ill of the dead when I tell you your father, Randolph's father, was not much of a hotel administrator. My father was the comptroller here then, so I speak from firsthand knowledge. This hotel didn't really become anything significant until Mrs. Cutler became actively involved.

"So," he said, eager to leave the topic, "I'll always be available to you. If I'm not here and you need me for anything, anything at all, you have my home phone number at the top of the packet of papers I just gave you."

I rose from my chair in a daze, thanked Mr. Dorfman and slowly walked out, moving like a somnambulist down the corridor. Where was I going? It suddenly occurred to me that it was time for me to take over Grandmother Cutler's office.

I paused before her doorway almost as if I had to knock. Then I opened it slowly and stood just inside for a long moment, my heart pounding as if I anticipated her miraculous resurrection. I could almost see her standing firm and tall with her steel-blue hair cut and styled to perfection. She was standing behind her desk as always, her shoulders pulled back firmly in the bright blue cotton jacket she wore over her frilly blouse. She turned her cold gray eyes on me, and in my imagination I even heard her chastisement: "What are you doing here? How dare you enter my office without knocking first?"

I gazed around. The dark-paneled office still had its lilac scent, everything about it still suggesting Grandmother Cutler, reflecting her austere personality, from the hardwood floors to the tightly woven dark blue oval rug in front of the aqua chintz settee. Her dark oak desk was just the way she had last left it: the pens in their holders, papers neatly piled to one side, a small bowl of hard candies in one corner and the black telephone in another. Her memo pad was open at the center of the desk.

Firm and resolute, I finally stepped forward and went to the partially opened curtains and pulled the cord to open them wide. Sunlight burst into the office, washing away the shadows that covered her high-back, blood-red, nail-head leather chair, the bookcases and standing lamp. Particles of dust danced in the air. Then I stepped back and looked up at the portrait of Grandfather Cutler, the man who I had learned was my true father.

It appeared the portrait had been painted in this very office with him at this very desk. Right now he seemed to be leering down at me, his head slightly tilted forward, his light blue eyes fixed on me. As I crossed to the other side of the room the portrait gave the illusion of his gaze following me. I thought that even though the artist might have been instructed to capture a strong, authoritative and distinguished look, he had also managed to replicate some lightness and charm in the way he had drawn and painted my father's lips.

What sort of a man could he have been? I wondered. How could my father have been a conniver, deceitful and lustful? What had made him decide to rape my mother, if it was indeed a rape? What sort of morality

50

did he have if he could make love to his son's wife? Obviously he had had some pangs of conscience, for he had tried to atone for his act by giving me this inheritance and making a full confession after his death. And he had been compassionate enough to worry about how it would all affect Grandmother Cutler and so left instructions for none of it to be revealed until she had passed away, too.

As I gazed into my father's eyes – eyes strikingly like my own – I wondered what, if anything – beside some physical attributes – I had inherited from this man. Would I now become as ambitious as he was? Would I live up to the responsibilities placed on my shoulders and develop into a good administrator? Did I have his charm when it came to pleasing guests? Had he been fair with the help and liked by them, and would I be? I realized I had developed a great hunger for knowledge about him and hoped I could get those members of the staff who had worked under him and were still here to talk to me about him. I certainly didn't expect Mother to tell me anything worthwhile, and as for Randolph . . . well, from what I understood and saw, Randolph couldn't be counted upon for anything these days.

I went around the desk and sat in Grandmother Cutler's chair. Looking over the large desk from this point of view, I began to see things in a more natural and realistic perspective. It was as if sitting in her chair and taking her position imbued me with the confidence I would need to carry on. The office wasn't as large as it had always seemed to be to me. I could do a great deal to brighten it up, I thought. I would replace the rug and the furniture. Then I would hang up some bright paintings.

I sat back. I could almost feel Grandmother Cutler seething behind me and grinding her teeth. Maybe I can do this, I thought. Maybe I can.

Then I realized what time it was and jumped up to see about Christie. But as I was passing through the lobby Patty, one of the older chambermaids, stopped me.

"I think you had better go down to the laundry," she advised, and she nodded as if she were slipping me some secret.

"Something broken?" It was on the tip of my tongue to ask her to see Mr. Dorfman, but she shook her head vigorously.

"Someone ought to go down there," she repeated, and she left me standing in confusion. I asked Mrs. Boston to go up and see about Christie while I went downstairs to the basement of the hotel, where the laundry was situated.

At first I thought no one was there, but when I turned into the room where all the washing machines were housed I spotted Randolph off in a corner by a table used for the folding of linen and towels. He had dozens of measuring cups lined up on each side of the table, and he was using a measuring spoon – the kind used to measure flour or sugar in a kitchen – only he was using it to scoop soap powder into the cups. He had two different brands of soap powder in big vats beside him.

"Randolph," I said, approaching, "what are you doing?"

He didn't turn around. He kept scooping the soap powder carefully.

"Randolph?" I put my hand on his arm, and he looked at me, his eyes bloodshot and wild.

"I'm right about this," he said. "I suspected it, and I'm right." He turned back to the soap powder.

"Right about what, Randolph?" I asked.

He stopped and smiled maddeningly.

"This brand on my right is more concentrated. It takes less powder per pound of laundry, even though it costs more, understand? What this means is we can save a lot of money by buying the more expensive brand. I told Mother this once. I told her. She just shook her head, didn't listen, was too busy with something else . . . whatever," he said, waving in the air, "but I was right." He gazed at me, his eyes brightening even more and his smile even more maddening. "I was right."

"Will we really save all that much, Randolph? I mean, is it worth it for you to go through all this?"

"What?" He swung his shining blue eyes my way, totally devoid of any expression. He behaved as if he didn't know who I was. It sent icicles sliding down my spine. "I'm sorry," he said. "I've got to finish this study. I'll talk to you later, okay? Thank you, thank you," he muttered, and he went back to scooping the powder carefully and exactly into the measuring cups.

I watched him for a moment and then hurried out and upstairs. Mother had to know about this, I thought.

As I stepped onto the second-floor landing I was surprised to hear the sound of my mother's laughter. I approached slowly, for I also heard the distinct sound of a man's voice. I knocked softly on her outer door and then entered.

"Yes?" Mother called, her voice filled with annoyance. I peered in and saw her sitting on the settee, a most handsome and distinguished-looking man seated

53

in the wing-back chair across from her, his legs crossed comfortably.

Mother was dressed in one of her bright blue angora sweaters and a matching cotton skirt. She had her hair brushed down softly over her shoulders and wore long, dangling diamond earrings and a matching bracelet. She had returned to wearing makeup as well and looked as bright and happy as I had ever seen her.

"Oh, Dawn, I'd like you to meet Mr. Bronson Alcott, a dear, dear old friend of mine," she said, beaming. The flood of color in her lovely face made her even more beautiful.

"So this is the young lady I've heard so much about," Bronson Alcott said, turning his attention to me.

He was a tall, sleek-figured man with a light brown mustache under a perfectly straight Roman nose. He had his hair cut short and neat, the chestnut-brown strands glimmering under the light of the Tiffany lamp. A smile formed around his bright, laughing aquamarine eyes.

"Hello," I said.

"Bronson is the president of the Cutler's Cove National Bank," Mother explained. "The bank that holds the mortgage on this hotel," she added pointedly.

"Oh." I turned to him again. For a banker his skin was remarkably tanned. He wore an amused smile, as if he were about to wink at me. He kept his long, graceful hands crossed over each other on his knee. Even though he looked like a man in his mid-forties, I thought he could easily be older.

"I'm very happy to finally get the opportunity to meet you, Dawn," he said. His voice was deep and resonant,

54

which complemented his perpetually sexy smile. Mother looked mesmerized by his every word, his every gesture. He stood up and extended his hand. I took it and felt myself blush at how intensely he drank me in, gazing at me quickly from head to foot. He didn't release my hand quickly.

"Is this an engagement ring?" he asked, still keeping my fingers firmly in his.

"Yes," Mother said dryly. "It is."

"Congratulations. Who's the lucky young man?" he asked.

"No one you would know, Bronson," Mother replied before I could.

He tilted his head, his smile softening.

"Someone from out of town?" he pursued.

"I'll say he's out of town," Mother said, beginning to buff her nails. "He's in the army."

"His name is James Gary Longchamp," I said, eyeing Mother with daggers.

I saw that Bronson wasn't going to sit down until I did. He was the quintessential Southern gentleman who easily made every woman feel a little like Scarlett O'Hara. Reluctantly I sat beside Mother on the settee, and he returned to his wing chair.

"So when is the wedding?" Bronson asked.

"Soon after Jimmy – I mean James – is discharged," I replied, again flashing defiance at Mother. She uttered a short, nervous laugh and continued buffing her nails.

"I told her, tried to explain to her how she shouldn't rush into anything, how she would now be the center of attention for every distinguished, available bachelor in Virginia, but she insists on pushing ahead with this childhood romance," Mother complained.

"Let's not be too harsh, Laura Sue," Bronson said, his eyes twinkling. "You and I once had a childhood romance."

Mother blushed. "That was different, Bronson, entirely different."

"Your mother broke my heart you know. I've never really forgiven her. But," he added, nodding, "I suspect mine was not the only heart broken in those days. She had a trail of beaux that stretched from here to Boston."

Mother brightened, and her laugh became lighter.

"It's not hard to imagine you doing the same thing, Dawn," Bronson said, turning back to me. His gaze lingered, and out of the corner of my eye I could see Mother growing green with envy.

"I'm not interested in breaking hearts right now, Mr. Alcott," I said.

"Oh, please, call me Bronson. I have hopes that we shall become good friends as well as business associates," he said, this time winking. "Which reminds me," he added, pulling up on a long gold watch fob and snapping his gold pocket watch open. He gazed at it and turned back to Mother. "I should be on my way. I have played hooky from my responsibilities at the bank long enough." He stood up and turned back to me. "Perhaps I can hope that you and your mother will pay a visit to Beulla Woods," he said.

"That's the Alcott estate," Mother explained quickly. "It's a magnificent home just northwest of Cutler's Cove."

The way she said it and gazed at Bronson when she did gave me the impression she had been there many, many times and could find it in the dark.

"Yes, maybe all of us can go one day," I said, emphasizing "all." Bronson held his smile, but Mother smiled coyly. He reached out for my hand and brought it to his lips.

"Good-bye. It was a pleasure meeting you," he said, holding me in his gaze so long, I felt my heart begin to flutter. He seemed to want to memorize every aspect of my face. Finally he turned to Mother. "Laura Sue."

She rose, and they embraced, Bronson planting a kiss on her cheek, but a kiss that found his lips so close to hers, I was sure they grazed in passing. Mother glanced at me quickly and then released one of her nervous little laughs. Bronson bowed and left us. When I looked back at Mother I saw her face was flushed. She looked as though her heart was pounding harder than mine.

"Oh, dear," she said quickly, "I didn't realize how getting dressed to look decent and visiting with someone would tire me. I'm afraid I have to take a little rest, Dawn." She turned to go into her bedroom.

"Mother, wait. I came up here to see you for a reason," I said. She paused, a look of impatience on her face.

"What is it now, Dawn?" she huffed.

"It's Randolph. He doesn't look very good to me, and he's doing very strange things." I told her what had transpired in the laundry. She shook her head.

"There's nothing new about all that," she said. "Randolph is Randolph," she added, as if that explained it forever.

"But don't you think he's worse? I mean, he's no longer concerned about his appearance, and – "

"Oh, Dawn, he'll snap out of it. It's just his way of

mourning the death of his precious mother. Please, I have my own health to worry about these days."

"Yes," I said, "but yours appears to return on demand," I added caustically.

"I'm too tired for this," she replied. "Much too tired." She continued into her bedroom and shut the door quickly. I left and went to my room, where I found Mrs. Boston rocking Christie in her arms and singing a lullabye. The sight made me smile.

"Oh, Dawn," she said when she realized I was standing and watching her. "I was just putting her back to sleep."

"Thank you, Mrs. Boston. I know you have so much of your own work to do without adding mine."

"Oh, I don't consider this work, Dawn," she said, carefully placing Christie back in her cradle. "Has your mother's guest gone yet?" she asked.

"Yes, he just left," I said, catching some disapproval in her voice and eyes. "Do you know him, Mrs. Boston?"

"Everyone knows Mr. Alcott. At one time, a long time ago," she said, "he was a frequent visitor at the hotel."

"Is that right?"

"Yes. Your mother had many gentleman callers," she said, "but he was the only one who came around after she married Randolph."

"Isn't he married himself?" I asked. Now that I recalled, I hadn't seen a wedding ring on his finger.

"Oh, no. He's still one of the most eligible bachelors in Cutler's Cove."

"I wonder why he never married. He's a very handsome man," I said. Mrs. Boston had that look

58

on her face that told me she knew the gossip. "Do you know why?"

She shrugged. "You know how it is around the hotel – people talk."

"And what do they say, Mrs. Boston?" I pursued.

"That your mother broke his heart so bad, he couldn't love anyone else if he wanted to. But that's enough of this idle chatter," she added quickly, pulling her shoulders back. "I do have work waiting."

"Mrs. Boston," I called as she started toward the doorway. She turned. "When did Mr. Alcott stop being a frequent visitor?" She tightened her lips as if she wasn't going to add any fuel to the fire.

"Right after you were born and stolen away," she said. "But that don't mean they stopped seeing each other," she added, and then she bit down on her lower lip as if to stop a runaway mouth. "Now don't make me into some gossip monger and ask me any more." She pivoted before I could and was gone, leaving all sorts of questions dangling in my mind.

Learning the Ropes

During the months that followed, Christie grew rapidly. The features of her tiny face became more and more distinct, as did her personality. She continued being a contented, happy baby who cried only to let us know her diaper was wet or that she was hungry, but she wasn't one who craved a great deal of attention and had to be doted upon, even though everyone in the hotel enjoyed doing so. Whenever I brought her down with me the receptionists, the chambermaids, even the dining room staff were drawn to her, eager to hold her or pinch her plump cheeks. She would smile and pummel their faces gently with her tiny pink fists.

Her curiosity and remarkable perception kept her occupied. There was nothing she looked at that didn't attract her interest. She could be content sitting for hours turning a toy in her hands, tasting it, testing its firmness and tracing its shape with the tips of her fingers. Whatever she reached, she explored, and when something made her laugh she slapped her hands together and widened her eyes, revealing a joy of life that made everyone around her feel good. On the grayest of days Christie brought sunshine and warmth.

When I sat her in my lap she would inevitably explore

my face with her fingers, touching my nose, my lips and occasionally going "Ooooh." If I smiled, she smiled. If I stopped to gently chastise her, she would grow serious and always listen. Often I would play peekaboo with her, lowering the blanket to reveal my hair and forehead. But she would laugh only when she saw my eyes. Then she would explode in delight.

By the time she was nine months old her hair had grown down to the base of her neck, and I could comb and brush it. She was already very feminine, a little lady, eager to sit quietly to have her hair brushed, happy to be bathed, and attracted to any affection or loving caress. Whether it was I or Mrs. Boston who sang to her, she would lie quietly and listen intently, her eyes so still, we both felt she had already memorized our songs and was waiting to hear the parts she knew would come.

Any musical expression interested her, whether it be our singing or the radio and records. Crib toys that played tunes were her favorites, and if she cried for anything to be done, other than to be fed or changed, it was to have me pull the cords that set the toys tinkling. Everyone knew she had a propensity for music, and on her first birthday she was flooded with picture books that had built-in music boxes, windup toys that played children's songs, recorders and a toy piano for her to play. That was her favorite. She was already fascinated with her ability to produce melodic sounds.

In the beginning I tried to look after Christie and learn about the hotel business every day, but as it drew closer to spring and the business and activity increased for the hotel, I decided I needed help with her. I found out that Sissy, the young black girl who had been my chambermaid partner when I had first come to the

61

hotel years ago, was in need of employment again. Grandmother Cutler had fired her for helping me find Mrs. Dalton, the woman who had taken care of me when I was born.

Mrs. Boston knew Sissy and her mother very well, and she thought Sissy would be ideal as a mother's helper. Sissy was overwhelmed with the changes that had come about for me since she and I had last seen each other. She didn't look much different from that day. We sat and talked for a while, reminiscing. She told me Mrs. Dalton had passed away.

"She was a very sick woman when I met her," I said. Sissy nodded sadly. "I was very sorry to hear that Grandmother Cutler had punished you for helping me, Sissy. I hope it didn't create too much hardship for you and your mother."

"No, we've been all right. I worked in a department store for a while, and that's where I met Clarence Potter."

Sissy explained that she and Clarence were practically engaged, and as soon as they had both saved up enough money they would get married.

"But I'd love to help take care of Christie until then," she emphasized.

Christie took right to her. Sissy was patient and gentle and almost as thrilled with every new thing Christie did as I was. She couldn't wait to come down to the office to tell me Christie had stood up and taken a step, and she was claiming that Christie said her own name when she was only eleven months old. Christie was precocious and did develop faster than normal babies. She was barely over thirteen months when I distinctly heard her say, "Momma."

As soon as I heard her pronounce "Momma" with some clarity I began to teach her other words, and everyone who heard her utter the syllables remarked at how brilliant she was. One of the words I wanted her to be able to pronounce was "Daddy." I was hoping that when Jimmy pulled his next leave and came to the hotel, she would greet him with it.

Not a week went by that Jimmy didn't call, or write when he wasn't able to get to a phone. My letters to him were volumes. I filled page after page, first describing all the things Christie had done, and then I described my activities at the hotel. I'm sure I bored him to death with my details concerning accounts and purchase orders and meetings with Mr. Dorfman, but Jimmy never complained.

"Everyone here's jealous of the mail I receive," he told me over the phone. "Some guys get nothing from their families."

Jimmy had tried to return on leave a number of times, but something always came up that kept him away. Finally he was able to get a weekend free. What he didn't tell me until he was about to leave again was that he had volunteered for a final six months of duty to be spent in Panama, guarding the canal.

"The deal is that I can get discharged six weeks earlier than I'm scheduled if I do this, so I figured it was worth it," he said. He kissed my trembling chin. "That means we'll be married six weeks earlier, you know. Aren't you happy about that?"

"I am, Jimmy," I said. "But I don't like the idea of your being so far away again."

"Well . . . you're going to be so busy now. Time

will pass quickly for both of us. Anyway, we can make definite plans, wedding plans," he pointed out.

I knew he was right, and we did have a wonderful weekend together. The hotel had two sailboats and a motorboat down at the dock, and we went motorboating. It was nearly summer, so it was already very warm. We anchored the boat a mile or so offshore, and I went swimming while Jimmy did some fishing. Mrs. Boston had packed a picnic basket for us. We stayed out all day and watched the sun begin to fall below the horizon, making the sky orange and turning the ocean into a dreamy dark blue. He and I sat in the boat with his arm around me, and we just let the waves rock us soothingly as we gazed back at the shore. The Cutler's Cove Hotel was visible on the hill overlooking the sea.

"It's very beautiful here," Jimmy said. "I'm sure we're going to be happy. That is," he warned, "if you don't turn into one of those crazy businesswomen who work, work, work all the time. I've heard about them, and Grandmother Cutler was like that, from what I've learned."

"I'll never be like that, Jimmy."

"Yeah, you promise now," Jimmy said, "but I can see in just the short time I've been here watching you around the hotel – signing this, talking to some department head about that, listening to this one complain and that one – that you like it already."

"I'm just trying to learn everything as quickly as I can, Jimmy. You saw Randolph and how terribly distracted he is. He doesn't do anything to help run the hotel, not really. It's fallen on Mr. Dorfman, Mr. Updike and me," I explained. "But I'll always have time for you."

"Don't make promises you can't keep," he admonished.

"I won't. Jimmy, you're scaring me. Now stop it," I said. He laughed and kissed the tip of my nose.

"All right. We'll take it as it comes, Mrs. Longchamp," he said. I smiled at the sound of that, and we talked about our wedding and about our honeymoon. Jimmy wanted us to go to Cape Cod.

"It will be nice at that time of the year, spring, and I remember how Daddy used to talk about going up there all the time," Jimmy said.

"He talked about going to a lot of places, Jimmy," I reminded him. Daddy Longchamp was full of dreams in those days, dreams and hopes.

"I know, but this one was kind of like the magical place for him. Well, he and Momma never got there, but we will. Okay?"

"Yes, Jimmy. I can't wait."

And I couldn't, but I buried myself in work, and time did pass more quickly. That summer both Philip and Clara Sue went abroad on student programs. I was glad Clara Sue wasn't around; I could never forgive her for what she had done with Christie. I let it be known that I thought it had been cruel and sick. Of course, she continued to deny she had done it. Whenever she did return to the hotel for a weekend the following fall, she didn't miss an opportunity to mock my upcoming marriage to Jimmy.

"Is he going to get married in his uniform?" she taunted one day, "and say 'Yes, sir' instead of 'I do'?"

One of her favorite things was to belittle my engagement ring. "It looks like a piece of glass," she would say, "but I'm sure Jimbo thought he was buying a diamond."

"Don't you dare call him Jimbo," I flared, my eyes full of fury. She would just throw her hair over her shoulders, laugh and saunter away, satisfied she had gotten a rise out of me.

I thought she grew meaner and meaner with each passing day, and I found it hard to accept that we shared any blood at all. True, we had similar hair color and eyes, and there were characteristics in both our faces that resembled Mother's facial features, but our personalities were like night and day. And Clara Sue continued battling her weight. Though her figure was fuller and more voluptuous than mine, if she wasn't careful, she put on extra pounds. She had no self-control when it came to sweets and was constantly on a diet. She never lacked interest from the opposite sex, and because of her increasingly promiscuous behavior – so I heard – she had a following of boys at school.

Philip rarely came home. He was doing exceedingly well at college, making the dean's list, becoming president of his fraternity and captain of his rowing team. Occasionally, when Mother decided to act like a mother, she would show me and Mrs. Boston some of the clippings about him in the college newspaper.

Neither Philip nor Clara Sue seemed concerned or interested in their father's increasingly bizarre behavior and physical degeneration. I could tell that they both viewed him as an embarrassment. I tried bringing him out of his depression by asking him to do real work from time to time and bringing him real problems, but he rarely completed any task, and eventually someone else had to do it.

The only time he seemed to snap out of the doldrums was when Sissy or I brought Christie around to see him.

He would permit her to crawl around his cluttered office and touch everything. By the time she was fourteen months old she was picking things up and holding them out, saying, "Waa?" We all knew that meant she was asking, "What is this?" Randolph had great patience for her. I realized she was providing him the only respite in his otherwise dark and dreary day. He would answer every time. She could spend hours in his office questioning him about every single item, from a desk weight to a small baseball trophy he had won in high school. He would sit there and talk to her as if she were twenty years old, explaining the history behind everything, and Christie would stare at him, wide-eyed, her body still, listening as if she understood.

Mr. Dorfman had been right about the hotel running itself. It was as if Grandmother Cutler had tossed a ball into space and it continued to fly under that initial momentum. Of course, guest after guest pulled me aside to tell me how much he or she missed her. I would have to pretend I did, too. What did interest and fascinate me were some of the stories the old-timers told about her. Some of these guests went back thirty years or more at the hotel.

The woman they described was clearly a different person. Their descriptions were filled with adjectives like "warm" and "loving." Everyone talked about how she made that extra effort to make him or her feel at home. One elderly lady told me that coming to Cutler's Cove was like "visiting with my own family." How could she have put on one face with these people and another, drastically different face with me and with Mother? I wondered.

Despite my distaste for her, I couldn't help being

intrigued, and I would often spend hours thumbing through papers in the file cabinets, reading letters from guests and copies of letters she had sent to guests, searching for clues, for an understanding of the woman who loomed so hatefully in my mind even now, nearly two years after her passing. No one except Randolph – not even Mrs. Boston – had gone into Grandmother Cutler's room upstairs in the family section of the hotel after her death. Her things remained just as they had been the day she had died – her clothes still hung in the closets, her jewelry was still in the jewelry cases, her perfumes and powders were still on her vanity table. I never passed her closed doorway without getting a chilling feeling, and I couldn't help but want to go in and look at her possessions. It was like being fascinated with the devil. I resisted the temptation for as long as I could, and then one day I tried the door impulsively and was surprised to discover it was locked. When I asked Mrs. Boston about it, she told me it was what Randolph wanted.

"Only he has the key," she said, "which is fine with me. I don't fancy going in there," she added, and she shook her body as if just talking about Grandmother Cutler's old room filled her with bad feelings.

I left it at that. I had too many other concerns now that I was forced to take on more and more responsibility in the running of the hotel. The staff heads grew more confident in me, too, and came to me more often with their problems and questions. One day Mr. Dorfman came into my office pur-posely to compliment me for how well I had taken on my duties.

"I heard the guests talking about you," he said. "They

said you were very warm, very personable, and very much like your grandmother."

I stared at him, not sure I was happy with the compliment.

"And all the older guests just love the way you bring Christie around to greet them. You make them feel as if they're all her grandparents. That's a very nice and a very smart thing to do," he added.

"Christie loves people," I said. "I'm not doing it for the sake of business."

"That's good. You're doing just what's natural. Mrs. Cutler was the same way – not afraid to share her personal world with her guests. It's a large part of what made this place so special to them and continues to make it so."

"How are we really doing now, Mr. Dorfman?" I asked.

"We're doing all right," he said. "Not breaking any records, but holding our own real well. Congratulations," he added. "You've almost earned your diploma at Cutler's Cove University."

I had to smile. For Mr. Dorfman to attempt a joke, it had to be something special. Despite myself, despite how I wanted things to be and what I wanted to become, the hotel had a way of taking over. Was that another part of Grandmother Cutler's legacy, or was it just the way things were destined to be?

I gazed up at my father's portrait and once again felt his eyes on me, only now they seemed filled with glee, as if he knew the secret and enjoyed my longing to know and discover the answers, too.

As soon as Jimmy was given the date of his discharge

I told Mother the date of our wedding. Once my mother understood that Jimmy and I were really going to marry, she took on the arrangements for our wedding eagerly and excitedly, seeing the preparations as a way to distract herself and everyone else from all the embarrassing revelations that had occurred. I marveled at how resilient she seemed to be. Even though she knew that by now most of the hotel staff and a number of people in Cutler's Cove had learned the secret revealed in the reading of the wills, she did not behave like a woman who had suffered any sort of disgrace.

On the contrary, Mother moved about the hotel like a restored princess, especially since Grandmother Cutler was no longer hovering over her, glaring at her and terrorizing her with her gaze and words. She was confident that none of the staff would dare laugh at her in her presence. She still believed she could become the new queen of Cutler's Cove.

But to me she had become someone to pity, even though she had never dressed more elegantly or looked more beautiful. Her blond hair had never looked as radiant and soft, or her cerulean eyes more crystalline. Rather than appearing pale and sallow, her cheeks were rosy, her complexion peaches and cream. Looking like an animated, hand-painted Dresden doll, she moved about the hotel bestowing smiles and small talk. It was as if she felt she could shield herself from the looks of derision and words of gossip by being more ebullient and sparkling. She would dazzle the world with her jewelry and fine dresses, her beautiful hair and her graceful manner.

And nothing fit into this new plan of hers better than her playing the role of the mother of the bride and staging what she was determined would be Cutler's Cove's most glamorous affair. She turned the sitting room of her suite into the headquarters for arranging, organizing and designing the wedding. Here she sat regally in her blue-patterned chintz chair with her small hands resting palms down on the heavy, dark mahogany frame, behaving very much like a queen, greeting the service people and tradespeople, photographers, printers and decorators. She summoned a number of them to present their ideas, products and prices, and then she made her choices like a monarch relegating those who were rejected to a beheading. Once she had made a decision to go with one or the other, the others no longer had access to her, even by phone.

"You know, Dawn," she said to me one day, "I still have my wedding dress, and with only the most minor alterations it would fit you like a glove. It would make me so happy if you would wear it. Will you? I assure you it's quite stylish, even by today's standards."

I was reluctant to do so, but in the end I agreed, knowing it would make her happy. Although I hadn't forgiven her for all her lies and weakness, I permitted her to plan the ceremony and reception. After all, I had to give the devil her due – she knew more about such things than I did. She had grown up in fine society. She knew what was considered elegant; she knew protocol. She knew how to plan an important social occasion, right down to how the napkins were to be folded.

I suppose it all didn't strike me as real until she called me into her suite to show me the proofs for our invitations. The card was designed in the shape of a cathedral with the figures of the bride and groom embossed. She had decided that wedding-dress white

71

was an elegant color. I opened the invitation slowly and read:

> *Mr. and Mrs. Randolph Boyse Cutler*
> *Cordially Invite You to the Wedding*
> *of Their Daughter Dawn to James Gary Longchamp*
> *on Saturday, October 26th at 11 A.M.*
> *at the Cutler's Cove Hotel*
> *Reception to Follow*

Mother studied my face to see how I would react to her having used Randolph's name, implying he was my father. In his confused mind, poor Randolph probably still thought he was, I mused. And he and Mother were paying for the wedding.

Practically every day during the weeks preceding Jimmy's and my wedding Mother held a meeting with those people on the hotel staff who would be in charge of different aspects of the affair: Nussbaum, the chef, Norton Green, the headwaiter, Mr. Stanley, and others. I often heard them whining to one another about how many times she changed her mind about things like the hors d'oeuvres for the cocktail party or the main dishes for the dinner and then reverted back to the original ideas – in short, how much harder "Little Mrs. Cutler" was making things for everyone.

It amused me that even though Grandmother Cutler was gone, the staff still referred to Mother as "Little Mrs. Cutler." She would never overcome the lingering shadow and presence of Grandmother Cutler as far as the hotel staff was concerned, no matter how flamboyantly she conducted herself in the hotel.

Randolph was of little or no value during any of this.

He had never really recovered from his deep melancholy over Grandmother Cutler's death. One night, as I was walking past Grandmother Cutler's old room, I thought I heard weeping from within and stopped to listen. I was sure it sounded like Randolph, and I knocked softly. The weeping stopped, but he never came to the door. Yet I hadn't realized how bad things were with him until he came to see me one day.

I was working in the office. I heard a gentle knock and looked up to see Randolph open the door tentatively to peer in.

"Oh, you're here. I thought you might be. Are you busy?" he asked.

"Busy? No," I said, smiling. "What is it?"

"Oh, it's nothing serious," he said, coming in quickly, clutching a paper bag to his chest, "but I've been going over and over this, and you were right," he said.

"I was right? Right about what?" I sat back, a smile of confusion on my face. Randolph had the excited look of a little boy who had discovered a cache of toy soldiers in the attic.

He turned the bag over and dumped a half dozen or so paper-clip boxes.

"What is this?" I asked when he had stepped back, smiling as if the mere emptying of the bag was a major achievement.

"Just what you said. You were right about these people. They cheat us in little ways. You see what I've discovered," he said, pointing to the paper-clip boxes. "Each one of these is supposed to contain one hundred clips, but every one I've counted out so far is five or six short. Five or six! And we order them by the case. Do you realize how many clips we are being shorted?"

73

"Randolph, I never – "

"After our discussion the other day, I knew you would be very happy to hear about this," he said.

"Discussion?" I said. "What discussion?" He didn't blink an eye. Instead he began to put the boxes back into the paper bag. Then he closed it and stepped back, looking like a grade-school child who had just spelled the hardest word in the spelling bee. I sensed he expected me to say something complimentary, but I didn't know what to say.

"Randolph, I'm sorry, but I really don't know what you're talking about."

"Oh, yes, that reminds me," he said, hearing different words. "I have started to look at the butcher's receipts, and I suspect you might be correct about that, too." He reached into his pocket and produced a small packet of bills so old their ends looked brown and crumbling. "The meat and poultry people have not given us the bulk discount we were promised. I don't know exactly how much we've been bilked, but I'm on it. I'll have the numbers for you by the end of the week. Then we'll have a session with them, huh? All right. I won't take up any more of your time, Mother," he said, pivoting to leave.

"Mother?"

He stopped at the door and turned back.

"I'll see you at dinner, Mother," he added, and he left.

I sat back in the chair, astounded. He wasn't simply refusing to accept Grandmother Cutler's death; he was imagining her still alive. But to look at me and think I were she! Was it simply because I was sitting in the chair in this office? It was eerie, as if Grandmother Cutler could reach out from the land of the dead and influence everything through her old possessions. I made up my mind that Mother had to understand how serious the problem with Randolph was.

I left the office and started through the lobby to go up to her suite to speak to her. Randolph was standing by the receptionist's desk talking to someone when he saw me crossing toward the old section of the hotel. He waved and started toward me. What would he do and say now? I wondered. And in front of everyone?

"Hi," he said, his voice lighter and much different from what it had been in the office. "Laura Sue tells me the wedding date has been set."

I stared at him. He saw me as I really was. But how could he make such a rapid and dramatic reversal? I looked back toward Grandmother Cutler's office. It gave me a sharp chill. Did her spirit truly still linger there?

"Aren't you excited?" Randolph asked when I didn't respond immediately to what he had said.

"Yes," I said softly, but I couldn't help but be frightened at how quickly he could change the expression in his eyes, turning off one emotion and turning on another as one would turn on and turn off a faucet.

"Good, good. Mother loves big family events. It will be a wedding like no other wedding you've seen before, that's for sure. Well, I'd better get back to work. I've made Mother promises," he said. "Promises . . ."

I watched him rush off toward his office. Then I went directly to my mother's suite and interrupted her meeting with a decorator. She wanted to do something special in our ballroom for the dance reception after the wedding ceremony.

"I must speak with you now," I said. "I'm sorry," I said to the decorator, "but this is a matter of some urgency."

"Of course." He gathered up his samples and left quickly.

"What is it, Dawn?" Mother demanded impatiently as soon as the man was gone. "I was right in the middle of something very important, and I'm on a very tight schedule today."

"I'm sure it can all wait. Mother, why haven't you done anything about Randolph and the way he behaves?" I demanded.

"Oh, that," she said with a wave of her hand. "What can I do? Anyway, why worry about it now, and especially in the middle of all this?" she said, making her eyes big.

"Because he's getting worse," I replied. I described what had just happened in Grandmother Cutler's office and told her the things he had said. She sighed.

"He won't accept his mother's death or face up to it. I've spoken to him repeatedly about it, but he doesn't hear those words, or doesn't want to." She pressed her lips together and shook her head. Then she sighed. "We're just going to have to ignore him right now, Dawn. He'll snap out of it soon."

"Ignore it? How can you ignore it? You should have a doctor see him," I suggested.

"What for? He just misses his precious mother," she said bitterly. "What's a doctor going to do for him? He can't bring her back. Thank God," she added under her breath.

"Well, something has to be done for him. He's only going to get worse," I insisted. "The staff can humor

76

him for a while, but it's not natural, not normal. He has dark shadows around his eyes, and he's lost so much weight that his clothes just hang on him. I can't believe you haven't noticed how serious all this has become."

"He'll be all right in time," she replied coolly.

"No, he won't," I insisted. I stood directly in front of her, my hands on my hips.

"All right," she finally said when I wouldn't budge, "if he doesn't get better soon, I'll ask Dr. Madeo to look at him. Does that satisfy you?"

"I would think you would be the one worrying, Mother. He isn't really my father, but he is really your husband."

"Oh, Dawn, please don't start all that again," she begged, dramatically raising a hand to her forehead. "We have so much to do right now. Please send the decorator back in to see me."

I saw there was no point in carrying this conversation any further with her. When she wanted to be an ostrich with her head in the ground, she could be. She saw and heard only what she wanted to see and hear. That was the way she had lived her life up until now, and nothing that had happened or that would happen would change her. Disgusted, I shook my head and left her arranging and designing my wedding.

Mr. Updike provided Mother with a list of important guests to invite. Subtly, he made the point to her and to me that the wedding would serve as my coming out, the equivalent of a debutante's ball. I was to be formally introduced to Virginia's high society. Mother didn't hesitate to use his words to stress the importance of all she had done and was doing. The Cutlers had gained some undesired infamy, and we had to show the

77

world that we were still one of the most sophisticated and elegant families in Virginia. The hotel was and always would be a desirable resort for the wealthy and influential who made up the bulk of the wedding guests.

Jimmy and I had few names to add ourselves. I sent Trisha, my best girlfriend at the Sarah Bernhardt School, an invitation, requesting that she attend as my maid of honor. We sent an invitation to Daddy Longchamp, but he called as soon as he had received it to tell us he didn't think he would be able to travel because his new wife Edwina was pregnant again and having some serious complications.

"Pregnant again?" Jimmy replied. It was a shock for both of us to think of Daddy Longchamp as having a whole new family with a new wife. Edwina had already given birth to a boy they had named Gavin about a month or so before Christie had been born. "I was hoping you'd be my best man, Dad," he told him.

"I hate to make promises, Jimmy. If I can, I'll be there, but if Edwina doesn't improve before, I'll have to stay by her. You understand, don'tcha, son?"

"Yes, Dad," Jimmy said, but after he hung up and told me the conversation, I saw that Jimmy didn't understand. Neither of us understood a world in which we grew up thinking two people were our parents and we were brother and sister, only to learn it wasn't so. Neither of us understood a world in which we could both inherit new families practically overnight. And neither of us could put Momma Longchamp out of our minds and see a new wife and family for Daddy Longchamp. In this way I supposed we weren't much different from Randolph – clinging to the things we

78

had loved and cherished and blocking out the changes, trying desperately to reject them. Only we couldn't drift off into a world of our own. We had to go on with our lives.

One weekend two weeks before the wedding, Philip returned from college. I was upstairs dressing Christie in one of her little sailor-girl outfits when Philip arrived.

"You look like you've been doing that for years and years," Philip said from the doorway. I hadn't heard him come down the corridor. He wore a dark blue jacket, striped tie and khaki slacks with his fraternity pin on his jacket lapel. His face was still tanned from his rowing team activities, which made his blue eyes even more beguiling.

"I've had lots of experience, Philip. Did you see Randolph?" I asked quickly.

"Actually, no. Mother told me about all the wedding plans, and I came directly here to wish you and Jimmy luck, and to see if I can be of some help."

"Some help?" I shook my head. "You should be very concerned about your father," I emphasized. "He's behaving very strangely."

"I know. Mother has told me some of it. May I come in?" he asked. He was still just outside the doorway.

"All right," I said, not hiding my displeasure and reluctance.

He stepped up beside me quickly and gazed down at Christie.

"Hi, Christie," he said.

She gazed up at him as I brushed her hair gently behind her ears and over the back of her head.

Christie had bright, inquisitive eyes and always gazed

curiously and intently at people she wasn't used to seeing regularly.

"This is Philip," I said. "Can you say 'Philip'?"

"She talks?" he asked with surprise.

"Of course she talks. She's nearly two years old, and she's an incessant babbler when she wants to be. 'Philip,' " I repeated. She shook her head. "She's teasing us," I said.

"She's beautiful. A lot like her mother," he added. I glanced up at him and then carried Christie to her playpen. As soon as I placed her inside she went for her toy piano and began tapping out notes, looking up occasionally to see if Philip appreciated her recital.

"That's great," he said, clapping. She laughed at him and continued.

"Seriously, Philip," I said, "you should insist something be done about Randolph. He's lost too much weight, there are dark shadows around his eyes, and he's not taking care of himself. He's even untidy, which is quite uncharacteristic of him. He was always concerned about his appearance. Now he's pretending Grandmother Cutler is still alive. He's even mistaken me for her."

"He's in a depression," Philip said nonchalantly, and he shrugged. "He'll snap out of it soon."

"I don't think so," I said, infuriated by his attitude. "But I'm not going to nag you about it."

"Well, thank goodness for little things," he said, his eyes twinkling.

"You won't ever change, Philip. You're too much like Mother: self-centered."

He laughed. "I'm not here to argue with you, Dawn. I don't ever want to argue with you again. I don't expect you can forgive me for everything I've said and done to you in the past, but – "

"No," I said quickly, "I can't."

"But I hope to win back your . . . your friendship, at least. Earn it," he added. "I really do."

I turned to gaze at him. He wore a look of repentance, the glint gone from his eyes, his mouth firm.

"What do you want, Philip?" I asked.

"Another chance. A chance to do something brotherly, perhaps. For starters, I'd like to be a real part of your wedding," he said.

"Part of my wedding? I don't understand. How?"

"Well, Mother told me that Ormand Longchamp can't come and be Jimmy's best man. I was wondering – that is, I was hoping I could be," he said.

"Best man?"

"I'd consider it an honor, of course," he said, his face full of sincerity. "I know Jimmy won't agree to it unless you do," he added.

"He still might not agree to it," I said.

"I just want us to have normal family relationships," he emphasized.

"Normal family relationships?" I nearly laughed. "I don't even know what that means anymore."

"Nevertheless, I'd like it," he insisted.

I studied him. Was he really sincere? Perhaps he, too, had grown tired of the deceptions and the conflicts. Perhaps he, too, hungered for the kind of family life so many people simply took for granted, but which seemed beyond the Cutlers. He did look older, wiser, more settled. I was sure the revelations and the aftermath of the reading of the wills had had a traumatic effect on him as well. After all, he had learned that his grandfather

81

had made love to his mother. That wasn't something to be proud of. The Cutlers had a long way to go to win back the respect and admiration of the world they lived in. Maybe it was now up to us, the next generation.

"All right, Philip," I said. "I'll speak to Jimmy about it."

"Great. So," he said, sitting down, "you've really taken to the hotel business, I understand."

"I'm still learning, but I'm doing more and more every day, yes," I replied proudly.

"When I graduate I intend to return to help you run this place. I've got some great ideas about changing some things, making them more modern and expanding business," he said.

"We've got to remember we're an old, established and distinguished hotel, Philip, catering to a definite clientele who expect certain things to remain as they are, as they always have been," I replied. Philip's eyes widened.

"For a moment there," he said, "you sounded just like Grandmother Cutler."

"I hardly think I could ever sound like her," I snapped back, not liking his comment.

"You never know," Philip said, standing up. "Grandmother Cutler made this place into what it is today, and if you don't change anything, then it will change you," he said prophetically.

"We'll see," I said. Was Philip right? Was I still in a struggle with Grandmother Cutler, even after her death? He smiled.

"All right. I'll go see my father and see what I can do about him. May I join you and Jimmy at dinner tonight? I'm going back to college tomorrow, and I

82

won't have all that much time to visit with you two before the wedding," he explained.

"Yes, you can join us," I said.

"Thanks." He started out. "Oh," he said. "I forgot to tell you. I've met someone at college. Her name's Betty Ann Monroe. We've sort of become an item on campus, if you know what I mean. I'm giving her my fraternity pin this week, and in college that's equivalent to becoming engaged."

"Congratulations."

"I think you'll like her very much. She's bright and very sensitive."

"I'm happy for you, Philip. I look forward to meeting her someday," I said. I was really very happy to hear that he had developed a love interest in someone else. It fueled my hope that he was really changing. Perhaps what he had suggested – normal family relationships – wasn't so out of reach after all.

"Thank you." He stepped closer to me. "Dawn, I . . . well, I hope that what happened between us can somehow be buried and . . ."

"I'll never tell anyone, Philip, if that's what you mean," I said. It was. He immediately looked relieved. "I'm too ashamed of it myself," I added, wiping the smile off his face.

"Yes, well, I'd better go see about my father. I'll see you at dinner," he added, and he left quickly.

When Jimmy came up a little while later I told him what Philip had requested. I had never told Jimmy about Philip raping me. At the time, I was afraid to tell him what Philip had done, and as time passed I'd pressed the memory of Philip's attack on me in the shower deeper and deeper into my memory, where I hoped to keep it buried forever.

"Best man, huh? Well, that's considerate of him. I guess it's okay. As long as it's okay with you," he added, looking at me slyly. Did he know anything? Had he sensed it somehow? Of course, he remembered when Philip had been my boyfriend at Emerson Peabody, but that was before Philip and I had discovered we were related.

"It's your best man, Jimmy. It has to be your decision," I replied, shifting my eyes down quickly.

"He still has a crush on you, doesn't he, Dawn?" Jimmy asked perceptively.

"I don't think so, Jimmy," I said, and I told him about Betty Ann Monroe.

"Um," Jimmy said, thinking. "We'll see. I guess for now it's all right for him and me to be friends. After all, he's my future brother-in-law, and the future's coming up real fast." Jimmy kissed me and started for the shower.

"Oh," he said. "Something peculiar. Randolph came to the workshop just before and asked me about our inventory of screws and nails. I think he's fixing to count them out one at a time. Can you imagine?"

I told Jimmy what had happened between Randolph and me and my conversation with my mother about it.

"Well, someone better do something about him soon," he said. "It's very sad."

Jimmy had more compassion and concern for Randolph than his own son and wife did, I thought. That was what was sad.

While Jimmy was showering the phone rang. It was Trisha. She was all excited about my wedding and had loads of gossip to tell me about the other students at the Sarah Bernhardt School, as well as about Agnes Morris, our resident mother.

"Nothing's really changed with Agnes," she said. "She's more dramatic than ever and wears cakes and cakes of makeup. Oh, Mrs. Liddy asked after you and was happy to hear the good news. She sends her best," Trisha said.

"Mrs. Liddy. I do miss her. She was so nice to me. Perhaps one day I'll invite her to spend a weekend at Cutler's Cove," I said. "Oh, Trish, I'm looking forward so much to finally seeing you again."

"Same here." There was a pause in our conversation, a short, heavy silence. I knew she had something to tell me. "There was some news about Michael Sutton," she confessed, "but I wasn't sure you wanted to hear it."

"I don't mind," I said quickly. "What is it?"

"Oh, there's always a bunch of gossip in the trade papers about his romances, but he's landed a starring role in a new musical opening in London, and the preview reports have been quite laudatory."

"I'm happy for him," I said quickly.

"I think he's horrible for what he did to you," Trisha snapped.

"I don't want to think about that part of it anymore, Trish. I'm very happy now, and I have Christie. That's all that really matters. Michael couldn't be more out of my life. Why, hearing you talk about him now doesn't even affect me," I lied. Deep in my heart of hearts I would never forget the way Michael had betrayed and abandoned me. I had loved him so, but my love had meant nothing to him.

"I'm glad. Do you think you will ever sing again, Dawn?" she asked.

"I hope so, someday. Right now I have plenty to occupy me between Christie and the hotel."

"I can't wait to see the baby. Who does she look like more?"

"She has some of Michael's looks, but right now she looks more like me," I said, adding another lie, remembering the times when I looked at Christie and saw Michael and how much it hurt as old memories returned to haunt me before I banished them.

"I have to get going," Trisha said. "Oodles of silly things to do. I'll speak to you soon. Bye."

"Bye, Trish."

I sat there for a moment with the receiver still in my hand, Trisha's voice trailing off in my memory like a leaf being carried off in a wind, growing smaller and smaller and smaller until it was gone.

Once I was young and innocent and full of dreams. It brought a smile to my face to recall first arriving in New York, being afraid of the traffic and the people and the tall buildings, and not knowing how to react to the eccentric retired actress, Agnes Morris, who ran our residence. And then Trisha burst into my life and introduced me to all the excitement, the nightlife, the cafés, the shops and museums and the theater. She had come with me to audition for Michael Sutton, who was choosing only a few lucky students to be in his vocal class. Trisha and I had squealed with delight that morning and run up the sidewalks and across the streets, holding hands, our hearts beating madly.

And then we saw him. He looked as if he had stepped off the cover of a fan magazine. I would never forget how light my heart felt when he turned to gaze at me and our eyes met. There were so many promises hanging in the air between us, ready to be snatched and savored. We had a dream romance, the kind of romance depicted in songs and stories. What music we made when we sang together.

Even now I could still hear his voice.

"Hey," Jimmy said, stepping out of the bathroom with a towel wrapped around him. "Why are you sitting there with the phone in your hand, smiling? Is anyone on the phone?"

"Oh . . ." I looked at the receiver as if just realizing I held it. "Trisha just called," I said quickly. "She's so excited about the wedding."

"Good." Jimmy stared at me. "You all right?"

"Yes," I said weakly, and I placed the receiver in the cradle. "No," I added, looking up at him. "Oh, Jimmy, hold me, hold me as if you were holding me for the last time."

He came to me quickly and embraced me. I rested my head against his cool chest, and he kissed my hair.

"Don't talk like that," he said. "We have a long, long way to go before I hold you for the last time."

His words were meant to be like drops of warm, gentle rain, soothing. But I felt as if I were sitting with my face pressed against a windowpane and the drops streaked over the glass like tears.

Even so, I raised my face so his lips could find mine and fill me with hope.

My Wedding Day

As Jimmy's and my wedding day drew closer an air of excitement developed in and around the hotel. Preparations swallowed up everyone's attention. I felt as if I were walking on air or parading across a giant stage. I sensed people staring at me all the time and saw them smiling. My heart was in a state of perpetual flutter, and I couldn't help suffering periodic dizzy spells. All I could do was sit down and try to calm myself whenever that happened.

The only unpleasant event that occurred was when Mother came running to tell me about Clara Sue's problems at school. I knew that Clara Sue was bursting with jealousy. Whenever she called home, the wedding was all Mother or anyone would talk about. She hated that I was getting all this attention. Even Philip was excited about it now, and he told her so when he spoke with her. She refused to come home and instead got herself into more and more trouble.

Mother came flying into my room while I was putting Christie to sleep. It was Sissy's night off.

"I don't know what I'm going to do," she cried, with real tears escaping those dainty lids. She wrung her handkerchief in her hand and paced. "Mrs. Turnbell has phoned twice already. Clara Sue's failing all her subjects and being very disruptive in class. She's a major problem at the dormitory, violating curfews, and . . . and she was caught smoking and drinking whiskey in her room with two other girls.

"Now," Mother continued, gasping and falling back into a chair as if she were in the first stages of a heart attack, "she's been found in the boys' dormitory, alone with a boy in his room!"

She started to bawl. Christie sat up and stared at her, wide-eyed. Mother was a mystery to her as it was, barely acknowledging her existence.

"I can't turn to Randolph for help. He's a pathetic creature who won't listen to me when I tell him how ludicrous he appears and how he is becoming the laughing-stock of the Cove. Half the time he doesn't hear anything I say," she moaned. "He's draining me, killing me, and now Clara Sue . . . I can't stand all this tension and controversy, Dawn," she complained. "You know I can't."

"I told you to have the doctor examine Randolph," I said dryly.

"I called him. He saw him," she confessed.

"You never told me that. I didn't know. When was this?" I asked in surprise.

"Last week," she said, waving away the topic. But I didn't want to wave it away.

"And? What did he say? What did he do?" I demanded.

"He wanted me to have him placed in a mental hospital for observation and treatment. Can you imagine? An asylum! Just think of the gossip – a Cutler in the loony bin. How people would look at me, married to a raving lunatic! It's degrading," she cried.

"But how about what's good for him, Mother?" I asked pointedly, my eyes glued hotly on her.

"Oh, he'll be all right." She waved a hand dismissively. "I told the doctor to prescribe some pills, some sedatives, and he's considering it, but until then all of it is falling on my shoulders, Dawn. Can't you help me, do something?"

"Me? What do you want me to do?" I asked with surprise.

"I don't know. Call Mrs. Turnbell and speak to her about Clara Sue. They want to expel her from Emerson Peabody."

"Me? Call Mrs. Turnbell?" I started to laugh. "She hated the sight of me and did everything she could to get Jimmy and me out of there," I said, recalling how unfairly we had been treated.

"But that was in the past. Now you're the owner of a major resort. You can promise her a bigger donation. Anything. What will I do if Clara Sue is expelled? Another disgrace on top of . . ."

"Your own," I said coldly.

"That's just like you, Dawn, to turn on me when I need you the most," she said, her eyes narrowing hatefully. "And here I'm working day and night to make your wedding successful. I would think you would show a little gratitude and treat me with more respect. After all, I am your mother. You seem to enjoy forgetting that fact."

I shook my head. There was no limit to her nerve. She had no shame when it came to certain things, especially if it had to do with her own comfort and happiness.

"Mother," I said, "even if you and I were closer and I wanted to help you with Clara Sue, I couldn't. You're

90

not listening to me. Mrs. Turnbell probably won't even accept a phone call from me. And what makes you think Clara Sue would listen to anything I said? She hates and resents me and hasn't hesitated to let me know it.

"No," I said, "you're going to have to assume your parental responsibility and go see Clara Sue and Mrs. Turnbell. Have a meeting and discuss the problems."

"What? What an outrageous idea! Me? Dragged into that school, into this mess?" She ground the tears out of her eyes with her small fists and laughed. "How ridiculous."

"*You're* her mother. Not me. You must bear the responsibility," I insisted.

"I'm her mother, but that doesn't mean I'm to be made to suffer because of it." She sat there a moment thinking. "All right," she said. "If you refuse to help, then I'll send Mr. Updike. Yes," she said, liking the idea more and more, "what's the point of having an attorney if we don't use him for these things?"

"Our attorney is not supposed to serve as a surrogate parent, Mother. He's supposed to give us legal advice and take care of our contractual needs," I replied.

"Nonsense. Mr. Updike has always been a part of the family, in a way. Grandmother Cutler treated him as if he were, and he likes it. He'll help me. I just know he will. He'll call that principal and stop them from expelling Clara Sue," she concluded. She rose and saw herself in my vanity-table mirror.

"Just look," she moaned. "Just look at the effect all this has already had on me. There's a wrinkle trying to get deeper and longer," she said, pointing to the corner of her right eye. Of course, I could see nothing. Her skin was as smooth and as perfect as ever. She appeared immune to age.

"And my hair," she said, pulling on some strands and spinning around to me. "Do you know what I found this morning while I was brushing my hair . . . do you?" I shook my head. "Gray hairs. Yes, they were gray."

"Mother, everyone gets older," I sighed. "You can't expect to look like a young woman for your entire life, can you?"

"If you don't let other people's problems affect you and you take good care of yourself, you can look young and beautiful for a long, long time, Dawn," she insisted.

"Clara Sue's problems and Randolph's problems are not other people's problems, Mother. Clara Sue is your daughter; Randolph is your husband," I pointed out sharply.

"Don't remind me," she said, and she started out. Then she turned in my doorway. "Someday you will understand me and see that I'm the one for whom you should feel the most sympathy," she predicted. Then she sniffed back her tears and walked out.

I wanted to shout after her and tell her that I did pity her. I pitied her for being so selfish that she couldn't love other people, not even her own children. I wanted to tell her I pitied her for trying to stop what was natural and wished she could grow older gracefully, instead of battling every gray hair. She would wake up one day and feel like a prisoner in her own aging body. Mirrors would become torments, and pictures of herself when she was younger would be like pins sticking into her heart. But I stopped myself from uttering a single syllable. Why waste my breath and my strength? I thought.

She did call Mr. Updike, and he did manage to get Clara Sue a reprieve. Mrs. Turnbell agreed to put her on probation, but I had no doubt that it was only a matter of time before she would get into serious trouble again. And I was against making any additional donations to Emerson Peabody to insure they kept her when Mr. Updike suggested it to me. Jimmy was pleased to hear about that.

"I'd love to walk back into her office one day," he said, "and see the look on her face."

"She's not worth the trip, Jimmy," I said.

"Yeah, but next time we're in the area," he said, laughing.

Life was filled with so many ironies, so many turns that led you to places you never imagined. A few years ago, when I had been whisked away from Jimmy and Fern and Daddy Longchamp, driven through the night to be returned to my real family here at Cutler's Cove, I felt terrible fear and dread. I remember being led into the hotel through a back entrance and brought directly to Grandmother Cutler, who made me feel lower than a worm and who tried to strip me of any dignity by forcing another name on me and making me clean toilets and make beds. And now I sat in her chair and signed the checks and made the decisions. I had my beautiful baby, and Jimmy and I were about to be married. No, I thought, this wasn't the time to cloud my heart with hate and dream of sweet revenge. This was a time to be forgiving and loving and hopeful.

I didn't even lose my temper when Clara Sue phoned me a few days before my wedding to inform me she wouldn't be able to attend.

"I have a date I can't break," she said. Perhaps she had expected I would beg her to do so.

"Well, I'm sorry to hear that, Clara Sue," I said.

"No one will even notice I'm not there," she added petulantly, still trying to get me to sound upset.

"Maybe," I said. "But I'll do my best to remind them," I added. She missed my sarcasm.

"I think it's stupid to marry the boy you once thought was your brother!" she exclaimed. "No one here who remembers you can believe it."

"Well, I'm sure you will do your best to convince them it's true," I said.

"That's not what I mean!" she shouted.

"I'm sorry, Clara Sue, but there are so many things for me to do right now. I'll have to hang up. Thanks for calling and wishing us good luck," I added, even though she hadn't. Then I cradled the receiver before she could reply, and I sat back, smiling. She was probably fuming so badly there was smoke coming out of her ears, I thought. The image made me laugh and turned a potentially unhappy moment into a jovial one.

There wasn't much time to sulk over anything anyway. The next day Trisha arrived. We were so glad to see each other, we both nearly burst with happiness. I knew exactly when she would arrive and waited at the front entrance. When the hotel car brought her up she flew out almost before it had come to a complete stop, and we hugged each other and cried and laughed, both of us talking at the same time.

Trisha's personality hadn't changed a bit. She was still her exuberant, effervescent self, her bright green eyes filled with excitement. Of course, she looked older and more elegant. Her dark brown hair was swept softly to one side and curled under her ear. She wore a pink and white cardigan sweater and a light pink shirt.

"You look so beautiful," I said.

"Thank you, and so do you. And this place!" She spun around, gazing excitedly at everything. She had arrived on one of our warmest early spring days. Flowers were blooming everywhere; the lawns had just been cut, and there was the wonderful scent of freshly trimmed grass. Just across the way the ocean was calm and glimmered like glass in the bright sunshine. "It's so beautiful here, and it's yours," she added, widening her eyes and squeezing my arm. "I want to see everything right away," she exclaimed. "Especially the chapel where you'll be married, and the ballroom and your wedding dress. Oh, I can't wait to see your wedding dress."

"The maid of honor is supposed to help plan my trousseau for the honeymoon," I told her. "My mother has given me specific instructions."

"I know." Trisha giggled, and grabbed my hand. "Come on, show me all of it."

It was like holding hands with a whirlwind. I no sooner brought her to one part of the hotel than she was crying for me to take her to another. She wanted to meet everyone we accosted and just had to know what each person's duties were. When I brought her to the kitchen, Nussbaum insisted she taste a new strudel he had concocted. Her eyes rolled, and she licked her lips with such emphasis, even he had to laugh.

Afterward I brought her up to my suite. On the way we stopped so she could meet Mother, who greeted her with such a haughty air that we looked at each other and swallowed our laughter. How she could put on that high-toned manner like a hat and then just as easily discard it. When we were safely in the confines of my room Trisha and I burst into laughter.

"Oh, she's everything you described," Trisha said. "She reminded me of Agnes demonstrating how she played Queen Elizabeth in *Mary, Queen of Scots*."

I told her about Randolph and what to expect when she was introduced. She shook her head sadly.

Then I showed her my wedding dress, which she insisted I put on. Afterward we went through my wardrobe, planning my honeymoon trousseau as if each day were another act in a play. We giggled over the lingerie, especially the sheer nightgowns. While we chatted and plotted Trisha made me turn on the radio. I had been buried in my work and responsibilities so intently that I had lost track of what was popular.

For a while, laughing and renewing my friendship with Trisha made me feel young again. My baptism by fire in the hotel had aged me in ways I didn't appreciate or desire. I felt like the princess who was given a chance to be a real young girl before she had to be returned to the palace and behave as everyone expected royalty to behave. Trisha and I could moan and swoon over movie stars, thumb through fashion magazines and giggle and squeal over stories she related concerning boys we had both known at Sarah Bernhardt. Cautiously, we both skirted any reference to Michael Sutton, gingerly circling those days I spent with him and in his vocal class. We talked a blue streak until Sissy arrived with Christie.

"Oh, she's beautiful," Trisha said after I introduced them. Christie's eyes brightened instantly. I was afraid she had inherited some of Mother's vanity, as well as her father's. She behaved coyly for a few moments, pretending to be shy, but watching Trisha out of the corner of her eye, waiting to be coaxed along. Then, as usual, she turned her charm on, smiling and eagerly accepting Trisha's hugs and kisses.

"She's darling," Trisha whispered. "And she has Michael's beautiful eyes," she said.

"I know."

It was the only mention either of us made of him the entire wedding weekend.

Afterward, we all went down to look for Jimmy, who was supervising the grounds people and working on the pool equipment. He and Trisha had a nice reunion. When we left him, she whispered in my ear how handsome and mature Jimmy had become.

"You're so lucky," she said as we started back into the hotel, Christie holding both our hands. "You have all this – a beautiful hotel, a handsome man who loves you and a beautiful child. And don't forget, you're still very talented. You can still do something with singing. Don't you feel lucky now?" she prodded when I remained silent. "Don't you feel that all the hardship and unhappiness is behind you?"

"Sometimes," I said. I looked back at Jimmy, who waved. "And sometimes I feel like I've just moved into the eye of a storm. It's calm, beguiling, deceptive. For no reason I can think of, my heart begins to pound, and I feel dizzy, frightened. I wish I could freeze the moment like a camera snapping a photograph and lock us forever and ever in today."

Trisha stared at me a moment, her eyes fixed curiously on mine. Then her smile returned.

"That's just because you had such a hard life before.

97

You can't believe your good luck. It's just natural," she insisted.

"Is it? I hope so, Trish," I said. "I hope so."

She hugged me for reassurance, and we went in to complete the preparations for my big day.

The day before my wedding we rehearsed the ceremony. Philip returned from college that morning. He was in charge of looking after Randolph and being sure he was where he was supposed to be. Mother took command almost the moment the minister arrived. She choreographed everyone's movements: when this one would come in from there, who should hold whose hand and where and how we should all stand. Randolph fidgeted terribly the entire time and was relieved when he was finally excused and could go back to his "critical" work. Mother sighed deeply to let everyone know how difficult things were for her with Randolph behaving this way. Naturally, his behavior upset her so much that she had to retreat to her bedroom to rest and prepare for the actual wedding.

I awoke very early the next morning, even before the sun had risen, but I lay in bed staring up at the ceiling. Because of the significance of the day, a mixture of some of the saddest and happiest moments of my life flashed before me. I couldn't help but recall Momma Longchamp brushing my hair when I was just a little girl and describing her dreams and hopes for me. She imagined I would grow up to be a beautiful woman and would eventually win the heart of a prince.

"You'll live in a beautiful place and have an army of servants just waitin' on your every beck and call," she said, and in the mirror I could see her tilt her head and gaze at me, her eyes twinkling with sugar.

And then I remembered her pale and sickly face, her eyes a dull silver like old dimes, and filled with trepidation the last time I had seen her alive in the hospital. I could still feel her hand clutching mine. I could still hear and see Jimmy sobbing. Daddy Longchamp's gray face rose out of the darkness behind my closed lids, all the pain of sorrow in his dark eyes.

I swallowed back my own sobs and felt my eyes fill with tears. Today I was getting married, and even though my real mother had done so much to prepare an elegant and fancy affair, I longed for Momma and Daddy Longchamp and wished that somehow they could be at my side. To me it was as if I were being married without my parents present. Randolph was a pathetic soul, hardly a father figure, and Mother . . . well, for Mother, this was as much her party as it was my wedding.

Despite my reluctance to do so, I couldn't help but think about Michael and about the wonderful, romantic times we had in his apartment in New York. That was when he had made all sorts of promises to me, when we had planned our own storybook wedding, when he had filled my eyes with visions of glamour and excitement – a wedding ceremony attended by all sorts of celebrities and covered by the newspapers and magazines, a honeymoon on the French Riviera, a chalet in Switzerland, cruises, parties on yachts and a triumphant return to the stage, singing our hearts and souls out to each other in a way that would make us both superstars.

All of that popped out of my mind like a soap bubble.

If it wasn't for Christie, I would try to convince myself none of it had actually happened.

But it had happened, as well as all the horror I endured during my pregnancy at The Meadows. I couldn't erase it from my mind like some words scribbled in pencil. The events, the pain and suffering, the tears and the laughter, the heartbreak and the relief, all mingled together to form a potpourri of memories I would drag with me forever and ever.

These depressing thoughts drifted from my mind as the early rays of sunlight found the openings in my window drapes and began to brighten the room with new warmth and hope. I heard Christie stir in her crib. A few moments later she was whispering her baby gibberish to herself as she lifted the curtain of sleep from her eyes and began a new day of discovery. Just thinking about the wonder and astonishment that would be revealed in her face when she was dressed and brought to my wedding made me smile in anticipation.

I rose from my bed and went to her. She looked up, surprised because she sensed how early it was. I took her in my arms and kissed her and brought her to the window, where I opened the curtains wide so we could look out on what was beginning to be a glorious late-spring day. She was as fascinated as I was by the way the darkness and the shadows retreated from the rising sun. Small clouds, like puffs of smoke, seemed to emerge from the blue sky behind and around them. Everywhere birds were coming to life, rising from their nests and branches to greet the warm morning and begin their efforts to find food.

"Isn't it a beautiful morning, Christie? A beautiful day for Momma to get married," I said. The sun shone through the window, casting diamond strands of light on her hair. She turned to me inquisitively, as if she really understood what I was saying. Then she focused her blue eyes on the scene still unfolding below us, and her little lips folded into an angelic smile, making her look like a cherub. I kissed her cheeks and decided since we were already up, we might as well get started.

Sissy arrived to help with the baby, and then Mrs. Boston brought me a breakfast tray. The first thing Mrs. Boston did was whisper to me about Mother.

"I got up in the middle of the night," she told me, "as is my habit these days, and I caught sight of this light on. So I went to see what it was, and that's when I saw her. It was easily four o'clock in the morning!"

"What was she doing?" I asked, amazed.

"She was already up and fixing herself at her vanity mirror. I didn't let her see me looking in on her. Maybe she just got confused about the time, with all the excitement and everything," Mrs. Boston added, shaking her head. But nothing Mother did at this point really surprised me.

A little while later Trisha arrived to help me prepare myself. Sissy dressed Christie and took her away so we wouldn't be distracted.

"Nervous?" Trisha asked.

"You mean because my fingers are trembling and I don't dare put the lipstick to my lips?" I replied, laughing. She helped me brush and style my hair. Mother looked in on us just before she was about to go down to begin greeting the guests. I had to confess she looked very, very beautiful.

She wore a strapless off-white satin gown with a lace bodice lined with pearls. Over her shoulders she

101

wore a sheer shawl, and around her neck she wore her thickest diamond necklace. Matching teardrop earrings dangled from her lobes. On her left wrist she had her thick gold bracelet studded with emeralds and diamonds and rubies, a bracelet she once bragged was worth half as much as the hotel.

"You look beautiful, Mother," I said.

"Yes, Mrs. Cutler. You do," Trisha chorused.

"Thank you, girls. I just came by to wish you good luck and to see if there is anything you need, Dawn. After this I will be very busy," she said.

"No, we're fine, Mother. Thank you for your good wishes," I said.

She flashed a smile and left, eager to take her position as queen of the hotel.

Jimmy surprised me with his adherence to tradition and refused to see me or let me see him until we saw each other in the chapel. "We've had enough bad luck to last a lifetime," he had told me. "I'm not doing anything to bring about any more."

I was shaking so much when Trisha and I took our positions to wait for the start of the music that I was positive I would trip and fall on my journey to the altar. Philip brought Randolph in only moments before the music began. Both of them wore tuxedos. Philip's fit perfectly, and he looked very handsome, but Randolph's illustrated just how much weight he had actually lost. The jacket seemed to float around him, and his pants looked rather baggy. Philip had managed to get him to have his hair trimmed and his face cleanly shaven. He did smile and look excited, but moments later he was fidgeting again and appearing very distracted. I noticed how he kept whispering in Philip's ear.

"Is he all right?" I asked.

"Yes, yes, don't worry," Philip said. "He'll do his small part okay," he assured me. "You never looked more beautiful, Dawn," Philip said. "Can I give you a good luck kiss now, before the rush?" he asked.

"Yes, Philip."

His eyes brightened, and he leaned forward to kiss me on the lips, but I turned my cheek to him. Disappointed, he planted a quick kiss there and pulled back.

"Good luck," he whispered.

"Thank you, Philip."

"I'd better get with the bridegroom. He looks like he's going to pass out any moment."

Randolph appeared to panic for a moment after Philip left, but I took his hand, and he smiled at me.

"It's a big day, big day," he said. "The hotel's just buzzing with activity. Mother's always been best when she's under pressure," he assured me, patting my hand.

Trisha and I exchanged worried glances, but thankfully, before any more could be said, the music started, and we began our march.

Jimmy looked so handsome waiting for me at the altar. As I drew closer and closer to him his eyes brightened. No one will ever love me as much as Jimmy does, as much as Jimmy always did, I thought. I'm so lucky to have him.

I was so terrified of doing something clumsy, I barely glanced from side to side, but I did catch glimpses of some of the guests. I recognized the faces of many of the dignitaries from the area and their wives, people I had met at different formal occasions. I saw Mr. and Mrs. Updike and Mr. and Mrs. Dorfman seated together, the men smiling, the women studying everything intently. Some looked very disapprovingly at me, I thought. They made me feel like an intruder, like a poor girl who had put on a rich girl's clothes and assumed a rich girl's identity and life.

I saw my mother flashing her smile at everyone, her jewelry sparkling on her soft-looking neck and perfect skin. Mr. Alcott was standing beside her and gazing warmly at me. He looked very dapper in his stylish tuxedo with a carnation in the lapel. Across the aisle Sissy held Christie in her arms. She looked darling in her white dress with the crinoline insert. Her golden hair was brushed softly and looked radiant. She stared intently, drinking in everything, fascinated with the scene taking place before her. Her eyes brightened with wonder the moment she saw me.

Here and there I caught sight of some of the hotel's department heads and their wives. Their smiles seemed more sincere.

I took my place beside Jimmy. His hand slipped around mine, giving me support. The minister began with a short prayer, giving thanks for this wonderful occasion. My heart began to thump like a drum. I was sure everyone in the chapel could hear it beating in my chest every time the minister paused and there was a moment of silence.

Finally he began, but just before he asked, "Who gives this woman to this man," Randolph leaned forward to whisper in my ear.

"I don't see Grandmother Cutler," he said. "Something must be detaining her. I'll be right back."

104

"What? No, Randolph." I turned to stop him, but he was already charging down the aisle. A murmur of amazement rippled through the congregation, and Mother looked as if she would faint. Bronson put his arm around her waist. The minister waited a moment and then looked at Mother. She said something to Bronson, and to my surprise and shock he stepped forward, nodding at the minister, who then said, "Who gives this woman to this man?"

"I do," Bronson Alcott replied. Once again there was a ripple of surprise in the audience, but the minister continued with the ceremony. Almost reluctantly, I thought, Philip gave Jimmy the ring to slip on my finger.

I looked into Jimmy's eyes when he was asked to repeat his words, but I was distracted by Philip because I saw Philip's lips move, too. He was mouthing the oath: "To have and to hold, in sickness and in health . . ." It was as if he thought he was marrying me through Jimmy. He, too, mouthed, "I do." I was so shaken by it that for a moment I lost my wits and didn't hear the minister ask me to repeat my vows. But I got hold of myself, slipped his ring on his finger, and concentrated on Jimmy's eyes as I said the words that would link us together for ever and ever, "Till death do us part."

We kissed, and there was applause as we hurried down the aisle together. It was over. I was Mrs. James Gary Longchamp.

The cocktail party and reception was set up in the hotel lobby. Mother, Jimmy and I stood in a reception line as the guests entered. It was Mother's idea that

Mr. Updike stand beside Jimmy and myself so we could be introduced to some of the important guests that I hadn't met yet. It saddened me a bit because I knew it was something Randolph should really do but was incapable of doing. In fact, I didn't see him anywhere. When I asked Philip if he knew how he was, he said he would see.

Once the guests passed through the line they could go to either side of the lobby, where two bars were set up for drinks. Waiters and waitresses were dressed in the new uniforms Mother had designed especially for the occasion. The waiters wore bright red vests, white shirts and red bow ties with red slacks, and the waitresses wore white vests, red blouses with white bow ties and white skirts. They threaded through the crowd, offering guests hot and cold hors d'oeuvres: fried and boiled shrimp, egg rolls, won tons, caviar and pâté. Some waiters carried trays of champagne.

In the far corner was the five-piece cocktail band. Once everyone had passed through our reception line, Jimmy and I and Trisha got ourselves some food and drink. Christie was down by the band with Sissy, clapping her hands and swaying to the music. It was a very lively cocktail party. Everyone seemed to be enjoying it immensely. Philip returned from looking for Randolph and told me he was all right, just doing some small things in his office.

"He's a bit confused, but nothing more," he explained.

"Isn't he coming out?" I asked.

"Sure. Soon," Philip said, and he mingled with some of the younger guests he knew.

Just before the announcement was made for everyone to proceed to the ballroom for the dinner and the

106

dancing, Bronson Alcott came up to me and pulled me aside.

"I hope you aren't angry about what I did during the ceremony," he said. "Your mother was in a panic and begged me to do something when Randolph wandered off at the most inappropriate time."

"It's all right," I said. "I understand and appreciate it."

He smiled widely.

"Might I give the bride a congratulatory kiss?" he asked. I nodded, and he kissed me rather softly and lovingly on my cheek, squeezing my hand as he did so. "The very best of luck to you," he said. "You two make a very handsome couple."

"Thank you," I said, and I watched him stroll over to Mother, who was obviously having the time of her life greeting people who were showering her with lavish compliments. She had already gathered a small herd of male admirers about her and was holding court.

A little bit later the band stopped playing and the bandleader went to his microphone to announce that he had been asked to tell everyone to proceed to the ballroom. As people entered they had to pass through a giant arch covered with red and yellow roses that spelled GOOD LUCK DAWN AND JAMES. On the other side of the arch, the maître d' awaited at a desk upon which he had everyone's name and assigned table. The entire ballroom had been decorated in a wedding motif. Enormous white, green, blue and yellow styrofoam cutouts of bells and flowers, chapels and angels were hung on the walls. At the far end were gigantic cutouts of a bride and a groom at an altar.

All of the tables had real flower centerpieces. Beside

them were bottles of champagne set in silver ice buckets. The guests received small mementos of the wedding: gold-trimmed matchbooks with "Dawn and James" printed on them in a gold heart and the date underneath, real leather bookmarks with our names embossed and figures of a bride and groom at the top and small makeup mirrors for the women with DAWN AND JAMES AT CUTLER'S COVE printed on the back.

While the guests were parading in I asked Mother if she shouldn't go see about Randolph.

"What for?" she said, grimacing as if I had shoved a tablespoon of cod-liver oil into her mouth. "He's so depressing," she added, "and he has already embarrassed all of us to no end."

"But . . ."

Before I could say anything more she saw someone turn her way and wave. She released a peal of laughter herself and hurried away.

"I'm going to see about Randolph, Jimmy. It will take these people a few minutes to get seated anyway," I said.

"Okay. I'll wait right here." He kissed me on the cheek, and I rushed out to Randolph's office.

I found him seated at his desk, scribbling over a pad. He didn't look up when I knocked.

"Randolph?" I said, approaching him. "Are you all right?"

He lifted his eyes toward me and then looked at the pad. I could see he had just been doodling. Suddenly a single tear broke free of his left eyelid and began to trickle down his cheek. His lips trembled, and his chin quivered.

"She's gone," he said. "Mother's gone."

"Oh, Randolph," I said, both happy and sad that he was finally willing to face up to it. "Yes, she is."

He shook his head and looked at Grandmother Cutler's picture on his desk.

"I never really had a chance to say good-bye," he said. "We were always so busy . . ." He looked back at me and shook his head. "We never really said the things that we should have said to each other. At least, I didn't say the things I should have said to her. She was always protecting me, looking after me."

"Randolph, I'm sorry," I said. "I know you have been avoiding the reality for so long, but maybe this is good. Maybe you can achieve things again, become what she would have wanted you to become."

"I don't know," he said. "I don't know if I can. I feel so lost."

"You will get better with time, Randolph. I know you will."

He smiled at me gratefully.

"How pretty you look," he said.

"Thank you, Randolph. You know it's my wedding day," I said softly. "The ceremony and the cocktail party are over. Now we're all going into the ballroom for dinner. Don't you want to come and celebrate with us? It's time for us all to enter together," I emphasized.

He nodded. "Yes," he said, looking around. "I'll be there," he said. "In a moment. I just want to get myself together." He lifted his heavy, dark eyes toward me again. "Good luck to you," he said, as if he would never see me again.

"Don't be long, Randolph. Please," I said. He wiped his cheek with the back of his hand and nodded.

"I won't," he promised. "Thank you," he said.

Mother was waiting impatiently beside Jimmy when I returned.

"It's time for us to enter," she said. "Where were you?"

"I went to see Randolph. He's snapping out of it, facing the truth," I told her.

"Well, good for him. It's about time," she said sharply.

"He needs you, needs someone to help him," I said.

"Oh, Dawn, why bring up all this dreary business at a time like this?" she moaned. "It's your wedding day, for goodness sakes! Enjoy it!"

"He said he would enter with us," I told her, and I looked back for him.

Just then we heard the band inside stop, and then a drumroll begin. The master of ceremonies took the microphone and announced us.

"Ladies and gentlemen, your hosts, the Cutlers, and the bride and groom, Mr. and Mrs. James Gary Longchamp."

"Where is he?" I cried.

"We can't wait any longer. He's probably forgotten what you told him by now anyway," Mother said, starting toward the door. "Dawn," she snapped when I hesitated.

"I guess we'd better go in," Jimmy said.

I nodded and put my arm through his. I looked back one more time before we went under the arch, but Randolph was nowhere to be seen. Mother, undaunted, passed through first, bathing in the applause. The guests were all standing. Jimmy and I walked in after her,

110

smiling and waving to people. The three of us went directly to the dais.

Seated with us were Mr. and Mrs. Updike, Mr. and Mrs. Dorfman, Philip and Bronson Alcott, who was placed on Mother's right. Randolph's empty chair was on her left. Sissy and Christie were on the far right end with Tricia beside them. Jimmy and I took our seats in the center, and everyone sat down. Almost as soon as we did, Mr. Alcott stood up.

The first thing the waiters and waitresses had done was to be sure everyone had his or her glass filled with champagne. Mr. Alcott lifted his.

"It's appropriate at this time," he began, "for someone to have the honor to offer a toast to the bride and groom. I am truly honored to be the one selected."

He turned toward us.

"The people of Cutler's Cove joyfully welcome Mr. and Mrs. James Gary Longchamp to our community and wish them health, happiness and success. May you two have a long and wonderful marriage and be blessed from this day forward. To James and Dawn," he cried, and the crowd of guests repeated, "To James and Dawn."

Immediately someone began to tap his glass, and the entire place reverberated with a chorus of tinkles. We knew that meant they wanted to see us kiss. We did so quickly, because Jimmy was quite shy about it. There was laughter and applause, and then the music and the meal began.

There was fresh melon and salad and a cup of soup. The main dish was filet mignon with baked potatoes and stir-fried vegetables. Mother had had the baker design bread in the shape of wedding bells. The courses were

111

well spaced so that people could get up and enjoy the dancing while they feasted.

Jimmy and I got up and danced twice, and then Philip requested a dance. I looked at Jimmy. His eyes narrowed, but he nodded gently, and I accepted.

"I have to hand it to Mother," he said while he held me close to him, "she outdid herself this time. I've never seen such an affair at the hotel. You can be sure Grandmother wouldn't have spent this much."

"Mother doesn't know a thing about money and costs, nor could she care."

"Spoken like a true Cutler," he said, smiling.

"Stop saying that, Philip. I'm just trying to be realistic. I see the plus and minus columns every day," I replied. He looked impressed.

"Anyway," he said, "I'm glad she didn't spare the expense. I can't think of anyone I'd like to see enjoy it more than you.

"I wonder," he continued, "if my wedding will be anything like this. I expect it might."

"Have you become formally engaged?" I asked.

"Not yet, but soon," he said. "My fiancée's parents are very wealthy."

"I'm happy for you, Philip."

"Of course," he said, swinging me to the side, "money isn't important if you're not with the one you want to be with."

"But you are, aren't you, Philip?" I pursued.

"You know, I'll always wish it was you and I, Dawn," he replied. His eyes were soft, limpid pools of desire.

"Well, we both know that can't and never will be. So there's no sense talking about it, is there?"

112

"No, you're right," he said. "It's only painful to do so."

When the dance ended I asked him if he would go look in on Randolph.

"See what's keeping him," I asked.

"Your wish is my command," he replied, bowing like a dutiful servant, and he left. Before I could return to the dais the music started again, and I felt myself being turned. I looked up into Bronson Alcott's eyes.

"May I have this next dance?" he asked. I looked toward the dais. Jimmy was talking to some of the hotel staff.

"Yes," I said. He took hold of me firmly, and we began.

"You know," he said, "I'm quite envious of James. He's landed the best catch at the shore."

"It's the other way around, Mr. Alcott. I've landed the best catch."

He laughed.

"Please, call me Bronson," he said again. "I don't like feeling older than you."

"No wonder you and my mother get along so well," I said petulantly. His smile widened. "She never wants to act her age either."

He roared and swung me around. I had to admit to myself that in his arms I did feel like a princess. He was so graceful. Our dancing caught the attention of a number of the guests, many of whom stopped dancing themselves to watch us. Before long it seemed as if the entire wedding party was staring our way, especially Mother, who wore the most unusual look on her face – a mixture of jealousy and sadness. When the number ended there was some applause.

113

"We're a hit," Bronson said. "Thank you."

"Thank you," I said, and I hurried back to Jimmy, who looked overwhelmed.

"I can't wait to get out of here," I whispered, "and be on our honeymoon."

He brightened and kissed me softly. Then Sissy brought Christie to us, and we took her out on the dance floor and held her between us as we danced and enjoyed the music.

Philip returned to tell me that Randolph had fallen asleep on the sofa in his office.

"I didn't have the heart to wake him," he said.

"Maybe it is for the best," I admitted.

Suddenly the band stopped playing and the emcee came to the microphone.

"Many of you know," he began, "that our beautiful bride is a very talented singer. Perhaps we can coax her into coming up here and singing at her own wedding."

"Oh, no," I cried. But the guests all cheered. I looked helplessly at Jimmy and Trisha.

"Go ahead," he said.

"Yes, show them what a Sarah Bernhardt student can do," Trisha added excitedly.

"Oh, Jimmy . . ." Reluctantly, I let myself be led to the microphone. The band waited for instructions. I remembered an old love song Momma Longchamp used to hum sometimes. To my surprise, the band knew it, too. They started playing, and I began.

"I'm confessing that I love you . . ."

The guests grew quite attentive. Many swayed to the melody. When I was finished there was thunderous applause. I looked at Jimmy and saw him beaming with pride. To his right Bronson Alcott sat staring at me with a wide smile. Mother fluttered about, accepting congratulations from everyone near her. I hurried back to Jimmy's side.

Shortly afterward the wedding cake was wheeled out, and Jimmy and I had to go down to do the traditional cutting. Once again our guests applauded, and the waiters and waitresses began taking pieces of the cake around to the different tables.

The dinner and the dancing lasted well into the early evening. I was so tired from the excitement and from getting up so early, I was frankly glad to see it coming to an end. Mother, who often cried and moaned over doing such simple things as brushing her own teeth, seemed to have endless energy. She fed on all the attention she was receiving, especially the male attention, and tried to talk people out of leaving when they came to say good-bye.

"But it's so early!" she exclaimed.

Gradually, though, the guests began to thin out until there were just a dozen or so remaining. Mr. Updike, Mr. Dorfman and Bronson Alcott were the last to go.

Jimmy and I were all packed for our honeymoon. We had our plane tickets, and the hotel car was set to take us to the airport after we both changed. I helped Sissy put Christie to bed, explaining to her that Momma would be away for a while and asking her to be a good girl for Sissy. She seemed to understand, for she hugged me tighter than usual and kissed me longer.

"Don't you worry none, Dawn," Sissy said. "I'll take good care of her."

"I know you will, Sissy. Thank you."

"You was a beautiful bride," she said, tears coming to her eyes.

"You will be one, too, Sissy."

She smiled, and we hugged. Jimmy had already gotten our bags down and was waiting in the lobby. On my way to meet him I met Mother, struggling to get herself up the stairs.

"I'm so tired," she said. "I'm going to sleep a week."

"Thank you, Mother," I said. "It was a wonderful wedding." Once again, I had to give the devil her due. She beamed.

"It was, wasn't it?"

"All except for Randolph," I said. "I do hope you will look after him now," I added. Her smile withered.

"Please," she said. "Don't remind me." She pulled herself past me, moaning about her feet. I bounced down the rest of the stairway and rushed out to join Jimmy. Trisha, who was going to ride to the airport with us, was waiting beside him at the door.

As I started across the lobby Philip, who was leaning against the reception counter, stepped forward.

"Have a good time," he said.

"Thank you."

"I wish I were going with you," he added.

I ignored him and ran into the waiting arms of Jimmy, the waiting arms of my husband.

Honeymoon Heartache

Exhausted, I was happy to lay my head against Jimmy's shoulder in the hotel limousine and close my eyes. I felt his fingers brush strands of my hair away from my forehead, clearing a place for him to place his warm, loving kiss. I smiled with my eyes closed.

"You look like a young woman having a wonderful dream," Jimmy whispered.

"I am," I replied, my smile widening.

"As long as I'm in it, I don't mind," he said. My eyelids fluttered open, and I looked up into his soft, dark eyes. I sensed his concern. After all, I had once fallen deeply and passionately in love with someone else and borne that man's child. Jimmy had reason to wonder if my dreams included him.

Suddenly I realized the immensity of his love for me. He had never asked me outright if I had stopped loving Michael Sutton after Michael had deserted me. He never seemed to wonder if I still thought often about Michael. He never asked. Maybe he was afraid of the answers. Maybe he knew I couldn't lie to him and deny that Michael came to my mind occasionally, especially when I held Christie in my arms.

But Jimmy was willing to put all this aside. He believed our love for each other would grow stronger and stronger with every passing day. I meant so much to him that he was willing to risk his own heart. I did love him, I thought, and that love could only grow stronger.

"You will always be in my dreams, Jimmy. Now and forever," I promised him. I lifted my head so our lips could touch, and we held a long kiss. Then I closed my eyes again and let my head fall against his chest. He held me snugly until we were nearly at the airport.

Our flight took us directly to Provincetown, at the tip of Cape Cod. From there we hired a cab to our motel, which was on the beach. It was nearly midnight when we were finally settled in our honeymoon suite, and we were both quite tired, but quite excited. Our room had a patio door that opened on a small balcony. We were only two flights up, but the unobstructed beachfront provided us with a sweeping view of the ocean. It was a clear night, with the stars blazing like diamonds on black velvet. I felt as if we were at the top of the world. Jimmy came up behind me. Sensing my thoughts, he put his arm about my shoulder and drew me closer.

"Happy?" he asked.

"Oh, yes, Jimmy. I feel like Alice falling into a wonderland of rainbow dreams."

Something boyishly wistful and sweet visited his eyes.

"The stars seem so close," he said, and he kissed me on the cheek.

"And bright. Even when I close my eyes, I still see them!" I exclaimed. Jimmy laughed and turned me around to kiss me on the lips. "Mrs. James Gary Longchamp," he whispered, and he scooped me into his arms to bring me to the bed. He hovered above me, stroking my hair, and stared down at me.

Once before, when he had visited me at school in New York, we had gone to his hotel room and almost made love. This was before I had met Michael. Jimmy's and my memories of being brought up thinking we were brother and sister were still quite strong, and even though I had closed my eyes and had told myself over and over that we weren't blood-related and we had no reason to feel dirty wanting and loving each other, it was very hard to overcome years and years of living as siblings.

It had been the same for Jimmy, and he had decided it was too soon. Although we had hugged and kissed and petted each other affectionately, we had held off consummating our love. I knew that once we did it, we would shatter the wall that still lingered between us, a wall comprised of mistaken guilt and confusion, a wall built out of lies and deceit, a false wall that never should have been between us in the first place.

"Are you too tired?" Jimmy asked, once more providing a way for me to avoid the moment.

"No," I said, and I brought my fingers to my blouse to begin undoing the buttons.

"Let me," he said. "You can just lie there with your eyes closed, seeing those stars."

I smiled, but the moment his fingers touched the buttons, my heart began to pound. It thumped like a tin drum, and my stomach filled with feathers. Gently he peeled my blouse away and slipped it down my arms. Just as gently, almost magically, he unfastened my bra. I didn't open my eyes. I felt him move down the bed to take off my heels and slide my skirt over my legs. When he plucked my panties away I opened my eyes and looked up at him. He was gazing down at me with such desire, I felt myself grow faint.

"Do you remember," he said in a voice barely above a whisper, "how you would catch me from time to time watching you dressing?"

"Yes," I said, recalling the way his face would redden when I did see him looking my way.

"I couldn't help but become fascinated with the way your body changed – how your breasts blossomed and your curves became more gentle. I didn't want to look; I told myself it wasn't right, it was dirty, but you were like a magnet, and my head was like iron."

"And how you would jump if our bodies touched while we shared those sofa beds, remember?"

"Yes," he said, bringing his hands to my awaiting bosom. He followed them with his lips. I closed my eyes and listened to the rustling of his clothing as he stripped the garments from his body. Moments later he was naked beside me, and something we had both seen in dreams, in fantasies that had made us feel guilty and evil, became real.

Real now were his lips, moving softly but quickly over my breasts. Real now were his hands, stroking me and bringing me closer and closer to him. Real now was the touch of his manliness, hard and ready. We both hesitated one more time, as if finally closing the door on a fraudulent past, and then we became what man and wife were supposed to become, joined in an ecstatic embrace, all our love for each other rushing up from where we coupled, his love driving deeper and deeper into my soul and my love welcoming him, drawing him, demanding more and more until we were both moaning. I held onto him as if I were on a roller coaster. He took me up and down, and I felt myself falling so quickly, I became dizzy. My heart beat so fast, it became one continuous whir, sending my blood rushing through me, making my fingers tingle.

When it was over we lay beside each other, panting, both of us surprised at the intensity of our passion. His fingers opened to entwine with mine, and we lay there, silent, holding hands, looking into the darkness, while outside our window the stars burned even more brightly, their light twinkling on the ocean surface, making it seem as if all the world was happy that Jimmy and I were finally man and wife.

Both of us slept soundly that night. Even the morning sunshine streaming through the slit in the curtains didn't interfere with our sleep. The ocean breezes lifted the curtains and nudged us until we finally parted our eyelids and gazed into each other's faces.

"This is your first morning waking up as Mrs. James Gary Longchamp," Jimmy said. "How do you feel?"

"Ravenously hungry," I replied, and he laughed. We showered and dressed quickly to have breakfast. The motel restaurant had a large patio with ice-cream-parlor tables and umbrellas. We had freshly squeezed juice and coffee and bacon and eggs.

Afterward, we took a long walk on the beach and hunted seashells, surprising each other with one colorful find after another. By the time we returned to the motel we had a sackful.

"Christie will love them," I said.

In the afternoon we lay on the beach and swam in the ocean. Our activity renewed our appetites, and we were both eager to sample Cape Cod's famous lobster. Jimmy had done a lot of research on the area and had planned our every move. He had made reservations in a seafood restaurant down at the harbor. Over the door there was a sign that said, "The lobster you eat today, yesterday swam in Cape Cod Bay."

It was delicious and very romantic, for we sat at a table lit only by candlelight and looked out at the ships in the harbor, many with their lights on, and some so far out they looked like stars that had fallen. After dinner we took a nice walk through the town, window-shopping and planning some of the gifts we would buy to bring back.

Our lovemaking that evening was no less passionate than it had been the night before. Along with the sunshine and the swimming, the walks and the feasting, it brought us once again to the portals of restful and contented sleep. We drifted off in each other's arms and woke to the same caress of warm ocean breezes and bright sunlight the next day.

Jimmy had planned for us to rent kayaks and paddle our way across the calm harbor, so soon after breakfast we changed and went down to the beach. The owner of the concession outfitted us with life jackets and then gave us lessons. A little while later we pushed off and began our fun-filled sea journey. Jimmy was reckless a few times and spilled over. It was great fun and great exercise. We were lucky that the ocean was so calm, but we were both happy to see the shore again after we paddled our way back.

As we drew closer and closer, however, I noticed one of the receptionists at the motel was standing with the owner of the boat concession and gazing out in our direction. He had his arms folded across his chest. As we approached the beach he stepped toward us, waving.

"What does he want?" I wondered aloud. Jimmy hopped out of his kayak first and helped me with mine.

"We just received an emergency phone call for you, Mrs. Longchamp," the receptionist said, "so I came right down to see if you and your husband had returned."

Dread filled me. I looked worriedly at Jimmy and then turned back to him.

"Do you know who the call was from?" My heart began to pound, and my nerve ends twanged.

"A Mr. Updike," he replied, handing me the slip of paper with Mr. Updike's phone number on it. "He asked that you call him immediately."

"Oh, no, Jimmy. Something must have happened to Christie," I cried.

"Now, don't jump to any conclusions," Jimmy said firmly. "It could just be something to do with the hotel – some decision that has to be made immediately."

I nodded hopefully, and we hurried up the beach to our motel room to make the call. Mr. Updike answered after only the first ring.

"I'm sorry to have to call you on your honeymoon, Dawn," he began, "but a tragic event has occurred."

"What is it, Mr. Updike? What's happened?" I cried. I shivered and turned icy with apprehension. Jimmy was at my side, holding my hand.

"Randolph is dead," he replied.

"Randolph? But how . . . what?"

"Apparently, all this was finally too much for him. He left the hotel some time early last night. No one even knew he had left. He rambled about all evening,

123

from what we can tell. Eventually he ended up at the cemetery."

"The cemetery?"

"Yes, and collapsed over his mother's grave. The caretaker found him there late this morning. He called for an ambulance and all, but . . . it was too late. The doctor says he literally pined away. The official cause of death will be heart failure," he concluded.

"Oh, I'm so sorry," I said. "Poor Randolph. He suffered so much, and no one really helped him."

"Yes," Mr. Updike said, and he cleared his throat. "Well, you can just imagine what's going on here now. Your mother – "

"Must be carrying on to no end," I said dryly. "I imagine she has her stream of doctors pouring up and down the stairs."

"Well, there's quite a bit of turmoil. She insisted Mr. Dorfman ask all the guests to leave and close the hotel. Naturally, he didn't want to take on all this responsibility, so he phoned me, and I told him I would phone you to confirm the next stage of action," Mr. Updike explained.

"What do you suggest we do, Mr. Updike?" I asked.

"Mrs. Cutler wouldn't have closed the hotel," he said plainly. "To her it was like show business – the show must go on."

"Then close it," I insisted, not caring what that horrid old woman would have done. "The guests will understand, and it's the decent thing to do. Jimmy and I will start home immediately. When is the funeral?"

"Your mother wanted it to be tomorrow, but the minister has talked her into waiting until the day after. A

124

number of people will want to attend," he said. "Philip and Clara Sue are already home," he added.

"Very well," I said. "How tragic," I repeated, and I cradled the receiver slowly. I gave Jimmy all the details.

"I told my mother how serious it was; I warned her," I said, "but she just didn't care. His own children didn't care!"

"You did what you could, Dawn. Don't start blaming yourself," Jimmy warned.

"I know. How horrible," I thought aloud. "Poor Randolph." I felt the tears sting behind my eyes. "She reaches back from the grave and destroys people," I said. A worried frown drew his eyebrows together.

"Don't talk like that. Soon you will believe it yourself," he said.

"But why is it, Jimmy, that evil things linger longer than good things, that the stench of something rotten lasts longer than the aroma of something sweet?" I asked.

"That's not true, Dawn. It just seems so, but it's not," he insisted. "Our good memories live with us, don't they?"

I shook my head. "Yes, but the bad ones cut into us and scar us, and those scars stay with us forever and ever. Somehow I've got to find a way to shut that dreadful old woman out of our lives," I said, my eyes narrowed in determination.

"When you talk like that," Jimmy said, "you scare me. Your whole face changes, and I don't know who you are, for the Dawn I knew wouldn't be worried about revenge," he said.

"It's not revenge I'm worried about, Jimmy. It's survival," I replied.

He swung his eyes away sadly.

I was sorry to have said those things, but I couldn't help believing that somehow Grandmother Cutler was reaching back from the dead and finding ways to ruin everyone's happiness, especially mine.

The motel manager helped us make emergency travel arrangements. In order to leave immediately we had to take a small airplane to Boston, and in Boston catch a bigger airplane to Virginia Beach. The hotel car was waiting for us when we arrived a little after nine in the evening. Julius Barker, the driver, stood at the doorway to the baggage area, his hat in his hands, his eyes drooping with sorrow.

Most everyone at the hotel had been fond of Randolph. Despite his ineffectiveness as a hotel administrator and his drifting into madness after his mother's death, he was a gentle, kind soul, the epitome of Southern geniality and grace. Before his depression he always wore a smile and had a nice word for anyone he met, be it a chambermaid or a rich hotel guest. The staff, as well as frequent guests, had been saddened by his physical and mental degeneration. It seemed that only the people who were supposed to care the most for him were not upset and concerned.

Julius rushed forward to get our bags.

"I'm sorry you had to come right back, Mrs. Longchamp," he said.

"It's very sad, Julius."

"Yes, ma'am. Everyone's just moping about the hotel, talking low and sniffling back tears. Mr. Dorfman made us cut back most of the lights," he added, and when we drove up we saw why he had mentioned it.

There was a funereal pall over the building and grounds. An overcast sky had begun to drop a cold rain through the darkness, making the air gray and chilly. The hotel loomed like a big, deserted house, its windows vacant and dark. The great porch looked as if a black shroud had been draped over it. It was very strange to enter the big lobby and find it empty and dim. Only one receptionist, Mrs. Bradly, was behind the counter to cover the telephones. Robert Garwood, one of the older bellhops, rushed forward to take our luggage and carry it up to our suite.

"I'll go see what's been shut down and what hasn't," Jimmy said. He went off with Julius, and I followed Robert to the family section. My mother's door was shut tight as usual, but as I started down the corridor Philip opened the door to his room and stepped out to greet me.

"I didn't think you would come back," he said. He was dressed in a blue velvet robe with the Cutler insignia, a large gold C, on the breast pocket, but his hair was brushed neatly, and he looked quite rested and relaxed. He smiled and then stepped forward close enough to kiss my cheek. His hand lingered on my shoulder.

"Of course I had to come back. Why wouldn't I come back?" I said, not hiding my indignation and shaking his hand off my shoulder.

"Well, he's not really your father, and you were on your honeymoon," Philip said. "Weren't you enjoying yourself?" he asked, his grin small and tight, amused. How could he be so lighthearted only a short time after

127

his father had died so sadly? I wondered. I couldn't help feeling disgust for that otherwise handsome and beguiling smile.

"Really, Philip, don't you have respect for anything, even your own father's memory?" I snapped. My sharpness wiped the leer from his face as quickly as my slapping him would.

"I'm upset. Of course I'm upset," he said defensively. "I had to rush back from college, didn't I?" he pointed out.

"You're still thinking only of yourself, Philip," I replied, shaking my head. "What about Randolph?"

I didn't wait for his reply. I left him standing there with his mouth gaped open, and I walked on to Christie's nursery to see how she was doing. Sissy greeted me at the door. Christie was fast asleep.

"It was so terrible," Sissy said, wiping her eyes. I pulled her out of the room so we wouldn't waken Christie. "Clarence told me he heard Mr. Cutler's clothing was ripped and torn like he had been running through barbed wire. He died with his hands clutching Mrs. Cutler's tombstone, his face pressed into the dirt." She shook her body to shake out the chill. "That poor man."

"I know," I said. "How's Christie been?"

"She knows something bad's happened. She's seen and heard all the people cryin' and snifflin' and lookin' downhearted, but Mrs. Boston and me tried to keep her in her room most of the time. 'Course, she's always askin' after you."

I nodded and entered the nursery quietly. I looked down at her asleep in her crib, a curl of her golden hair spun over her forehead. Her perfect little face looked like the face on a porcelain doll. I fixed her blanket and left to put away Jimmy's and my things. But Mrs. Boston, who had heard about our arrival, was already there, doing just that.

"I'm just looking for ways to keep busy," she said, shaking her head, her eyes drowning in tears. We hugged.

"How's my mother?" I asked suspiciously. Mrs. Boston sucked in some air and pulled back her shoulders.

"She shut herself up in the suite and hasn't come out ever since. All she will do is call down for things. I don't think she's gotten out of her bed."

"Who's seen about the funeral arrangements?" I asked.

"I imagine Mr. Updike," she said.

"Well, I guess I've got to go in there sooner or later," I said, and I went to my mother's suite. She had the door to her bedroom closed. I knocked on it softly.

"Mother? Are you awake?" I called. There was no reply for so long a moment, I was about to turn away. But then I heard her small cry.

"Dawn . . . is that you?" she asked.

I opened the door and entered. Mother had never looked tinier in the king-size bed with her head sunk into her oversized satin pillows and the comforter drawn over her. There was only a small table lamp lit, casting a weak, pale glow over everything. Despite her period of mourning, she looked as if she had been brushing her hair for hours and hours. She wore lipstick and some rouge and pearl earrings with a matching pearl necklace.

She sat up slightly and held her arms out for me to

run into them and comfort her. I walked slowly to her bed and let her embrace me.

"Dawn, I'm so happy you've come back. It was horrible, just horrible. Have you heard all of it?" she asked, falling back on her pillows as if hugging me had drained her of all her available energy. "How he wandered God knows where, through back alleys, under docks, spoke to complete strangers, babbling about his mother? Can you just die?" she said, throwing her eyes back. "People in Cutler's Cove will be talking about this for generations."

"I don't think Randolph was worried about that, Mother," I said caustically.

"No, of course he wasn't. He's gone. None of this will matter to him anymore," she flared. Then she used her small fists to grind away her thick tears and pulled herself into a sitting position. "Mr. Updike keeps calling me to ask dreadful questions concerning the funeral," she moaned. "I don't want to hear another word about it. You will have to take charge."

"What about Philip or Clara Sue?" I asked.

"Clara Sue won't come out of her room," she said, "and Philip is getting to be more and more like his father. He says whatever I want. Well, I don't want," she said flatly, without emotion. "What I do want is for all this ugly business to end," she concluded firmly.

"I feel so sorry for him," I said, "but I told you how serious it was getting. I told Philip, too. No one seemed to care," I said, a bit more sharply than I had intended. But I was getting tired of how Randolph's death was inconveniencing all his loved ones.

"Don't you start blaming me for this, Dawn," Mother said, pointing her forefinger accusingly. "There was nothing I could do for him. He was obsessed with his mother and her memory. He was always in awe of her, worshiping her as if she were some goddess and not just his mother. He never saw her for what she was; he never saw her meanness or her viciousness. Everything she did was all right, according to him. All she had to do was nod in a direction, and he would rush off to do her bidding. He wanted to be with her, so he's with her," she asserted, nodding.

"I'm sure he didn't want to die on her grave like that, Mother. He wasn't well," I said softly.

"Believe me, Dawn. He wanted to die that way," she said, waving away my protest. "He was crazy, yes, but he knew what he was doing. Well, it's over," she said, taking a deep breath and sighing. "At least that part is. Now there is this unpleasantness to face. Well, I'm not well either, so I can't be pressured with dreadful details. I want it all to go as quickly as possible. Will you see that it does? Will you?" she begged.

"We'll do what is proper and what shows respect, Mother," I said, pulling my shoulders back. I couldn't help it. I knew I must look like I was mimicking the one woman I despised the most. The way Mother's eyes widened with surprise confirmed it. "And you will find the strength to perform as a loving wife should at her husband's funeral. You can expect it will be heavily attended, and many of the people you admire so much will be watching you."

"Oh dear, dear," she moaned, closing her eyes. "How will I have the strength?"

"Somehow you will find it, I'm sure," I said sharply. "I will phone Mr. Updike immediately and see what's left to be done, and then I'll tell you what you are to do," I said, and I turned to leave.

"Dawn," she cried.

"What is it, Mother?"

"I'm so happy you're here . . . to lean upon," she said, smiling through her crystal tears.

"Well, you can thank the security guard who recognized Daddy Longchamp and told the police so they could come and get me," I replied. Her smile wilted.

"How can you be so cruel to me at a time like this?" she cried.

Jimmy's words returned: ". . . for the Dawn I knew wouldn't be worried about revenge." Was he right? Was I changing? Was I permitting Grandmother Cutler to make me into someone like her and, in effect, destroy me?

I softened.

"I'm sorry, Mother," I said. She looked pleased. "I'll do what I can to make things easier for you."

"Thank you, Dawn. Dawn," she called again as I reached the doorway. "I did love him . . . once," she said in a small, sad voice.

"Then when you mourn him, Mother, mourn the man he was and not the man he became," I advised, and I left her sobbing into her lace handkerchief.

Both Mr. Updike and Mr. Dorfman thought that just like Grandmother Cutler's funeral procession, Randolph's should stop at the front of the hotel for a last good-bye. The minister would say a few words from the front entrance. Mother moaned as if in dire pain when I told her.

"Not that again. Oh, what dramatics," she cried.

132

But she went along with it. In fact, once the funeral arrangements were all confirmed, she suddenly had a burst of new energy. She decided that the dress she had worn to Grandmother Cutler's funeral was not good enough for Randolph's.

"I didn't care what I looked like then," she explained. "But this is different."

One of the dress designers she favored was summoned to the hotel with an emergency air and was put to work creating a fashionable black dress. Mother wanted a tight waist and fluffy sleeves with a rather low-cut bodice. The designer was surprised but did what she asked. When I saw the way she was dressed on the morning of the funeral, I thought she had prepared herself for some sort of costume ball. All that was needed was a black mask. She had had her nails manicured and polished, her hair washed and styled, and had even called the beautician to give her a facial because she claimed hours and hours of crying had made her look like an old woman.

Not once during the entire time between Jimmy's and my return from our aborted honeymoon did Clara Sue show herself. Like her mother, she insisted on all her food being brought to her room. I was told she was on the telephone constantly, speaking with her school friends, however. When I did see her on the morning of the funeral, she turned away.

The family was supposed to ride together in the hotel limousine, but some of Clara Sue's local friends were there, and she decided she would ride with them. I was surprised Mother didn't protest.

"I don't have the strength for that sort of thing this morning, Dawn," she told me when I pointed out how insensitive it was for Clara Sue not to be at her side. "Let's just get underway and get it over with as quickly as we can."

The sky was mostly overcast and gray, but fortunately the clouds held back their rain. The crowd of mourners was so great it overflowed out the door of the church. People stood on the steps and around the lawn listening to the minister's eulogy. Clara Sue at least joined us in the family pew, standing beside Philip. Directly behind us sat Mr. and Mrs. Updike, Mr. and Mrs. Dorfman and, at Mother's request, Bronson Alcott. From time to time I caught him patting her sympathetically on her arm. Once she reached back to squeeze his hand.

I had to admit that she looked elegantly beautiful, like a dazzling bright pearl encased in a black shell. Periodically, almost as if she had it timed, she would dab her eyes with her lace handkerchief and take a small breath, closing her eyes. Then she would open them and gaze at someone to smile gratefully at his or her look of condolence.

After the eulogy, during which the minister stressed the great contribution the Cutler family had made and was making to the community, the mourners streamed out to get into their cars and follow the hearse to the hotel. The entire hotel staff gathered around. There the minister spoke about the great traditions the Cutler family had created and how the hotel had been more than a business for Randolph; it had been a home. There was barely a dry eye in the crowd when the minister said, "And so we bid you a final farewell, Randolph Boyse Cutler, and now take you to your place of eternal rest. Your work here has ended."

Some of the staff members cried openly and had to be

134

comforted by others. When we passed through the arch of the cemetery I closed my eyes, for the memory of that day when I had discovered the small tombstone, placed there to symbolically indicate my own death, returned sharply.

Randolph was to be buried right beside his mother and father. My mother gazed at me as the coffin was brought to the grave. I could see her thoughts. Once again she was telling me Randolph was where he wanted to be. But no matter how much he loved and admired his mother, I didn't think he wanted this sort of end for himself. He was a troubled, lost soul, wandering through a maze of memories, searching for some meaning to his life after the light of it had been dimmed.

The minister offered his final prayers, and the crowd of mourners began to disperse. As Jimmy and I turned to go, Clara Sue, who had been standing just a little ways down from us with her friends, spun on her heels and glared at me. Her face wasn't filled with sorrow so much as it was filled with anger and jealousy at the way people were shaking my hand, embracing me and offering their expressions of sympathy. It was her own fault for not standing with her family, I thought.

Surprisingly, she stepped right in my path as I began to leave the cemetery. She seemed to pull in her breath and straighten her spine.

"Are you satisfied?" she cried. Her face flamed furiously.

"What?" Stunned, I looked from her to Jimmy and back to her. A small crowd of mourners had heard her outburst and stopped to listen.

"Ever since they brought you back, this family's been falling apart piece by piece. Then they gave you

135

control of our hotel, and my father became nothing . . . *nothing!*" she screamed, her eyes blazing and wide.

"That's not true, Clara Sue," I began. "Randolph was suffering long before – "

She shoved her face closer to mine and narrowed her eyes to sinister slots as she continued to lash out.

"Don't you tell me about *my* father. You have everyone else fooled, but not me," she spat. "You caused trouble for all of us and made my grandmother sick to death. Now you've done the same thing to my father."

"That's not fair, Clara Sue, and this is not the time or the place to – "

"Clara Sue, you're behaving like a fool," Jimmy said.

"He's right, Clara Sue," Philip added. "You're acting like a spoiled brat."

Clara Sue laughed, a wild, thin, hysterical laugh that carried over the heads of the nearby mourners, who widened their eyes in shock and surprise.

"Of course you two would take her side. You're both in love with her," she accused. The crowd of onlookers drew closer, their murmuring growing louder.

Philip's face reddened, and he drew his shoulders up as if he had been sharply slapped in the face.

"Shut your mouth," he commanded, and he stepped toward her threateningly, his hands clenched. Clara Sue stood firmly in place, not budging an inch, challenging him with her wry smile. I felt certain he was about to strike her, and all this at the foot of their father's freshly dug grave.

"Oh, Clara Sue," I heard Mother cry. I turned to see her swoon and faint into Bronson Alcott's waiting arms.

136

Philip turned to go to her, too, and Clara Sue stepped forward toward me.

"Now look what you've done," she sneered.

"I've done?"

"Well, I won't rest until I've driven you out of here," Clara Sue continued, not in the least concerned about Mother. Those who had remained behind were gathered around as Bronson fanned her with his handkerchief.

"I'll hire lawyers; I'll find a way to get rid of you," Clara Sue promised hatefully.

"Do what you want," I said. "You have no respect for anything or anyone but yourself, and you are a disgrace to your father's memory," I added, turning to join the others around Mother. She still had not regained consciousness.

Bronson Alcott finally lifted her in his arms and began to carry her from the cemetery. People stepped aside and gaped in astonishment. Word of Clara Sue's outburst and vicious attack on me was spreading with electric speed through the throng of mourners, and all eyes were on us as we followed Bronson down the path and through the arch to the hotel limousine. Julius opened the door for him, and he carefully slipped Mother into the rear seat.

Mother's eyes began to flutter. They opened and closed, opened and closed.

"You'd better get her back to the hotel quickly," Bronson whispered. "I'll be right behind."

"Yes, thank you," I said. Jimmy, Philip and I got back into the limousine with Mother. Philip patted her hand, and to me, he looked just like Randolph used to look whenever he comforted her. She opened her eyes slowly and tried to smile.

"I'm all right," she muttered. "But is it over . . . is it finally all over?"

"It's over, Mother," Philip said. Mother smiled and closed her eyes again.

Bronson Alcott was already waiting when we reached the hotel. Philip and Jimmy helped Mother out of the limousine, but Bronson took her from them immediately, and she accepted his support. She was able to walk, leaning on his shoulder. Staff members stepped aside and watched as we all entered the hotel. At the far end of the lobby Mrs. Boston came forward to take Mother from Bronson Alcott. Mother turned and smiled appreciatively up at him, her eyes filled with more than mere thanks, I thought. Then Mrs. Boston led her into the family section and helped her up the stairs and into her suite.

"I'm sorry about the things Clara Sue said," Philip told Jimmy and me before we parted. "She's become a real problem for everyone, but I won't let her bother you."

"Maybe she just doesn't know now to handle her grief," I replied. "I don't want to think about it right now. I'm very tired myself," I said, "and I want to freshen up and rest before we have to greet people."

Jimmy and I went up to our suite and changed out of our mourning clothes. Later in the day the family's closest acquaintances, as well as others who wanted to pay their respects, arrived. Mr. Updike, Mr. Dorfman and I had decided we would provide some cakes, tea and coffee in the lobby. Mother remained upstairs in her suite, but Jimmy, Philip and I accepted sympathies and spoke with people. Clara Sue was nowhere to be seen, and, in fact, we learned later that she hadn't returned to the hotel.

Finally, hours later, Mother made one of her miraculous recoveries and came down to greet people, too. She was still wearing her rather stylish funeral dress. Condolences, expressions of sorrow, kisses on the cheek and the pressing of hands fed her need for attention well, and instead of growing fatigued as the day wore on, Mother gained strength. I heard her laugh once or twice and saw her beam her smile, especially at Bronson, who remained faithfully beside her the entire time.

After nearly all those who were going to pay their respects had done so, Jimmy, Philip and I retreated to a table in the kitchen to have something to eat. Like most everyone at the hotel, Nussbaum had put his sorrow into work and had cooked and baked enough food for an army of mourners. Despite my emotional fatigue, I was starving.

Mother retreated to her suite to have her dinner brought up to her as usual. No one spoke about it, but we knew she had invited Bronson Alcott to dine with her.

"Clara Sue's not coming back to the hotel," Philip told us when he sat down at the table, "which is probably a good thing."

"What do you mean, Philip? Where is she?" I asked.

"She sent word with one of her spoiled-brat friends that she was returning to Richmond," he said.

"Back to school so soon? But – "

"It's all right," Philip said. "I'm going to leave myself in the morning. There's no point in my remaining any longer," he continued, "and I can't miss my final exams."

Jimmy and I glanced at each other quickly and then looked down at our food.

"As far as Mother goes . . . she'll recuperate from her sorrow as rapidly as she sees fit. My presence won't change that. Of course," Philip continued, "if there are some business reasons why you think I should remain . . ."

"No, no. Mr. Updike and Mr. Dorfman have things pretty much under control. We'll reopen the hotel for the weekend," I said. "It's better that everyone gets back to work."

I hated to admit it, but Grandmother Cutler's philosophy was probably correct when it came to that. I was glad, however, that we had shown some respect for Randolph's memory by closing the hotel a little while.

"Right," Philip said. "That's why I want to get back to the books myself." Philip played with his food for a moment and then gazed up at both of us. "I want to apologize again about the things Clara Sue said at the cemetery. She really has become a nuisance. I'll try to keep her from bothering everyone," he promised.

Jimmy nodded. I wanted to say more, but I didn't. I wanted to say Clara Sue wasn't much different from the first time I had met her. She was self-centered and vicious then, too. She probably always would be. But I didn't want to add any more unpleasantness to an already disagreeable time. It was better to put it all to rest.

Afterward, Jimmy and I went up to check on Christie and then retire for the evening. As we walked down the corridor we heard Mother's laughter coming from behind the closed doors of her suite.

"Mother's already begun her spectacular recovery from sadness," I muttered. Jimmy nodded and smiled.

Later, though, when we lay together in bed, I felt very sad, and I snuggled up inside his arm and rested my head on his shoulder. We could gaze out the window and up at the sky. The heavy overcast that had hovered above us all day, adding to the mood of depression and sorrow, now began to break up. We could see a star or two twinkling between the misty clouds.

"I can't help remembering the day Momma died," Jimmy said. "I thought my heart had shrunk so small in my chest it wouldn't have the power to pump my blood, and I would just die from sadness."

"I remember how you ran all the way home from the hospital," I said.

"I just wanted to pound the earth with my feet, strike out at something, someone. I just can't imagine burying your father and going off with your friends like Clara Sue did. I don't even understand how Philip can return to college so fast and get back into things so quickly," he said. "This has never been much of a family, has it, Dawn?"

"No, Jimmy."

"You think something like this is going to happen to us if we stay here and bring up our kids in the hotel?" he asked.

"I hope not, Jimmy. I think we care about each other too much for that to happen anyway," I added quickly. He nodded, but even in the darkness, with just a twinkle of starlight coming through the window, I could see the anxiety in his eyes. It made my heart do flip-flops and brought a lump to my throat. How I wanted to assure him, to promise him, to guarantee him that for us, happiness and love were as certain as the seasons.

But I couldn't shake off the memory of Grandmother Cutler's steel-gray eyes. Would they haunt me forever? Would she do something more to hurt us?

I tightened my embrace around Jimmy, and he kissed my hair and stroked my hand.

Across the grounds and up the street Randolph lay beside his mother. Was he finally at peace? And if he was, why did he have to pay so dearly for it?

An Evening at Beulla Woods

During the days immediately following Randolph's death I noticed a rather dramatic change in my mother. She had barely begun a period of bereavement when suddenly she no longer wanted to be shut up in her suite all the time. In fact, she burst out of her state of mourning with an explosion of startling new energy. But her attention and interests were not directed toward anything to do with the hotel. On the contrary, she seemed to avoid every aspect of it. She had no desire to meet guests or become involved in the hotel's activities. I knew she hated walking through the lobby even to get to the hotel limousine. She didn't want to see the critical eyes of the staff and others focused on her, so she began leaving via a side entrance, almost as though her exits and entrances were clandestine. Sometimes I thought they were, even though she claimed she was only going shopping or to have lunch or dinner with old friends.

Yes, suddenly Mother had old friends again. I could count on my fingers how many times anyone she knew in the vicinity had come to visit her socially since I had been brought back to the hotel, and I couldn't recall a single time she had gone to visit anyone else. But all that quickly changed.

One day I met her in the hallway as she was leaving for

one of these engagements. She had been digging into the depths of her closets to come up with some little-worn but quite stylish outfits. It was as if her having to wear the black gown of mourning, even one she had had designed especially for herself and even for so short a time, had left her craving colors and brightness. Her pinks and blues and greens were almost luminous. This particular day she also wore a matching blue bonnet. With her hair primped and curled, her face made up and her jewelry sparkling, she practically bounced down the stairs. I even thought she was humming.

"Oh, Dawn," she said when I surprised her in the hall. A guilty look flashed momentarily through her blue eyes. Then she smiled and spun around. "How do I look?"

I had to admit she looked years younger. Her face had a lightness to it, a rosy radiance that made her sparkle with exuberance. It was as if some dark shadow implanted in her soul had been lifted.

"Very nice, Mother. Where are you going today?" I asked.

"Oh, I'm meeting some old finishing-school girl-friends for lunch, and then maybe we'll go to a fashion show," she recited as if she had memorized the reply for anyone who would have the nerve to ask. She saw the look of confusion and skepticism on my face and continued, more forcefully.

"Well, why shouldn't I get out? I've grown tired of my suite. It's become more like a prison to me. I spent so much time shut up in there, recuperating from one illness or another, that now I can't bear to stay in there a moment longer than I have to. Besides," she added, the corners of her mouth drooping, "there are

144

too many sad reminders of poor Randolph. I must get rid of his things, give some to Philip and some to the Salvation Army so poor souls can at least benefit from the tragedy," she said.

"Yes, that would be nice, Mother," I said dryly.

"And have you ever noticed how little sunlight comes into my suite?" she moaned. "It's just the way it's situated, I'm sure, but it can get so dismal and dreary in there. No wonder Grandmother Cutler gave it to Randolph and me and kept the one across the way for herself. That one gets sunshine most of the day," she added.

"Maybe you should move into hers, then," I suggested, half in jest.

"Heaven forbid. I don't want anything whatsoever to do with that dreadful woman's things. Don't even joke about such a thing," she said, and then as quickly as her face had turned sour, it turned sweet. "Well, I must be off," she said. "I have Julius waiting in the hotel limousine outside. Perhaps," she said, calling back to me as she left, "I'll see something new and fashionable for you to buy."

I watched her hurry away and then went up to get Christie. Because the summer season was in full swing, I had become more and more involved in the day-to-day administration of the hotel. Occasionally Jimmy gently reminded me of my promise not to become so involved in my hotel work that I neglected him and Christie. A few times I had been called away from dinner to solve a problem or two, and each time, when I returned to the table, Jimmy gazed up at me, that "I told you so" glint in his eyes.

But both Mr. Dorfman and Mr. Updike were growing

more and more confident about leaving things up to me. Phone calls and requests, questions from staff members and suppliers were increasingly directed to me. Every morning now my notepad was filled with things to do and people to call. It had become far more tiring and mentally draining than I had ever imagined it would be. It made me wonder how Grandmother Cutler had run this hotel so firmly when she was so much older. I couldn't believe that someone that age, especially someone like her, could outlast someone my age. And yet precisely because I had all these things distracting me, I felt more and more guilty about not spending enough time with Christie.

She was developing so rapidly that one day I would look at her and think of her as a pretty little baby, and the next day I would see her as a precocious infant with a remarkable curiosity about her surroundings. She missed Randolph enormously – probably missed him more than anyone. Sissy told me how often she asked to go to his office. He had been so patient with her and so happy to have her interrupt his bizarre activities.

Finally I told Sissy to bring her to my office, only I found it more difficult than Randolph had, for my work was real, and the people who waited to speak to me on the phone or came to see me about problems in the hotel weren't as happy about waiting for me to first explain something to Christie. But if I didn't explain it, she would pull on my skirt or ask her question repeatedly until she was satisfied.

Sometimes, when Jimmy was in one of his more charitable and forgiving moods, he would come by and take her out with him to ride on the mowers or watch the men painting and cleaning. Nothing bored her, whether it be manual labor or simply watching the bookkeeper work away on an adding machine. People were always interesting to her.

We bought her educational toys, and her speaking vocabulary grew by leaps and bounds. Guests were astounded when they were told she was only a little more than two. Growing up in the hotel environment, surrounded by different strangers weekly, she became quite outgoing and was shy only when someone complimented her clothes or her hair or her beautiful blue eyes.

I couldn't help wondering if she had inherited Mother's coyness. She was certainly quite enamored of herself and would spend hours before her mirror with her first brush and comb set. She sat patiently, too, when Sissy did her fingernails for the first time, and she couldn't wait to be paraded through the hotel to show everyone.

Only Mother paid her scant attention. If she did come upon her in the hallways or lobby, she would flash a smile, but I felt she was doing it because she was aware there were other people watching. She never volunteered to spend time with Christie or permitted Sissy to bring her into her suite. The one time Christie had wandered in there, Mother had shouted for Sissy to take her out because there were too many expensive things she might break accidentally.

Mother's busy new schedule increasingly kept her away from the hotel. She rarely ate a meal with us in the dining room and saw guests only as she was passing through to come and go. Philip called me one day to ask me if I knew why she hadn't returned his phone calls.

"I'm just wrapping things up at college and wanted to

147

take a short holiday with Betty Ann and her parents in Bermuda. They've invited me, and I wanted Mother to know," he said, but I also felt he wanted me to know.

"When did you call her last, Philip?"

"At least a week ago, and I called twice before that. Where is she? Is she all right?" he inquired.

"She's fine. I've never seen her looking healthier or more energetic. The fact is, I don't see her all that much these days. She's always going somewhere, and wherever she goes, she stays away for most of the day. Even most of the evenings sometimes," I added.

"Hmmm," he said. "That's not like her. Anyway," he said, "please give her my message. I'll send you postcards from Bermuda," he added.

"Well, I hope you have a good time," I said.

"Thank you. I do expect that when I return I'll pick up my share of the work," he promised.

"There will be plenty for you to do," I advised him. He laughed.

"Becoming the new Mrs. Cutler?" he teased.

"Hardly," I said. "I'm my own person."

I felt I had done much to make that happen. As I had planned, I changed the office decor considerably, replacing the dreary dark curtains with bright blue ones, tearing up the carpet and putting in a thick, beige one that gave one the feeling that he or she was walking on marshmallows. I added more light and put up some paintings that had color and brightness. The only painting I let remain was the portrait of my father on the wall behind the desk. It just didn't feel right taking that down.

I had pictures of Christie and Jimmy in frames all over my desk, and I let Sissy leave some of Christie's

148

toys in a corner of the office. Jimmy made sure there were fresh flowers brought in and placed in vases every few days, so that the scent of lilac – a scent that had been Grandmother Cutler's – was replaced with the scent of roses and carnations, jasmine, or whatever was in bloom, except lilacs.

"I hesitate to ask this," I said before Philip and I ended our conversation, "but what is Clara Sue doing?"

"She won't return my phone calls either, but she passed word through some mutual acquaintances that she intends to spend the summer with a friend whose parents have a home on the Jersey shore. I'm sure that leaves you heartbroken," he concluded, laughter in his voice.

"Has she told Mother?" I wondered aloud. "If she has, Mother had said nothing about it to me."

"Her only contact with Mother will be to have her send money, I assure you," Philip said.

I wished him a good time once more, and we ended our phone conversation.

Early in the evening, when I had gone up to shower and change for dinner, Mother came to my door and knocked. Apparently she had returned from wherever she had been and showered and changed herself for another one of her evenings out. She looked quite smart in her crimson dress with its slender waist, billowing full skirt and boned bodice. I had just come out of the shower, and I had my head wrapped in a towel and wore a robe.

"Knock, knock," she sang, peering in.

"Come in," I said.

"I just bought this today. How does it look?" she asked, turning to model the dress.

149

"You look very nice," I complimented.

"Thank you." Her face bloomed as it did whenever she received praise. "I feel very nice," she added, giggling. She looked drunk on herself and whatever good times she was having. Never had a husband passed so quickly from a wife's mind, I thought.

"Where are you going tonight?" I asked, expecting one of her vague responses.

She pulled herself up as if to make a formal announcement.

"Tonight I have agreed to go to dinner at one of the finest restaurants in Virginia Beach," she replied.

"Oh. And with whom?"

"Bronson Alcott," she confessed. And then as quickly as she did, she burst into justification. "I don't think it's horrible for me to be seen out with a proper escort. People don't expect me to pine away like Randolph did. I'm still quite young and attractive, and it wouldn't be fair.

"Besides," she continued, barely taking a breath, "Bronson is an old friend, an old family friend. It's not like I couldn't wait to rush out and see one beau after another."

"You're old enough to do what you want, Mother," I said. She nodded.

"Yes, I am. Exactly." She paused to look at herself in my mirror and patted her hair where she thought some strands had rebelled.

"Philip called today," I told her. "Did you call him back?"

"Philip? Oh, no. What did he have to say?" she asked, her interest minimal. She continued studying herself in the mirror.

150

"He wondered why you haven't returned his calls," I said.

"Oh, I haven't?" She followed her statement with a short giggle. "Was he very upset?"

"He was curious and a little worried," I said, "but I told him how you were getting out and about and not pining away in your suite," I said, unable to keep myself from sounding sarcastic.

"Good," she said.

"He wanted to tell you he was going on a holiday with his girlfriend's parents. They're taking him to Bermuda immediately after his last final exam."

"That's wonderful," she cried. "It's nice that he's become involved with a girl whose family has such high standing and wealth. I'm very happy for him. At least someone has listened to me and learned about life."

"He also said he heard Clara Sue wasn't coming home for the summer," I continued, ignoring her innuendo. "Did you know that?"

"Not coming home? No. Where is she going?" she asked, her face in a grimace.

"She is going to spend the summer with a friend at the Jersey shore."

"Well, that's fine," Mother said quickly. "I really don't have the patience for her right now. I'm trying to put my life back together." She beamed a smile. "I feel a little like Humpty Dumpty. I've fallen off a wall, but fortunately, all the king's horses and all the king's men *can* put me back together." She laughed again and spun around to gaze at herself once more, tapping her teardrop diamond earrings and then running her fingers over her diamond necklace. Her eyes seemed to draw and absorb the sparkle from her precious gems.

151

"I'm happy for you, Mother," I said, and I went to my closet to choose something appropriate to wear to dinner. We had nearly a full house, and there were many guests to greet.

"Thank you. Oh," she said, turning. "With all our chatter, I nearly forgot why I came in here to see you. Isn't that silly of me?"

"Oh? I thought you came in here to show me your new dress," I said.

"Yes, that, too."

"What else brought you in here, Mother?" I asked, turning back to her, sensing she had something up her sleeve.

She paused and took a deep breath. "Bronson would like to have you and James accompany me to his home for a formal dinner this coming Tuesday night, if that's all right with you."

I stared at her a moment.

"A formal dinner?"

"Yes. It will be wonderful, I assure you. And I would like so much for you to see Beulla Woods. Also," she added, her eyes narrowing, "it would be smart to accept an invitation from the man who is president of the bank holding the mortgage on the hotel."

"If I agree to go, it won't be because I feel threatened not to," I snapped back. She pulled herself up as if I had spit in her face.

"I didn't mean . . . it's just good sense to do the proper things now that you are a woman of some position, Dawn," she explained.

"All right," I said. "I'll speak to Jimmy about it."

"Well, why shouldn't he want to go?" she asked quickly.

"Jimmy's not impressed with these things, Mother, but I don't anticipate him refusing, so relax."

She brightened immediately.

"That's very nice, Dawn. I so want us to become good friends, despite all the unpleasantness that has occurred between us in the past."

Unpleasantness? I thought. Her permitting Grandmother Cutler to arrange for my kidnapping, and then her not coming to my defense while the dreadful old woman made my life miserable after my return? Unpleasantness? Her never coming to see me in New York or doing anything to interfere with Grandmother Cutler's sending me to give birth at The Meadows, under the control of that horrible sister, Emily? Unpleasantness? Her failure to do anything about poor Randolph and her permitting her children to fall away like pieces of some delicate china?

"I have to get ready for dinner, Mother," I said, turning away so she couldn't see the two tears that had lodged themselves in the corners of my eyes.

"Of course." She started out and turned in the doorway. "Isn't it remarkable," she said, "how well you are doing?" She laughed. "Grandmother Cutler is surely spinning around in her grave." Her laughter trailed after her.

Perhaps Mother was right about that, I thought. Perhaps that was really why I was working as hard as I could to fill her shoes, and maybe even do better. I wanted to keep her spinning in her grave.

"Forgive me, Jimmy," I whispered, "but I can't help wanting sweet revenge."

To my surprise, Jimmy was more than just willing to

go to dinner at Bronson Alcott's home. He was looking forward to it.

"I've heard so much about that house," he told me, "especially from Buster Morris, who does some grounds maintenance there as well."

I smiled. Jimmy had become very popular with the hotel staff, especially the men and women directly under his authority. He put on no airs of superiority and didn't act as if he knew everything. He relied heavily on the advice of the old-timers and didn't attempt to change anything they had been doing for years and years.

"What have you heard about Beulla Woods, Jimmy?" I asked. Curiosity filled me. I couldn't help but be interested in Mr. Alcott, not only because of Mother's friendship with him, but because of the debonair and suave way he had swept into my life, flashing that charming smile, drinking me in with those laughing blue eyes. Whenever I saw him he seemed to have an alluring and provocative grin.

And there was a mystery about him. He was a handsome and engaging man who carried himself with the self-confidence of a famous movie star. Well-to-do, important and obviously well educated, he presented a striking figure. Why, then, had he remained unmarried all these years? Was it what Mrs. Boston thought – he was too brokenhearted over not marrying Mother?

"Well, for one thing, Buster says that the house is enormous for one man to be living in it alone. He's got some servants, of course, but the house has ten bedrooms, a sitting room, a formal living room, a library and an office. He says the kitchen's half as big as our hotel kitchen, and it's all on one hundred and fifty rolling acres with a view of the cove and the sea that will take your breath away. He has a pool and a tennis court in the rear, too.

"Buster says his father built the house after he returned from the First World War. It's one of those Norman cottages."

"Cottage?"

"Well, that's what they call the style. It's French, but it looks a little like English Tudor, too," he added, proud of his new knowledge.

"It sounds like you and Buster talked a lot about Mr. Alcott's home," I teased.

"Yeah, well, I'm interested in houses and construction and stuff. I told you," he added, his face a little crimson, "I intend to build us a house someday. I've even got a piece of the hotel property picked out — up on a little rise at the northwest end. Buster says it's perfect for the sort of house I'm designing."

"Really? Oh, Jimmy, that would be wonderful." He beamed.

"Anyhow," he said, "I don't mind looking at Beulla Woods close up."

And so on Tuesday we got dressed up to accompany Mother in the hotel limousine. I hadn't really bought any new clothing since my days in New York City attending the Sarah Bernhardt School of Performing Arts. At Mother's suggestion I took off Monday afternoon and went shopping for something appropriate to wear to a formal dinner. I found an elegant-looking black satin gown with spaghetti straps and a black silk sash. Mother was literally ecstatic when she saw what I had bought.

"It's perfect," she cried, holding it up against herself and gazing in my mirror. "Absolutely perfect.

We're almost the same size," she commented. "Maybe you'll let me borrow it one day."

"Of course, Mother," I replied.

"Oh, let me help you dress tomorrow night," she begged. "Please."

"I know how to get dressed, Mother," I said. Her smile wilted so much I thought she might burst into tears. "But I don't mind you giving me some hints," I added charitably.

"Good," she said, hugging my new dress to her bosom. She closed her eyes. "We'll be like mother and daughter getting ready for an important ball . . . like a debutante's ball. Oh, I can't wait," she cried.

True to her promise, she was at my side the following day as I began to prepare to go to Bronson Alcott's dinner. Following her suggestion, I changed my hairstyle somewhat by brushing and pinning one side. I let her brush and trim my bangs. Then she insisted I go back to her suite and sit beside her while we did our makeup together. Jimmy shook his head, laughing as she seized my hand and pulled me away.

But as she sat there giving me instructions on how to do my eyes, how to work in the makeup, what color lipstick to choose and what perfume to wear, I couldn't help wondering what it might have been like if she and I had been together since my birth. It made me feel a bit guilty to wonder, for I truly missed Momma Longchamp and mourned her passing; but I couldn't help longing for the feminine things.

I would have had beautiful dresses and stylish clothes. As I grew up, Mother and I would have been like two princesses in the hotel. Maybe she wouldn't have become so self-centered if she had had a daughter with whom she could really share things. We could have been good friends, confiding in each other, sharing hopes and fears.

All these things I longed for, I vowed Christie would have. She and I would sit before a vanity mirror like this when she was older. I dreamed about helping her prepare for her first date or dance. I would be the mother to her that I had never had.

"There," Mother said when we were finished, "just look at how much more beautiful you are now."

I gazed at myself. I did look older, more alluring. Was Mother like the devil making me as vain as she was? I thought. I couldn't stop gazing at myself.

"Thank you, Mother," I said. "I'd better finish dressing and see how Jimmy is coming along."

"Don't worry," she sang. "It's fashionable to be late. Bronson expects it of me anyway," she added, laughing. "He told me if I came to my own funeral on time, the minister would be shocked to death himself."

Jimmy looked sincerely impressed when I stepped back into our suite. He whistled and nodded.

"You look great!" he said.

"So do you, Jimmy." He wore a dark blue sports jacket, matching tie and slacks. After I put on my dress I took his arm, and we stood before the full-length mirror gazing at our images.

"Is this the little girl who used to streak mud all over herself while playing with her toy teacups in the backyard?" he asked.

"Is this the boy who fell off his bike and smacked his head so badly he had to have stitches?" I responded.

"Hey," he said. "You've never forgotten that. You were so frightened." He started to laugh.

157

"The blood was streaming down your face. I thought you were going to die," I protested. "And you shouldn't have laughed at me."

"I had to," he confessed. "I was so scared myself at the sight of all that blood. I was glad I had to calm you down first."

"I was only – what, four, five?"

"Five," he said. "Daddy was so mad. 'We ain't got money for this kind of nonsense,' he said. Remember?" I shook my head. "I couldn't ride my bike for weeks after that. That old bike," he said, shaking his head and recalling. "I had to leave it behind when we packed up and moved. No room for it in the car. I'll never forget how I felt when we pulled away and I looked back and saw it leaning against the side of the house." He swallowed back his tears, and I kissed his cheek.

"Maybe we shouldn't think about those days so much, Jimmy. Maybe we should think only about the future," I suggested.

"Yeah, I know. Once in a while, though, I can't help remembering, and then I think about Fern and wonder what happened to her. Mr. Updike still can't find anything out, huh?"

I had asked him to try, but he had had no luck. I didn't want to tell Jimmy how pessimistic Mr. Updike was about it, but I explained it to him the way Mr. Updike had explained it to me.

"No, Jimmy. When people adopt children like that they want it kept secret just so the baby's old family doesn't come around, and so they can tell the child she's their own. Then if she does find out she's adopted, she can't go off looking for her real family and trying to find out why they gave her away."

"I understand," Jimmy said. "I just wish we could see her, see how she's grown, what she's like. I bet she looks more and more like Momma, huh?"

"Probably. She had Momma's dark hair and dark eyes."

"I'm ready," Mother sang from the corridor.

"The queen is calling," Jimmy said, smiling. "Shall we?" he added, and he held out his arm for me to take.

Mother hadn't shown me her newest dress until this moment. It was a pearl-white satin strapless gown with a bodice that dipped scandalously low on her bosom, easily revealing half her cleavage. Her crimson breasts bubbled over, raised by an uplift bra. Yet the hem of the skirt was quite conservative, a little below the ankle. Around her neck she wore a necklace I had seen only once before. It was an enormous pear-shaped diamond in a white-gold setting with a white-gold chain, and I would never forget it, for Grandmother Cutler had worn it. Mother had the earrings to match.

Mother threw her crochet lace shawl over her shoulders and ran it over her arm before stepping toward us.

"Do I look beautiful?" she asked, spinning around.

"You certainly do," Jimmy said. He nodded appreciatively.

"Thank you, James. And Dawn, you look so pretty, too," Mother said.

"Where did you get that necklace, Mother?" I asked pointedly.

"Necklace? Oh," she said with a nervous little laugh, "this was one of the last things poor Randolph gave me before he . . . before he passed on," she said.

159

"Wasn't it Grandmother Cutler's necklace?" I pursued.

"So? What if it was? What good did it do her anyway? She never cared about it, or about anything that any normal woman would care about. Go look in her closet and you will see the sort of garments she owned. She hardly ever wore makeup," Mother said, and she leaned toward us to add, "I don't think she even wore perfume. Just used Ivory soap and a Brillo pad," she said, laughing. "That's why she filled her office with lilacs."

"I can't believe Randolph would have given any of his mother's things away," I muttered, loud enough for her to hear.

"Well, he did. Actually, I asked him for it, and he went into her room and got it." She shook her head. "He told me she wanted me to have it, and I said, 'Next time you see her, thank her for me.'" She started to laugh.

"Oh, Mother, you didn't," I said, grimacing. To feed Randolph's insanity like that . . . it was immoral.

"Oh, what difference does it make now? Whatever is in that room is yours and mine anyway, Dawn," she claimed.

"What about Philip and Clara Sue, Mother? Clara Sue certainly would want to be included," I said.

"Well, yes, theirs, too."

"But I thought you didn't want anything to do with Grandmother Cutler's things," I reminded her.

"Not these things!" she exclaimed, her eyes wide. Then she settled into a smile. "Oh, let's not talk about anything that is unpleasant in the remotest way tonight, okay? Just look," she said, stepping closer to Jimmy. "We have such a handsome escort. Can I borrow an

160

arm, James?" she asked. He blushed and glanced at me before nodding.

Mother threaded her arm through his quickly.

"Now won't we three look like something going through that lobby!" she exclaimed.

The stairway wasn't wide enough for the three of us to descend abreast, but Mother didn't seem to want to relinquish her hold on Jimmy, so I backed up and let them go first. At the bottom Jimmy turned and smiled, offering his arm again.

"Mrs. Longchamp," he said.

"Thank you, Mr. Longchamp," I replied, and we made our entrance into the lobby.

It was just as Mother had envisioned. Guests and staff all turned our way, their faces lighting up with awe as we paraded through to the front entrance where Julius waited. As soon as he saw us he opened the doors, and we left the hotel. Julius ran to the limousine and opened the rear doors. Mother got in first. She insisted Jimmy sit between us.

"To Beulla Woods," Mother commanded.

"Yes, ma'am," Julius said, and we were off.

It was still light enough for us to get a clear view of things as we drove up the long, winding road that led to Bronson Alcott's home. Beulla Woods stood on a high hill looking down on Cutler's Cove like a castle. Just as Jimmy had described, it was a spectacular house built with gray stone wall cladding and decorative half-timbering. It had a prominent round tower with a high conical roof. The tower housed the main entrance, which was a dark pine door set in a single arched opening. The tall two-story building had a steeply pitched roof. There were two sets of three double-hung windows on each level facing the front. Under each set of windows on the second floor was a small wrought-iron decorative balcony. The chimney was on the side, and there were round hedges all about the house.

The driveway took us around the rich, elaborately landscaped front with its gardens and fountains. Julius jumped out of the limousine and opened the rear doors, helping Mother out. Jimmy and I got out and joined her.

"Isn't it wonderful?" she said, turning and sweeping the air with her arm. We looked down at the ocean below, the boats, the docks, the cars and people on the street – everything looking toylike and precious. The sun was sinking below the horizon, the last rays of sunlight shining toward the center of the sky, making the world below celestial and angelic.

"I could stand here forever and look," Mother said.

"Well, you'd better not, or our dinner will get cold," Bronson Alcott said.

All three of us spun around to see him standing in the doorway, his arms folded, a white meerschaum pipe in his right hand. He wore a dark blue velvet jacket with a gold lining on the collar and above the breast pocket. Instead of a tie, however, he had on a ruby cravat. In the twilight his chestnut hair and mustache looked a shade darker, like dark honey. The laughter around his sapphire eyes rippled down to widen his smile.

"Bronson," Mother cried. "Spying on us?"

"Hardly that," he said, stepping forward quickly to take her hand. "I did see your car drive up and wondered what was taking you all so long to ring my chimes. Poor Livingston is standing in the entryway

162

fidgeting like an expectant father," he said, and Mother laughed.

"Livingston," Bronson explained to Jimmy and me, "is my butler. He's been with me . . . well, he's been around longer than I have. He actually worked for my father," Bronson said. He shook Jimmy's hand quickly. "Welcome. And you," he said, dropping his gaze to my feet and climbing up my legs and over my bosom to my face, "look absolutely beautiful. Like mother, like daughter," he declared, still staring at me.

"Now who's keeping us from dinner?" Mother asked, not hiding her annoyance at being ignored.

"Oh. Sorry. Right this way," Bronson directed, and he led us into the beautiful house.

Livingston, in coat and tails, stood just inside. He was a tall, lean old man who bent forward, making him seem to be climbing hills even while standing on a flat surface. His hair was candle white and his eyes a pale, watery blue.

"Good evening, Livingston," Mother said.

"Good evening, ma'am," he replied in a somewhat raspy voice.

"This is Mr. and Mrs. Longchamp, Livingston," Bronson introduced. Livingston nodded.

"Hello," I greeted.

"Hi," Jimmy added.

Livingston went to close the door, and I turned my attention to the inside of the house. As we followed Bronson into the house I saw that there were paintings on all the walls, from Renaissance to modern. Colors and elegance were everywhere in evidence throughout the house, particularly in the hall, with its maroon velvet curtains, its marble floors and marble bench.

We stopped first at the library, which was filled with rich leather furniture and dark oak tables and bookcases. Bronson showed us his office, where he had an enormous portrait of his parents above his desk. There was something vaguely familiar in his mother's face. She reminded me of someone, but I didn't have time to dwell upon it, for my attention was quickly drawn to the portrait of a young woman on the wall to our left.

She looked as though she was in her late teens. She had light brown hair brushed down over her shoulders and had a soft oval face with kind, light green eyes and a gentle smile. In the portrait she was seated on a wide cushioned chair. She had her graceful-looking hands crossed over each other on her lap, but there was something about her posture, the way her shoulders turned, that seemed odd. I thought she looked uncomfortable.

I looked at Bronson and saw the way he gazed admiringly at the portrait. There was a soft smile around his lips that resembled the smile on the young woman's face. In fact, as I studied him and the girl in the portrait, I realized there were enough resemblances to make me suspect they were brother and sister.

"That's my sister Alexandria," he said, confirming my suspicion.

"Oh, she's very pretty," I said.

"Was," Bronson said, and he sighed. "She died a little more than two years ago."

"Oh, I'm sorry."

"What happened to her?" Jimmy asked quickly.

"Despite what you see there, she was constantly in pain. She suffered from a degenerative bone disease. Posing for that portrait was a difficult thing for her to do, but she insisted on it. She wanted me to have it," he added, smiling at the memory.

"It's so depressing to dote on these tragic things," Mother said.

"What? Yes, yes, of course," Bronson said. "How rude of me, especially in light of Randolph's recent passing."

"Let's not talk about death and sickness tonight," Mother pleaded.

"Of course not," Bronson agreed. "Let me show you the rest of the house," he said to Jimmy and me. The tour continued. We passed under and to the right of the semicircular stairway with its white marble balustrade. He showed us his sitting room with its elegant French furnishings and even took us in to see his kitchen, where at the moment two chefs worked on our meal. The aromas were sumptuous.

"It's a gourmet feast," Bronson promised.

We went directly to the enormous dining room that had windows that soared up to the ceiling, framed by deep rose velvet swags lined with gold. There was a great teardrop crystal chandelier hanging over a table that could easily seat twenty people. The chairs were all high backed with arms and cushioned seats. The moment we sat down, servants appeared as if from out of the woodwork. There was a waitress and a waiter. The waiter brought out the iced champagne, and the waitress followed with our glasses on a solid silver tray. The bottle was uncorked and the champagne poured.

"I should like to begin by offering another toast," Bronson said, looking at me. "From everything I have heard . . ." He leaned toward Mother to speak sotto voce. "And as you know, I have spies everywhere . . .

I understand," he continued, sitting back and raising his glass, "that the new young owner of Cutler's Cove is proving to be a success. So," he said, "to the Cutler's Cove Hotel, whose future now looks bright again."

"Oh, Bronson, how can we toast a hotel? Toast people, not buildings," Mother complained.

"Very well," he said, undaunted. "To the two most beautiful women in Cutler's Cove."

"Now that's a toast," Mother said, and we drank.

The moment our glasses touched the table, the feast began.

We started with escargots and then had a radicchio salad with an absolutely delicious dressing and loaves of home-made French bread. Bronson warned me that every recipe was his chef's secret, and I would not be able to steal anything to bring back to the hotel.

"Don't worry, Nussbaum wouldn't appreciate my suggesting someone else's recipe," I said, just imagining. "He has too much pride."

"Oh, that egotistical Hungarian," Mother moaned. "He can be such a bore."

After we were served a few tablespoons of sherbet to cleanse our palates, the main course was served. We had duck à l'orange and wild rice with a side dish of asparagus in a hollandaise sauce that was sumptuous. The waiter served us wine, and the waitress hovered about, just waiting for the opportunity to refill our water glasses.

I noticed that as usual, Mother ate like a bird, despite the delicious food. But Jimmy and I stuffed ourselves and nearly burst when the waiters brought out our dessert: baked Alaska. How we found the room for it all, I'll never know. But by the time we finished having our coffee, I thought I would need a crane to lift me out of the chair.

"Why don't we all take a walk about the grounds," Bronson suggested, "before we have our after-dinner drinks? I think we could all use the exercise."

"Sure," Jimmy said, eager to continue his study of the house and grounds.

"I need it," I confessed.

"Well, I don't," Mother said. "And I've seen the grounds. I'll wait for you all in the French room, Bronson."

"Everyone could use the exercise, Laura Sue," Bronson coaxed. His eyes twinkled with persuasion. Mother sighed deeply.

"Oh, well, if everyone insists, I'll go," she said, making it look as if she was doing us all a great favor. Somehow, Bronson didn't mind Mother's performances. If anything, I saw a look of amusement in his face.

He took us back out the front, where Livingston rushed as best he could to open the door, and we followed a slate walkway around the house, past gardens, a gazebo and a small pond, to the rear of the house, where we found the tennis courts and a rather large swimming pool. Everything, including the walkway, was lit up.

Jimmy walked ahead with him and talked about the house and the grounds, while Mother complained to me that the shoes she was wearing were not designed for hikes.

"I would hardly call this a hike, Mother," I said, but that didn't dissuade her from whining until we made our way back and she could drop her body into the soft cushions of the settee in the drawing room. Moments later Livingston arrived with a tray bearing a bottle of sherry and four glasses. He poured us each a glass and brought the tray around. Jimmy and I were seated in the two wing-back chairs to the right of the white marble fireplace. Bronson remained standing. As soon as Livingston left, Bronson raised his glass again, this time smiling in a conspiratorial way at Mother.

"It's time for the main toast of the evening," Bronson said, "and an announcement."

Mother followed that with one of her nervous little laughs.

My heart began to thump like a lead drum against my chest. Some little voice within me had been whispering suspicions all night, but I had chosen to ignore it, chosen to ignore the way Mother and Bronson Alcott gazed into each other's eyes, chosen to ignore the way he placed his hand over hers and held it there at the dinner table.

I looked at Jimmy, who gazed back at me with eyes betraying a similar suspicion. There had been ulterior motives for this dinner after all.

"We wanted you two to be the first to know," Bronson said. "Right, Laura Sue?"

"Yes," she said, smiling.

"We're announcing our engagement tomorrow," he declared. "It won't be much of an engagement, however," he added quickly. "We intend to be married within a week."

"A week!" I couldn't help my exclamation. "But it's been less than two months since Randolph's death," I cried.

Like a tender flower without the admiration of rain to nourish her faith in herself, Mother wilted before me.

"I knew it," she moaned. "I knew she would say something like that. I just knew it! My happiness means nothing to you, does it, Dawn?"

"Well, how can you expect me to say anything else?" I looked up at Bronson and then turned back to Mother. "How can you do this so soon after Randolph's death?"

"You of all people should know, Dawn," she replied coldly, "that my marriage to Randolph was not much of a marriage anyway. He was married to his mother, her every shadow, her every word. You don't know how much I suffered," she added, her throat choking and her eyes filling with tears and quickly overflowing in streams down her dainty cheeks.

"Now Laura Sue, don't," Bronson chided gently, putting his glass of sherry down and going to her. He sat beside her and put his arm around her shoulders.

"Well, she doesn't know. She hates me because she doesn't know what I went through." She looked up at him, gazing into his eyes through her tears now.

Bronson turned to me, his eyes showing such intensity and purpose, it made my breath catch and a lump come into my throat.

"Perhaps," he said, "it's time she knew it all, then."

Mother looked up sharply, fear shadowing her face. Bronson patted her hand.

"It's time, Laura Sue," he repeated.

"I just can't," Mother cried. "It's too painful for me even to think about and remember these things, much less talk about them anymore," she pleaded, and she shook her head vigorously.

"Then let me," Bronson said. "If possible, I don't want any hard feelings among us – not now, not at the beginning of a new start. I want us to all feel like family."

Mother closed her eyes and sucked in her breath. Then she pulled herself to her feet.

"Do what must be done," she said. "I'm exhausted and too upset to listen. I want to go back to the hotel," she said.

"All right," Bronson said. "Perhaps James will escort you, and Dawn can stay here and talk. I'll send her home with my car and driver."

"Sure," Jimmy said, rising.

"Jimmy should hear anything that has to be said, too," I declared. Jimmy stepped in front of me and leaned down to whisper.

"Maybe he wants to talk to you alone, Dawn. Maybe he'll be uncomfortable with another man listening. You can fill me in later." He squeezed my hand reassuringly and then turned and nodded to Bronson and Mother.

"Thank you, Bronson," Mother said, relieved. "It was a wonderful evening, and I would like to keep it that way in my storehouse of memories." She flashed a smile at me. Bronson escorted her and Jimmy out.

Moments later he returned, sat down across from me, crossed his legs, lifted his glass of sherry to his lips and began.

More Secrets from the Past

"First I should tell you a little about myself," Bronson said, "so that you will be able to better understand how and why events unfolded as they did."

That charming yet provocative smile left his face, and his manner turned very intense as he leaned forward to lock his eyes with mine.

"I was born into money and position and had a rather comfortable childhood. My father was a firm man who came from hardy stock, but my mother was a very warm and devoted person, devoted to my father, devoted to her children and devoted to the Alcott image.

"Right from the start, both Alexandria and I were taught how important that image was. We were made to understand that we had a responsibility to maintain our high standing. We were told that people looked up to us, that we were, in a sense, the new ruling class of the South. We had money and power – power to affect other people's lives.

"As an investor and a banker, my father controlled the destinies of many. In short, I was brought up believing I was some sort of prince, and some day I would inherit my father's throne and rule in the Alcott tradition."

He leaned back, templing his fingers under his chin a moment, and then smiled.

"It was all a bit overdramatized, but as it is with most people of some position and wealth, they began to believe their own publicity. Father certainly did.

"Anyway," he continued, his eyes somewhat wistful now, "as I told you, Alexandria was born with a crippling ailment. Because of that and because of how self-important we were made to feel, she became more and more melancholy. She felt the disease was somehow her fault and always believed she was disappointing my parents, especially my father.

"Despite her sickness, she was an excellent student, always trying harder and harder to achieve. I loved her dearly and would do anything in my power for her."

He smiled softly.

"She was always chastising me for spending too much time with her. 'You should be off doing things with your friends,' she would say, 'chasing after pretty girls and not spending all your time with your crippled sister.' But alas, I couldn't desert her.

"When no one asked her to the high school prom, I took her myself and forced her to go, even though she couldn't dance. I would be the one to take her to movies or shows, the one who insisted she go for motor rides down the seashore or into the mountains. I took her sailing and even horseback riding, when she was still well enough to do those things. After a while anything she saw or did, she saw or did because of my insistence.

" 'Oh, what difference does it make, Bronson?' she would ask when I would stubbornly persist. I didn't want to say it, but I wanted to squeeze everything into her life

172

that I could, knowing she didn't have long to live. But then again, it didn't have to be said; she understood.

"Anyway, I suppose my devotion to Alexandria put some young women off. There were snide remarks and ugly rumors spread about us – to most it was unnatural that a brother and a sister should be so close – but I wasn't about to turn my back on Alexandria just to please some gossips and chase some conceited, pretty young skirt."

"My mother was one of those young women, wasn't she?" I asked confidently.

He stared at me blankly for a moment or so, drumming his fingertips on the arm of his chair before he got up to stand before the wide wall of windows, staring out at the gardens and beyond toward the sea. Finally he turned back to me, his eyes revealing a deep inner agony I could understand, for I recognized it as the agony a man feels when he longs for a woman who seems forever beyond his reach. I had seen this look in Jimmy's eyes occasionally when we were growing up together, believing we were brother and sister, and feeling emotions and longings we thought were indecent.

"Your mother," he began, "was and still is one of the most beautiful women in Cutler's Cove, and like all beautiful women, she has a certain amount of vanity."

"Mother," I said dryly, "has far more than her fair share of vanity."

He started to smile but stopped and shook his head.

"I won't deny that, but I understand why it is so." He paused for a moment and thought. "You don't know much about your mother's family, her childhood, do you?"

"No. She never talks about it, and whenever I did ask her questions she always answered quickly, impatiently, as if I were annoying her, so I stopped. All I really know," I said, "is that she was an only child, and that both her parents are dead."

"Yes, she was an only child, a young girl who adored – no, practically worshipped her father. But Simon Thomas was a rake if there ever was one and didn't give her the attention she needed so desperately. His reputation for womanizing was always a topic of conversation. Her poor mother suffered so and tried to pretend all was well. Laura Sue," he stressed, "comes from a world of illusion and deceit, distrust and betrayal.

"Consequently," he continued, his eyes serious, "she craved attention, craved love, and was far more demanding than any other woman I knew.

"But I was desperately in love with her from the first moment I set eyes on her. I remember," he said, a smile returning to those aqua eyes, "parking my car at the corner of her street and sitting in it for hours just to catch a glimpse of her coming and going."

He paused, as if the image of my mother as a young girl was projected on the wall across from him.

"Anyway," he said, snapping out of his reverie, "I began to court her, and for a while we were quite a striking couple. But after my mother contracted a rapidly destructive blood cancer and died, I felt even more of a need to spend time with Alexandria. She was so shattered by my mother's unexpected passing."

"And your precious Laura Sue, my mother," I said, jumping ahead, "was upset about all the attention you were giving your sister?"

"Laura Sue needed a man who would make her the very center of his existence," he explained. "I wanted to be that man, desperately wanted it, but I couldn't turn my back on Alexandria."

"So Mother turned her back on you," I said. "Why do you still care for her, knowing how self-centered she is and was?" I wondered aloud. "Is love so blind? Are men really such fools?"

He laughed.

"Perhaps," he said. "But for a young woman who has suffered something of a tragic romance herself, you don't show very much compassion and understanding."

I blushed. Was he right? Was I turning into the hard, cold person Jimmy was afraid I would become?

"I'm sorry," I said.

He returned to his chair and sipped some more of his sherry. Then he leaned back and templed his hands under his chin again.

"Laura Sue went off to finishing school, and I directed all my energies into my work. I tried to hide my emotional pain from Alexandria, but she was a very perceptive person, especially when it came to anything concerning me. I know she suffered terrible guilt, thinking she was destroying my life, and she tried to get me to spend less time with her. She even begged my father to put her into a facility for the handicapped, but he was embarrassed by her illness and refused to acknowledge it.

"Not long after, I heard that Laura Sue had become engaged to Randolph Cutler. It was strange," he said, shaking his head and smiling warmly, "but it was as if a cloud had been lifted. Now that there was no longer

175

any chance of my having Laura Sue, the torment ended for a while."

"Did you have another romance?" I asked quickly.

"Nothing serious. Perhaps I had a distrust of love by then," he added, his eyes sparkling mischievously. "It was a particularly hard period of life for me anyway. My father suffered a heart attack. He lingered for weeks in the hospital until he finally died. After his death I assumed his position in the bank.

"Now there was only Alexandria and me. But her condition was growing worse. I hired a full-time nurse, took my meals with her in her room, wheeled her about in her wheelchair whenever I could; in short, spent even more time with her, knowing her days were limited. She never complained and did all that she could to make herself less of a burden.

"Finally, one night she died in her sleep. Even in death she had this gentle smile on her lips." Tears filled his eyes and began to descend down his cheeks. He didn't wipe them away; he stared ahead as if oblivious to his own crying.

I couldn't keep back my own tears, which had begun to burn behind my eyelids. When he saw me grinding them away with my small fists, he straightened up. His tears had stopped, but the anguish in his eyes remained.

"By now, of course, Laura Sue and Randolph had married, and Philip had been born. Because the bank had such a close financial relationship to the hotel, I was often invited to dine with Mrs. Cutler and would sit at the table with her, Randolph and Laura Sue."

"That must have been difficult for you," I said, "knowing how much you had loved her."

"Yes," he said, happy with my understanding. "Actually, it was exquisite torment. I longed for those times, those opportunities to be at her side, to see her and talk with her and feel her hand in mine when we greeted each other. And I was soon convinced that I saw something burning for me in her eyes when we gazed at each other.

"Those were particularly difficult days for Laura Sue. Mrs. Cutler was never happy about Randolph's marrying her, and Mrs. Cutler was not one to hide her feelings. You could cut the air between her and Laura Sue; that's how thick it was with the dislike they had for each other.

"But Mr. Cutler was a different story. Randolph's father had a reputation for being something of a rake. He loved to charm the young women who came to the hotel, and there were always stories about his illicit affairs. Of course, no one dared say anything about it in front of Mrs. Cutler. She was quite a woman — diminutive in body, but towering and impressive."

"I'm quite aware of how impressive she was," I said sharply.

"What? Oh, yes, yes. Anyway, late one night I heard the chimes ring and then heard Livingston go to the door. I threw on my robe and slipped into my slippers quickly and came down the stairs to see Laura Sue. It was immediately evident that she was distraught to the point of hysteria. She had thrown on any old clothes, her hair was wild; she wasn't wearing any makeup, and her eyes were bloodshot. Livingston was literally terrified by the sight of her.

"I took her into this room and got her some sherry. She gulped the glass down and then fell back on the sofa and burst into tears, gasping words. Gradually I put everything she was saying together into some sensible order and realized she was telling me her father-in-law had raped her.

"Naturally, I was shocked. My mood moved from astonishment to pity to outrage. Twice I started out of the house to go to the hotel and tear the man apart, but twice she begged me not to do it.

"Finally, we both calmed down. I held her in my arms for hours, kissing her and reassuring her that I would be at her side to help her in any way I could. I promised her I would get her the finest attorney. I offered her my home, but she was frightened, and no matter how much I pledged my support, she couldn't be persuaded to take legal action.

"But" – he looked away and then turned back – "we knew we loved each other, and we admitted it openly. She stayed with me that night," he confessed.

"After she had just been raped?" I asked incredulously.

"We only held each other. The next morning she returned to the hotel, but she was to come back to me often from time to time. We thought it best I not go to the hotel. Mrs. Cutler stopped inviting me anyway." For a moment he blushed with shame and guilt. Then he straightened up in his seat and took a deep breath.

"Mrs. Cutler was not someone who missed anything that was going on around her, no matter how furtive and careful we were. Soon afterward, Laura Sue realized she was pregnant with you, and, counting back the weeks, also realized you were Mr. Cutler's child. When Laura Sue announced her pregnancy, Mrs. Cutler accused her of having an affair with me and assumed I was your father.

"She and Laura Sue had it out, and Laura Sue told her what her husband had done to her. Of course, Lillian Cutler refused to acknowledge it openly, but Laura Sue and I both feel that inwardly Mrs. Cutler knew it was true. Threats were exchanged, Mrs. Cutler pledging to cause a scandal for Laura should she as much as whisper this tale to anyone. She said she would simply bring witnesses to testify that Laura Sue and I were having an affair, showing that you had to be my child, and Laura Sue would be disgraced for falsely accusing Mr. Cutler. Laura Sue was no match for Mrs. Cutler. I often tried to get her to leave Randolph and marry me, but she was afraid.

"Not long afterward, Mr. Cutler suffered his stroke, and after a week or so he passed away. With him gone, Laura Sue felt she had no way of ever proving what he had done.

"As the date of your birth drew closer and closer Mrs. Cutler tightened her grip around Laura Sue, even to the point of bringing her attorney in to outline for Laura Sue what sort of things she would do to her if she didn't obey her every command.

"She terrorized her into accepting the kidnapping hoax, thus eliminating you from the scene. You know the details of that story," he added.

"Yes," I said sharply. "Unfortunately, I do."

"But you don't know the pain and the sorrow Laura Sue felt afterward. She was haunted by guilt," he said.

"I still find that difficult to believe," I responded. "I think I always will."

"I know," Bronson said, nodding. "How can a child ever understand why her mother would give her away? Perhaps, though, you will find it in your heart to forgive her someday."

I bit down on my lower lip and shifted my eyes. Numbly, I shook my head.

"Maybe it's because you are a man and you are so in love with her still that you can find it easy to forgive her for her selfishness. I can't make any promises," I said.

"All that I ask is you try," he replied. "Would you like some more sherry?" he asked, rising and going to the bottle.

"Yes, thank you," I said. He poured me a glass and gave himself another.

I waited until he sat down again.

"Tell me," I said, "how much of all this did Randolph know?"

"Laura Sue told him everything, but he refused to hear. Early on, he withdrew into his own world, but it was his mother more than anyone who drove him into it. I knew him well enough to see that he was very insecure and even ashamed that he wasn't living up to his mother's expectations. She punished him in little ways for his having married Laura Sue against her will. It was the only thing he had ever done in defiance, and she wouldn't forgive him for it.

"My feeling is that she made him feel less than a man, and that was the reason he became what he became. I don't think Mrs. Cutler minded. In fact, she was probably happy about what he turned out to be when it came to Laura Sue."

"What do you mean?" I asked, catching something hidden between the lines.

"Randolph still doted on Laura Sue, pretending as if they were still man and wife in every way. I think in his own way he still loved her very much, but he and Laura Sue had stopped sleeping together soon after his father had raped her," he said.

"Stopped sleeping together." I let the sherry warm my chest, and then I sat up. "But that can't be," I said, realizing the chain of events. "Clara Sue . . ."

"Is my child," he confessed.

Bronson sat back, exhausted from his revelations. His face was flushed from that and from the glasses of sherry he had drunk, one after the other, to fortify his courage. His story had left my mind in a turmoil. My heart was racing. I felt as if I were drowning in a sea of conflicting emotions. I hated my mother and I pitied her; I pitied Randolph but hated his weaknesses. I thought less of Bronson for permitting Mother to torment him so and keep him on a string all these years, yet I admired him for the loyalty and love he gave to his sister.

Most importantly and most tragically, I saw that there was always something keeping people from doing the right things, the things their hearts told them to do. Ironically, if Mother had been less self-centered, she might have married Bronson and had a wonderful life. She would have avoided the horror of living under the thumb of Grandmother Cutler.

"I'm tired," I said, breaking the deep silence that had fallen between us. "I'd better go home."

"Of course," he said, jumping up. "Let me have my driver bring up the car."

While he was gone, Bronson's confession reverberated in my mind. Clara Sue was his. Now I knew why

181

there was something familiar in his mother's face in the portrait. I had seen resemblances to Clara Sue. Since we had different fathers and her father was not a Cutler, the cords of blood that tied us together weren't as thick as I had once thought. I found myself feeling grateful about that. She and I had such different personalities. I didn't think I was capable of being as hateful or as vicious and cruel, not that Bronson struck me as a father from whom she could have inherited such qualities.

Another irony that didn't slip past me involved Clara Sue and me. She would end up living with her real parents, but not knowing it; and I, because of the turn of events, had lived with people who were *not* my parents, and I didn't know it for most of my life. For both of us, family had been built on deception.

That was why I was so silent when Bronson, escorting me out of his house and to the car, turned to me to say, "I hope that now we can all be more like a family." I stared at him bleakly, as if he spoke of pipe dreams made of smoke. To me the concept of family had become mythical. It was like a fairy tale. What was it like having parents and brothers and sisters whom you loved and who loved you? What was it like caring about one another, remembering one another's birthdays and celebrating each achievement, each wonderful new thing each of you did? What was it like being in a home on a holiday like Thanksgiving and having a family gathered around a full table with everyone laughing and smiling and being thankful all were here?

"Dawn," he said, seizing my arm as I started to get into the limousine. I turned to him, and he riveted his pleading eyes on mine. "I hope you can find it in your heart to forgive us all our weaknesses and sins."

"It's not for me to forgive anyone for anything," I said. I lowered my eyes and then lifted them to meet his agonized gaze again. "Thank you," I said, "for trusting me with your story and caring enough to want my understanding."

He smiled, his blue eyes now gleaming.

"Good night," he said.

"Good night. The dinner was wonderful," I added. The driver started the engine and took me away. When I looked back, Bronson was still standing in front of his house, watching me go.

As we careened around the turns going down the hill from Bronson's beautiful home I could see the lighted windows in houses below. Inside, perhaps, families were gathered in their living rooms, talking or watching television or listening to music. The children had no doubts that they were with their parents. Again ironically, many of them probably wished they owned a glamorous and famous resort like Cutler's Cove. They thought their lives were boring and uneventful, and they longed for the excitement we had.

Yes, we lived in castles, but the moats that surrounded us were filled with lies and tears. The rich and the famous lived behind billboards; their houses were like movie sets, facades, glittering but empty. What person living what he considered a mediocre life would want to trade places with Bronson Alcott once he knew the truth about how the man had suffered?

Suddenly, looking out over the ocean and seeing the quarter moon peek through two soft white clouds, I became melancholy. I wished I could fall back through time and be a little girl again, the little girl who thought she was running home to her real mother when she cut her finger and needed love and attention. I wanted to burst through the front door of whatever poor and shabby cottage or apartment we were living in at the time and throw my arms around Momma Longchamp and feel her arms around me and her kisses on my hair and face. I wanted all the scratches and cuts and bumps to go away in seconds.

But they don't go away in seconds anymore. They linger in our hearts, I thought, because we have no one but ourselves to comfort us.

As we turned into the driveway and climbed toward the hotel I felt some of the gloom lift from my heart, for I knew inside that Jimmy and Christie were there for me. It was important – more important than ever, I thought – that we hold on to one another and love and cherish one another dearly.

The hotel was quiet. Most of the guests had gone to their rooms. Some lingered in the lobby, talking softly, and a few sat outside. I hurried up to our suite, stopping first to look in on Christie. She was fast asleep, her face turned. She still embraced her teddy bear. I fixed her blanket and kissed her cheek and then went in to tell Jimmy everything Bronson had revealed.

He listened attentively, shaking his head in amazement every once in a while. When I was finished I made him hold me tightly.

"Oh, it was terrible, Jimmy, terrible to sit there and listen to him describe how cruel and mean the people who were supposed to love one another had been to one another," I cried.

"Our lives won't be like that," he promised.

"Maybe there's a curse here, Jimmy. Maybe we won't be able to help ourselves," I said fearfully.

"The only curses here are the curses people make for themselves," he said.

"Jimmy," I said, pulling back from him, "I want us to have our baby right away."

He didn't answer, and I saw that darkness around his eyes that always suggested something sad.

"What is it, Jimmy? Why doesn't that make you happy?" I asked.

"It makes me happy. It's just" – he stared at me a moment – "I got a letter from Daddy yesterday."

"Daddy Longchamp? Why didn't you say so? What did he say? Is he coming to see us?" Jimmy shook his head. "What is it, Jimmy?"

"Edwina had a miscarriage," he said. "I didn't want to tell you because of all that was happening here. She's all right, but they were both upset."

"And so you're afraid of my becoming pregnant now?" I asked.

"It's not that. You're so involved with what you're doing that you barely have time for Christie and me at the moment."

"Having our baby is more important than anything else I'm doing."

Jimmy lay back against his pillow and watched as I got undressed. Naked, I crawled in beside him and cuddled up against him, feeling his desire for me quickly stir. Even so, he remained a bit hesitant.

"Don't do this because you're feeling gloomy, Dawn," he warned. "There should never be any regrets."

"There never will be," I swore, and then I brought

185

my lips to his and kissed him long and hard, making my embrace more and more demanding until whatever reluctance he had in him evaporated under the heat of my passion. He pressed on lovingly. As he drove me higher and higher, the despondency that had invaded my heart began to retreat. I turned to look out the window and saw that quarter moon slip past the clouds and blink brightly against the inky sky.

The past can't hurt us, I thought, if we build a fortress out of our love.

Mother did not emerge from her suite the next morning, nor did she come out for lunch or go anywhere. Jimmy had told me she had cried softly in the hotel limousine all the way back to the hotel once they had left Bronson's house. Bronson had tried to paint a different picture of her for me; he painted a portrait of a little girl to whom her father barely paid attention, a little girl who grew up to become a beautiful but fragile and insecure person, trapping herself in a marriage that proved horrifying. I knew that much of his description evolved from his desperate and undying love for her, and that she wasn't the lily-white victim he had portrayed her to have been; but I was also haunted by the fear that I was becoming too hard and too cold.

Tired of hating and fighting, I got myself to go in to see her.

She was lying in bed, looking much like she used to look before my wedding and Randolph's passing: weak and despondent. The tray of food Mrs. Boston had brought in to her lay on the nightstand, barely touched. She had her eyes closed, her head sunk in the large pillow, her hair falling around her. I was surprised to see that she hadn't put on any makeup.

"What's wrong with you today, Mother?" I began. She let her eyelids flutter open and stared at the ceiling for a moment before responding.

"I'm just so tired of arguments," she said. "So tired of hateful words. It's made me sick. I was never a very strong person to begin with, Dawn," she added, lifting her head and sliding up slowly, "and years and years of turmoil have taken their toll. I feel like surrendering to Father Time and his despicable companion, Age. Let what will be, be," she said, and she let her head fall back on the pillow again.

Her performance brought a smile to my face, but I turned quickly to hide it.

"But Mother," I said, "what about your plans to marry Bronson and start a wonderful new life? Bronson won't want to marry a wrinkled-up, gray-haired hag, will he?" I teased.

"Bronson won't marry me if you oppose it and make it seem like another scandal," she said sadly, with funereal eyes. "He says we must all like one another or it won't work."

"I'm not opposing it," I said. "I'm not one to cast stones. If the two of you want to get married, get married," I said, and at my words she lit up like a Christmas tree.

"Oh, Dawn, do you mean that? Do you really? That's wonderful," she cried, sitting up again.

"Are you going to have a wedding here, too?" I asked, wondering how it could all be planned in a week's time.

"Oh, no, no. We're past that sort of thing. We're

187

going to New York to be married by a supreme court judge and then see dozens and dozens of Broadway shows!" she exclaimed. She reached for the food tray and brought it to her bed table. "I've already bought an entire new wardrobe for the occasion," she continued, pecking away at her salad. "That's what I've been doing afternoons these past few weeks."

"So you knew that far back?" I asked.

"What? Oh. Well, I always thought . . . yes," she confessed, unable to think of an excuse quickly, "I did. I know it doesn't sound nice, but what was the point in deceiving ourselves and pretending something we knew would happen wouldn't? We knew what we wanted and what we were going to do eventually. I wanted to prepare and be ready."

"I see. Have you told Clara Sue anything?" I asked, wondering if that might be another reason why Clara Sue had refused to come home for the summer. Mother shifted her eyes back to the food quickly.

"Not yet."

"How much will you tell her, Mother?" I asked.

"Just that we're getting married," she said. "That's all that's necessary for now. Why complicate things any more than they already are?" she asked.

"That's for you and Bronson to decide," I said. "I can tell you that it's very painful to learn that someone you thought was your mother and someone you thought was your father are not."

"I agree," Mother said, missing my point. "Why add additional pain? Poor Clara Sue has already suffered in losing the man she thought was her father. Why . . . why, it would be like making him die again," she

188

said. She looked up, smiling, her blue eyes shining with excitement.

"And I don't want anything unpleasant to happen when Bronson and I start anew. I hope you will come visit us often, Dawn," she said. "We'll have wonderful dinner parties and invite all the important people in Cutler's Cove. Bronson knows everyone who's anyone."

"We'll see," I said. "When do you intend to leave?"

"Why, I think" – she looked around as if she had forgotten – "I think Bronson will come by late today."

"Today!" I cried, astonished. If it all depended on my attitude, how did she know what I would say and think? I laughed to myself and wondered if it were possible that Bronson did not know how much of a conniver Mother was. Of course, it was possible he did but was willing to live with it, or even believed he could change her. Love makes us all into dreamers, I thought. Or in Mother's case, schemers.

"Yes. So please see if you can find Mrs. Boston for me, will you, Dawn? I want her to help me pack, and I want to tell her how to arrange my things to be moved."

"What about Philip? Have you told Philip?" I asked. Now that it was settled, I couldn't believe how quickly things were going to change.

"Philip? But Philip is still away with his girlfriend and her family," she said. "I'll have to wait to tell him. Or, if he should call while I am in New York, you can tell him," she said.

"Isn't that something you want to tell him yourself?" I asked.

"News is news," she said, shifting the tray off her lap.

189

"Besides," she added, "Philip never gets terribly excited about anything affecting me. He's a bit too much like his grandmother in that respect," she concluded.

"Very well, Mother," I said. "I'll see about Mrs. Boston."

"Thank you, Dawn. And Dawn," she called as I started out, "thank you. Thank you for being so understanding. You have become quite a young lady."

"I hope you will be happy, Mother," I said. "I really do."

I left her scurrying about her room, revived, a resurrected corpse. I couldn't help laughing.

Late in the afternoon Bronson's car pulled up in front of the hotel. By now, because of Mrs. Boston and some of the other members of the hotel staff Mother had drafted to help her prepare for her departure, word had spread throughout the hotel. Everyone in the lobby looked up expectantly when Bronson made his entrance. There was whispering in every corner.

All of Mother's things had been carried down and were at the side of the door in a half dozen suitcases and two large black trunks. The bellhops and Bronson's driver proceeded to load them into his limousine. When I realized Bronson had arrived, I came out to greet him. Mrs. Boston had gone up immediately to tell Mother, as she had requested.

"Well," he said, a little embarrassed by the attention he was receiving, "it looks like we've made the evening news."

"Headline story," I said. "When do you two actually get married?"

"Tomorrow," he replied, shifting his weight from one leg to another and smiling nervously.

"I want to wish you luck," I said, and I offered my hand.

"Thank you. I meant what I said yesterday. I hope we will all be family now," he replied.

Before I could respond we heard one of Mother's high-pitched laughs and then saw her make her entrance. Her face radiated happiness and excitement. As she crossed the lobby to join Bronson I saw the way she gazed about, drinking in the curiosity of onlookers like a flower, for the attention only made her blossom more. Bronson held out his hands, and she took them so that he could pull her to him. He put his arm around her shoulder and kissed her on the cheek.

"You look like a fresh spring day," he said.

"Do I?" she asked with obvious false modesty. "I thought I looked horrible from rushing about so much." She turned to me and reached for my hand. I let her take it into hers. She smiled.

"Good-bye, Dawn," Mother said in a voice barely above a whisper. Her face was flushed now and her eyes sparkling.

Gazing into her radiant face, I realized that Mother saw herself escaping. She was getting out from under the shadow of Grandmother Cutler and the weight of all those unpleasant memories. And for a moment I envied her. What had I done to myself by accepting my inheritance and sacrificing my dreams and ambitions?

She hugged me and kissed my cheek.

"Good-bye and good luck, Mother," I whispered.

"We'll call you as soon as we return," Bronson promised. I followed them out the door. Jimmy, who was supervising some work being done on the fountains in the front, came rushing over to shake Bronson's hand. Mother kissed his cheek, and he blushed with embarrassment. Then he stood by my side and watched them get into the limousine.

I saw the way Mother looked up at the hotel. I saw the strange mixture of sadness and happiness on her face. Tears began to zigzag down her cheeks. Then Bronson embraced her, and she turned into him to bury her face against his neck. Clinging to each other, they drove off . . . two lovers who had missed their moment years and years ago and had somehow found a second chance.

The limousine left the dark shadows cast by the afternoon sun and the hotel. For Mother it was truly as though she had slipped through the fingers of Grandmother Cutler's ghost. Sunlight beamed off the top of the limousine as it turned and disappeared.

"Well, that's that," Jimmy said, embracing me. "Funny," he said, looking around, "old lady Cutler's gone, and poor Randolph's followed in her footsteps. Now your mother runs off to be married and live in that great house, and Clara Sue is sure to live with them."

"Oh, she'll live with them, all right," I said. "I'll see to that."

"Then there will just be us," he said.

"And Philip," I reminded him.

"Oh, yes, and Philip."

A few days later – a day before Mother and her new husband returned from their whirlwind marriage and honeymoon in New York City – Philip arrived. He was darkly tanned and rested from his vacation in Bermuda. The first place he came to was my office. I heard him knock and looked up to see him peek around the door.

"Hello," he said.

"Philip. Did you just arrive?"

"Yes," he said, entering. "Rested and ready for duty," he said, saluting me. I sat back. His eyes scanned me quickly, and he stopped jesting.

"Something wrong?" he asked.

"I don't suppose anyone's told you the news yet," I said.

"News? What news?" He held his smile, but his eyes were filled with worry. "Something's happened to Mother?" he asked.

"Something's happened, all right. She's remarried and is still on her honeymoon," I replied. He held his smile, but it drifted into incredulity.

"You're kidding," he said.

"No. She and Bronson Alcott left about six days ago to be married in New York City. Most of her things have already been moved to Beulla Woods," I added.

"Well," he said, gazing down at the floor. After a moment his smile returned, and he shifted his gaze back to me. "*C'est la vie*. That's Mother. No grass grows under her feet," he said. I wondered how much he had known, or if he knew anything. "Are you and Jimmy going to move into that suite now?"

"No," I said. "We're happy where we are."

"Good. Then I'll move in there. That's where Betty Ann and I will eventually live," he added.

"Oh?"

"We've decided we will get engaged in the fall and marry a week after we graduate," he said.

"I'm very happy for you, Philip. Congratulations," I told him. He stood there staring at me, his eyes fixed so intensely on my face, I couldn't help but look down.

"Just imagine," he said, almost in a whisper, "some-day soon we'll be sleeping right beside each other."

"You mean in rooms beside each other, Philip," I corrected.

"Yes," he said, widening his smile, "of course. In rooms. Well," he said, slapping his hands together, "a lot's happened and is happening. I wonder if dear Clara Sue knows. Does she?"

"If she doesn't, she will soon," I said, my eyes hard and cold now.

"Oh? What do you mean?"

"I've taken the liberty of moving all of her things to Beulla Woods," I said.

Philip stared with even more incredulity in his face than he had had before. Then he burst into laughter.

"How ruthless but decisive of you," he said. Then he shook his head and added, "You really have become Grandmother Cutler. Well, I've got to see to my things," he said before I could reply, and he started out, his laughter trailing behind him.

I stood up and went to the window to think about what he had said. I didn't care, I told myself. This is one time I don't mind being compared to her. There's got to be a little of Grandmother Cutler in us all if we are to survive, I thought.

But when I turned and looked up at my father's portrait it seemed his face had grown darker around the eyes.

An Elusive Rainbow

The morning after Mother and Bronson returned to Beulla Woods, she called to tell me all about her wedding and honeymoon in New York. The excitement in her voice when she described the lights of Broadway, the elegantly dressed theater patrons, the crowds and traffic, and the lights and music, all of it, brought back my own memories of the theater; and of course, with that, memories of Michael.

Mother babbled on and on, describing every last detail. She barely paused for a breath before going on to describe the museums and art galleries they had also visited.

"I never realized how cultured a man Bronson is," she finally said. Then, in an almost wistful tone, she added, "Funny, you can know someone almost all your life and not really know him."

"That's very true, even about your closest relatives, Mother," I replied, finally getting a word in. "Have you spoken to Philip since you returned?" I asked quickly before she went on to describe more of her New York honeymoon trip.

"Philip? No. I called you," she said. "You can tell him I'm home, and if he wants to call, he'll call," she said. Then, after a moment's pause, she asked, "How did he react when he learned about my marriage?"

"He's not upset, if that's what you mean. He was surprised, of course," I said.

She laughed her thin, nervous laugh.

"That's Philip. That's why I don't worry," she sang.

"You saw that Clara Sue's things have been moved to Beulla Woods, I imagine," I said. I knew that must have been one of the first things Livingston had told her and Bronson when they had returned from their honeymoon.

"Yes," she said, tagging on a long "S" sound. It was almost a whistle. "Did she call and demand that be done already?"

"No," I replied in a casual tone. "I decided to do it myself."

"Clara Sue may be upset about that," she mused.

"Well, better that she be upset there then. I have no time for her immature behavior here," I stated firmly. "She belongs with you," I asserted. Mother did not disagree.

"Bronson expected she would live with us. He wanted it," she added, but I could feel her pouting. Mother expected her new marriage would restore her youth magically. She didn't want the obligations of family, of children. She wanted truly to be a newlywed and, in every sense of the word, rejuvenated.

"That's good," I said. "Well, I have to get back to work. Welcome back, Mother."

"Oh, Dawn," she cried before I could say good-bye, "when can you and James come to dinner? Philip will come, too, of course. Bronson would like you all to come this Saturday night, if you can. We've already

196

started planning it. I'm having the Steidmans." She put on a haughty tone. I could just see her lifting her nose in the air. "Mr. Steidman is building that new complex outside of Virginia Beach. It's a multimillion-dollar construction project."

"I can't speak for Philip, Mother, but you know Saturday nights are our big nights at the hotel. We have a full house this weekend, too. For the first time in a long time we've had to turn people away," I said proudly.

"Really," she said without any interest. "Well, suit yourself, but you will be missing an important dinner."

"I'm sorry. It can't be helped," I said. "It is the resort season, you know."

"Oh, don't become a dreadful bore, Dawn. And don't let that place dictate your life," she warned, her voice becoming impatient.

"I'll let you know as soon as we can break free one night, Mother," I said, too tired to argue with her.

"Let me know soon," she demanded. "I want an invitation to Beulla Woods to mean something special. I'm going to be very selective about whom I do and don't invite. Bronson knows who really has money and who simply puts on airs, you know."

"That shouldn't be important to you, Mother. If the people are nice, don't hold their low incomes against them," I said.

"Oh, Dawn, you still don't realize the significance of your associates, do you? And you're in charge of such a famous resort," she said, followed with one of her silly, thin laughs.

"Good friends, true friends are more valuable," I

said. "It doesn't matter how important their jobs are or how big their houses are. Not to me," I emphasized.

"You'll learn," she insisted. It was just as if I had no voice and Mother had no ears for all the effect my words had. She was silent for a moment and then went on to babble for a few more minutes, describing her plans for the Saturday night dinner menu. Finally I was able to say good-bye.

Mother was true to her word. Almost immediately after she and Bronson returned to Beulla Woods we began to hear about her extravagant dinner parties. It seemed she was in a furious campaign to win back any social acceptance she had lost because of the revelations and scandals that haunted the Cutlers. Jimmy, Philip and I finally gave in and went to one of her dinners, but she continued to call to invite us again and again.

We were all very busy, however. It was turning out to be one of the hottest summers on record, the economy was good and our reservations phones were ringing off the hook. Philip did prove to be a valuable assistant and quickly picked up some of the managerial responsibilities. He took over Randolph's old office, and I began to appreciate the relief he provided because it allowed me to spend more time with Jimmy and Christie. Jimmy had grown to love the work he did around the hotel. He wasn't afraid to get his hands dirty; in fact, he sought opportunities to do so, and despite the title he carried – supervisor of maintenance – it wasn't unusual to find him alongside grounds workers digging a trench or sitting on a lawn tractor. It didn't pay to buy him fancy uniforms, for he would only get them stained and smeared with paints and oils and varnish. He had to have hands-on contact. When a hot-water heater broke down, he was the one ripping it apart. And when the pool filter gave us trouble, Jimmy was out there sitting in the middle of parts.

One summer afternoon he came into my office with his cheeks smeared with grease. His hands were dirty, but he wiped them on a rag he carried in his back pocket so he could tear open a manila envelope and remove its contents in front of me.

"What is that, Jimmy?" I asked, sitting back and smiling. Jimmy loved surprises and especially loved surprising me.

"It's from Daddy," he said, and he pulled out the photographs, handing them to me one at a time without speaking. There was a letter, too. The photographs were pictures of Daddy's wife Edwina and their son Gavin. Some pictures were just of Gavin. They had named him after Daddy Longchamp's grandpa. "Daddy says as soon as they get a chance they're going to travel up to see us," Jimmy declared, and he handed the letter to me along with the pictures.

"Oh, that would be wonderful. Gavin looks just like Daddy Longchamp," I said. Gavin did have Daddy Longchamp's coal-black hair and dark eyes. "And Edwina's very pretty," I added. She was a slim brunette with light brown eyes. From the way she was depicted in the photograph, I thought she was almost as tall as Daddy.

"Yes," Jimmy said, but we looked at each other and silently agreed she wasn't as pretty as Momma had been.

"Daddy seems very happy now," I said, gazing at the letter. "And very proud of his new son."

"Yes. And I suppose I should be happy about having a

new brother," Jimmy declared, a sad look washing over his face and dimming the light in his eyes. "Of course, Fern's got a new brother, too," he said, "although she doesn't know it and may never know it. Did you speak to Mr. Updike about what I suggested, about hiring a private detective?" he asked.

His dark eyes held a quiet, waiting look, as if his entire life depended upon my answer. I didn't want to tell him Mr. Updike was not enthralled with the suggestion and had tried to talk us out of it.

"Yes. He said he would look into it for us and get back to me later this week."

"Good," Jimmy said. "Well, I'd better get back out there. I'll leave all this with you," he said, handing me the envelope and the letter.

I sat there gazing at the photograph of Daddy Longchamp with his new family. He looked so much older to me, and a lot thinner. It was almost as if he were the ghost of the man I had once known as my father. His smile seemed forced to me; he looked like a man desperately trying to hold back gloom and doom, slamming the door on the past and clinging to the doorknob while the memories battered and pried, trying to get back at him. I was sure it would be very difficult for him to come here to see me. He carried a ton of guilt on his shoulders, and confronting me might only weigh him down. It was better he remain where he was, in a new world, in a new life, the past off beyond the horizon.

I didn't realize I was crying until a tear dropped on the photograph. And then suddenly my sorrow began to upset my stomach. I felt a wave of nausea come over me. The blood drained from my face, and my heart began to pitter-patter so quickly, I had to gasp for breath. I got up quickly and rushed to the bathroom, where I emptied my stomach of everything I had eaten for breakfast and lunch. It brought me to my hands and knees. Finally I was able to retreat to one of the sofas and lie down. The nausea eased up enough for me to sit up and catch my breath.

I didn't feel as though I had a fever, but the vomiting had left me weak and tired. I tried to go back to my work but found the nausea returning. I had to rush back to the bathroom. Later that afternoon I decided I had better go see the doctor. I didn't want to worry Jimmy, so I didn't tell him. I just had Julius bring the hotel car around.

But keeping secrets at Cutler's Cove was a nearly impossible thing to do. I had to tell Mrs. Bradly at the reception counter that I was leaving the hotel. She saw I wasn't feeling well, and she told Mrs. Boston, who told Robert Garwood. The chain of gossip ran out to Jimmy rather quickly, so that when I emerged from the examination room I found him waiting in the lobby, pacing nervously about. He hadn't even stopped to wash the grease off his forehead and cheeks.

"How did you find out where I was?" I began.

"What's wrong, doctor?" he demanded, looking quickly from me to Dr. Lester, the physician I had been using to care for Christie. He was a very gentle man who had a way of putting his patients at ease with his comforting smile and methodical manner.

"Nothing's wrong, Mr. Longchamp," he said, and then he smiled. "Unless you didn't want your wife to be pregnant."

"Pregnant!" Jimmy's look of concern transformed into a look of shock and happiness. He smiled with a dazed expression in his eyes and started to stutter. "But I . . . I . . ."

"Congratulations," Doctor Lester said, laughing.

"Is she all right? I mean – "

"Everything's fine, Mr. Longchamp," he assured Jimmy quickly.

"Now, don't you feel foolish running down here like this, James Gary Longchamp?" I playfully chastised with my hands on my hips. Jimmy started to stutter again, so I took his hand. "Come on, Jimmy," I said. "We have lots of work to do."

"Work! You're not working as hard as you've been working. No, sir. Things are gonna change around that hotel. And don't you start arguing about it, Dawn," he warned, placing his forefinger on my lips. "I'm about to be a daddy, and I've got a say in these matters."

"Well, it's not going to happen tomorrow, Jimmy," I said, laughing. "And being pregnant isn't like being sick. I'm not going to lie around like Mother and be waited on hand and foot. So don't you start," I said firmly.

"We'll see about all that," he replied.

"Uh-oh," Doctor Lester said, "I'm stepping out of this." He retreated to his office, and Jimmy and I returned to the hotel, where we knew the news would spread and everyone would want to share in our happiness. I still couldn't believe it. I was pregnant with Jimmy's baby. At last it seemed all our dreams were coming true.

Mother found out two days later and called. Bronson had told her. Sometimes Bronson knew things about events at the hotel before I did. He had his spies, his

202

informers who kept him aware of how we were doing. I suspected Mr. Dorfman might be his source. I didn't blame Bronson; I imagined he wanted to be up on the news at the Cutler's Cove Hotel because it was such a big investment for his bank. Maybe some of the members of his board were pressuring him to keep tabs on how the new, very young owner of the Cutler's Cove Hotel was bearing up under her responsibilities.

"I'm not surprised you hid this news from me," Mother began. She didn't even say hello or ask me how I was. She went right into her tirade. "Why you would want to make me a grandmother again, I'll never know. You just got married recently, and you're so young. You have so much to live for, so much to do, and here you go having another baby."

"Mother, getting pregnant and having children is not sentencing yourself to death," I replied quickly.

"That's what you say now, but just wait," she moaned, as if it were she who was having the baby. "It takes months, years to get your figure back; most women never do," she warned.

"I'm not worried about that, Mother. I had no trouble getting my figure back after Christie was born, did I?"

"You say that now because you are young and naïve, but oh, how you will change your mind. Believe me. What are you going to do," she snapped, "have a half dozen babies?"

"Mother, you had three children, didn't you?" I pointed out.

"Don't remind me," she said, and then she gave out a deep sigh. "I suppose everyone in the community will be talking about it soon," she added, once again speaking as if my becoming pregnant was a scandal.

"I think they will have more interesting subjects to amuse them, Mother. If they don't, their lives must be terribly boring."

"You don't realize who we are in this community," she lectured. "Everything we do, everything that relates to us is news here. Why – why, we are their royalty, their celebrities. Like it or not," she said, "we live in a fishbowl."

"You didn't always think that way, Mother," I said. "You certainly didn't worry about being under glass," I reminded her. It came out a great deal sharper than I had intended, but Mother was making me angry. I didn't ask to be put on display and have my every little action and decision put under a microscope.

"I was young and foolish and very unhappy then," she retorted. "I thought you understood that," she added, with tears in her voice. "Oh, do what you want. You never listen to anything I say anyway," she complained. "I'm always wrong in your eyes, no matter what I say or try to do."

"I listen, Mother. I just don't agree," I said.

"Why must our conversations always degenerate into arguments?" she asked, her voice dreamy, wistful, as if she were asking someone else in the room with her. "Anyway," she said, jumping to another topic, "Bronson and I have decided to go on a cruise in the fall . . . Italy, the Greek Islands. Bronson suggested I ask you if you and Jimmy wanted to go along, but I suppose now, with your new motherhood on the horizon . . ."

"Thank Bronson for thinking of us, Mother," I said. "I'm tired now. I have to go lie down."

"That's just what I mean," she snapped. "You're in the middle of your high season, and you go and get yourself pregnant. You don't even have the strength and energy to talk to me on the telephone. Honestly, I don't think any of my children has a brain."

"It must be so hard for you, Mother, to have all this wisdom now and not have anyone listen," I said, but she didn't understand my sarcasm.

"Exactly. That's it exactly," she agreed. By the time I cradled the receiver I was laughing.

I suppose I had really anticipated what Mother's reaction to my being pregnant again would be, but I had no way of knowing how Philip would react. When I told him, he stood staring at me for a moment, his eyes far off. Then he blinked and smiled, and his eyes gleamed. He rushed forward to hug and kiss me and offer his congratulations, but everything he said sounded odd. It was as if I were having his baby and not Jimmy's.

"We're going to have to adjust some of the work around here and make sure you're not stressed. We can't have our little mother made tired. No more standing for hours in the dining room doorway at dinner to greet the guests, and no more parading around to see how their food is. Let me handle all that. And just buzz me in the office if someone calls you to go all over the hotel to check something," he pleaded. "Our new baby's got to have the best care and protection."

"Thank you, Philip," I said. I shook my head in astonishment after he kissed me on the cheek again and rushed out to check on a room assignment problem I was about to solve. Was there something about this hotel that forced people to dwell in illusions? First Randolph, and certainly Mother, and now Philip? I hoped it would never happen to me.

With Jimmy hovering around me all day to be sure

I wasn't doing too much, and now with Philip popping in and out to check on my condition, I began to feel like the specimen under glass Mother suggested I was. Both Philip and Jimmy had the staff spying on me and reporting to them if I went traipsing up and down stairs or into the basement to see about something. Every time I went outside and walked over the grounds I saw bellhops and chambermaids gawking out of windows or around corners. Moments later either Jimmy or Philip would be at my side to see what it was I had intended to do. If I so much as lifted something that weighed more than a pound, someone would drop whatever he or she was doing and fly over to assist. Carrying Christie up or down the stairs was enough to set off an air-raid siren. Sissy did her best to intercept and finally confessed that both Philip and Jimmy had ordered her to prevent me from doing anything that could in the least way be thought of as work.

At first it was amusing, but after weeks and weeks of it I began to get annoyed, and I let both Jimmy and Philip know in no uncertain terms one evening when they both showed up to escort me to dinner. First Jimmy arrived at my office, and then Philip popped in behind him.

"I just came by to see if there's anything I can do," Philip said.

"What can you do, Philip?" I cried, rising up and out of my seat behind the desk like a fountain of anger, gushing. "Can you carry me to the dining room? Can you eat my food for me? And you," I said, spinning on Jimmy, "why did you forbid Sissy from letting me carry Christie anywhere and tell her not to let me lift her out of her playpen or her crib?"

"I just thought" – he held his hands out – "Dr. Lester said – "

"He said, 'Don't do anything you wouldn't ordinarily do.' That's what he said. He didn't say turn me into an invalid!" I screamed.

Unlike my last pregnancy, this one was making me somewhat irritable and blue. I had stopped having nausea, but my temperament had undergone a change. Was it just the pregnancy? I wondered. Or did it have something to do with the work, the hotel, making decisions, becoming the administrator Grandmother Cutler once was?

"Okay," Jimmy said, holding up his hands like a man surrendering. "Okay, I'm sorry."

"We're just trying to look after you," Philip insisted.

"Well, don't," I snapped.

Both wore the same shocked expression.

"I'll just . . . see about tonight's dinner," Philip stuttered, and he left quickly. I sat down again and dropped my head in my hands.

"Dawn," Jimmy said, coming around to put his hand on my shoulder. I started to cry. That was happening to me more and more often, but I kept it hidden from everyone, especially Jimmy. For no reason at all I would suddenly find myself bursting into tears. I had no reason to; the hotel was doing well, Christie was growing more and more beautiful every day, Jimmy and I loved each other very much and wanted our new child very much; but all it would take was a dark cloud slipping over the sun or a point on my pencil breaking, and I would sit there and bawl like a baby.

Often I would awaken during that dim and lonely hour that comes before dawn, and I would lay in the semidarkness and stare around me, feeling strangely out of myself. Was I going mad?

My shoulders shook when Jimmy's hand touched me.

"Hey, what's wrong, honey?" Jimmy asked. He squatted down beside me and lifted my arm away so he could look into my face.

"I don't know," I cried through my tears. "I can't help it. I just . . . can't help it," I added, and I began to sob again. Jimmy raised me to my feet along with him and embraced me, stroking my hair softly and kissing my forehead and cheeks, kissing away the tears as fast as they emerged.

"It's all right," he whispered. "It's all right. You're just tired. Maybe not physically tired, but mentally tired, emotionally tired. A lot has happened in a short time, Dawn. You have to realize that," he coached.

I took a deep breath and swallowed back my sobs. Then I ground the tears out of my eyes and looked into Jimmy's soft, dark eyes, now filled with worry and concern.

"I'm scared, Jimmy," I confessed.

"Scared? What are you scared of? Being pregnant again?" he asked.

"No, not that. I'm happy about that. Really I am. I'm just frightened sometimes, frightened of changing, of becoming someone I'm not, someone I don't want to be. I'm not changing, though, Jimmy, am I? I'm still the same person. I'm still Dawn Longchamp, the Dawn Longchamp you fell in love with, right?" I asked frantically.

"Of course you are," he said, smiling. "I'll tell you when you've become someone horrible, don't worry."

I didn't tell Jimmy, but it felt as if the office were closing in on me, as if Grandmother Cutler could still reach me here, even though I had altered and replaced almost everything, down to the color of the pens. One day, for no reason whatsoever, I had suddenly had three chambermaids come in and wash and polish and vacuum every corner. It was as if I was afraid there was still some trace, something of her that could affect me. I never told Jimmy, but I had nightmares about it. If he had heard about my mad cleaning of the office, he didn't bring it up.

"Oh, Jimmy, I don't want to become someone horrible," I cried, throwing my arms around his neck. He held me tightly.

"You won't," he whispered. "I won't let you. I promise."

"Do you, Jimmy? Do you promise?"

"Absolutely," he said. "Now wash your face. Sissy's brought Christie down to sit with us tonight. She's already greeting guests like a small princess."

I laughed.

"I bet she is. She thinks she's a princess," I said. I put my fingers on Jimmy's cheek and stared into his eyes. "Thank you, Jimmy. Thank you for loving me so much."

"Hey," he said, shaking his head. "I couldn't stop even if I wanted to."

We kissed, and then I washed my face, and we went to play our roles as the hosts of Cutler's Cove.

The rest of the summer flew by, maybe because we were so busy and I was so occupied with Christie and with my pregnancy. One day it was the middle of July,

209

and then it seemed like only the day after and we were looking at plans for our Labor Day weekend. As had happened every weekend this summer, we had a full house booked. Twice during the high season I had let the bandleader talk me into singing for the guests on Saturday night. He made me promise to do the same thing on Labor Day weekend, claiming that some frequent guests had actually requested it. I did have guests stop to compliment me on my singing and ask when I was going to do it again. This happened especially at dinner, when I made the rounds to greet people at their tables.

I often missed my music and tried to keep up with my piano playing. I was so happy when Trisha returned for a weekend when she was able to get away from her summer performing arts program. Just listening to her describe her acting classes and her vocal classes made me long to return to those days. As she did every time we spoke or saw each other, she brought me a tidbit of news concerning Michael Sutton.

"His show closed in London earlier than was expected," she told me when she had come to the hotel. "There have been some rumors about him."

"Rumors?" I knew how quickly show business gossip spread and that it was often exaggerated, but Trisha didn't seem to consider this a product of the rumor mill.

"About his drinking," she said. "They say he's actually had to go for treatment in Switzerland."

"How sad," I said.

"I hope he gets whatever he deserves," Trisha responded, but despite all he had done to me, I couldn't harden my heart against him. After all, every time I looked at Christie I saw his face. Her features were getting more and more distinct, and she was getting to look more and more like him. It was as if he were reemerging through our daughter, so it became impossible to hate him. I couldn't help but wonder what it would be like for her when she was old enough to understand and I had to explain who her real father was. I would do it as soon as I could, because I knew her aunt Clara Sue wouldn't hesitate to tell her the first chance she got.

Because Clara Sue had stayed with her friend in New Jersey all summer and because neither Mother nor Philip made any mention of her, I rarely if ever gave her any thought. But on the Thursday before the Labor Day weekend she came to the hotel. I was upstairs taking a nap. I had reluctantly agreed to break up my day with naps, only when Philip and Jimmy promised they wouldn't hesitate to wake me if something important happened. I didn't really believe either of them, but even though my pregnancy had yet to show and I had gained only three pounds, I was feeling more and more fatigue these days, and I found myself stopping to catch my breath more often than I would have liked.

A clap of thunder woke me, and I opened my eyes and gazed out the window to see the sun suddenly take a fugitive position behind an oncoming wall of dark clouds. The thunder crashed again and swiftly came closer, with the swollen, heavy sky zigzagged by frightening electrical bolts, so I didn't hear Clara Sue come pounding down the corridor after she had gone into her old room, now stripped bare.

Apparently, from what I gathered in the first few seconds of my confrontation with her, Mother had not told her I had had her things moved to Beulla Woods. I sincerely wondered if Mother had spoken with her more than once or twice the entire summer.

Once she discovered what had been done, she shoved open my bedroom door and burst in like an angry whirlwind.

Spending her entire summer lying on a beach, eating and partying with her friends, Clara Sue had added more pounds to her voluptuous figure. She looked ten pounds heavier than the last time I had seen her. She was wearing a clingy violet silk dress that fit her like a second skin and showed a great deal of her cleavage. She'd permed her long blond hair and wore heavy mascara and ruby-red lipstick. I thought she looked extremely trashy, but Clara Sue probably didn't care a bit about my opinion. She was darkly tanned, and her cold blue eyes were hard and sharp, sending daggers my way.

I sat up quickly, frightened by the bang of her hand on my door. She stood there fuming, fists clenched at her sides.

"What are you doing?" I demanded. I swung my legs over the bed and slipped on my shoes while she stood there staring hatefully at me. Her eyes narrowed dangerously, and it looked as if smoke might soon emerge from her ears.

"How dare you! How dare you touch my things!" she cried. "What have you done with them?" she demanded, stepping forward.

"Hasn't Mother told you?" I said calmly. "All of your things have been moved to Beulla Woods. That's where you're going to live now," I said.

"Who decided that?" she asked through clenched teeth. I fixed my eyes on hers.

212

"I decided," I answered calmly, despite the fear growing inside me.

Suddenly she screamed, a high-pitched howl like some animal caught in a steel trap. She slapped her hands over the sides of her head and ripped at her own hair, her fingers clutching the strands.

She lowered her head, her eyes rolling back, and then she charged at me. Her action took me so much by surprise, I didn't move.

"You bitch!" she cried. "You can't run my life, too! I won't let you!" Without warning she swung her clenched right fist and caught me squarely on the side of my head. The unexpected blow with all her weight behind it sent me reeling to the side. I fell over the vanity chair and slammed down hard on the floor, the chair turning over beside me. Stunned, I struggled to get back to my feet. I righted the chair and got to my knees to pull myself up, but Clara Sue came at me again.

"I'll teach you to touch my things! I'll teach you to try to give me orders! I'm going to make you pay, Dawn! I'm going to make you feel the same pain I've felt since the day you came back into our lives!" she screamed, and then she kicked me hard in the stomach. The blow sent a storm of pain around my sides and up to my chest. It knocked the breath out of me. I fell forward, and Clara Sue kicked me again and again in the side, screaming like a madwoman at the top of her lungs as she delivered each blow. When I opened my eyes the room began to spin. I felt as if I were falling down a deep tunnel, falling toward the darkness below. I tried crying out and waved my arms and hands desperately to ward off any additional blows.

Vaguely, before I passed out, I heard Jimmy's and

Philip's voices. One of them pulled Clara Sue back. Someone – maybe Sissy, maybe Mrs. Boston – was screaming in the hallway. Clara Sue continued to rant and rave. Either Jimmy or Philip started to lift me up, and then all went black.

I regained consciousness in the back of the hotel limousine, but the voices I heard around me sounded thin and distant. I tried to cry out, but it was as if my own voice was trapped inside my chest. It ached so in there, and the pain that had begun in my stomach had turned into a hand of fire with fingertips made of hot coals, spreading itself over my body, expanding, growing, invading the walls of my heart, which alternately pounded and fluttered. My lungs felt as if they had filled with air so hot that I couldn't breathe. I saw that my head was resting on a pillow, and the pillow was on Jimmy's lap. He was looking down at me, petting my hair, his eyes filled with tears. I tried to smile, but my face was like plastic. My lips wouldn't move, my skin wouldn't fold.

"Easy," I heard Jimmy say. "We're almost there."

"Almost there . . . almost there . . ." The words trickled down the back of my mind. My eyes wouldn't stay open.

The next time I did get them to open I was on a gurney and being rolled down a hospital corridor. I saw the ceiling lights flash by, and I heard the voices of the nurses and the distinct voice of Dr. Lester.

I'm with Dr. Lester, I thought, and I felt reassurance. I'll be all right now. Everything will be all right now.

"She's hemorrhaging, doctor," I heard a nurse say.

"In here, quickly," Dr. Lester responded. Something warm was running down my legs. The panic began to creep up my body again, and my heart began to pound in long, deep thumps that reverberated up into my head. I felt myself being lifted, and as my body was lowered onto a bed I lost consciousness again.

When I awoke this time, I was in a hospital room, and Jimmy was at my side. He had his head down, and his shoulders slumped. He didn't know I was awake, so he didn't hide the tears, nor did he keep them from dripping off his cheeks. I gazed around the white-walled room and saw one large window to the left. The plain cotton curtain rose and fell with the slight breeze that drifted in. I could smell that cool dampness that followed a brief but hard summer storm.

"Jimmy," I said, my voice surprisingly weak. He lifted his head and quickly scrubbed the tears from his face. Then he grabbed my hand between both of his.

"How are you doing, honey?" he asked.

How was I doing? I wondered. I felt numb all over. The sharp pain had gone. If anything, there was only the sense of a dull ache in the walls of my stomach.

"Jimmy," I said, my lips trembling.

"I know, I know. She was wild; she was horrible. We couldn't get her off you. It was like she was possessed. I threw her out, and she went screaming through the hotel. I want to press charges against her," he said angrily. "I want to see her put in jail. She deserves nothing less than to be treated as a common criminal . . . as a . . ." Jimmy's tongue stumbled over the words.

Oh, no, please, no, I thought. Please . . .

"As a murderer," he said, and it was as if Clara Sue was still there, kicking me again and again.

"The baby . . . I had a miscarriage?"

Jimmy nodded and bit down on his lower lip.

215

I closed my eyes and turned away. It was no use, I thought. That black cloud that had always seemed to hover above us when we were young was still hovering above us. I would never be happy, and that meant that Jimmy would never be happy. I wished I had never agreed to marry him, for when I did, I tied him forever to whatever curse had been cast over me.

"Dr. Lester says you're going to be all right," Jimmy said reassuringly. "He says in time we can try again. He says there's no reason why – "

"Oh, Jimmy, there will always be a reason," I cried, turning back to him. "There will always be something making life miserable for us, turning everything sweet into something sour. Why hope? Why care?"

"Don't talk like that, Dawn," he begged. "Please don't. It's not true anyway. Good things have happened to us and will continue to happen. Why, we've got the hotel and – "

"The hotel," I spat out hatefully, unable to lock in the bitterness. "Don't you see? It was Grandmother Cutler's ultimate revenge, my having inherited so much."

Jimmy shook his head.

"Yes, Jimmy," I said more firmly. I tried to sit up, but the pain in my abdomen kept me down. Even so, I continued. "The hotel is a weight, a burden, not a blessing. In the end it will destroy us. I want to sell out. Yes, that's what we'll do. We'll sell out and take whatever money we can to start a brand new life someplace else . . . you and me and Christie."

"We'll see," Jimmy said, trying to calm me. "We'll see."

"She's still there, Jimmy," I insisted. "She was the

216

one striking at me through Clara Sue, don't you see? It was she!"

"Easy, Dawn. You're only getting yourself more upset and making yourself sicker."

"She was the one kicking me. She was the one who killed my baby," I muttered, closing my eyes. "It was she." I must have fallen asleep again and dreamed. In my nightmare it was indeed Grandmother Cutler who was kicking me over and over, smiling as she drove her tiny foot with a sharply pointed shoe into my stomach. I shuddered and woke with a start. I knew I had slept for a while, for it was dark outside. Jimmy was standing in the doorway talking softly to Philip.

"She's awake," Philip said. They both returned to my bedside.

"Hi, Dawn," Philip said. "How are you?"

"Tired," I replied. "Very tired, but very thirsty."

Jimmy reached for my plastic cup of water and straw and brought it to my lips immediately. The cool liquid felt good, felt as though it was putting out the simmering ashes of the fire that had been started inside me. I made myself smile for Jimmy.

"She's become a monster," Philip began. "I told her I don't ever want to consider her my sister again. As far as I was concerned, she could go jump off a cliff."

"We still might press charges against her," Jimmy said.

I shook my head.

"You should," Philip agreed. "She needs to be locked up someplace and the key thrown away."

There was a knock on the door, and we all turned to see Bronson and Mother.

Mother wore a sable wrap over a scarlet dress. She

had her hair pinned up and had so much makeup and jewelry on that I thought she and Bronson must be stopping by after attending a formal function or the theater.

"It's so cold out. There's such a bitter chill in the air," she said, pulling the fur wrap tighter around herself as she entered. "Why is that window open?"

"It's all right," I said softly.

"Well," she said after taking a deep breath and pulling her shoulders back, "how are you?"

"I'll be all right," I said.

"Good, good. I just can't stand being in hospitals. They smell so . . . medicinal. It makes me want to faint. I didn't even go to the hospital to visit my own mother until I had to," she said, as if that was something to be proud of.

Bronson stepped up beside Philip and smiled at me.

"I was sorry to hear what happened," he said, shaking his head sadly. "When she came to Beulla Woods I forbade her to leave her room."

"She's probably gone by now," Philip said, "doing whatever she wants. She's a wild animal."

"That will change," Bronson said sharply. He fixed his eyes on Philip so firmly that Philip had to swing his eyes away. "Your mother found out just yesterday that she failed almost every subject at school," he added, and Mother released a tiny cry that sounded like the whimper of a mouse. "Somehow she had intercepted all the school reports and kept them from us," Bronson added, but when I gazed at Mother I wondered if that was so, or if Mother herself had simply put it all aside and ignored it until she had to face up to reality.

Bronson patted my hand and smiled down at me.

218

"If there is anything we can do for you . . ."

"Thank you," I said. My lips began to tremble.

"Well," Mother suddenly said with a burst of energy, "perhaps after you are released from here you and Jimmy can consider joining us on that cruise."

"Sure they can," Philip chimed in. "I'll take care of things at the hotel if you guys want to get away. Don't worry about that."

"I don't think I'm in the mood to go on a cruise," I said quickly.

"Well, you have to get your mind off all this somehow, and a cruise is just fine for that, isn't it, Bronson?" Mother asked.

"I think we had better take things one step at a time," he said wisely.

"Well, now that we see you're all right," Mother said, ignoring the fact that I was lying prone because my body was full of aches, that I was pale and weak because I had lost blood and had a miscarriage, "we'll leave. I'm not one for staying in hospitals long. If I ever get very, very sick, they will just have to bring the medicines and machinery to me. Bronson?"

"Right. Feel better, Dawn," Bronson said, and he leaned down to kiss me on the cheek. Mother blew me a kiss, and then the two of them departed.

"I'd better go, too," Philip said. "I'll check on you in the morning." He kissed me and left.

Jimmy and I stared at each other for a moment.

"What did you tell Christie?" I asked him.

He shook his head.

"She thought you were coming here to have the new baby already," he said. "That kid's something else," he added, and he started to laugh.

219

"Oh, Jimmy . . ." I couldn't stop the tears from gushing.

"Don't, Dawn." He was at my side quickly.

"But I should have been coming to the hospital for that one thing only," I cried.

"I know. You will. Someday soon you will," he promised. "Come on," he coaxed, "you and I have been through some hard times, and we've always managed to see the rainbow at the end of the storm. We'll find it again, as long as we have each other."

I smiled up at him. He was so handsome and strong now. I was lucky to have him.

"That's better; that's the Dawn I remember," he said.

I closed my eyes.

"Getting tired again?" he asked. I nodded.

"All right. I'll let you sleep, but I'll be close by," he assured me.

"Go home, Jimmy. I'll be all right. Get some rest yourself," I told him.

"Now don't go being the boss again," he chastised. "You're off duty."

I didn't have the strength to argue. I closed my eyes and felt his lips on my lids and then on my lips. My eyelids fluttered open as he backed away. He waved, and I closed my eyes, locking his image within, an image that brought back memories.

We were somewhere, a long time ago. We had been dragged from one place to another so often, I couldn't remember exactly where we were, but I had been running, and I fell and scraped my knee badly. I hurried home to show Momma, but she was at work, and there was no one to comfort me, so I sat on the floor crying. Finally the door opened, and Jimmy came in. He rushed over to me and looked at my knee. Then he went into the bathroom and came out with a wet washcloth to clean it. He fixed a bandage for me, too. And then he lifted me up and took me to our sofa bed and made me comfortable.

So much of the time we lived like two orphans, and orphans have less time to be children. It's as if some strange adult, someone with a dark face, takes our hands and makes us run faster, pulls us along and then suddenly lets go and leaves us dangling, wandering, searching for our identities, hungering for a place to call home. I wondered if we would ever find it.

All I could do was hope that Jimmy was right. We had been through so many storms, and we had always managed to find a rainbow waiting.

Where was the rainbow waiting now?

Part Two

Life Goes On

Despite my hopes and expectations, the recuperation from my miscarriage took months and months. Even though Dr. Lester assured me I was recovered physically, I was continually tired and listless. Even after I had become pregnant, I was used to working an endless stream of hours without so much as pausing to go to the bathroom, but now I found a mere hour or so seemed to exhaust me. I had to retreat to take frequent naps. Sometimes I would just lie there with my eyes open, wondering and dreaming about the baby I had lost.

Jimmy tried to get me to take a winter vacation. He wanted to go fishing in the Florida Keys, but I kept postponing it until he finally gave up.

"You're behaving like a bear in hibernation," he told me. I did welcome the gray, cold days because they drove me to sleep, and sleep seemed to provide the only hours of relief.

Nothing excited me, not even Jimmy's plans for our house. I tried to show interest, but he took one look at my face as he explained the architectural drawings and saw that I wasn't really listening. I knew he had deliberately thrown himself into this project soon after my miscarriage in the hope that it would plant new seeds of happiness and joy in the garden of our marriage. He was trying so hard, every way he could, to pull me out of the doldrums.

Finally, one spring afternoon when he came up to our room and found me staring blankly up at the ceiling, he exploded. I hadn't seen him in this sort of a rage since our early days when Daddy Longchamp would rip us abruptly out of one place to speed us through the night to another, making us leave treasured possessions and new friends behind.

Jimmy threw up his hands and almost made me jump out of my skin with his outburst.

"This can't go on, Dawn!" he exclaimed. He paced in front of me, pounding his feet down so hard, the whole room shook. "You're letting everything get the best of you. Everyone's noticed it and is upset. It's even affecting Christie."

"I'm sorry, Jimmy," I said. My tears began to rise against the floodgates, threatening to overflow and send torrents down my cheeks.

"It's not enough to apologize, to lie there day after day, night after night, for months and months, feeling sorry for yourself. A terrible thing has happened, I know. I hate that it has happened, but we can't change that now. We've got to go on and build anew," he lectured.

"I've spoken repeatedly to the doctor, and he assures me there's no physical reason for you to be this way," he added. "What you've been doing," he fumed, "is letting Clara Sue win, giving her the satisfaction of knowing she's succeeded in destroying you, and in destroying you, she's destroyed us." He flopped into a chair, lowered his head to his chest and folded his hands in his lap, exhausted.

226

I couldn't stand to see Jimmy so unhappy, looking so beaten down. I hated myself for doing this to him. He had been so patient and loving and understanding, but even he had limited tolerance. For the first time I realized that I could very well drive him away from me. What was I doing? I had to get hold of myself.

"Oh, Jimmy, I'm sorry," I repeated, sitting up. "I don't mean to be this way. Really, I don't. But every time I try to snap out of it a dark gray cloud sweeps in and makes me feel as if I will live under stormy skies forever."

"Dawn, you're beginning to sound and act more and more like your mother," he replied. "Is that what you want to happen to you? Do you want to become that sort of invalid, just lying around all day and night moaning and groaning about how hard life has been to you?

"Well, it has been hard, and it might even be harder before we're through, but we're still very young, and we've got to be strong and do the best we can to overcome every defeat. What about Christie? What about our new baby when he or she finally comes? What about each other?" he pleaded, his eyes filled with tears.

I swallowed mine back and bit down on my lower lip. Then I nodded.

"You're right, Jimmy. I am being like Mother, self-centered, self-pitying. It's not fair to you," I confessed.

"Not just me," he corrected quickly. "It's not fair to yourself, either. Now I insist," he said, rising, "that you get yourself up from that bed and follow me outside."

"Outside?"

227

"I'm about to break ground for our new home," he announced, "and that requires some celebration."

"You're about to break ground?" I asked incredulously. All this was going on around me, and I hadn't even noticed. Before the miscarriage I had gotten so a doorknob wasn't changed on a room without my knowing about it.

"Yes. I rushed things along as soon as the warm weather permitted," he admitted. "I want us to be living in our own home by this summer season. I've come to the conclusion that you might have been right about our lives in the hotel. Not that I believe in ghosts and all that sort of thing," he added quickly, waving the idea away. "But I do believe that being in these same surroundings day and night might be taking its toll. Grandmother Cutler left her mark on too much here. We don't have an opportunity to get away from it for a while, no relief. And I know how it plays on your mind all the time.

"Living in our own home, away from the hotel, even though it's still technically on hotel grounds, we'll feel free, more like we're in our own world – a world we're designing, and not one we're inheriting already designed by someone else," he explained.

"Besides, Philip is getting married at the end of his last college term and wants to live here with his wife. I think," he said, perceptively and perhaps prophetically, "it will be better for us to be further apart, better for all of us to have some privacy."

Suddenly what Jimmy was saying and doing did excite me. I would never forget how Mother looked when she left the hotel to marry Bronson Alcott, how she seemed to have had a burden lifted from her shoulders, escaping from under Grandmother Cutler's shadow. She was happier, more energetic and alive. Why couldn't the same be true for me?

"You're right, Jimmy. Let me just wash my face and freshen up. I do want to be part of it and see the ground-breaking."

"Well, that's why I came up here to get you, and when I saw you laid out again and moping about, I just couldn't stand it. I'm sorry I was so angry," he said.

"No, Jimmy. You had every right to be. In fact, I'm glad you were," I said, and I kissed him. I washed my face and threw on a cable-knit blue sweater, and then we went down and out a rear entrance of the hotel.

Jimmy had chosen a house lot a good half mile or so south of the main building. It was on a rise and provided an unobstructed view of the ocean, yet there were enough trees and bushes to give us a sense of privacy.

"I thought we'd get a couple of those golf carts to ride back and forth to the hotel," Jimmy said as we walked toward the lot. "Not that it's so far."

"It isn't, and I know I'll enjoy the walk," I said. I was enjoying this one. The early-spring day was clear and crisp with just a few scattered clouds drifting across a sharply blue sky. Leaves had begun to turn rich green, and bushes were filling out. The brightness and fresh air brought a crimson tint to our cheeks. I could feel my skin tingle at the welcome daylight. I felt like a flower that had been kept on the windowsill and teased by the sunlight. Finally I was outside, blooming again.

The bulldozer operator was waiting and talking with Buster Morris when we arrived. They both looked up expectantly. Then Buster produced a bottle of champagne and four glasses he and Jimmy had kept hidden, awaiting my arrival. I laughed. It felt so good to do it. It was as if I hadn't laughed for ages and ages.

Jimmy poured the champagne and lifted his glass to make a toast.

"To our house. May it be the home of love and happiness forever and ever."

"To our house," I said.

"Hear, hear," Buster said, and we all drank.

"Okay," Jimmy announced. "Let'er rip."

Buster stepped back to watch with us as the bulldozer began to clear the land and tear out the ground for our foundation. Jimmy took my hand.

"Congratulations and good luck, Mrs. Longchamp," Buster said.

"Yes, Mrs. Longchamp. Congratulations and good luck," Jimmy said, and he kissed me.

At least once a day after that I would either go out with Christie or join Jimmy to watch the construction of our new home. Working closely with an architect, Jimmy had designed a two-story classical revival with a two-tiered entry porch supported by four simple columns.

The house would have five bedrooms, a den, a living room, an office, a large dining room and a large kitchen with maid's quarters right behind it. He had been impressed with Bronson Alcott's marble entryway floors and stairway and included both in our design. Once the structure was planned, the details for the interior were to be left up to me. Bronson, and especially Mother, came around often to offer their suggestions. Anyway, Jimmy's ulterior motives worked. I became very involved with the house once it was underway and buried myself in design and decor magazines. It was very exciting as more and more of the house was completed and I began to envision it.

Once Christie understood this was going to be our new home, she had to know immediately where her room would be. After Jimmy pointed it out and walked her through the framing, she was after both of us all day to take her out so she could visit her future residence. And when the house was more than half completed it became one of the regular sights for hotel guests. Neither Jimmy nor I was ecstatic over the idea that guests would be coming by to look things over, but for the time being it was hard to keep them away. Jimmy decided that afterward, when the house was completed, we would build a pretty fence around it so that the guests would understand it was not really part of the hotel property.

"One of the bedrooms is for your younger brother or younger sister, when she comes," Jimmy told Christie one afternoon when the three of us were inspecting the day's work.

"Where is she?" Christie asked. "I can't find her," she said, holding her hands up and shrugging. She was almost three by now and quite precocious. Developing by leaps and bounds, she astounded everyone with the things she would say and do. She had begun to explore the piano keys herself and tap out combinations of notes that were far more than musical gibberish. Sissy complained that she knew all the children's stories by heart and would announce the endings before she was halfway through reading them to her. We had to get her books and toys designed for a child twice her age.

"I don't know where your little brother or sister is,

Christie," Jimmy told her, shifting his eyes to me as he spoke. "She or he is hiding in your mommy."

I knew what he meant. We had been trying for months to get me pregnant again, but for some reason it hadn't happened. Dr. Lester had told us both on more than one occasion that there was no reason I shouldn't get pregnant. I knew Jimmy suspected I was somehow mentally against it and that that was preventing it from happening.

"You're not afraid of getting pregnant again, are you, Dawn?" he asked me one night a few days later.

"No," I said, but I said it too quickly. Deep inside I guess I was afraid. I had snapped out of my depression and become actively involved with the hotel and our house, but I couldn't throw off this dreary, heavy feeling that a curse hovered over me. It made me worry about bringing another child into the world.

"You shouldn't be," Jimmy insisted. "There are only good things ahead for us."

"I'm trying, Jimmy. I am," I said, but instead of thinking about it and hoping for it, I buried myself in the impending summer hotel season. Along with finishing the house, that kept all of us quite busy.

Then, about a week after the formal invitations for Philip's wedding went out, Mother and Bronson decided to throw a small dinner party for just the family as a way to introduce Betty Ann Monroe, Philip's fiancée. I wasn't going to attend if Clara Sue would be there, but Mother guaranteed she wouldn't.

Clara Sue had been sent away to a finishing school, and Bronson had made a sizeable donation to it as a way of insuring that they accept and keep her. It was far enough away, too, in Florida. From what Philip told me, he had had no contact with her since she had attacked me.

"I'm still quite ashamed of her," he explained to me on the telephone, "and I don't intend to invite her to my wedding. Not that she cares."

"I don't know how you can do that, Philip," I said. "No matter what, she's still your sister, and it would just fan the flames of gossip around here. You know what that would do to Mother," I reminded him.

"But you won't come to the wedding if I do invite her, will you?" he asked.

"I don't know. It's been nearly a year. I suppose I can ignore her in a ceremony and a party this big," I said.

"I don't want to take that chance," Philip replied. "Your coming means far more to me, Dawn."

Finally I promised him I would come even if Clara Sue attended as well. He was so grateful, I became embarrassed and looked for an excuse to end the conversation.

I still had a hard time accepting compliments from Philip. I could sense his underlying passion for me, the words between words, the feelings just below the surface that behaved like little animals threatening to break out any moment. I only hoped that his marriage to Betty Ann would put an end to it. But when I finally got to meet her, I wasn't optimistic.

Mother staged one of her most elegant dinner parties. Although she had proposed the dinner party as a way to introduce Betty Ann to the family, she decided to invite some of the more prominent citizens of Cutler's Cove as well. I knew we were in for a more elaborate evening when she sent out formal invitations describing the affair as "black tie." She began with a catered cocktail party and had a three-piece band providing the music. It seemed Mother never missed an opportunity to reestablish her social standing in the community.

So when Jimmy and I arrived we were not surprised to see a line of limousines parked along the driveway. It was a warm evening with barely a cloud in the sky, so that the stars were twinkling everywhere, especially over the ocean. The chauffeurs were gathered in a small circle conversing, and Julius went to join them. Bronson greeted us immediately after Livingston had opened the door.

"Your mother is in top form tonight," he informed us. To me it sounded more like a warning. Moments later she pulled herself away from some of her guests in the marble corridor to receive us. She wore a black velvet gown with her usual low-cut neckline. I recognized a dazzling new diamond necklace and matching earrings. She was as radiantly beautiful as ever, her hair styled in an elegant upsweep. Her eyes were full of glitter, borrowing the sparkle from her gems.

"Dawn, darling," she cried, "and James. How nice to see both of you looking so well."

She hugged me to her quickly and then gave Jimmy her hand to kiss.

"I just saw you day before yesterday, Mother," I said dryly. She flashed a smile at some of her guests before responding.

"Was it only two days ago? It seems like ages and ages. Oh, Dawn, Jimmy, you know Mr. Parkins, the president of Seaside Savings," she said as an elderly gentleman passed nearby. He stopped to be introduced.

As soon as he left us I seized Mother's hand and pulled her to me.

"Mother, I thought this was supposed to be a simple family gathering to introduce Philip's fiancée and give us a chance to get to know her, and her a chance to get to know us. How do you expect that to happen with all these people here?"

"It was my intention," she said, batting her eyelashes. "But after giving it some more thought, I realized it would be foolish to waste an opportunity to introduce some of our finer citizens to Betty Ann and she to them before the wedding. We'll all have plenty of time to get to know one another . . . lifetimes. Besides," Mother added, "I think we all need some extravagance in our lives these days. It drives away the gloom and doom."

"Where are Philip and Betty Ann?" Jimmy asked, looking around. A waiter came by with a tray of champagne, and Jimmy took a glass for himself and one for me.

"They haven't arrived yet," Mother revealed, leaning in to whisper. "I told them not to come until I was sure all my guests had arrived. It's more dramatic, don't you think?"

"Where do you have them waiting – in the shadows outside?" I asked.

Mother laughed and scooped us both under the arms.

"Come into the living room. I have some more people to introduce you to," she said. I looked at Bronson, who gave me his "I told you so" smile.

A good half hour later Philip and Betty Ann finally arrived. I hadn't seen Philip for quite a while. I thought he had grown to resemble Randolph even more. He

235

looked taller, his face more mature. He had kept himself slim and had his usual tanned, rich look, his debonair smile and his laughing blue eyes. He looked handsome, successful and very rich in his black tux.

I think Philip's handsomeness and buoyant appearance sharpened and emphasized his fiancée's ordinary face. If anything, her mouth was too small and her brown eyes too close. Her pale complexion looked positively sickly beside Philip's tanned skin. She had lackluster brown hair brushed too far back, thus revealing the wideness of her forehead. Her black satin gown did little to enhance her figure, even though it was obviously an expensive designer dress.

With nothing about her looks to recommend her, I wondered what it was that had first attracted Philip to her. I imagined she had a winning personality and must be quite bright. But when we were finally introduced, even those areas seemed deficient.

She followed everything she said with a silly little laugh and pronounced my name "Don" instead of Dawn. I felt like a dentist when we spoke because it was just like pulling teeth to get her to say more than one or two words. She answered every question with a simple "uh-huh" or "no." I thought it was probably because she was distracted and overwhelmed by all the attention.

Mother seized her by the wrist as soon as she could and dragged her around the large room to introduce her formally to each and every guest. When she introduced her, she spoke about her as if she were a prize or something Philip had bought at Tiffany's, and during the descriptions of her father's estates and vacation homes, their yacht and plane,

Betty Ann stood with that idiotic smile frozen on her face.

At first I felt sorry for her, but after a while I became amused. Nothing Mother did or said seemed to change or warm Betty Ann. She resembled a life-size doll that could curtsy properly, bat an eyelash on cue, smile as expected and recite the same polite lines. She had perfect posture, took measured steps, sipped her champagne with clockwork regularity and punctuated her sentences and things said to her with nods and laughs. It was as if Philip had laid claim to some human trophy awarded to the outstanding member of a college fraternity in an Ivy League school.

"What do you think of her?" he asked me as soon as we had a private moment together.

"It's too soon to make any judgments, Philip," I responded diplomatically. "But if you love her and she loves you, what other people think shouldn't really matter."

He fixed his eyes on me, his lips trembling into a small smile.

"You're not other people, Dawn. You never will be other people to me," he said. There was pain in his deep blue eyes. I had to look down.

"You know what I mean, Philip."

"Of course," he said, restoring a note of happiness to his voice. "Betty Ann's devoted to me," he said. "She never stops telling me how lucky she is to have me. She's very sweet. And very, very rich," he added.

"I'm happy for you, Philip, if you're happy," I said. His eyes moved to clash with mine.

"Despite what I say, you know anyone I choose will always be second best. And," he added, a wry smile cocking his lips, "whenever I look at her I will see you. But don't worry," he added quickly, "Betty Ann doesn't know. She doesn't know that once upon a time, a hundred years ago, you and I were boyfriend and girlfriend. Oh, she knows your story," he said, "but not that part. That part is locked here," he whispered, patting his heart. "I can't help it. Don't hate me for confessing. Please," he pleaded.

I was unable to respond. He locked his gaze so intently on me, I could feel the passion and desire radiating. Numbly, I shook my head. I was deceived, I thought. It would never end . . . Philip's lust for me would linger forever and ever. Jimmy was so right to want us to have a home separate from the hotel and away from Philip and Betty Ann, but even that, I feared, would not be enough.

Now, when I looked at Betty Ann, I thought I understood what had attracted him to someone so plain. He had deliberately sought a girl who had little to distinguish her physically. It made it easier for him to see me in her eyes and feel my lips instead of her lips when they kissed. Just the thought of it made me tremble.

I was happy when Mother called him away to meet someone else.

"What's wrong?" Jimmy said, approaching. He had been talking with Bronson. "You look upset. Aren't you feeling well?"

"I'm all right," I said. "Just too much champagne."

"Too much champagne would turn your face crimson, not white," he insisted. He gazed across the room at Philip. "Is it something to do with Philip? Did he say something?"

"No, it's nothing, Jimmy. Please. I'm all right," I repeated more emphatically. Jimmy raised his eyebrows. "Philip was talking to me, and I didn't even hear what he said," I lied. "For a moment I just drifted off and felt a little nauseous. It's nothing."

"Nauseous? Maybe . . ." His eyes lit up with hope.

"No, Jimmy," I said. "I'm not pregnant. Remember, I just had my period."

"Oh," he said, disappointed. "Right. Well, if it happens again, you'd better see the doctor," he said.

A little while later we were all called in to dinner. There were twenty guests, and Mother had arranged the seating so that Betty Ann and Philip were at her sides. Consequently, I didn't get to speak to Betty Ann very much. After dinner I finally had a real conversation with her. We stepped out on a patio to get some air. She was more relaxed.

"What a beautiful house and beautiful view," she exclaimed. "And your mother is so beautiful, too. It's hard to believe she has children your age and Philip's."

"Mother will love you for saying that, Betty Ann," I said. She smiled and giggled.

"I'm so excited about living in the hotel," she said. "From the way Philip has described it, there's always something to do, something happening. It's never dull."

"He's right about that."

"And I'm so impressed with what you do. Philip says you haven't even been to college. He's told me so much about you. I know all about how you were kidnapped and returned. Philip's always talking about you," she added, but without any note of envy.

"About how talented you are musically and how bright you are."

"He exaggerates, I'm sure," I said, unable to hide my embarrassment.

"Oh, no. Not Philip. He's known for his honesty. Besides, he's always playing that tape recording of you singing, and you do have a beautiful voice."

"Tape recording?" I wondered when Philip had taped me singing. "What am I singing?" I asked. After she told me, I realized Philip had taped me singing for the guests at the hotel one night, and he had never told me. It made me feel funny, as if I had been eavesdropped upon. Why had he kept that a secret?

"He's so proud of you. It's so nice for a brother and a sister to like each other as much as you two like each other, especially when you consider what happened to you," she added.

"Yes." I smiled weakly.

"Someday I hope you will sit down and tell me all about it. Will you? I want to know all the details – what it was like for you before, how you were found, what it was like to return . . ."

"It's not as exciting or interesting a story as you might think," I replied.

"Oh, no, I know it is. Philip always has tears in his eyes when he talks about it . . . especially when he describes that first day you were at the hotel and you and he met for the first time as brother and sister. I cry myself," she confessed.

"Philip's so romantic," she continued. "He's so handsome, and he has a wonderful sense of humor. All my girlfriends are dying with jealousy. And my parents love him – especially my father, because he

240

knows so much about business and investments. I'm so lucky," she said. "Don't you think?" she asked me, and suddenly I felt a great sorrow for her. How horrible it would be for her to know that whenever Philip looked at her lovingly he was looking at me, and whenever he kissed her passionately he was kissing me.

She was being deceived and lied to and used. Philip had found himself an innocent, naïve young woman who just happened to fit all the social criteria. She was incapable of seeing or understanding the deception. A handsome, debonair young man – a hero on campus who came from a famous resort family – had chosen her. Her fantasy, her dream had come true.

I wanted so much to say something, to stop her from beginning a life of illusion, but then I thought that even if she knew the truth, she might accept it just so she could have Philip. Obviously, he meant that much to her.

I could almost hear Mother telling me, "Everyone accepts a certain amount of deception and illusion, Dawn. It's the price we pay for what little happiness we can achieve."

It was the way Mother had lived her life; it would be the way Betty Ann and Philip would live theirs. And deny it or run from it as much as I would, I was sure, in the end, it was the way I would live mine as well.

"I'm very happy for you, Betty Ann," I said. "Happy for both of you."

"What are my two favorite women doing out here alone?" Philip cried, coming up behind us. He moved himself between us and embraced both of us at the waist. "Not exchanging notes about me, I hope," he said, eyeing me suspiciously.

"What an ego. Why should we be talking about

241

you?" I asked. Muscles near his lips worked almost spasmodically, hovering near a smirk or a laugh, I couldn't tell which.

"A little bird told me," he said, squeezing us both tighter to him. "That's all right. I want you two to get to know each other as quickly as you can so we can all be a happy little hotel family again."

"I'm looking forward to being of some use at the hotel," Betty Ann said. "I want to contribute, even if it's only in some small way."

"I'm sure we'll find something appropriate for you to do, darling," Philip said. He smiled at me again. "Even if it's just standing by the dining room door greeting our guests as Mother and Grandmother used to do."

"Oh, I'd love to do that," Betty Ann said. Philip gazed down at me and winked.

"I will be a very lucky man to have two beautiful women around me day and night," he said, and he kissed Betty Ann on the cheek and then turned to kiss me. But I pulled out of his grasp.

"We had better return to the dinner party before Mother has a fit," I said quickly, and I rushed off, feeling as if I were fleeing a dirty dream.

Claudine Monroe, Betty Ann's mother, held tight reign on the planning of Philip and Betty Ann's wedding. Mother tried to insert her opinions and ideas often, but her attempts were continually thwarted. As the wedding date drew closer Mother's complaints about the way she was being treated intensified.

"I feel as though I'm just another guest," she told me on the telephone one morning. "Now that woman (Mother had taken to calling Betty Ann's mother 'that woman') won't even answer my phone calls. I can only get her secretary . . . her secretary! She has a secretary to look after her social affairs, do you believe it? And I'm curtly told my messages will be delivered, yet that woman doesn't return the calls. Isn't that discourteous?"

"It's her wedding to plan, Mother. You had mine," I reminded her.

"Well, who else would have done it, if I hadn't? Besides, these people think they're above us, Dawn. I can't stand the way that woman talks down to me whenever we do talk. They think just because they live on the outskirts of the nation's capital and socialize with congressmen and senators, they're somehow better than we are," she complained.

"I'm sure it will be a very nice wedding, Mother. Why don't you just relax and enjoy having someone else do all the work for a change? If Betty Ann's mother is treating you like a guest, be a guest," I suggested.

"Yes, you're right. I shouldn't give her the benefit of my expertise. Let that woman do it on her own."

"I'm sure she has many professional advisers, Mother, and actually does very little on her own."

"Um . . . have you chosen the carpet for the master bedroom?" she asked, jumping to an area in which she felt she could have some input – my new house.

"I'm going with the beige," I said.

"Oh, that's such a mistake. You don't know how hard it is to keep that looking clean. Now, I think . . ."

It had gotten so that I could listen and not listen to Mother at the same time. I usually did paperwork while she babbled over the telephone, sensing when to respond with an "uh-huh" or a "yes." However, during this particular phone conversation she suddenly switched to a third topic with the shock of a headline announcement and seized my full attention. First she began to cry.

"What is it now, Mother?" I asked wearily.

"Clara Sue has left finishing school and moved in with a man," she announced, her voice crumbling.

"What? When?"

"It's been over a month, but I haven't had the strength to talk about it. I still don't, but I feel if I keep it all bottled up inside me, I will simply explode one day. All that money we've spent on her finishing school has been wasted. Bronson says there's nothing we can do or should do. She's over eighteen now."

"He's right, Mother. Not that she listened to anything you or Randolph told her before she was eighteen. What sort of man is she living with?" I asked. What I really meant was, what sort of a man would want to live with her?

"A man fifteen years older! And divorced, too," she cried. "With two children, a boy ten and a girl twelve!"

"Where did she meet him?" I wondered aloud.

"She went bowling," Mother replied, sighing. "Fortunately, people here don't know yet, but can you imagine what it is going to be like when they find out? And she intends to bring this man to Philip's graduation and wedding. I will be so disgraced – so embarrassed – but do you think she cares? Not one bit."

"Look at it this way, Mother," I said dryly, "someone else has to put up with her now."

"This is no time to be flippant, Dawn. It's a serious problem. At this period in my life I don't need anything

244

to speed up my aging process. I'm thinking of taking those new skin treatments I read about."

"Mother, if I've told you once, I've told you a hundred times: anyone who wants to see wrinkles in your face has to use a magnifying glass," I said.

"I know you're just being nice, Dawn, but I can see myself in a mirror, can't I? Oh, this thing with Clara Sue," she moaned. "It will be the death of me. What should I do?"

"There's someone knocking on my office door, Mother," I said.

"I'm sure there's no one there, Dawn. You just want to get rid of me. Everyone just wants to get rid of me these days . . . Philip, that woman, Clara Sue, and now you, too," she sobbed. "Thank goodness I have Bronson."

"There really is someone knocking, Mother. We're in the season now," I reminded her.

"Oh, that hotel. It will always be my competition. First it was with Randolph, and then with Philip, and now with you."

"Responsibilities don't take care of themselves, Mother," I said.

"You sounded just like her when you said that, Dawn. Do you know that? Just like her."

"Mother . . ."

"No, Dawn, the hotel's all you think about or care about these days. Honestly, I don't know why it should be so important to you. Well," she said, sighing deeply, "goodbye, then. As soon as the gossip about Clara Sue begins, tell me so I can prepare myself for the worst," she added before hanging up.

When I told Jimmy he thought the whole thing was

amusing, but I couldn't imagine why Philip hadn't told me about Clara Sue. He called at least once a week now, sometimes twice. I was surprised to discover he didn't know.

"Mother never said a thing," he claimed, "and I haven't spoken to Clara Sue for months. An older man? And divorced? Well, what do you know about that? I wondered what she would eventually do with herself. She has no aptitude for anything, never cared much about the hotel, did terribly in school and wasn't interested in going to any college . . . oh, well," he said, "at least she will be out of everyone's hair."

Somehow I doubted that.

Family Affairs

There were a great number of people at Philip's graduation. Jimmy and I drove down with Bronson and Mother in Bronson's limousine. I wanted to bring Christie, but Mother insisted it was no place for a child. When we arrived and took our seats, however, we saw dozens of children, many younger than Christie. I was sure she would have enjoyed seeing the ceremony.

It was a beautiful and warm spring day, so the college had the ceremony outside. Mother was a nervous wreck, of course, looking around expectantly every five minutes, anticipating Clara Sue's arrival with her "male friend," as Mother now referred to him.

The Monroes did not sit with us. They had a contingent of their own friends and relatives to sit with, and we had only a passing meeting with Betty Ann's parents. I decided Mother was right in referring to Claudine Monroe as "that woman," for she showed little interest in meeting me and Jimmy and was rather abrupt. After the introductions she was off to meet and greet other people. Stuart Monroe was a great deal warmer and friendlier. I decided that Betty Ann had inherited her plainness from her mother, who, although tall and stately in posture, was quite unremarkable in looks and had that same pale complexion and unshiny hair.

We took our seats only moments before the coordinating director gave his signal for the band to play the march.

"Where is she?" Mother muttered, her head turning every which way like a weathervane in a crosswind.

"Perhaps she decided at the last minute not to come," Bronson suggested.

"I hope so," Mother replied.

The music started, and the audience rose as the graduates began their walk to the stage. Philip smiled our way as soon as he appeared. Strands of his gold hair uncovered by his cap caught the sun's brightness, as did his blue eyes. Bronson had brought a camera and snapped pictures. As soon as all the graduates were on the stage we sat down, and the commencement festivities began. I had all but forgotten about Clara Sue until the middle of the main speaker's talk. He was a state senator and had everyone's rapt attention when suddenly we heard a wave of murmuring behind us, and we all turned to look.

Clara Sue and her "male friend"were coming down the center aisle, Clara Sue giggling at the disruption she was causing. She held her older man's hand and charged ahead, looking as though she were dragging him to a seat. But that wasn't what shocked everyone. It was what she was wearing – a short, tight black leather mini skirt and a flimsy white silk off-shoulder blouse that revealed more than just the top of her full bosom. In fact, as she bounced down the aisle in her spiked heels, it looked as if her breasts might pop up and out of the garment any moment.

Her hair was still permed, but fluffed out in a wild mane. She wore pounds of makeup: heavy blue eyeliner, a deep red lipstick and layers and layers of rouge. Her long gold leaf earrings dangled and swung as she pranced, deliberately turning every which way to smile at the gawking men.

Her "male friend" was tall and thin with prematurely graying hair. He had a thin nose and round eyes with an abundant mouth and sharply clipped jaw. Dressed in a gray suit and tie, he looked like some businessman Clara Sue had fished off the street to accompany her.

When Clara Sue finally found our aisle she stopped. Bronson had saved two seats beside him, which would keep Clara Sue as far away from Jimmy and me as possible. She disturbed everyone in her way, falling over one elderly gentleman as she approached us. His eyes goggled as her breasts spilled toward his face. Flustered, all he could do was wait until Clara Sue's "male friend" helped her back to her feet and guided her along, his hands on her hips. She plopped into the seat beside Bronson, laughing. Eyes glared angrily from every head around us. The commotion had reached the senator, who paused in his speech. Mercifully he continued, taking the attention from us.

If Mother could have crawled under her seat, she would have. She had slumped back and down as far as she could and stared ahead as though what was going on had nothing whatsoever to do with her.

"Sorry we're late," Clara Sue told Bronson in a giggle loud enough for anyone within five rows of us to hear, "but I misplaced the invitation and forgot the time."

"Shh," someone said.

"I've got to introduce Charlie," she moaned.

"After the speech," Bronson advised, and he put his forefinger to his lips. Clara Sue pouted and then caught my gaze. She glared hatefully at me, her eyes turning crystal hard and cold, and then she folded her arms under her scantily covered bosom and sat back like a sulking child.

Right after the speech ended the diplomas were handed out. Clara Sue, not interested in any of it, again attempted to introduce her "male friend." I could see Bronson thought it was best to get it all over with.

"This is Charlie Goodwin," Clara Sue said. "He owns his own bowling alley in Tampa. My stepfather and my mother," Clara Sue said, indicating Bronson and Mother.

Bronson shook his hand, but Mother simply batted her eyelashes and flashed a quick smile. Of course, Clara Sue made no attempt to introduce Jimmy and me. Bronson had to do that after the diplomas were handed out and the graduates began leaving the stage. When we were introduced, Charlie Goodwin moved his eyes over me as if he had the power to undress me with his gaze. I didn't like the way he tucked his mouth in at the corner when he smiled.

"Pleased to meet you," he said. His slim, bony hand seemed to slide over mine. I couldn't wait to pull my fingers away. He gave Jimmy only a passing glance and looked at me again. Immediately Clara Sue rubbed up against him and whispered into his ear. His eyes widened, and he laughed. I could see he was titillated and thrilled by everything Clara Sue did and by the attention this young, voluptuous woman showered on him.

Just before Philip arrived Mother pulled Clara Sue aside. I couldn't help but overhear their conversation.

"Don't you realize what you're doing to me, dressing

like that and making such a shocking entrance?" she cried. "And coming here with that – that man," she sputtered.

"Oh, please, Mother," Clara Sue responded. "Don't start. I'm very happy with Charlie."

"Happy? How can you be happy with a man twice your age?" Mother complained.

"He's not twice my age, and I like his gray hair," Clara Sue said. "It makes him look distinguished."

"Distinguished! That man hardly looks distinguished," Mother spat.

"Here comes Philip. I've got to introduce him," Clara Sue declared, and she rushed off before Mother could say another word. Mother was practically swooning with embarrassment at this point anyway, and we had to leave the graduation ceremony as soon as we had met and congratulated Philip and Betty Ann.

All the way home Mother moaned and cried about how much she had been disgraced by Clara Sue's behavior.

"Can you imagine what the Monroes must think of us? And what their friends must think? Poor Philip. I felt so sorry for him, too, especially when Clara Sue introduced that man in front of all Philip's college friends. What could she possibly want with such a person? Can anyone tell me?"

When neither Bronson nor I responded, she turned to Jimmy.

"What do you think, James?" she asked. "You were in the army; you should know about such things."

What Jimmy's being in the army had to do with it none of us knew, but Jimmy had an answer ready for her.

"It's just a rebellious fling," he said. Mother nodded.

Then Jimmy leaned toward me, and under his breath he added, "I'm sure it won't be her last."

Philip insisted on returning to the hotel and working during the week before his wedding. Jimmy thought he would have too much on his mind to be of any real use, but Philip said if he didn't keep busy, he would go mad. We were only two weeks or so away from moving into our new house, and Philip spent a great deal of time over there with Jimmy checking on the finishing touches.

"I think the anticipation of getting married is driving Philip mad," Jimmy told me one evening.

"Why do you say that, Jimmy?" I asked. We were getting ready for bed.

"I don't mind him following me over to the house, and I don't even mind him hovering over my shoulder every time I look at something, but the questions . . ." Jimmy shook his head.

"Like what, Jimmy?"

"Like where exactly will our bed be located in our room? What side do you sleep on? Which closet is yours and which is mine? Why should he care about that? Today he sat at the vanity table and stared into the mirror the whole time I was in our suite. I left, and when I came back I thought he was gone, but I found him in the master bathroom, standing by the tub, just gazing down at it. He was in some kind of daze, because I had to call him three times to get his attention.

"I've heard about men acting that way when they're in love, but . . . What's the matter, Dawn?" Jimmy asked. "You have the strangest expression on your face." He laughed. "Actually, you look like someone who's seen a ghost. Is something wrong?"

"No," I said quickly. I smiled up at Jimmy. "Actually," I said, making it up as fast as I could, "I was just remembering how I was that day you came to New York to visit me at school. I was on pins and needles the whole time, and when you were late – "

"I remember," he said. "I was so nervous, but the moment I set eyes on you I stopped worrying. I knew we just had to be together; it just had to happen.

"Do you think Philip and Betty Ann have that kind of love?" Jimmy asked.

I turned away.

"I don't know, Jimmy. She appears to love him very much."

"Well, I'm just happy now that things ended up the way they did – that you turned out to be his sister and not mine. I don't know if I would ever have found anyone else," he said.

"Oh, Jimmy." Half undressed, I sat on the bed.

"Hey . . . you're crying. Why are you crying?" he asked, sitting beside me and putting his arm around my shoulder.

"I'm just happy I'm with you and you're with me," I said. "Really I am."

He smiled, and we kissed.

That night we tried once more to have our baby. I couldn't have wanted it any more than I did when we made love this time, but after we were finished and had kissed and turned away from each other to sleep, I had this empty feeling inside, this knowledge that we hadn't found the magic moment yet. I began to wonder if we ever would again. It was a frightening thought. What if the only child I would have was the one I had had with Michael? It would surely break Jimmy's heart.

He craved family so and was constantly inquiring as to whether Mr. Updike's detective had made any headway in his search for Fern. I couldn't tell him that we had stopped searching because we had run into one dead end after another. I didn't have the courage to tell him that the facts were simply inaccessible to us; it was the law, and Mr. Updike had advised me that to pursue it was verging on something illegal.

My mind was in such a turmoil, I tossed and turned, unable to sleep. Every time I closed my eyes and tried, I saw Philip standing in my nearly completed new bedroom, gazing licentiously at my vanity table and tub – but in my imagination I saw myself in the tub, taking a bath. I lifted my head, and suddenly there was Philip in the doorway, smiling down at me. I tried to get him to leave, but he stepped in further and offered to wash my back. I couldn't help but imagine him forcing himself on me again, running that washcloth over my shoulders and then down and over my breasts.

I moaned, frightened that these thoughts had even entered my mind. But it wasn't my fault, I told myself. It was Philip's. Somehow, slyly, surreptitiously, with the stealth of a fox in a chicken coop, he was creeping through the shadows and entering my world, first in little ways, and then bursting in upon me, upon my very thoughts.

I couldn't help but relive his sexual attack on me in the shower. I had been so frustrated, so trapped; I had been unable to shout out for fear I would bring attention. In the end I had been unable to hold him off.

And here I was feeling muzzled once again. I was afraid to mention anything to Jimmy, terrified of what he would do if he discovered any of this. In my heart

254

I sensed he had some suspicions that just hadn't found their way into words yet. But someday they would, and when that day came . . . I groaned just imagining the crisis.

"Dawn?" Jimmy said. "Are you all right?"

"What? Oh, yes. I just had a bad dream," I said.

"What was it about?"

"I don't want to talk about it. I'm all right. Really," I said.

He kissed me to reassure me, and then I did finally fall asleep, hoping that somehow I could put these fears to rest.

But one afternoon late in the week Philip wandered into my office and sat down. When I asked him what he wanted, he said nothing in particular; he just wanted to watch me work for a while. I sat back, unable to hide my annoyance.

"I don't think well under glass," I said. "Really, Philip, if you have nothing to do, why don't you go visit Mother? She's the one who's on pins and needles these days and could use your company."

Mother just dreaded the thought of attending Philip's wedding now that she knew for sure that Clara Sue and Charlie would be there. She was positive Clara Sue would do something terrible again, just as she had done at Philip's graduation, and embarrass the family. But despite her reticence, she couldn't help but be intrigued with the gala event. She went out of her way to find the most expensive, and most striking new gown. She had her personal hairdresser experiment with a half dozen different styles until she settled on one. Every day so far during the entire week before the wedding she had had facial treatments. She went on an intensive diet because she thought her waist was a little wide and her arms a little flabby. One day she was in a panic because she thought she saw the beginnings of a double chin. She came to the hotel to have me confirm it wasn't so.

"Are you kidding?" Philip cried out, laughing at my suggestion. "Mother would simply pile on her complaints and recommendations about the wedding. We would drive each other crazy. No, thank you."

"Well, I can't work with you just sitting there, Philip," I insisted. He nodded and rose from his seat.

"Your house is looking beautiful," he said, not with any real enthusiasm.

"Thank you."

"Actually, I'm kind of upset about it. Now that Clara Sue's gone and Mother's remarried and you're moving out, everyone will be gone from the family section but me," he complained.

"You have Betty Ann," I reminded him. "And I'm sure you will be raising a family. You should be happy you have all that privacy."

"Yes," he said, looking down at the floor. Then he looked up at me and smiled, but it was a queer, shadowy smile.

"You haven't asked me about it, so I imagine you don't know where we're going for our honeymoon, do you?" he asked.

"No." I sat back, a ripple of apprehension creeping up my spine. "Where?"

"The exact same place you and Jimmy went in Provincetown on Cape Cod," he replied. "I got the information from Jimmy. I'm surprised he didn't tell you. Or did he?"

"No," I said, shaking my head. My heart began to

256

thump in my chest. Jimmy hadn't told me because he knew it would upset me, I thought. "Haven't you been to Cape Cod?" I asked.

"Oh, I have, and so has Betty Ann, dozens of times. Matter of fact," he said, "her parents have a house in Hyannis Port."

"So why are you going there? Why don't you go someplace neither of you has been so you can see new things?" I asked, afraid of the answer.

"When you're on a honeymoon," he said, his eyes twinkling, "you don't care about the surroundings, do you? Don't tell me you and Jimmy did a lot of sightseeing," he said, his eyes and his smile full of suggestion.

"We didn't have time to do much, if you will recall. Randolph had just died," I reminded him sharply.

"Uh-huh," he said, unflappable. He kept his eyes trained on me, a wry smile cocking his lips. "Is Jimmy a good lover?" he asked.

"That's not the sort of thing I care to discuss with you, Philip," I replied. My voice took on the steely edge of a razor, but his smile widened.

"I bet it was hard for you two, continually reminded of yourselves as brother and sister. How did you get over that, or didn't you?" he asked, his head tilted slightly, his eyes narrowing.

"I said I don't care to discuss it, Philip," I flared.

He stared at me a moment and then nodded.

"Okay," he said. "I'm sorry. I guess I'm just nervous. Maybe I will follow your suggestion and take a ride up to see Mother. I need the amusement," he said. "Sorry I bothered you." He turned and headed for the door. After he opened it he paused. "But I meant what I said about being lonely in the family section now. I'll miss you, miss listening to you move about your suite." He raised his eyebrows. "I can hear almost everything through those walls, you know."

I reddened.

"Not that I'm trying to listen. I don't have my ear up against the wall," he added quickly. "It's just that after a while you get used to certain sounds." He shrugged. "Who knows? Maybe someday soon Betty Ann and I will be in a house, too, and not far from you and Jimmy. Then the only one left living in the family section will be Grandmother's ghost," he added with a laugh.

I stared, feeling a scream in my throat that just stayed there. He shook his head and walked out, closing the door softly behind him. The silence that rained down around me filled me with a terrifying chill. I embraced myself and sat back. It was as if the cold was coming from inside me, as if an ice cube in my stomach was building and building. Finally I had to get up and go outside into the warm sunlight. I walked around the hotel and found Jimmy talking with some maintenance men who were about to wash windows.

"Hi," he said, seeing me approach. He took one look at the expression on my face and his face became somber. "Something wrong?"

"Oh, Jimmy," I said. "I want to move into our new house right away – tomorrow, if we can."

"Tomorrow?" He started to laugh.

"Yes, tomorrow," I insisted.

"But I don't have all the plumbing fixtures, and we haven't even connected our phone lines, and – "

"Well, when can we move in?" I demanded.

"We're on schedule, but I suppose I could rush a few

things and get us in comfortably in, say, a week. Why? What's the rush?" he asked.

"Nothing. You were right about living in the hotel," I said quickly. "I need to feel I'm in my own place."

"Okay. I'll see what I can do to rush it even more. In the meantime, maybe you ought to start thinking about packing our things, getting that part organized."

"I will. I'll see Mrs. Boston and Sissy about it right away. Thank you," I said, kissing him on the cheek. "I don't mean to be a burden."

"You're no burden; you could never be a burden. A pain in the you-know-where once in a while, but a burden – "

"All right, James Gary Longchamp," I chastised playfully. He laughed, and then I felt the cold and the trepidation lift out of my body. It was so good having Jimmy. He was my strength, the rainbow at the end of every storm, the sunlight breaking through every cloud.

I returned to the hotel to resume my work and put all my dark concerns at the very bottom of my trunk of thoughts where they belonged.

But dark thoughts and trouble seemed to have a way of finding my doorstep. Two days before Philip's wedding I had an unexpected visit from Clara Sue and Charlie Goodwin. I was in the office reading Mr. Dorfman's weekly financial report and recommendations when my door was thrown open and Clara Sue appeared like the queen of nightmares, wearing the same tight-fitting violet silk dress she had worn the last time we had been alone together. For the rest of my life I would never forget any of the details of the nightmarish day when Clara Sue had stolen my most precious possession: my unborn baby. The horror would haunt me until the day I died.

At first, because of the way she stood there with her hands on her hips, I didn't see Charlie Goodwin behind her; but when she stepped in he appeared, hat in hand, that sly smile cutting a crooked line from the corners of his mouth through the sides of his lean cheeks.

"Well, look at how you've changed Grandmother's office!" Clara Sue exclaimed. "I bet this cost a pretty penny to do, and for what? Just to make you happy, I suppose."

"It's my office now, Clara Sue," I said, glaring back at her. "What is it you want? Make it quick. I've got work to do."

"Me and Charlie want to talk to you, right, Charlie?" she said, turning back.

"Uh-huh," he said, continuing to smile.

"Charlie's a businessman," Clara Sue bragged. "He knows about all this stuff," she added, waving at the walls of my office as if they were covered with Wall Street ticker tape.

"Talk to me about what, Clara Sue?"

"About the hotel. What did you think?" She plopped herself down in one of the red leather chairs and crossed her stockinged legs. "Sit down, Charlie," she commanded. Charlie took the other chair quickly.

"So how's business?" Clara Sue demanded.

"We're doing well," I said. "If you have any – "

"You know," Clara Sue said quickly, leaning toward me, "Grandmother Cutler loved me the best. She wanted me to be the real owner of this place some day."

260

I sat back and smiled.

"I hardly think so, Clara Sue. Whatever I say about Grandmother Cutler, I will never say she was stupid," I replied. My comment had the effect of slapping her across the face, and I relished the look of outrage washing over her features. She snapped back in her seat, her smile washed away.

"That's what you say, but I had many a talk with her before you came here and ruined our lives," she insisted.

"I don't want to go through this with you again, Clara Sue. You and I have nothing to say to each other. I'm really going to have to ask you to leave. I'm busy."

"I'm not leaving so fast. We've still got unfinished business. And I've told you before, Dawn" – her eyes glinted maliciously – "especially that last time we spoke, not to try giving me orders." A sly smile twitched across Clara Sue's lips. "You remember our last conversation, don't you, Dawn? Surely you haven't forgotten the details of that day." She laughed cruelly. "We were in your bedroom, and I was wearing this exact same dress – "

I cut Clara Sue off before she could continue. "Don't you *ever*, *ever* mention that day to me again, you murderer!" I lost control of myself as my rage toward Clara Sue and what she had done to me suddenly burst forth. "As long as I live I will *never*, *ever* forget that day or forgive what you did to me. The only reason I can tolerate the sight of you is that I know it was all a tragic accident. You didn't know I was pregnant, yet what happened that day could have been avoided if only you would let go of the hatred you hold against me. I've never tried to hurt you, Clara Sue."

261

"Accidents happen," she sneered. "My heart was broken when I heard the news. To think I missed out on being an aunt again. By the way, how's the brat? Does she miss her Auntie Clara Sue? I'd love to see her. I've got some stories I'd love to tell her. One's about a princess named Dawn and a big bad wolf named Michael." Clara Sue grinned at me wickedly.

"Get out!" I shouted, outraged at the audacity of her threatening to tell Christie the truth about her parentage before she was ready to hear it. "Get out before I have you thrown out! How we can even be related is beyond me."

"I'm not leaving," Clara Sue spat in a steely whisper. "Not until you hear what Charlie and I have to say, right, Charlie?" She turned sharply on him, and it was as if she held some string attached to his head. He straightened up quickly and nodded.

"She's right, Mrs. Longchamp," he said.

"Call her Dawn, or better yet, Eugenia," Clara Sue said, smiling maliciously. "That's what Grandmother Cutler wanted her to be called."

"What is it you have to say, Mr. Goodwin?" I asked. It was my turn to be demanding.

"Well, Clara Sue's been telling me about the situation with the hotel – the wills and all – and, well, to be direct, Mrs. Longchamp, it sounds to me like she hasn't gotten her fair share of things. I'm familiar with estates and wills and deeds and – "

"Clara Sue knows very well that we have an attorney, Mr. Updike, and if she has any legal complaints to make, those complaints should be directed to him," I said curtly.

"He's just going to do whatever you want him to do,"

262

Clara Sue hissed. "You've managed to fool him the way you've fooled everyone else."

"I would hardly do anything other than what my attorney recommended, Mr. Goodwin," I said, ignoring Clara Sue completely. "So if you feel you want to present something on her behalf, he is the man to call. I'll be glad to give you his phone number," I said, opening a drawer to get one of Mr. Updike's business cards.

"We don't want his phone number," Clara Sue snapped. "Tell her, Charlie," she demanded.

"Tell me what, Mr. Goodwin?"

"Well, I discussed Clara Sue's situation with my own attorney, and he says there's real cause for contesting the wills, especially the grandfather's will that leaves a majority interest in things to you.

"I don't mean any disrespect," he continued, "but facts are facts, and the fact is that you're a child born out of wedlock, whereas Clara Sue here is a legitimate child. It seems to us she should be getting a bigger piece of the pie," he concluded.

"Is that so?" I said.

"Yeah, that's so," Clara Sue said, smiling. She looked at me triumphantly.

I looked from her to Charlie Goodwin and suddenly realized what it was that drew this man to her. Surely she had described her family situation to him, and he had thought there was gold to dig. Now that Charlie Goodwin believed he was so close to getting his hands on some big money, he looked like he could taste it. The tip of his tongue moved over his lips in anticipation of my surrendering some lucrative percentage of Cutler's Cove to Clara Sue.

"I'm afraid it isn't so, Clara Sue," I said. I rose from my chair, ready to divulge my own little surprise.

As I moved around the desk I couldn't help but recall the way Grandmother Cutler had looked down at me and spoken to me that first time we had met. Queenly stiff, she rained her orders and commands over me with a torrent of authority and power that made my knees knock. As slight as she was in build, she had a tremendous aura of authority about her and looked as if she could command the sky to clear or the clouds to storm. She wore her confidence like a steel rod in her back and filled her voice with strength and superiority. To challenge her seemed futile, even dangerous.

"What isn't so?" Clara Sue cried. I leaned back on my desk and folded my arms comfortably.

"That I'm illegitimate and you're legitimate."

Clara Sue started to laugh.

"I'm not kidding," I said quickly. Her laughter ended. "For years you've called me a bastard, and all along you've been no different yourself."

"What the hell are you saying?" she demanded. She rose up in her seat, ready to confront me. "*What the hell are you saying?*" she shrieked as my words sank in.

"What I'm saying, sister dearest, is that the man you thought was your father, wasn't," I said, relishing the shock on her face. "In fact, you have no Cutler blood in you at all." I turned to Charlie, whose face seemed to sink in, his cheeks growing hollow, his lips turning toward his mouth. Only his eyes remained wide, bulging.

"No Cutler blood . . . this is ridiculous!" Clara Sue screeched, gazing quickly at Charlie. "Don't believe anything she says. It's lies. All lies!"

264

"You don't have to believe anything I say; you don't have to listen to me. Just go to Mother and ask her outright who your real father is. Better yet," I smirked, standing away from the desk, "go ask Bronson Alcott."

Clara Sue glared up at me, the confidence draining from her face as the possibility took shape in her thoughts. Charlie squirmed in his seat.

"Bronson," I continued, returning to my seat, "will tell you the truth now."

"You're lying. You're a filthy liar!" Clara Sue spat.

"There's only one way to find out. As I said, go – "

"You go. You go to hell!" Clara Sue screamed. "None of this is true!"

"Hold on, Clara Sue," Charlie said. "Easy. Calm down."

"Easy? Calm down? She's making this all up just to stop us from getting my fair share."

"You never knew that Mother and Bronson had been lovers even before Mother married Randolph?" I asked. I saw from the way her eyes blinked that she had heard some rumors.

"That doesn't mean anything," she replied.

"No. Not in and of itself, it doesn't. But after my birth and subsequent disappearance Mother went to Bronson, and their love affair was revived. As a result, you were born. Up until now the truth didn't matter, but if you and Charlie are going to pursue some legal vendetta, I guess it all has to come out."

"You bitch," Clara Sue said, standing. "You bitter, bitter bitch! You're just like her now. Just as hateful and . . . and mean. Come on, Charlie. We'll tell Mother what she said. You'll see. She's lying. Come on!" she shouted when Charlie didn't rush to get up. He rose quickly now. Clara Sue grabbed his hand and tugged him toward the door.

"You're not finished with me, and I'm not finished with you," she threatened. I stared at her coldly.

"I think you're wrong about that, Clara Sue. Very wrong. We couldn't be more finished with each other than we are now," I said calmly. My glare and my controlled voice overwhelmed her. She simply turned and pulled Charlie out of the office with her, slamming the door behind her.

I sat back in my chair, my heart thumping. It felt good; I couldn't deny it. Shattering Clara Sue like that had been enjoyable. The shoe was on the other foot. Now she was the one to learn her life had been a lie, not me. The sad thing was that the only reason she would be upset was that she couldn't squeeze any more money out of me or the hotel, and not because her family was disrupted. Of course, it would probably lead to the end of her little romance with Charlie Goodwin, who, once he had it confirmed that Clara Sue wasn't the gold mine he had hoped she was, would drop her like a hot potato. Sadness and hardship, disappointment and pain would be the new building blocks of her world, I thought.

A few hours later Mother called me. I had been expecting it.

"Clara Sue and her friend just left here," she said. "How could you tell her? Why did you tell her?" she cried.

I explained how they had come to blackmail me into giving them money, and Mother's self-pity came to an abrupt stop.

"I just knew it," she said. "The moment I set eyes

266

on that man, I just knew what sort he was. Still, it was hard to tell her these things. She used to put me up on such a high pedestal," Mother moaned. "Now she thinks so much less of me."

"She never respected you, Mother. Don't delude yourself. And as for loving Randolph . . . I don't think she loves anyone but herself."

"Perhaps," Mother admitted. She sighed and then described how Clara Sue had ranted and raved. I enjoyed hearing about it until she concluded with, "In the end Bronson gave her some money."

"It won't be the last time she comes for money," I said, disgusted with Clara Sue's antics.

"I know, but we felt . . . guilty. I pulled her aside and told her in no uncertain terms that if she persists in living with a man twice her age, there will be no more money coming."

"You don't have to worry, Mother. Charlie Goodwin won't be hanging on to a lost cause long," I said.

"You're probably right. You're a lot wiser about these things than I was," she said. "Oh, well, one good thing came out of it, I suppose."

"What's that?" I asked.

"She says that since Philip isn't a whole brother and Randolph wasn't really her father, she and Charlie are not going to attend the wedding. At least she won't be there to embarrass me."

I had to laugh at the way Mother could always manage to find her rainbows.

The day of the wedding we all flew to Washington, D.C. The wedding ceremony itself was held in a beautiful church, and the reception was held in the ballroom of one of the most luxurious hotels I had ever seen. We had invited nearly three hundred people on our side, and the Monroes had invited close to five hundred. It was a most impressive wedding party.

But for me and for a number of people, the sensational thing about the affair was Betty Ann herself. I was shocked when I first set eyes on her coming down the aisle of the church.

She had dyed her hair blond.

"I did it for Philip," she told me when we had a private moment together at the reception. "He had been asking me to do it for weeks, and I thought I would surprise him. Does it look okay?" she asked.

I didn't think it did, especially with her eyebrows still dark brown, but I could see how important it was for her to please Philip.

"Yes; it's just such a surprise," I said. "I'll have to get used to it."

"Philip's already used to it. You should have seen the pleased expression on his face when he saw me. I never saw his eyes so bright or his smile so deep. We're going to be very happy together, don't you think?" she asked, searching for reassurance.

"I'm sure you will," I said.

Mother didn't seem to notice any significance in Betty Ann's dyeing her hair, but she was in quite a daze. Everything overwhelmed her: the richness of the ballroom, the number of guests, the army of servants, and the abundance of food and champagne. The cocktail hour itself was equivalent to most wedding dinners. Chefs were slicing roast beef and handing out enormous shrimps. There were trays and trays of hot hors d'oeuvres and two bands just for the cocktail hour.

The dinner had seven courses and went on and on until after midnight, with toasts being made by senators and congressmen. There was even a governor present. Of course, we were occupied with our own guests, but Stuart Monroe took the time to introduce us to many of his important guests as well.

Philip was very busy with his college friends and with all the guests the Monroes brought around to meet him, but before the evening ended he managed to ask me to dance.

"Doesn't Betty Ann look beautiful?"

"Why did you ask her to dye her hair, Philip?"

"Don't you know?" he responded, and my heart began to pound. Of course I knew, I thought. "If I can't have you," he whispered, "I can at least imagine it."

I didn't realize how serious he was about this until after we had returned to Cutler's Cove and I met Mrs. Boston in the corridor outside my suite.

"Did it all go well?" she inquired.

"It was an overwhelming affair, Mrs. Boston. Mother is still spinning," I added, smiling.

"Mr. Philip was so nervous. He nearly panicked when you weren't here to give him what you had promised. We had packed many of your things away in those cartons in preparation for your moving."

"Promised?" I held my smile.

"Yes. I helped him find what he wanted. We went through the cartons together until he located it."

"Located what, Mrs. Boston?"

"Why . . . one of your nightgowns, and the perfume."

I stared at her.

"Philip took one of my nightgowns and my perfume?"

"Didn't you want him to?" she asked. "He said he needed it for his honeymoon." Mrs. Boston saw the shock in my face. "Did I do something wrong?"

"Oh, no," I said, reassuring her. "It's nothing to do with you, Mrs. Boston. Don't give it any more thought."

She smiled.

"Well, then, good night," she said.

I walked into my suite slowly.

Philip was off on his honeymoon. He had made reservations at the exact motel where Jimmy and I had gone on Cape Cod; he had gotten Betty Ann to dye her hair my color and now he was going to dress her in my nightgown and make her wear my perfume. When he held her in his arms and closed his eyes he would see and feel me.

Somehow, the thought of it made me feel unclean and unfaithful. It was as if Philip was raping me again, even if it was only in his mind.

Days of Happiness, Days of Sorrow

Two days later we moved into our new house. Christie was so adorable, insisting she be permitted to carry her own little suitcase. In it she had her hairbrush, two of her rag dolls, a pair of blue cotton socks, one of her summer dresses, and a book of nursery rhymes. She had decided herself what she would put into it. It reminded me of myself and my own little suitcase, only when I had packed, I had stuffed in everything I owned. I did it from the time I was Christie's age until the day they brought me to the hotel. That suitcase was still somewhere in the hotel attic with other old things.

"I'm ready," she declared as soon as she closed the little suitcase. Jimmy picked her up and carried her along with him to help supervise the moving. There was a great deal to do at the hotel as well, so I remained in my office throughout the morning. Mrs. Boston surprised me by coming to my office to ask if she could be our maid. Sissy and her fiancé had saved enough money to set the date for their wedding, so Mrs. Boston knew Sissy wouldn't be with us much longer.

I was flattered by her proposal and her decision to stay with Jimmy and me rather than continue at the hotel, taking care of the family section for Philip. She had been there for years and years. I thanked her and told her to pack her things and move into the maid's quarters in the new house immediately. From the way her face lit up, I thought she might even feel as I did: that she was getting away from old ghosts and unhappy memories, which seemed to be resurrected as soon as the day's work was over for us and we retreated to our suites.

"Fresh walls is what I need now," Mrs. Boston said. "I'm tired of the same shadows behind me and around me."

Fresh walls is what she got, for our house was bright and airy. I had chosen as many light colors as I could for all the rooms. With the large windows letting in as much sunlight as possible, the marble floors, white staircase and mauve curtains looked resplendent even on gray days. Everyone commented favorably about my choice of furnishings. Those who paraded through our hallways and rooms the first week or so spoke about the "dazzling chandeliers," the "radiant colors" and the "happy and warm feelings" they felt while there.

Philip surprised me with a phone call from Provincetown the first night we spent in our new house.

"I wanted to be sure to call you and wish you good luck," he said.

"It's very nice of you to think of us on your honeymoon, Philip," I replied, keeping my voice as formal and as cool as I could.

"The weather here hasn't been as nice as we hoped," he said quickly. "I'm tempted to cut our honeymoon short and return to Cutler's Cove."

He then proceeded to complain about the restaurants and the beach. Nothing was as good as he had expected it to be. Jimmy was surprised when I told him about Philip's call.

"Why would anyone want to cut his own honeymoon short if he didn't have to?" he wondered aloud. "He was probably just talking," he said.

However, Philip did cut his honeymoon short by one day. He returned to the hotel at night, after Jimmy and I had retired to our house. We heard the buzzer, and Jimmy went to the door to greet Philip and Betty Ann. Philip had brought along a bottle of champagne.

"We weren't here to celebrate with you, so we thought we'd have a toast now," he said. "If we're not intruding, that is."

"Oh, no, no," Jimmy said, unable to hide the surprise in his voice. "Come on in."

I took Betty Ann through the house while Jimmy and Philip talked in the sitting room. Mrs. Boston had just put Christie to bed, but she was still awake.

"Do you know who this is, Christie?" I asked her when we popped our heads in.

"Uh-huh," Christie said, sitting up quickly. Her golden hair had grown down below her shoulders. "It's Aunt Bet," she said, and from that day forward it would be the way she would refer to Betty Ann. We both laughed about it.

"Your house is so beautiful," Betty Ann said. "Good luck with it."

"Thank you. I'm sorry the weather was so poor in Provincetown on your honeymoon," I said.

"Poor? It wasn't poor; it was magnificent every day. Some days there were hardly any clouds at all, and I was surprised at how warm the ocean was."

273

"What about the hotel in Cape Cod?" I asked, to confirm my suspicions.

"Oh, everything was beautiful. I didn't want to leave, but Philip got itchy and said he hated just lying around all day. He's so devoted to Cutler's Cove. I could see he regretted not being here when it's so busy, so I didn't complain when he asked to come home a day early.

"I think he was also very eager to see your home all finished and you and Jimmy actually living in it," she added.

We returned to the sitting room, where Jimmy and Philip had our champagne toast ready. After everyone took a glass, Philip raised his and said, "To Jimmy and Dawn's new home. May it be the place where dreams come true." Thoughtfully, with narrowed eyes, he stared at me and waited until I brought my glass to my lips. Then he drank.

"You know," Philip said, gazing around and nodding, "the idea of living outside the hotel is probably a very good one. You do feel more like real people with your own private life. Even when Grandmother Cutler was alive guests would wander into the family section.

"Maybe one day soon Jimmy and I can pace out a lot nearby," he added, fixing his eyes on me. His smile was small and tight, amused. He was toying with me and toying with his own passions.

"I hate to be the one to say it, but it's getting late," I said, "and we have another big check-in tomorrow. I have to be at the hotel early."

"And so do I, then," Philip echoed. He rose quickly and said good night. "Somehow," he added, gazing at me with those deep blue eyes twinkling, "I feel as if Betty is right: We're all about to start new lives."

"Well, what do you think?" Jimmy asked me when he returned from showing them out. We started upstairs. "Do they look like a happily married new couple?"

"I suppose," I said.

"You should have heard him talking about her when you were showing her the house," he said. "It got downright embarrassing at times."

"What do you mean?"

"I asked him why he returned home early from his honeymoon, and he said he was simply exhausted."

"Exhausted?" I paused on the stairway. Jimmy widened his eyes and shook his head.

"He went into great detail about their lovemaking, about how hungry Betty Ann was for sex and passion. I don't know why he wanted to tell me all those intimate details about her, do you?"

"No," I said. "And I don't think it's very nice of him to do that."

"It was almost as if – "

"What?" I asked quickly.

"As if he was trying to get me to do the same thing . . . compare notes or something. Locker-room talk," Jimmy said, shaking his head. "I never thought Philip was that type."

"Did you . . . say anything?" Jimmy smiled.

"As far as he knows," Jimmy said, "you're a nun and I'm a monk." He embraced me and kissed me on the neck.

I had to laugh, but my laughter was more of relief than of amusement.

After Philip and Betty Ann moved into the family section of the hotel, things settled down. Our work kept us occupied. The hotel was having one of its best seasons

275

in recent history. Grandmother Cutler had never really advertised the hotel in any magazines or newspapers. Her philosophy was that the hotel had its own special reputation and would exist solely on that and on word of mouth. For a long time that was sufficient, but as a new generation of vacationers came into existence I thought it was necessary to appeal to them, so I talked Mr. Dorfman into advertising Cutler's Cove in some travel magazines and big-city papers. We had immediate results – new bookings, inquiries from new travel agents and a boost in our income. For the first time in a long time Mr. Dorfman mused aloud about the possibility of expanding the hotel – adding on rooms and new facilities. I told him about the frequent inquiries I was getting from organizations looking for convention sites.

"That was something Mrs. Cutler would never do," Mr. Dorfman reminded me. "She thought it took away from the nature of Cutler's Cove."

"I know," I said. "But times are changing, and we might have to change a little to survive."

Mr. Dorfman nodded and looked at me so intently, I had to ask him if something was wrong.

"No, not wrong," he replied. "I was just recalling what you were like the first time we met and how much you have matured since," he said, and then he immediately turned crimson. "Oh, I'm sorry, I didn't mean to – "

"No, that's all right," I said. "I don't mind. I appreciate it, in fact. Thank you, Mr. Dorfman."

All of these thoughts and some of the changes excited Philip. He was ready to charge ahead and do anything, but I decided we had to be more cautious. I did tell him to do some studies, which, I was glad to see, kept him very busy.

One of the things that surprised me was how quickly Betty Ann adjusted to hotel life and how happy she was about it. She did prove to be a very good hostess, although a bit too formal for some of the older people at times. She never missed a dinner and was even at the dining room door to greet guests for breakfast. She began to dress more appealingly and went to the beautician in the hotel salon to get advice about her hair. They also helped her with her makeup. With a more flattering hairstyle and clothing that accentuated the good qualities of her figure, she did begin to appear more attractive.

Gradually we all fell into our routines. Mother continued to host her now-famous dinner parties and was very pleased when the four of us – Jimmy and myself, Philip and Betty Ann – could attend. Summer moved to fall and fall to winter without any major problems or incidents. And then, late one afternoon, Mrs. Boston called me at the office.

"I just want to check," she began.

"Check? Check what, Mrs. Boston?"

"That you did give Clara Sue permission to take Christie for a ride in the truck," she said.

"What? What truck?" I asked, sitting forward.

"Oh, dear," she said. "I wanted to call you immediately, but Miss Clara Sue insisted she had stopped at the hotel first and you had said it was all right."

"What are you talking about, Mrs. Boston? I haven't seen Clara Sue for some time. What truck?" Panic began building within me, but I fought it back. I wouldn't jump to conclusions. I wouldn't lose control. Not yet.

277

"She was with a man, a truck driver. They came to the house in one of those big trucks, and Miss Clara Sue marched around looking at your home. Then, on the way out, she asked Christie if she wanted to go for a ride in her friend's truck. I think she called him Skipper. He had tattoos all over his arms.

"Christie was timid about it until Miss Clara Sue said you told her she could take her for a ride. Then she scooped her up, and they left."

"My God," I gasped. "I'll be right there." I hung up and sent one of the bellhops to get Jimmy. He met me at the house, where I heard Mrs. Boston go through the whole story once more.

"What's going on?" Jimmy asked when he arrived, and I told him quickly.

"I can't believe she had the audacity to do something like this. She's gone too far this time. Who does she think she is?"

He asked Mrs. Boston for a description of the truck.

"A tractor trailer?" Jimmy asked, amazed. "That shouldn't be too hard to find. When I get my hands on the both of them . . ." he said threateningly, and he rushed out.

"Jimmy, wait!" I cried, but he wasn't going to hesitate.

"I'm so sorry, Dawn. I thought – "

"It's not your fault, Mrs. Boston. She lied to you. It's good that you had your doubts and called right away," I said, comforting her. As long as I comforted her I kept myself from getting hysterical.

Why would Clara Sue take Christie? What possible reason could she have? Where had they gone? Was this

278

her way of getting back at me for throwing the truth about her real father into her face?

I phoned Mother and Bronson to see if Clara Sue had gone to Buella Woods.

"I didn't even know she was in the area," Bronson said. "She and Laura Sue had an argument last week about this new boyfriend. Laura's taking a nap. As soon as she wakes I'll tell her what's happened. Call us as soon as you learn anything, and if we hear from her, I'll call you."

"Thank you, Bronson," I said.

"I'm sorry. She's getting to be a serious problem," he added before hanging up.

Afterward I sat with Mrs. Boston and waited to hear from Jimmy. More than an hour passed, and we heard nothing. Mrs. Boston made us both tea, and we sat staring out the window.

"Maybe you should phone the police," Mrs. Boston mused aloud. "And tell them . . . what happened."

I could see she didn't want to use the word "kidnapping." I didn't even want to think it, but at this point, with no word from Jimmy, I couldn't help but consider it a real possibility. Christie was not very fond of Clara Sue. She didn't even like calling her Aunt Clara Sue. I knew how uncomfortable she had always been in Clara Sue's presence, and it didn't take much to imagine her being afraid and unhappy right now. Just the thought of her trapped in that truck cab with Clara Sue and one of her sleazy boyfriends made my skin crawl. It felt as if some tiny hand with sharp fingernails was scratching away at the inside of my stomach. I did all that I could to keep from simply bursting out and screaming.

279

Finally, twenty minutes later, we saw Jimmy's car pull up, and both of us ran out to greet.him.

"I didn't see hide nor hair of them," he declared. "It's as if they simply disappeared into thin air. Mrs. Boston, you're sure about that truck description?"

"Oh, yes," she said and immediately she burst into tears. I had to embrace her and comfort her again.

"Jimmy," I said, "we'd better call the police."

He nodded and went into the house to do so.

"Please, Mrs. Boston, don't cry. No one blames you. Come on, let's go in and sit down," I coaxed.

Less than ten minutes later the police arrived, and we told them what had happened. They hurried out to radio a description of the truck to other patrolmen. Again time passed slowly. When it grew darker I couldn't help but go off by myself and shed tears. Finally, a little after seven-thirty, we heard the roar of a truck engine, and we all ran out to see a police patrol car, its bubble light going, escorting a tractor trailer truck up the driveway to our house. The moment it stopped the door opened, and Clara Sue lowered Christie to the ground.

"Momma!" she cried, running into my arms. I embraced her and held her tight, covering her face and head with kisses.

Jimmy was like a flash of lightning coming up behind me.

"How dare you take her without our permission?" he screamed.

"What's everyone getting so excited about?" Clara Sue asked nonchalantly, that wry smile on her face. She didn't get out of the truck. "Me and Skipper just took her along on a delivery and then took her to have hamburgers. Right, Skipper honey?" she said.

"That's right," the tall, lean man beside her replied.

"You had no right to do that!" I cried, holding Christie to me possessively.

Clara Sue smiled coldly and reached into her pocketbook to take out a hairbrush. She smiled at the police.

"I was just trying to be a good aunt," she said, shaking her head. "Everyone complains that I don't care enough about my family, and then when I go and try to do something nice I get yelled at. See, Skipper, see how it doesn't pay to be nice?" she said, smiling coyly at us. She began to run her hairbrush through her hair as if she were about to go on stage.

"You little witch," Jimmy flared.

"Hey," her boyfriend said, leaning over. "Watch yourself." He waved his fist.

"Come on out here and say that," Jimmy taunted. Clara Sue's boyfriend started to open the door, but the two policemen interceded.

"Just hold on here," the taller one said. He turned to me. "Mrs. Longchamp, do you want to press any charges against these people?"

"Charges against these people?" Clara Sue cried. "I'm her aunt. She can't press charges against us. I took my niece for a ride and dinner. She had a good time, didn't you, Christie honey?" she crooned.

Christie buried her face deep into my shoulder.

"You're so irresponsible and hateful," I spat. "To terrorize a child for your own satisfaction. You're despicable.

"I won't press any charges," I said, not wanting this ugliness to go on, "but don't you ever, *ever* set foot on this property again."

"That's the gratitude I get being a good auntie,"

Clara Sue chimed. "Come on, Skipper. These people are just ungrateful." She laughed. "Enjoy your life. It's built with the money that should have been mine," she added, slamming the truck door.

Jimmy fumed, but the policeman held him back. We watched the truck start off slowly and go down the driveway again. All the while Christie kept her little face buried in my shoulder.

"Are you all right, honey?"

She nodded. Then she lifted her head.

"Aunt Clara Sue made me sit and watch her and Skipper dance in the restaurant. He smells and has no tooth here," she said, pointing to the top of her mouth.

"Poor child," Mrs. Boston said. "Are you hungry, Christie?"

"We'll take her up and give her a nice warm bath, Mrs. Boston," I said.

"Of course. Come to Mrs. Boston," she said, holding out her arms. Christie went to her gladly.

"We'll make sure they're heading out of town, Mrs. Longchamp," the policeman said.

"Thank you."

"Where did you find them?" Jimmy inquired.

"Hoagie's Diner," the policeman said.

"I never thought to look there," Jimmy muttered. "Lucky for them I didn't," he added.

I took his arm, and we followed Mrs. Boston and Christie back into the house. Another crisis of Clara Sue's making had ended. She was like a dark cloud full of rain, always ready to spoil a nice day.

Late in the spring Betty Ann announced that she was

pregnant. I was happy for her, of course, and so was Jimmy, but it had the effect of accentuating my own failure to become pregnant. At Jimmy's insistence we went for another physical examination and had another session with Dr. Lester. After all the tests had been completed we met with him in his office.

"I'm not surprised at the results," he began, sitting back in his chair and templing his fingers under his chin. "Nothing much has changed. You're both in perfect health and both fertile."

"Then what is it?" Jimmy demanded. "It certainly isn't for lack of trying," he said, not realizing how forcefully he said it until he looked at my face. "I mean . . ."

"No, no, I understand," Dr. Lester said. He leaned forward on his desk and gazed at me intently. "Dawn, how are you feeling emotionally these days? I don't mean to pry, but are you happy?"

"Happy?" I looked at Jimmy, who was awaiting my answer almost as eagerly as the doctor. "Why, yes. Things are going very well for us. We have a new home. Christie, thank God, is a healthy, happy child. The hotel is doing very well, and we're all getting along . . . I'm happy," I insisted, but I sounded angry about it. The doctor's eyebrows rose.

"Uh-huh," he said. "Emotionally you're all right . . . none of those mood swings we talked about once before . . . periods of sadness coming over you for no apparent reason?"

"Well . . . hardly," I said. He nodded, contemplating. Then he sat back and shrugged.

"Nature has its ways," he said. "Medicine can do so much, but after a while it's up to forces beyond our control."

283

"I've heard about fertility drugs," Jimmy said. I was surprised. He had never mentioned them before.

"Oh, there are some I can give you, but that's not a concern, considering your own fertility, and there are some side effects and unexpected results, too. Why endanger yourselves and your offspring?"

"No, no, of course not," Jimmy said quickly. "I just thought – "

"I think," Dr. Lester said, nodding, "that it's going to happen in due time. When the right combination of events occurs – physical, mental, emotional – then it will happen.

"Let's not forget that Dawn has gone through a very traumatic experience with a pregnancy. The body works in mysterious ways sometimes, and it might still be – what should I say? – gun shy?" He smiled. "I think you know what I mean. Give it a little more time," he said, standing up.

"I'm sorry, Jimmy," I said after we left and we were in our car. "I know it's my fault. Dr. Lester has just about come out and said that."

"Oh, no. You can't blame yourself. You didn't ask for any traumatic experiences. Hey," he said, "we'll do just what he says . . . we'll keep on trying." He smiled and kissed me on the cheek.

The following January, a day after New Year's Day, Betty Ann gave birth to twins, a boy and a girl, both with strands of Philip's and my golden hair, but both with Betty Ann's brown eyes, only theirs seemed brighter, with specks of bronze. They had identical diminutive features: tiny button noses and wee mouths with soft but full upper lips. Side by side in their bassinets in the maternity ward, they still seemed to share the same womb, for when one began to cry the other joined in instantly. They swung their arms and clenched their doll-like hands in synchronization, their wails in harmony.

Jimmy held Christie up to look in at her new cousins. Her eyes widened with awe as her gaze moved from one to the other.

"We've named the boy Richard, Richard Stanley Cutler, and the girl Melanie Rose," Philip announced proudly. Then he looked at Christie and asked, "Can you say Richard and Melanie?"

Christie nodded, still too overwhelmed to speak.

"Go on, then," Philip coaxed. "Say it. First Richard."

"Richard," she pronounced perfectly.

"And Melanie Rose."

"Mell . . ." Christie paused and looked at me. I nodded encouragement, but in her excitement she had forgotten the rest. "Mellon," she said, and we all laughed.

"That's a nickname that will stick for sure," Philip said. "I even like it myself."

I could have predicted Mother's reaction to Betty Ann's giving birth to twins. Bronson was excited and happy for Philip and Betty Ann, but Mother looked dazed. The sight of two more grandchildren – two more reasons for her to be called a grandmother – depressed her. She smiled and kissed Philip. She even acted motherly toward Betty Ann, but she didn't want to linger over the babies. As if she needed to flee reality, she booked herself and Bronson on a cruise the day after and was gone for the next two weeks.

Philip hired a nurse to help Betty Ann after she and the children were brought home. The arrival of the golden-haired twins was a major event at the hotel. After they were old enough to wheel about they became a regular phenomenon, stopping the guests in the middle of whatever they were doing in the lobby or card room and drawing small crowds. The two seemed to understand their power. They smiled, cooed and grabbed fingers dangled before them. Everyone commented on their good nature.

Christie was never more in her glory than when Betty Ann or Philip would permit her to push the double stroller through the corridors of the main building or over the garden walkways. As soon as she woke up in the morning she would ask to go visit Richard and Mellon. Nearly five now, she was old enough to rush off by herself and go to the hotel. Betty Ann described and I saw myself how seriously and maturely she handled her infant cousins. Mrs. Caldwell, the nurse, a pleasant middle-aged woman, told me she felt very confident about permitting Christie to hold the babies and even feed them.

"And they appear to love her as much as she loves them," Mrs. Caldwell said. "I've seen them stop crying the instant Christie has one of them in her arms. It amazes me how when one stops crying, the other follows suit. I've seen twins before, but never a pair so in tune with each other's feelings and wants."

That fall, when it came time to send Christie to grade school, she was in a terrible turmoil. She wanted to go to school very much, but she hated the idea that she would be away from the twins all day. Both Sissy and Mrs. Boston had started her reading, and she had a natural curiosity about everything. Her eagerness to learn was only harnessed by the energy of those around her who

286

were forced to answer question after question. She could exhaust anyone with her inquiries. I couldn't help but recall poor Randolph talking to her for hours when she was barely old enough to form intelligible sounds. But she had a remarkable attention span and great patience and persistence. When she wanted to do something she remained with it stubbornly until she satisfied herself.

This was especially true when it came to music. Milt Jacobs, our piano player, asked me if he could work with her on the piano; he was that impressed with her abilities. He wanted to do it during his free time, just for the pleasure of seeing her grow and achieve, but I insisted he be paid for the lessons. The result was that Christie had quite a full day for a five-year-old. She was in school until two-thirty. Julius would pick her up in the hotel limousine. At three-thirty she would go to the ballroom and take her piano lesson. Then she would rush out in time to help Mrs. Caldwell with the twins' dinner.

By now Christie was everyone's darling. I could come into the lobby and find her behind the receptionist's desk, standing on a stool, greeting people. They even taught her how to answer the phone and field reservation inquiries. The guests who called got a big kick out of hearing her tiny voice tell them the price of a room with a double bed or single bed. Of course, any other questions had to be referred to the receptionists.

In short, the hotel had become her playground. She knew all the bellhops by first name, as well as many of the waiters and busboys. She had gotten so she recognized and remembered the names of frequent guests, most of whom lavished affection and praise on her. I would never forget the first time she received a tip.

She came running into my office, all out of breath, her golden pigtails swinging over her shoulders, and held up the dollar.

"Look, Momma!" she cried.

"A dollar. Where did you get that?"

"Mr. Quarters gave it to me for bringing him a glass of warm milk in the card room," she said. "And I didn't spill a drop."

"Quarters?" I thought a moment. "Oh, you mean, Mr. Cauthers. Well, isn't that nice? You'll have to go show Daddy," I said.

"And Aunt Bet, too. I'm going right now," she cried, and she ran out holding her dollar tightly and proudly in her fist.

What a different sort of childhood Christie was having from the childhood Jimmy and I had had, I thought. We had been more like the guests, staying in one place or another for a short period of time, making friends and then moving off. Faces and names blurred in our minds after a while. I couldn't recall a single girlfriend I had had throughout grade school, even middle school. Christie, on the other hand, had developed an enormous extended family – the hotel family. She had dozens of people looking after her, loving her.

And she loved them. She had certainly inherited Michael's desire to be the center of attention. She craved society, wanted to perform in any way possible, be it playing her piano or singing or reciting something she had just learned. It didn't take much coaxing to get her to do any of it, just a request and applause.

The hotel had surely become a happy place for all of us. Thankfully, my fears about problems with Philip had diminished with every passing day. With his heavy involvement now in the hotel's business, and with the birth of his twins, Philip seemed to settle down to the life he had chosen and, like me, had accepted the cards fate had dealt. Whenever he and Betty Ann and Jimmy and I did anything together, he paid proper attention to Betty Ann, and although he looked at me longingly from time to time, he didn't disturb or frighten me with references to his undying love and his continual torment.

One warm summer day, however, when I was out in the gardens talking to Mrs. Caldwell, who had taken the twins out for a stroll, Philip came up beside me and whispered in my ear.

"You know why I am happy we had twins, don't you?" he said.

"Why?" I asked, expecting some sort of joke. He had a wide, soft smile on his face.

"Because it's as if there's one for you and one for Betty Ann. I know you and Jimmy have been trying to have another child and haven't been successful," he added quickly, before I could respond. "You would have been successful with me," he said. I felt the heat rise into my face. ' 'Which one do you think would be ours?" he asked in all seriousness.

For a moment I couldn't speak, so he continued to talk as he gazed down at the twins.

"I often imagine Richard is our child. He reminds me of you. I don't know why; he just does."

I pulled him out of Mrs. Caldwell's range of hearing.

"Philip, that is a sick thing to say. Those children are yours and Betty Ann's. It would break her heart to think that you fantasize one of them to be mine."

"I can't help what I dream," he said.

289

"Well, you should try," I snapped, and I walked away from him, my heart pounding.

I think what terrified me the most was the way my inability to become pregnant had developed into community news. Of course, it was only natural for people to wonder why Jimmy and I hadn't had a child of our own since my miscarriage. In a community as small as Cutler's Cove it wasn't hard to imagine that most people knew there was no physical reason for me not to become pregnant. This old seaside town had its share of gossips, just like anywhere else. On more than one occasion, especially during our phone conversations, Mother confirmed that the topic was frequently on people's minds.

"Catherine Peabody asked me why you and James haven't attempted to have another child," Mother said. "Can you imagine the gall? I wanted to ask her what business was it of hers, but instead I told her bluntly that you and James were being sensible. I said you were both too young and too involved with your work to become bogged down with a brood of offspring."

"Tell them whatever you like, Mother," I said dryly. The topic was deadening to me. I felt beaten down, defeated, exhausted over worrying about it. I was at the point of giving up and accepting the fact that it would never happen anyway.

I think Jimmy was beginning to feel that way, too. Not that we stopped making love or thinking about it. He just stopped asking me how I was and if I had any symptoms. Actually, what the birth of the twins and my inability to become pregnant did was put Jimmy's mind back on Fern. I knew that he and Daddy Longchamp had kept up a correspondence about her. We continually invited Daddy Longchamp and his new wife Edwina to the hotel, but he always had one reason or another why he couldn't come. Finally, one day Jimmy decided we should visit him.

I had left the hotel early to go to sit on the bench in our newly constructed gazebo. The late-afternoon sun spread long, cool shadows over the lawns and gardens. In the distance the calm, silvery ocean glittered. I felt pensive and moody. All day I had been recalling things about Momma Longchamp and my childhood, a time that seemed more like a dream now.

"So there you are," Jimmy said, approaching. "I've been looking for you."

"I got lazy," I said, "and decided to come home earlier today."

"You should be taking more time off. This hotel can run itself. Anyway, that's why I was looking for you," he said. "I received a new packet of pictures from Daddy Longchamp today. Look at how big Gavin's getting," he said, handing me the photographs.

"He's getting handsome, too," I said, gazing down at the dark-haired, dark-eyed boy. He had Daddy Longchamp's lean, hard look, but a very nice smile.

"I should go to see my new brother," he said. "It's not right that he and I have never met."

"Of course you should go, Jimmy. But maybe you should go yourself," I said.

"What? Why?"

"I don't know . . . maybe Daddy Longchamp is still very uncomfortable about seeing me," I said. "That's probably why he doesn't come here. You can tell him I was just too busy at the hotel to leave at this time."

291

"You sure it's not the other way around?" Jimmy asked.

"What do you mean?"

"You sure you're not uncomfortable about seeing him?" he pursued, his eyes narrow with suspicion.

"Jimmy, how can you say that? I wanted him to come to the hotel, didn't I?"

"Yeah, but maybe you always knew he wouldn't come," Jimmy said. "And you were never terribly upset when he didn't show up." He fixed his eyes on me, and I had to look down. It was as if Jimmy could look into my heart and see my fears.

"You were the one who talked me into forgiving him and going to see him," Jimmy reminded me. "And here you're the one who still hates him."

"Oh, Jimmy, I don't hate him. I'm just . . . just . . ."

"What?" he insisted.

"Afraid," I said. "I can't help it. I don't know why I should be, but I am."

He stared at me, confused.

"What are you afraid of? Raking up the past?"

"Oh, Jimmy," I said, finally letting it all burst out of me, "he raised us as brother and sister, and here we are married. I'm afraid to look him in the face."

"But – but he knew the truth!" Jimmy exclaimed.

"Jimmy, all the time I lived with him and Momma Longchamp I never felt I wasn't their child. I think they got so they believed it themselves. Truth sometimes changes. Like a chameleon, it transforms itself to fit where it is at the time. Daddy Longchamp can't look at us and not remember us sharing a room, sharing our meager meals, even sharing some clothing. And when he looks at me and remembers the past he's

292

most likely to feel bad, even though I won't want him to."

"But – "

"Jimmy, you go yourself. Just this first time," I pleaded. "I promise I'll go the next time," I said.

He stared at me a moment and then shook his head.

"All right," he finally said. "I want to talk to Daddy about Fern anyway. He's been trying to find out about her, too. I can't understand why Mr. Updike has been unable to find out anything all this time, especially with the services of a professional detective."

"Jimmy," I said after taking a deep breath, "we don't have the detective working on it anymore."

"What? Why not?" he demanded, his face turning beet red.

"I told you, Jimmy. There are secrecy laws, and we just can't break them. Mr. Updike advised me to stop."

"As far as I can see, rich people break laws whenever they have the need to, and then they hire fancy lawyers like Mr. Updike to make it all right. Maybe we need a different lawyer for this," he suggested. "One who's not so law-abiding. Anyway, why didn't you tell me we didn't have a detective working on it anymore?"

"I didn't want to make you unhappy, Jimmy."

"That wasn't right, Dawn. You should have told me. Daddy's been thinking we had the detective working all this time, too." He shook his head. "It wasn't right."

"Jimmy, even if we do find her, it's going to be strange for her. She's almost ten by now," I reminded him. "And she's been living with another family under another name. Most likely they never told her she was

293

adopted. We might do more harm than good at this point."

"I'm surprised at you, Dawn," he said, his eyes full of pain and anger. "If she was really your sister again, you would think differently, I'm sure." He turned and charged off, leaving me sitting in the gazebo.

My heart felt like a chunk of lead in my chest, and I felt the blood drain from my face. Jimmy had never before looked at me that angrily, nor had I ever hurt him that deeply. I was dumbfounded, shocked at myself. Why did I wait so long to tell him, and how could I make such a cold statement to him? It was as if Grandmother Cutler had put the words into my mouth.

I hurried after him and found that he had gone to the other side of the house and was just staring off at the horizon.

"Oh, Jimmy," I said, embracing him, "I'm so sorry. I didn't mean to hide anything from you, and I didn't mean to say those things. Of course we should find Fern. Of all people, I should remember how important it is to know who you really are. I don't know what came over me in there. I guess I'm just frustrated and unhappy about not getting pregnant. I know how much you want it."

"Don't you want it, too, Dawn?" he asked, his eyes shifting toward mine, searching, penetrating, digging for the truth.

"Yes, Jimmy, I do. I really do," I said with all my heart. He let out a deep breath.

"Okay," he said. "I'll go see Daddy by myself this time."

"Jimmy, if you really want me to go . . ."

"No," he said. "You might be right about it. Anyway, I won't be there long."

"I'll miss you no matter how short the time you're away," I said.

He kissed me, but it was as if a tiny crack had started across the shiny veneer of our love and marriage. His kiss wasn't as long or as hard, and as soon as he had given it he hurried off to pack.

I went dead inside. I felt like a small bird left behind with winter rushing down over the hills.

Reliving an
Old Nightmare

Jimmy left early the next morning. It was completely overcast, with thick layers of soiled gray clouds hovering above and threatening rain. Even the ocean looked ashen and drab, its morning tide churning with a dreary monotony. The winds were rough, seizing and shaking the trees mercilessly. I embraced myself while we waited on the porch for Julius to pick up Jimmy and take him to the airport. Christie had already gone to school, and Jimmy had said good-bye to her. All that remained were our good-byes. We were both putting them off until the final moment.

At breakfast our conversation centered around the list of things Jimmy had left for me to check for him at the hotel.

"I don't like rushing off like this," he said, "but if I don't just up and do it, I know I'll postpone it again and again."

"Don't worry, Jimmy," I assured him, "I'll see to it that everything you want done is done."

He nodded. We had been avoiding each other's eyes all morning. I had had a restless and troubled sleep, still regretting some of the things I had said to him and my reluctance to join him on his visit to Daddy Longchamp and his new family. I wanted to wake Jimmy up and apologize again and again, but he was in a deep sleep. I finally fell asleep myself just before morning and didn't even hear him get up and get dressed. I woke when I heard Mrs. Boston getting Christie ready for school.

Now we stood together watching the limousine approach.

"Well, okay," Jimmy said, lifting his suitcase, "I'll call you sometime tonight."

He leaned in to kiss me. I tried to hold on to his shoulders. I wanted to keep his lips on mine for as long as I could, but he pulled away as the limousine came to a stop in front of us.

"Jimmy!" I cried, my hand out toward him. He turned back as Julius took his bag to put into the trunk.

"What?" His eyes met mine, and I saw tears there, unshed but shining.

"Be careful," I said.

"I'll try. I'll call you," he repeated, and he got into the limousine. I stood there feeling numb and tiny as Julius got back into the limousine and drove him off. I didn't go into the house until the car was gone from my sight. My heart felt so empty, hollowed out, each thump echoing louder in the vacant chambers.

I ran back upstairs and flung myself on the bed, where I cried and cried like a hysterical schoolgirl. Mrs. Boston heard me and came to knock on the door.

"Are you all right, Dawn?" she asked.

"Yes, Mrs. Boston," I said, sitting up. "It's all right." I wiped my cheeks. "Don't worry."

"If you want anything, let me know," she said, her voice full of concern.

What I wanted, she couldn't provide, I thought. I wanted to heal the scars of years and years of painful living. I wanted to bury the sad and bitter memories still clinging tenaciously to the walls of my mind, clinging like spiteful bats, eager to take advantage of every dark moment to fly about and torment me. I wanted to gain new courage, to be able to face all of the ghosts and drive them back into the shadows where they belonged.

Jimmy had been so strong; his love for me was so great that he could overcome these old feelings and fears. I had seen the deep disappointment in his eyes when he gazed at me just before he left. In my heart I felt the ache that had made a home in his, and I knew I was dissatisfying him in a serious way, but it was as if there were invisible chains binding me to my fears and weaknesses. I needed a little more time to break them, just a little more, I thought.

I decided the only thing to do now was to bury myself in work so I could keep my mind off the sadness I felt with Jimmy gone. I filled my eyes with words and numbers to prevent them from seeing Jimmy's dark, sad eyes again and again. Every time I finished something, I leapt to find something else to do, no matter how minor or how unimportant. At times I thought I resembled poor Randolph, who had become obsessed with insignificant details. Now I could understand why that had happened to him, I thought. He was only trying to keep himself from facing ugly realities.

Unfortunately, however, before the morning was over I could stop looking for things to do in order to occupy myself. Something serious came my way, and Philip had gone to Virginia Beach on business, so he couldn't be of any assistance. Mr. Stanley, who was in charge of the chambermaids, came knocking on my office door. He looked terribly flustered when he entered.

"What's wrong, Mr. Stanley?" I asked before he reached my desk.

"Mrs. Longchamp, something dreadful," he replied. "Mary White, one of our chambermaids, came to tell me that one of our guests has passed away in his room . . . Mr. Parker."

"Mr. Parker?" I knew him well. He was an elderly gentleman who had been coming to the hotel for twenty years at least. He was a very kind and distinguished man, a widower. Last year he had given Christie a hundred dollars for her birthday. "Are you sure he's – "

"I went up to the room myself and found him slumped in his chair by the window. I'm afraid it's true," Mr. Stanley said, fidgeting with his shirt collar.

"I see. All right. Keep the room closed, of course. I'll go speak with Mr. Dorfman and see how such things were handled in the past."

"I'm sorry," Mr. Stanley said, as if this was all somehow his fault. "I did tell Mary to keep it to herself for now," he added.

"Fine." I rose from my chair and walked out with him.

"I'll be in my office," he said. I went directly to Mr. Dorfman's.

"How unfortunate," he said when I told him what Mr. Stanley had discovered. "However, it has happened before. When you cater to older people – "

"What do we do in situations like this?" I asked quickly.

"Well, I'll call for an ambulance, of course. It's best the other guests not know that he's actually passed away. I'll speak to the ambulance attendants myself when they arrive. They'll understand and cooperate. This is a resort community."

"Understand? Cooperate?" I shook my head in confusion. "What do you mean?"

"They will wheel him out with an oxygen mask on his face, and we'll say that he's having some trouble breathing and is being taken to the hospital," Mr. Dorfman explained.

"What? Why would we do that?"

"It's the way Mrs. Cutler handled similar situations in the past," he replied. "That way . . . the impact of his death doesn't lie like a shadow over the hotel and the other guests."

"I don't know," I said. "It seems very deceitful."

"I can only tell you what Mrs. Cutler has done in the past. I think if she were here," Mr. Dorfman said softly, "she would tell you poor Mr. Parker wouldn't mind. You do have a house full of guests, many of them elderly.

"Something like this can get them thinking – wrongly, of course – that they should examine every morsel of their food, where their rooms are located, what kind of ventilation they have . . . believe me, it can create a host of problems. All of a sudden every ache and pain, every skipped heartbeat will signal serious illness, and the doctors will be running in and out, not to mention Julius carting people over to the hospital for checkups.

"I hate to put it so coldly," he concluded, "but it's not good for the hotel's image. This is a place where people relax, enjoy, have only good times and bring out only good memories." He paused and took a deep breath. "I

300

think I'm giving you Mrs. Cutler's speech verbatim," he added, amazed himself.

"Naturally," he continued, "I'll give Mr. Updike a call and keep him apprised of the situation. There are always legal considerations."

He sat there staring at me, just waiting for me to give him the go-ahead. Part of me wanted to be rebellious and contrary, just because we were handling it the way Grandmother Cutler would have handled it. I wanted to order him to call the mortician and have a hearse drawn up in front of the hotel. Somehow it would be like slapping Grandmother Cutler across her arrogant face.

But another part of me – the part that had been growing and developing – realized how immature and silly that would be. I would only hurt myself and the people I loved.

"All right, Mr. Dorfman," I said. "Carry on with this the way we have in the past."

He nodded and lifted the phone receiver. He had the ambulance come to the side entrance of the hotel. Some guests would see them take Mr. Parker out, of course, but it wouldn't be as big an event as it would if the ambulance was right in front and the attendants wheeled Mr. Parker through the lobby. Mr. Updike came by to make sure it all went according to plan.

Somehow it seemed appropriate that it continued to be a gray day with intermittent downpours of rain, yet I couldn't help but feel devious and underhanded when they wheeled the old man on a gurney through the hallways with an oxygen mask over his face. I especially felt this way when guests asked me what had happened and I told them Mr. Parker wasn't feeling well and

301

we thought it best he be taken to the hospital for examination.

"They're only going to ask about him later on," I told Mr. Updike. "And of course, they will learn that he has died."

"Yes," he said, "but somehow the impact of his death is lessened when it occurs at a hospital rather than right here." He patted me on the shoulder. "You did very well, my dear." I could see it was on the tip of his tongue to say, "Mrs. Cutler would be very proud of you," but he saw the glint of anger in my eyes and simply muttered, "Very well."

The events surrounding Mr. Parker's death and removal had taken my mind off Jimmy's being gone, but when I finally returned to my office after it was all over I regretted that he wasn't at my side during the crisis. I realized how much I leaned on him, needed his strength and reassurance. I was tempted to try to reach him in Texas to tell him what had happened, but I thought it wouldn't be fair. Looking at the clock, I realized he must have just arrived and was involved with meeting his new brother. My problems could wait until later.

By late afternoon I sat back in my chair. A feeling of exhaustion washed over me. All of the mental turmoil had taken its toil. I felt drained. I was sure I would sleep well tonight, despite myself. Christie had returned from school, taken her piano lesson and gone to be with the twins. She asked to eat her dinner with them, and I agreed. I wasn't very hungry myself and thought I would just have some tea and toast later. I began to close up my books and reports to leave the office and return to the house so I could dress to greet the guests at dinner. Tonight, because of what had occurred, that seemed to be more important than usual to do.

But just as I stood up I heard a gentle rapping at the door and called for whoever it was to enter. It was Betty Ann.

Betty Ann had gained weight with her pregnancy, of course, but it had filled her out and, I thought, made her more attractive. She hadn't lost much since giving birth. I thought she was still quite happy living at the hotel. She often had old college friends visit and had made friends with some of the more affluent members of Cutler's Cove, mainly because of the dinners Mother staged. In any case, what with caring for her twins, the work she did at the hotel and her social life, she appeared quite occupied and content. So I was surprised when she came in, closed the door softly behind her and proceeded to burst into tears.

This seems to be a day for sadness, I thought. It was as if the dreary sky, the rain and the gray world without had managed to seep into our lives through every crack and cranny in our walls of happiness. Every dark thought, every sorrowful and unhappy moment in our pasts was resurrected to bloom in this soil of depression. Melancholy would have its day today.

"What's wrong, Betty Ann?" I cried, coming to her quickly. She answered with louder and harder sobs. I guided her to the sofa and helped her to sit down. She had made her face puffy with so much crying.

"Oh, Dawn," she moaned through her sobs, "I can't stand it anymore. I've got to tell someone. I'm sorry."

"That's all right. There's no need to apologize. We're sisters," I said. "I don't mind your telling me your

303

troubles. What happened? Is it something to do with the twins?" I asked.

"Oh, no, they're fine, thank goodness."

"Something with your family?" I pursued, already understanding how her socialite mother might be giving her trouble about her life at the hotel. On more than one occasion Betty Ann had remarked to me that her mother thought it was beneath her to greet guests and work as a hostess.

"No," she said. She took a deep breath and then blurted, "It's Philip."

"Philip? What about him?" I sat back. He was telling her things about me, I thought fearfully.

"Every night for the last week he's insisted on sleeping in another room. I don't know why. I haven't done anything to him. We haven't had an argument; he just . . . gets up and leaves."

"Gets up and leaves? You mean he gets into bed with you and then – "

"Yes," she said, wiping her eyes and breathing in deeply again, "he just gets up and disappears. At first I thought . . . he was seeing someone else . . . going someplace to meet some nasty chambermaid or someone like that. I was too frightened to move, to do anything, even to ask him where he had gone."

"I can't see Philip going to meet any of our chambermaids," I said.

"No, he's not doing anything like that." She brought the handkerchief she had been holding tightly in her hands to her nose and blew into it. "I got up and followed him last night. He's just . . . just going to another room."

"Another room? What other room?" I asked.

"Your old suite," she replied. It was as if someone had tossed a pailful of ice water over my head. I felt the chilling streaks run over my shoulders, down the back of my neck and over my spine.

"My old suite?"

"Yes. Oh, Dawn, does this mean he can't stand being beside me for any length of time? Is this the way a divorce begins?" she asked, wide-eyed.

"No, I don't think . . . Didn't you ask him why he's doing this?" I inquired.

"I did. This morning. He said he just gets restless and has to move around. He told me not to make a big deal over it and forbade me to tell anyone, but I can't get it out of my mind, and I knew you wouldn't tell him I told. But what should I do? It isn't normal, is it? Nothing like this has happened between you and Jimmy, has it?"

I shook my head.

"You're just going to have to tell him how much it upsets you," I said. "Discuss it quietly and make him understand."

What else could I tell her? I wondered.

"Should I?"

"Of course. If you let him see how much it bothers you, he's sure to change," I promised, even though I had serious doubts deep in my heart.

She smiled.

"It's nice to have someone like you to speak to," she said. "I felt bad about coming to see you after all you've had to do today," she added, "but I couldn't help myself."

"It's all right." I patted her hand, and she looked quite reassured.

"I'll be with you to greet the guests tonight and

smooth things over," she promised. "Philip hasn't returned yet and doesn't know about poor Mr. Parker."

"He'll know soon enough," I said, standing. She rose, and we walked to the door.

"I'll go to the children's dining room to see how the children are doing with their dinner," she said, and she kissed me on the cheek. "Thank you again."

I smiled and opened the door. I watched her walk off, and then, after she rounded the corner and disappeared, I couldn't help myself. I hurried down the corridor and swung through the lobby to the family section. Quickly, before anyone would take much notice, I walked to the stairway and went up to my old suite. The door was closed but unlocked.

I opened it and entered. We had left all the old furniture here, having bought new things for the house, along with new linens, pillowcases and blankets. I stepped into the bedroom and stood staring ahead, my arms crossed, my hands on my shoulders. For a moment it was as if the air were too hot to breathe. My face felt absolutely feverish.

The blanket was pulled back on the bed. Neatly laid out on the side where I slept was the nightgown – my nightgown – Philip had taken for Betty Ann to wear on their honeymoon. I approached slowly, anticipating. When I stood beside the bed it was there, just as I had suspected: the scent of my perfume. The pillowcase and sheet seemed saturated with it. The other pillow still had the imprint of Philip's head on it.

I stood there, unable to move, both frightened and fascinated with the bizarreness of it all. Then I thought I heard footsteps in the corridor outside, and my heart began to race. I went to the doorway and listened. If

306

it was Philip coming home, I would hate to have him find me here, I thought. I didn't know how he would react; he would surely understand Betty Ann had come to see me to complain. The footsteps stopped at their door. I peeked around the jamb and saw it was Philip. He went into his suite.

The moment he disappeared I hurried out and down the stairs. I didn't look back. I felt as though I were fleeing from nightmares. I hurried through the family section and burst out into the lobby, never so grateful for the noise, the people and the activity. Catching my breath, I left the hotel for home to change for dinner.

Almost the moment I walked through my front door I felt how deeply I missed Jimmy. Perhaps it was because I was without him for the first time in our new home. So much of it had the feel of him. His favorite easy chair looked so empty to me, as did his seat at our dining room table. I was haunted by the clothing in his closet and the scent of his after-shave lotion in the master bedroom.

I dressed as quickly as I could and hurried back to the hotel to greet the guests for dinner. Betty Ann joined me, looking refreshed and happy again. Considering what she was going through with Philip, I was impressed with the style she showed, the poise, the ease with which she handled everyone and made them feel welcome.

"I asked Philip to meet me later. We're going to go somewhere private and have a cocktail and talk. Everything will be all right," she added, her eyes glimmering with hope.

"Of course it will," I said, but in the back of my mind I thought, She doesn't have any idea how deep her problem with Philip is.

He joined us moments later.

"I hear I missed a lot of excitement," he said, and then proceeded to tell me about another time a guest had died at the hotel.

"I don't think I was more than five or six, but I got a peek into the room and saw her sprawled out on her bed, her skin as white as fresh milk. But what I remember the most was how much makeup she wore. Apparently she had put it on just before she died."

"Let's not talk about these things anymore, Philip," Betty Ann begged. "It's too unpleasant and makes me dreadfully nervous."

Both Philip and I turned to her because she sounded so much like Mother.

"Fine. Dinner?" He held out his arms for us to take so he could escort us both in. "With Jimmy gone, I'm doing double duty tonight."

"No thank you, Philip," I said. "I'm taking Christie back to the house and just having a little something tonight. You two enjoy," I added, and I left before he could react.

It wasn't really until the evening that the impact of Jimmy's going away hit Christie, too. Never before had one of us left and the other remained behind. The novelty wore off quickly as her precocious mind drove her to question after question.

"Why did Daddy have to go now? Why doesn't his daddy come here to see us instead? Why couldn't we all go along?" None of my explanations satisfied her. In the end she pouted. She had Michael's intolerance of things that didn't go her way.

I nearly jumped out of my skin when the phone rang. I hoped and prayed it was Jimmy. I was never so happy to hear his voice. After I told him how much I missed him, I described what had happened to poor Mr. Parker and how we had handled it.

"Sounds just awful," he said. "I'm sorry I wasn't there to help you."

"You can't imagine how much I wished you were. But I'm glad you've finally met your new brother. How's Daddy?"

"Fine. He's very disappointed you're not here," he said, "but he promised he would come to the hotel very soon. Here," Jimmy said, "let him tell you himself."

My breath caught. Daddy and I hadn't spoken for so long.

"How you doin', honey?" he asked. My throat was so choked, I couldn't speak. It felt as if my heart had dropped into my stomach. All my memories of Daddy being loving and warm to me rushed over me. I pushed aside all the times he was angry or had drunk too much whiskey.

"I'm fine, Daddy," I finally said. "And you?"

"We're doin'the best we can. I'm sorry you couldn't get away," he said. "I think of you often."

"I think of you, too, Daddy."

"I know you had a lot to do with my getting out of prison as soon as I did. Always figured you were a smart one, Dawn. Always knew you'd be somebody," he bragged.

"I'm nobody important, Daddy. A lot of people help me here, and things were pretty much set before I started doing anything," I told him.

"No sense in being modest with me, Dawn, honey. I know you too well. You can't fool an old fool," he said, and he laughed. I remembered him saying that often.

Now that I heard his voice, I regretted not going with Jimmy even more.

"Jimmy's tellin' me all about your hotel. It sounds pretty nice. We'll get up there sometime this year. That's a promise and a half," he said.

"I hope so, Daddy."

"Here's Jimmy again."

"Dawn."

"Oh, Jimmy, I miss you something terrible, and Christie is acting like a spoiled brat just because you left and we didn't go. I'm sorry."

"I miss you, too, Dawn, but I might have some good news for you in a day or so. Daddy and I have been working on something, and I think it's going to pay off."

"What, Jimmy?"

"I don't want to say anything until I'm sure," he said.

"Let me talk," Christie cried, pulling on my skirt.

"Here's Christie," I said, and I gave her the phone. She hugged it to her as if she could feel Jimmy as well as speak to him through the receiver.

"Hi, Daddy," she said. "When are you coming home already?" She listened, and after a moment she gave me one of her little furious looks and then promised Jimmy she would behave. Then he said something that lit up her face.

"Daddy's bringing me something special when he comes home," she told me when she handed me the receiver.

"If you're good," I added.

"I'll be good," she said.

"Hi. It's me again," I said into the receiver.

"Hi, me. Kiss yourself for me tonight, will you?"
Jimmy said.

"Oh, Jimmy."

"Talk to you soon. I love you."

"I love you, Jimmy. Hurry back."

I held the receiver even after he had cradled his and
the dial tone had started. I was trying to hold on to his
voice for as long as I could.

"Why are you crying, Mommy?" Christie asked. I
hadn't even realized I was. I felt the tears on my cheeks
and then laughed.

"I'm just happy to speak to Daddy," I said.

"If you're happy, why do you cry?" she asked.

"Sometimes you do. You'll see. Come on. It's time
you put on your pajamas." I took her hand and led her
upstairs. It was Mrs. Boston's day off, and she was with
her sister in town. That morning she hadn't wanted to
leave when she heard I would be alone, but I insisted.

"I've been alone plenty of times before, Mrs. Boston," I told her bravely. Now I wished I hadn't. If I
ever needed company, I need it now, I thought.

"I want Daddy to kiss me good night," Christie
complained when I tucked her in and kissed her.

"You know he's not here, Christie."

"I still want him to kiss me. I'm not going to sleep
until he comes home and kisses me good night," she
insisted.

"Fine. Lie there with your eyes open all night," I
said.

She folded her little arms over her chest and glared
up at me defiantly. I knew I should have been more
understanding and sympathetic, but her unhappiness
only served to underscore my own.

I left but peeked in on her every fifteen minutes. Amazingly, she kept herself awake for nearly an hour before her eyelids grew too heavy and she had to fall asleep.

After I put Christie to bed I went into my bedroom and got into my nightgown. I decided I would read and read until I got so tired I would pass out. But my eyes were just sliding over the pages, the words meaningless to me. I was about to give up and turn off the lights when the doorbell sounded.

Who would come to the house? I wondered. Anyone who needed me at the hotel would simply call. Curious but apprehensive, I slipped into my silk dressing gown and started down the stairs, belting my gown as I descended. I opened the door and found Philip gazing in at me. He swayed and smiled widely.

"Evenin'," he mumbled, and he seized the door jamb to steady himself.

"Philip Cutler, are you drunk?" I asked.

"Drunk? Nooooooooo. Oh . . . maybe, just a trifle," he said, squeezing his thumb and forefinger together. "May I come in?" he asked, straightening up.

"It's late, Philip. What do you want?" I asked, not giving an inch of ground.

"Simply to . . . to . . . talk," he said, and he fell forward, stepping just in time to keep from landing on his face. I had no choice but to close the door.

"How could you do this, Philip? Don't you care what the guests will say if they see you? What's come over you?"

He covered his ears with his hands.

"My God, it's as if she rose from the grave," he

312

moaned. " 'How could you do this?' " he mimicked.
" 'What will the guests think if they see you?' "

"Philip!"

"I need something to drink," he muttered, and he
stumbled his way into our den. He knew where Jimmy
kept our whiskey and headed directly toward it.

"You've had enough to drink, Philip," I said. I cut
him off in the middle of the room and grabbed his right
arm, spinning him around.

"Dawn," he said, smiling, "you look lovely tonight.
Just the way I always imagine you, with your hair down.
You're wearing one of your sheer nightgowns under
that, aren't you?" he asked, licking his lips.

"Philip, you turn yourself around and march yourself
back to the hotel and your wife this moment, do you hear
me?" I commanded. He nodded, but he didn't move.

"My wife," he said, and he fixed his eyes on me,
his lips moving into a grotesque mockery of a smile.
"You could have been my wife if that security guard
hadn't recognized your father." He seized my shoulders
and pressed his forehead to my hair. "We would have
eloped before Grandmother could have said anything,"
he whispered. From the way he spoke, I knew it was a
fantasy he replayed time and time again.

"Philip, that's ridiculous; it's ridiculous to think and
to dream such things."

"No, it isn't," he replied. I couldn't stand the odor
of his whiskey breath and started to pull myself from
his embrace, but his fingers tightened, and he pressed
his right hand against my back, running it up my spine.
His lips brushed over my eyes. I struggled harder
until I broke from his hold. He staggered, his eyes
glazed.

313

"Wait, Dawn," he said, his voice nearly a whisper now, "it's not too late for us."

"What are you talking about, Philip? How can you even think these things?" I said, taking another step back. He shook his head vigorously.

"You don't understand. Listen . . . listen," he pleaded. He stepped toward me. "I know you and Jimmy have been trying to have a child and have failed all this time. But we wouldn't fail," he said in a loud whisper. "We wouldn't."

"What?" Instinctively I brought my hands to my bosom.

"We wouldn't fail, and no one would have to know, not even Jimmy. He'd think the baby was his own, don't you see? It would be our little secret, our precious little secret." His smile widened as the possibility of such a fantasy coming true suddenly loomed in his eyes. "Look at how pretty my children are. Ours would be no different, and if the child had golden hair, too, why, no one would think anything of it, seeing the color of your hair.

"I want to do this for you . . . for us . . . for the family," he pledged.

"Philip, you're mad, even madder than I ever imagined. I know that some of what you're saying, you're saying because you're drunk, but even to have these thoughts is terrible. I'm your sister. We share family blood."

"It won't matter." He closed his eyes and shook his head vigorously. "It won't. We have different fathers."

"Philip," I snapped. "Even if we weren't related, I would never betray Jimmy. I would never be unfaithful."

314

"Sure you would," he insisted, smiling licentiously. "You're like me. You've inherited some of Mother, too."

"*No,*" I cried. "I want you out of here now. I insist you leave. Go home to your wife and sleep off these distorted and terrible thoughts. Go!" I ordered, pointing toward the door. Desperation made my voice high and shrill. He staggered for a moment, and then his debauched smile returned.

"Dawn . . . our child . . ." He came toward me. I started to flee the room, but even in his drunken state he had quick enough reflexes to reach out and seize my left arm, pulling me toward him and toward the sofa.

"Philip! Stop this!" I screamed. He locked his arms around mine, holding me down. Then he began to flood my face with his wet kisses. "*Philip, you're doing a horrible thing again!*" I tried to kick my way free, but I only lost my balance and fell back to the sofa with him over me. Once again I screamed; I even tried to bite his ear, but he didn't release his viselike grip.

"Dawn, oh, Dawn," he chanted. His mouth began to nuzzle between my breasts. I grew dizzy with the struggle. I couldn't believe what was happening. When he started to bring his right hand to my thigh, I pummeled his head and shoulder with my free left fist, but it was like a fly attacking an elephant; his drunken stupor kept him from feeling any pain. He was drowning in his fantasy. It was almost too late.

And then I heard Christie's small voice. I stopped struggling and listened again. She was calling from behind us, from the doorway. Miraculously, Philip heard her as well, and it brought his attack to an end. He froze.

315

"*Momma!*" Christie called. I pushed Philip away and sat up, quickly straightening my robe and my hair. I couldn't let her see what was happening.

"What's wrong, honey?" I asked, forcing a smile. I swung my legs out from under Philip, who sat back on the sofa, his eyes sewn shut.

"I thought I heard Daddy," she said. "Is Daddy home?"

"Oh, no, Christie." I rose from the sofa, went to her and picked her up to hold her in my arms. "It's not Daddy. It's Uncle Philip."

"Uncle Philip?" Her sleepy eyes shifted toward the couch. Philip opened his; he was just sober enough to realize what was happening.

"Hi, Christie," he said, waving.

"Is Aunt Bet here, too?" Christie asked.

"No. Uncle Philip just stopped by to tell me something about the hotel. But he was just leaving," I added pointedly.

"Yes, that's right." He struggled to his feet and straightened his own clothing. "It's late. So," he declared, "I shall wander on home." He turned and started toward the door. "Home to my bed of dreams," he added. He stopped at the doorway and turned, bowing. "Good night, ladies."

Christie giggled. I said nothing until he opened the door and was gone.

"Uncle Philip's funny," Christie said.

"Not really," I replied, but she didn't hear or understand. "Let's go back to bed," I told her, and I carried her up. After I put her in again I went back downstairs to be sure the front door was locked. Then I put out all the lights and went up to bed, my heart still pounding. I pulled Jimmy's pillow close to me and pressed my face into it to stifle my tears. That was how I finally fell asleep.

In the morning the events of the night before seemed more like a nightmare. I got Christie dressed and ready for school; then I dressed myself, and we had breakfast together. After I sent her off I went to the hotel and my office. I wasn't there an hour before I heard a knock on the door. It was Philip. He looked tired, drained, his normally immaculate style flawed by loose strands of hair, a poorly knotted tie and drooping eyelids.

"Dawn," he began. I glared at him. "I just came by to apologize for my behavior last night. I drank too much, and . . . and I lost my sense of proportion," he confessed.

"Don't you *ever* come to my house without an invitation again, Philip," I snarled. I was not in any sort of forgiving mood. "To think that Christie almost saw – "

"I know; I know. I'm sorry, and I hate myself for it," he said. Humbly he bowed his head and gazed down at the floor. My anger abated, and the tension left my body as I relaxed back in my chair.

"You need to see someone, Philip. You're disturbed. I'm afraid if you don't, you'll end up like Randolph." He lifted his head and cut his eyes toward me sharply. "You're already doing strange things."

"She's told you, hasn't she?" he asked quickly.

"No one has had to tell me anything, Philip. I've seen for myself." He nodded.

"Are you going to tell Jimmy? About last night, I mean?"

"No," I said. "If I did, he would kill you."

317

Philip nodded again.

"I'm sorry," he repeated. "It won't happen again, I promise, and I will . . . try to find someone to talk to," he pledged.

"Good."

He gazed at me longingly for a moment and then turned and quickly left. The moment he was gone I released the breath I had trapped in my lungs. All I could do was hope what he said was true. I meant it when I said I wouldn't tell Jimmy. I knew he had always harbored some suspicions about Philip, and this would just confirm it all and send him into a rage.

When the phone rang an hour or so after Philip's apology and I heard Jimmy's voice, I had the terrible feeling that he somehow sensed something had happened, even over all the distance between us. But he was calling for another reason, a reason that would blind him to anything else.

"Dawn," he began, "I told you I might be calling you today with some good news. Well, I am!"

"What is it, Jimmy? I've never heard you so excited," I said, growing excited myself.

"Ready for this? I've been giving Daddy a little money to invest in a project of ours."

"What project?"

"Wait. Just listen. When Daddy was in prison he met a man who did some work from time to time investigating things. That's what got him into prison – he found out someone's deep, dark secret and tried to blackmail him.

"Anyway, Daddy put this person on our case as soon as he was released from prison, and guess what he has done."

318

"I can't imagine, Jimmy. What?"

"He's located Fern," Jimmy said.

For a moment I couldn't respond. My heart began to thump with excitement. Images of Fern as a baby flashed before my eyes. I recalled that first time I had looked at her in the maternity ward and the disappointment I felt when I saw she had no resemblance to me; but I also remembered the hours and hours I spent taking care of her, and how she used to cry for me to hold her and sing to her. Momma Longchamp had often apologized to me because I had to spend so much time taking care of Fern.

"You ain't got time to be a little girl yourself," she would say, "rushin' home from school every day to help me take care of a baby."

But I didn't mind. It was fascinating to watch Fern grow and discover things around her. For me, she was like a real-life doll, the ultimate little girl's plaything.

"Are you sure, Jimmy, absolutely positive he's located our Fern?"

"Absolutely," Jimmy replied.

"Have you seen her?"

"Of course not," Jimmy said. "She's not in Texas; she's in New York City. That's where her stepparents eventually moved. She lives in a townhouse in Manhattan, not very far from where you went to school and where you lived.

"Just think, Dawn," Jimmy said, "all the time you were there, you were so close to her. Why, you might have passed her on the sidewalk and not even noticed," he said. The possibility stole my breath away.

"Oh, Jimmy, what do you think we should do?" I asked, my heart pounding even harder.

"First I'll come right home, and then the two of us will go to see her. I'm sure it's just as you suspect – she doesn't even know we exist.

"But she will," Jimmy pledged. "She will very soon."

320

Seeing Fern Again

Jimmy sat on the sofa in my office and excitedly rattled off the details provided by the man he and Daddy Longchamp had hired. Right after Jimmy called me in the morning he had started out for home, and when he arrived he had come directly to my office. Christie hadn't even seen him yet, and very few people in the hotel knew he had returned.

"The couple's name is Osborne, Clayton and Leslie. Clayton Osborne is an investment broker on Wall Street. His wife has recently begun to enjoy some success as an artist, placing some of her paintings in galleries around the city. She has her own studio in Greenwich Village."

"How old are they?"

"They're both in their mid-thirties."

"Do they have any other children? Adopted or otherwise?" I asked.

"No. They have a townhouse on First Avenue in Manhattan and have been living there for nearly nine years. Before that they lived in Richmond. Fern goes to a very expensive private school," Jimmy concluded, obviously proud of accomplishing what Mr. Updike and his high-priced private detective had been unable to do.

However, listening to these details about people who had no idea we were snooping around them made me feel like an eavesdropper, a Peeping Tom. How would I like someone watching me, following me, taking notes? After all these years they probably had no suspicions they were being observed, no fears concerning themselves and Fern.

"They sound well-to-do and accomplished," I remarked. "Especially if they own a townhouse in that section of the city."

"So? What does that have to do with anything?" Jimmy snapped. I could see he was on a short fuse.

"Nothing," I said quickly. "I'm just glad she was able to have nice things and live comfortably."

"Yeah, I suppose we should be happy about that," he admitted.

"Well, what do we do now, Jimmy?" I asked.

"I'm going to pick up that phone on your desk and dial their number and tell them directly who we are and what we want," he replied firmly.

"What do we want, Jimmy?" I asked because I wasn't sure what we would do once we arrived in New York.

He looked surprised for a moment.

"Well, we want to . . . to meet Fern, of course, and see how she is, how she's grown, what she's like. She's my sister," he declared, sounding like someone demanding his rights.

But I couldn't help being nervous about it. Jimmy wasn't about to accept anything less, and any sort of rejection was sure to set him off like a firecracker. There was no telling what he would do then. I was sure he would make that clear to Clayton Osborne. Nevertheless, I couldn't help anticipating trouble. His

322

call was coming like a bolt of lightning out of a clear blue sky – no warning, no hints, nothing but sharp, sizzling shock.

He stood up.

"It's time to make the call," he announced.

I got up from my seat so he could sit behind the desk to use the phone. He moved right to it and began dialing the number he had been given. I couldn't help pacing about like a caged tigress, waiting, but trying to close off my emotions and clamp down on them.

"Is this Mr. Clayton Osborne?" he began as soon as the man had answered. I held my breath and listened. "My name is James Gary Longchamp," he said, pronouncing each part of his name like an oath, slowly, with determination and force. I could see from the look on his face that there was a dead silence on the other end. "Mr. Osborne? You know who I am," Jimmy prodded. "Fern is my sister."

In a way, Clayton Osborne had to be feeling a little like Daddy Longchamp had felt the day the police came to our door to arrest him and take me away, I thought. I meant what I had said to Jimmy before he had left for Texas: Daddy and Momma Longchamp had never done anything to make me feel I wasn't really their child, and surely after all those years they had come to accept it as so themselves. We believe in our own illusions if we live with them so long. I imagined Clayton and Leslie Osborne must have buried the truth and in their own minds made Fern their true child. Now here was Jimmy digging up the past and throwing the cold water of reality over their warm fantasies in one fell swoop.

There were more long periods of silence after things Jimmy said or, rather, demanded. The conversation continued for a while longer, and then Jimmy concluded by making an appointment for us to be at their townhouse tomorrow between five and six in the afternoon. When he cradled the phone and sat back he looked drained. For a long moment he was silent. Then he ran his hand over his hair and stood up.

"It's settled," he said. "We can see her, but only if we keep our identities secret. He insisted on that, and I had no choice but to agree. As long as we're going to visit as friends of theirs, he promises to have Fern present. Of course, her name is no longer Fern. They dropped that as soon as they got her."

"What's her new name?" I asked.

"Kelly, Kelly Ann Osborne," Jimmy disdainfully spat. It had a nice ring to it, but I was afraid to say so.

"What else did he tell you about her?"

"He says she's precocious for a ten-year-old. That's the way he put it, 'precocious.' From the way he spoke about her, I guess that means she's ahead of her age."

"Yes, like Christie."

"Ummm." He thought a moment.

"What's wrong?" I asked, seeing a familiar look of worry on his face. There was a depth, an intensity to his gaze, dimming the brightness in his otherwise pearl-black eyes.

"I don't know. He didn't sound proud of her. To tell you the truth," he added, looking up sharply, "he sounds like a stuffy type, speaking out of his nose." He shrugged. "Maybe he just has a cold."

"Maybe he's just in shock, Jimmy."

"Yeah. He kept asking how did we get his number, how did we get his name. I skipped over his questions and asked him questions of my own." Jimmy's eyes brightened, and he slapped his hands together. "Just think, Dawn. After nearly nine years we're going to set eyes on Fern again."

The radiance in his face set my own heart racing. What would it be like? Would she take one look at us and know, especially one look at Jimmy? By now the resemblances in her features would be clear, I thought, but wasn't there also some unseen thing, some magical feeling that would trigger her recognition? I recalled the first time I had set eyes on Philip, that feeling I had first mistaken for romance. There was something in his eyes that told me we were already very close, linked by blood, by heritage. I just didn't know it, didn't understand at the time. Perhaps, like me, Fern was too young to comprehend these feelings and would mistake them for something else. She would be confused, not enlightened, and we would move in and out of her life like ships gliding silently in the twilight, vaguely aware of each other in the semidarkness, but deaf to the inner voices that told us who we really were.

"Yes, Jimmy," I said. "I can't wait, but I won't lie. I'm a little scared, too."

He paused and looked at me in that special way that kept my love for him always alive and thriving.

"So am I, Dawn," he confessed. "So am I."

We made arrangements for our trip immediately. Christie was very confused, even angry about Jimmy's arriving and departing in less than a day. When she heard I was going, too, she demanded to go along and then cried and finally pouted when we said she couldn't. But fortunately, Jimmy hadn't forgotten to bring her back something from Texas: a model of a Texas ranch with tiny cattle and horses and ranch hands of all sorts, some with lassos in their fists. There were women and children, the women involved in household chores, one churning butter. There was even a tiny porch with tiny furniture, including a grandmother seated and knitting in a miniature rocking chair that really rocked. The model had to be put together. However, I thought Jimmy was happy about that – it took his mind off the trip to New York. He didn't come to bed until it was all finished and set up in Christie's room.

"Well, that should keep her occupied until we get home," he said, crawling in beside me. He snuggled up. "I really missed you when I was in Texas," he said.

"I missed you, too, and I was sorry I didn't make myself go," I admitted.

"Daddy's different. It's almost as if he's a completely changed man," Jimmy said.

"How so?"

"I don't know. He's . . . a lot more settled. He doesn't ever stay out drinking, Edwina says, and he just dotes on his new son. I wish," he added wistfully, "he had been this sort of daddy with me."

My heart nearly broke when I heard him say that. Tears burned behind my eyelids. All I could do was lean over and kiss him tenderly on the cheek. He turned to me and smiled. Then he lightly brushed the back of his hand over my cheek.

"I do love you so," he said, and he held me close. "Let's never get mad at each other again," he whispered.

"Never," I promised, but never was one of those words hard to believe in. Never again to be sad or troubled or lonely seemed like an impossible dream, something too magical for the world we were in.

We lay there quietly, both of us waiting and welcoming sleep to yank us back from the sad memories of yesterday.

Early the next morning I rose and went to the hotel to see about some things that had to be done before we left. We didn't say a word to anyone about the real purpose of our trip. Philip and Betty Ann simply thought we were going on a quick shopping spree. They were surprised, but not suspicious. We made reservations at the Waldorf and arrived in the hotel early in the afternoon. A mostly overcast sky cleared so that it was bright and blue by the time we had settled in. We had a late lunch, both of us fidgety and nervous. I did do some shopping around the hotel, mostly just to keep my mind occupied. Finally Jimmy said it was time to take a cab to the Osbornes' address.

Their brownstone was located in one of those clean and neat enclaves of New York City, a section that looked immune to all the noise and trouble. No loiterers lingered; no litter lined the gutters. The sidewalks were cleanly swept, and the people who walked up and down them didn't have that same frenzied gait and look that characterized most people hurrying through the busier sections of Manhattan. Of course, I remembered the area because it was close to the Sarah Bernhardt School and Agnes Morris's residence, where I had lived while studying.

The cab brought us to the address, and we got out. Jimmy paid the driver, and then we turned and contemplated the dark oak doorway with its stained glass window. Now that we were actually here we were both so nervous that we had to hold onto each other as we went up the steps. I saw the tension in Jimmy's eyes, the way the skin around them narrowed and tightened. He straightened into his military posture and pressed the doorbell button. We heard the chimes clang, and immediately a small dog began to bark.

Moments later Clayton Osborne opened the door, chiding the gray French poodle at his feet to be still, but the dog wouldn't stop barking until Clayton lifted him into his arms. It whined and squirmed in Clayton's long, graceful fingers but didn't bark.

Clayton was still dressed in his pin-striped suit and tie. He was tall and good-looking with dark brown hair and hazel eyes. He was a slim man who held himself confidently, perhaps exaggerating his stiffness because of the occasion.

"Good afternoon," he said. Jimmy had been right about his arrogant nasality. It wasn't a cold. He held his head back when he spoke and immediately tightened his jaw, as if he were anticipating an argument after each and every word.

"Good afternoon," Jimmy replied. "I'm James Longchamp, and this is my wife, Dawn."

"Pleased to meet you." He offered me his hand first, shifting the dog under his other arm. Then he shook Jimmy's hand quickly. "Come in," he said, stepping back. After he closed the door behind us he paused. "Just so we all understand clearly," he said, "Kelly knows nothing about her sordid past. As far as she is concerned, you two are friends of mine, friends I've made through business. You were in the neighborhood and stopped by," he instructed. "But you can't stay long. You're going to a Broadway show or something and have to get ready, if Kelly should ask."

I felt Jimmy stiffen beside me. I didn't like the condescending tone in Clayton Osborne's voice either. He spoke with a pompous air, as if we should be forever grateful for the favor he was doing us.

When neither of us spoke, he added, "I've had a discussion with my attorney, and he was not happy about this. However, your locating us was surely inappropriate, if not out-and-out illegal. There are laws protecting the parents of adopted children and the children themselves, laws specifically against this sort of thing."

"We're not here to cause anyone any trouble, Mr. Osborne," I replied quickly, before Jimmy could speak. "I'm sure you can sympathize with our feelings and understand why we want to see Fern now."

"Kelly," he corrected. "Her name is Kelly," he repeated firmly. "You must not say Fern," he snapped.

"Kelly," I corrected. His eyes fell more heavily on me as he shifted the dog to his other arm. "Are you two husband and wife?"

"That's right," Jimmy said. A tremor of confusion passed through Clayton Osborne's face, but he quickly recovered.

"One other thing," he said. "Don't refer to me as Mr. Osborne. My name is Clayton, and my wife's name is Leslie. Kelly is a very perceptive and" – he turned to Jimmy – "precocious young girl, as I explained to you on the phone. She would pick up something like that immediately and become suspicious."

"Clayton?" a female voice called.

We all turned. Leslie Osborne had come into the

hallway. She wore a jade-green blouse and jeans. I thought she had the figure of a dancer – small-breasted with a narrow waist and long, sleek legs. She had very light brown hair tied behind her head with a turquoise ribbon and wore no makeup, but she had the sort of face that didn't require much. Her lips were naturally bright red, her blue eyes crystalline and her complexion perfect, her skin as smooth and as clear as alabaster.

"Why are you staying in the entryway so long?" she asked.

"We were just greeting one another," he explained quickly. "This is my wife, Leslie," he said. She stepped toward us, extending her hand. I saw she wore two diamond stud earrings in her pierced ears.

"How do you do?" she said.

I took her hand in mine. Her fingers were long and thin, but her palms were puffy with muscle. Artist's hands, I thought. I felt she was a substantially warmer and less threatened person than her husband, and even though her eyes scanned me quickly, they were friendly eyes.

"Forgive me for staring," she said, smiling. "I often forget I'm doing it. It's an occupational hazard. You see, I'm an artist."

"I understand," I said. I had almost said, "I know," but I didn't, because I didn't want her to know how much spying we had done.

"Well, Clayton?" she said, turning to him.

"You take them into the living room, and I'll get Kelly," he instructed.

"Right this way," Leslie said, indicating the room to the right.

"Thank you," I said, and Jimmy and I walked into their living room.

The Osbornes' townhouse appeared to be a large two-story building with thick carpets and elegant old furniture immaculately maintained. From what I could see, every room was a showcase filled with expensive and beautiful things. There were paintings everywhere, and because of the signature I spotted on them, I knew most were Leslie's. But here and there were rural scenes painted by other artists. Fern had been brought up in this world, a world of elegance and art, a world filled with rich and good things, I thought. I wondered how it had shaped her.

"Please have a seat," Leslie said, indicating the chestnut silk sofa. "And quickly tell me something about yourselves before they arrive. Where do you live?" she asked, sitting on the matching settee.

"We live in Cutler's Cove, Virginia, where I manage my family's resort, the Cutler's Cove Hotel."

"Oh, I've heard of it," Leslie said. "It must be beautiful there."

"It is."

"And how did you two . . ." She gestured.

"Get together?"

"Yes," she said, still smiling.

I looked at Jimmy. We both understood how difficult it would be to tell our story quickly.

"I guess we always realized we were in love. After Jimmy joined the army we pledged ourselves to each other," I said, still looking at Jimmy. "When he was discharged we got married. By then I was living in Cutler's Cove."

"Oh, how nice," she said. Jimmy had yet to say a

331

word to her. She stared at him, but before she could say anything to him or he could say anything to her, Clayton Osborne and Fern appeared in the doorway.

Despite our promises to pretend to be people we weren't, neither of us could help but fix our gazes intently, almost hungrily on Fern. I saw immediately that she sensed we were looking at her in a way that was much different from how her parents' other friends might look. Her dark eyebrows rose like question marks.

She was tall for her age and looked more like a girl of twelve or thirteen, which made sense when I recalled how tall Momma Longchamp was. She wore her hair in a pageboy; it was as dark and shiny as black onyx. Momma Longchamp's hair, I thought. She had Jimmy's dark eyes, but hers were smaller.

Clayton was right to characterize her as advanced for her age. Although she was only ten, she had begun to develop a figure. The outline of her training bra was just visible beneath the light green cotton blouse. She had long arms and slim shoulders, her body trim and sleek like a cat's. In fact, I realized she had cat's eyes – narrow, sharp, searching, probing and poking, driven by a feline curiosity.

Even so, she was a pretty girl with a smooth, dark complexion. She had Momma's nose and mouth and Daddy's chin and jaw. It wouldn't be hard to see Jimmy beside her and not know they were related, I thought.

"This is Mr. and Mrs. Longchamp," Clayton said. "Our daughter Kelly."

"Hello," I said first. For a moment I thought Jimmy wasn't going to say anything.

"Hi," he finally added.

She studied us as if trying to decide whether to talk or just glare. Her mouth opened slightly, but she made no sound. She looked from Jimmy to me and then back to Jimmy.

"It's polite to return a greeting when you get one, Kelly," Clayton chastised.

"Hello," she said.

"Sit down, Kelly," Clayton commanded.

Reluctantly, she sauntered over to the easy chair and plopped into it, keeping her eyes glued to us.

"Kelly," Clayton snapped, "since when do you treat the furniture like that? And in front of guests?"

"It's all right, Clayton," Leslie said. "Kelly is just a little bit depressed today," she explained, turning to us. "She's had a bad day at school."

"It wasn't my fault!"

"This isn't the time for this discussion," Clayton said, fixing his eyes firmly on Fern. She shot a gaze at us and then looked away. "Mr. and Mrs. Longchamp are old friends who have come a long way and are here for only a few minutes," he continued.

The way he limited our visit caught Fern's attention, and she turned back to us with renewed interest.

"How far did you come?" she asked.

"From Virginia," I said.

"Did you drive or fly?" she followed.

"We flew," Jimmy said, smiling. His warm expression drew her gaze, and for a moment, a fleeting moment, I was sure I saw something in her eyes, some note of recognition, or at least some deep-seated curiosity.

"Wasn't I born in Virginia?" she demanded of Leslie. Leslie smiled softly.

"I've told you dozens of times, Kelly," Leslie

333

explained. "You were born in the emergency room of a hospital just outside of Richmond, Virginia. Your father and I had wandered off too far while I was in the ninth month."

Born on the road, I thought – the same sort of lie Momma and Daddy Longchamp had told me. When I looked at Fern to see her reaction, however, I found she was already staring intently at me, as if she wanted to see my reaction more than I wanted to see hers. Jimmy flashed a disdainful gaze my way. He didn't think much of their fabrication.

"And what do you do?" Fern asked. "Buy dozens and dozens of stocks and bonds like Daddy's other friends?"

"We own and operate one of the biggest hotels in Virginia Beach," I explained. "It's called Cutler's Cove."

"I've never been to Virginia Beach," Fern moaned.

"Oh, you poor, deprived child," Clayton said, cutting into her with his sarcasm. "You've only been to the beaches in Spain and France and all over the Caribbean islands."

"Do you have any children?" she asked me, ignoring Clayton.

"A little girl, Christie."

"How old?" she followed quickly.

"Kelly, it's not polite to cross-examine people like that," Leslie said. She turned to us. "She's a very inquisitive child. Clayton thinks she will become a journalist."

"Or work for the I.R.S.," he added, shaking his head.

"That's all right. I don't mind," I said, turning back

334

to Fern. "Christie's just over five, actually five and a half."

"How come you have only one child, too?" she demanded.

"Kelly!" Clayton glanced down at us and then stepped toward her. "Didn't your mother just tell you not to cross-examine? There are ways to carry on a civilized conversation and there are ways not to."

"I'm just asking," she said.

"I did try to have another child," I told her, "only I had a miscarriage."

Fern's eyes brightened.

"Wow," she muttered. I saw a smile take form on Jimmy's face.

"What's your favorite subject in school?" he asked her. From the way he held himself as he gazed at her, I could feel his frustration. How he would like to jump up and embrace her, I thought. It was evident he saw all the resemblances to Momma Longchamp in her face, too.

"English," she replied, "because I can make up stuff and write it sometimes."

"Why, then, are you doing so poorly in the subject?" Clayton inquired.

"The teacher doesn't like me."

"None of your teachers likes you," Clayton commented.

"Kelly's been having a little trouble adjusting to things this year," Leslie began.

"This year?" Clayton said, raising his eyebrows. Leslie continued, ignoring him.

"She happens to be a very bright girl who, whenever she wants to," she added, gazing at her, "can leap to the head of the class; but because the other students are a bit slower, she gets bored, and when she gets bored, she gets into trouble."

"She's bored a lot these days," Clayton inserted.

"Well, I hate the Marion Lewis School. All the kids there are snobs. I wish I was back in public school," she complained.

"I don't think your record in public school is much to brag about, Kelly," Clayton said. He turned to us. "We were hoping that if we enrolled Kelly in this private school, she would change, benefit from the special attention, but she has to want to change herself."

Fern pouted just the way I imagined she would. She embraced herself tightly and turned away, her lips pursed.

"Have you been having good hotel seasons at Cutler's Cove?" Leslie asked me.

"The last few years have been very good. We're going to expand the facilities next year. We're thinking of adding some tennis courts and buying a few more boats for the guests to use off our dock. We're getting younger guests these days," I explained.

"You own your own boats?" Fern asked, slowly drawn back by my description.

"Uh-huh," Jimmy said. "Sailboats and motorboats."

"What else does the hotel have?" she inquired.

"A large swimming pool, playing fields, gardens, a ball room, a game room, a card room . . ."

"Cool," Fern exclaimed.

"Kelly, I've asked you not to bring that juvenile jargon into the house," Clayton said. "One of Kelly's problems," he continued, "is her hanging around with children much older than she is. They are invariably bad influences."

"They're not children," Fern cried.

"Excuse me," he said. "Teenagers."

"How long are you staying in New York City?" Leslie asked, more to end the argument than to find out the answer.

"We're going to leave tomorrow," I said.

"Which hotel are you at?" Fern asked.

"The Waldorf," Jimmy said quickly.

"Coo . . . that's nice," she said, looking up at Clayton. All this time he had made no attempt to sit down, which underlined how short he wanted our visit to be. He gazed at his gold wristwatch.

"I think," he said slowly, nodding his head, "Kelly should go up and begin her homework, don't you, Leslie?"

"I got lots of time. I'm not going to school for two days," Fern said.

"What? Two days?" He spun around toward Leslie.

"We'll talk about it afterward, Clayton," Leslie said calmly.

"She's been suspended from school again?" he cried out in dismay.

"Later, Clayton," Leslie said, nodding in our direction. His pale skin flamed with a bright red fury as he bit down on his lips.

"Kelly," he snapped, "say good-bye to Mr. and Mrs. Longchamp. I want you up in your room."

Reluctantly now, I thought, Fern rose from her seat.

"Good-bye," she said. She stopped in front of Jimmy, who couldn't keep his eyes off her, and extended her hand. "Why do your eyes look so watery, like you're about to cry?" she asked.

"Do they?" He forced a smile. "Maybe it's because I had a sister who would be just about your age now," he said, "and when I look at you, I'm reminded of her."

It was as if the air around us was suddenly filled with static electricity. Clayton Osborne's mouth dropped open; his face flamed even redder, so it seemed he might go up in smoke. An icy look of cold fear washed over Leslie Osborne's face. My heart began to pound as if it wanted to break out of my chest, and my breath caught in my throat and seemed to stay.

Fern, however, didn't take her eyes from Jimmy. Her lips curled into a strange smile.

"What happened to her?" she asked.

"She died."

"How?"

"Kelly, that's enough," Clayton said forbiddingly. "You can't keep asking people personal questions, especially painful ones. It's not only impolite, it's . . . it's" – he glared down at Jimmy – "cruel."

"I didn't mean anything," she moaned.

"Just go up and do your homework, no matter how much time you have to do it," he commanded. She lowered her head and started away, turning once in the doorway to look back at us. Then she ran out and pounded her way up the stairs.

The moment she was out of earshot, Clayton stepped toward Jimmy.

"We had an understanding," he said. "That was the only way I would agree to this, and you knew it."

"I didn't say anything to ruin the farce," Jimmy replied disdainfully. Clayton shot a glance at Leslie, but she was looking down at the floor.

"I think you should just leave," Clayton said. "And

338

I warn you, if you try to make any further contact with Kelly – "

"Don't threaten me," Jimmy said, standing up abruptly. His face was swollen with fury, his dark eyes as luminous as hot coals. I saw that he had clenched his hands into fists. His neck stiffened. Clayton Osborne took a step back. He felt the heat of Jimmy's anger, and for a moment he couldn't respond.

"I'm merely pointing out to you that you're treading on thin ice here. I was kind enough to permit this visit, but we don't want to do anything that will disrupt our relationship with Kelly. If it means applying for legal remedies, you can be assured we will do so," he added, regaining his composure. Jimmy simply glared at him.

"Thank you, Mr. Osborne," I said, rising. "I'm sorry there's been any trouble at all. Mrs. Osborne, thank you," I added, turning her way.

She smiled and stood up.

"It's difficult for everyone now, I know, but events have taken their course, and we must follow through for Kelly's sake as well as our own. In the end I'm sure you will agree it's been for the best," she said softly.

Her soothing tones eased Jimmy. He relaxed, and the crimson left his cheeks. He nodded at her, and then we started out of the house. When we reached the front door I turned back and looked at the stairway. I was positive I saw Fern kneeling at the top, gazing at us from under the balustrade. Without so much as a good-bye Clayton Osborne closed the door behind us.

"I hate that kind of guy; I've always hated them," Jimmy muttered as we walked down the stone stairway. "Somehow, some way . . ."

"Jimmy, don't aggravate yourself now. I don't know

339

if you can do anything at this point. Just as he said, the law is on their side, not ours."

"It doesn't seem right, Dawn. Not to be able to tell her who we are, not even now," he complained. "Damn." He looked back at the townhouse door. "Even though they're obviously rich people, I don't feel we're leaving her in a good home," he added.

He took my hand, and we hurried up to the corner to catch a cab and return to our hotel. Shortly after we arrived there I called home to be sure everything was all right with Christie. Mrs. Boston put her on the phone, and we both spoke with her. She rattled on and on about her toy ranch house, but she didn't forget to ask if we were bringing her anything from this trip.

"Now, Christie Longchamp, you know it's not nice to ask for things," I said. "Especially after you've just gotten such a wonderful present."

"You sound just like Clayton Osborne," Jimmy complained from the sidelines. "We can bring her a little something."

"Your father is spoiling you," I told her, my eyes on Jimmy. He laughed at the fire in them.

"Okay, okay," he said, holding up his hands and backing away. "Whatever you say."

After we spoke with Christie and Mrs. Boston we decided to shower and dress for dinner. The emotional and traumatic events of the day had been overwhelming for both of us, and we both looked forward to a fine, elegant dinner and the chance to relax. I had been toying with the idea of calling and perhaps even visiting with Mrs. Liddy and Agnes Morris, but I decided that it was probably not a good time. Jimmy's mind was too occupied with Fern. I didn't even call Trisha, because

340

I knew she would want to meet us for dinner, and I didn't think Jimmy was in the mood for company, even though Trisha's effervescence might be just the antidote for melancholy we both required.

Jimmy couldn't stop talking about Fern while we were dressing.

"She sure looks a lot like Momma now, doesn't she?" he asked.

"Yes, she does. She reminds me of the one picture I have of Momma, the one with her standing under that tree," I said.

"That's right," he said excitedly. Then his face turned gray and sad again.

"At least we saw Fern and know she is healthy and well," I said.

"Healthy, yes. Well? I'm not so sure about her emotional and psychological health," Jimmy replied. "I've been thinking and thinking about the way Clayton Osborne spoke to her in our presence. I know he's a stuffed shirt and all, but it was like he was speaking to a servant or some orphan he was forced to take in. I didn't sense any love between them, did you?"

"I don't know, Jimmy. I don't know if it's fair to judge him on one meeting like this. He was upset with Fern's behavior at school. Apparently she has been in trouble repeatedly. Maybe she needs some discipline. Leslie Osborne certainly seemed like a nice enough person, didn't she?"

"Yeah," he admitted reluctantly, "but Clayton's the one who rules that roost."

"She is being exposed to fine things and will have wonderful opportunities," I said.

"Sometimes that's not enough, Dawn. Clara Sue

was certainly exposed to nice things and wonderful opportunities, and look how she turned out. No, there's something missing in that house, something warm and necessary. Hell, as mean and as bad as Daddy could be sometimes, he still looked at us in a way that made us feel he cared in a pinch, didn't he?"

"Jimmy," I said softly, "I'm afraid you're just reaching, looking for something wrong. There's nothing we can do now, nothing," I said.

He nodded and lowered his head in defeat. I didn't like saying it so firmly, but I saw no other way. In silence we continued to get dressed. However, just as we were both ready to leave and had started toward the door, we heard a knock. We looked at each other, wondering who that could be. We hadn't called anyone in New York, and we had just spoken with the hotel, so we didn't expect any messages. Jimmy stepped forward to open the door.

There stood Fern, dressed in a dark blue wool jacket and jeans with a beret on her head. Jimmy gaped in astonishment, and for a moment he couldn't speak.

"Kelly, dear," I said. "What are you doing here?"

"I ran away," she declared proudly.

"Ran away? Why? And why would you come running to us?" I asked.

"Because I know who you really are," she replied.

Together Again

My pounding heart took my breath away, and for a moment all I could do was speak in a loud whisper.

"Come in and sit down," I said. Fern glanced at Jimmy, who looked absolutely stunned, and then walked quickly to the sofa in the sitting room of our suite. She unbuttoned her coat, scooped the sock hat off her head, and shook out her hair. I sat down, but Jimmy remained standing, his eyes locked on Fern. From the way he stared, I knew he saw Momma in her eyes and hair, Momma in her gestures. Some of my own precious memories of Momma came rushing back. They brought tears to my eyes.

"It's pretty here," Fern said, gazing around. "A friend of mine, Melissa Holt, stayed here once with her father, and I came to visit her. Her father took us both to dinner and then to the circus! Her parents are divorced, but her mother has a new husband," she continued. "Melissa hates him. She wants to run away from home and live with her real father," she concluded.

Her lack of inhibition and her obvious comfort and ease in our presence brought a small smile to Jimmy's lips. He finally sat down and folded his hands in his lap.

343

"How did you find out the truth about yourself and us?" Jimmy asked.

"I snuck a peek at Clayton's important papers one day and found my birth certificate and the adoption papers," she replied with a shrug. "I didn't know I would find those things. I don't snoop," she said, turning more to me, "but I was bored doing tons and tons of stupid homework and just went exploring."

"Weren't you afraid your parents would find you looking into their things and be upset?" I asked.

"Leslie was at her studio, as usual, and Clayton was at a dinner meeting with some clients."

"They left you home alone?" Jimmy asked.

"Uh-huh. They do that a lot, because Clayton has to go somewhere and Leslie is supposed to come right home from her studio, but she gets so busy with her paintings, she forgets the time. Sometimes Leslie even forgets to eat! She forgot Clayton's birthday, too, and mine, and last week she forgot she left Snoogles in her bedroom, and he wet the carpet in three places."

"Snoogles?" I asked.

"Their poodle," Jimmy guessed.

"Leslie named him Snoogles, but Clayton named me Kelly Ann after his mother," Fern said. "She was dead before Clayton and Leslie adopted me."

"Do you always call your parents by their first names?" I asked.

"They're not really my parents," she replied, her dark eyes bright with anger. "So I don't care."

"You mean you started calling them by their first names after you made that discovery?" I pursued.

"Oh, no, I always called them by their first names. It's what they wanted. They're . . ." She paused to

344

search for the term. As she did so, she ran her tongue over her lips, a gesture that widened Jimmy's smile. It was something Momma Longchamp used to do, also without being aware of it, whenever she was deep in thought. "Progressive parents," she finally concluded. "They have loads and loads of these books on how to bring up a child and have studied up on it. I guess it's mostly Clayton, though. Leslie didn't read the books. She just listens to whatever Clayton says.

"Clayton's always complaining about her," she continued, "complaining about her missing appointments or being late or not looking after the house and me.

"That's one of his favorite complaints," she added, widening her eyes. "They even had a fight about it after you left today."

"What sort of fight?" Jimmy asked.

"He blamed her for what happened at school and told her she doesn't take enough interest in my education," she responded.

"What did happen at school?" I asked.

"Jason Malamud's science project burned up in the lab."

"What?" I looked with concern at Jimmy.

"Well, it was something electrical, and it shorted out or something, only he claimed I did it, and the teacher believed him because he's the teacher's pet."

"Did you do it?" I asked. She returned my gaze firmly.

"Absolutely not. And I'm tired of being blamed for things that other people do," she moaned. "I hate that school. It's full of . . . spoiled rich kids."

"Sounds like a complaint I once had about the Emerson Peabody School," Jimmy said, and he winked at me. He was pleased with the similarity of their complaints; it was almost as if he believed it was in their blood.

"Why would Jason blame you, though?" I asked.

"Because he hates me, ever since I told everyone how he made in his pants. He tried to hide it by saying he was sick and going to the nurse."

Jimmy laughed.

"How long have you known the truth about yourself and us?" I asked.

"A couple of years, I guess," she said, shrugging again. "I don't remember the exact date. It was before Christmas, I think. Uh-huh, before Christmas that year," she confirmed, nodding. "Clayton bought me a set of encyclopedias, but I wanted the dollhouse I saw in Macy's window."

"It's been years? Did you ever ask them about it?"

"Oh, no. Clayton would be furious if he knew I had gotten into his precious secret papers. He has them under lock and key, but one day I saw where he put the key. I never mentioned anything," she said, shaking her head, her eyes wide again.

"Well, they are still legally your parents," I pointed out. "They have raised you and provided for you, and – "

"I hate them!" she cried. "Especially Clayton."

Jimmy's smile evaporated, and he leaned forward, cutting his eyes toward me sharply and then looking at her.

"He just wants what he thinks will be good for you," I explained. "He seems like a very intelligent man and a successful man, so – "

"He's mean and cruel," she cried. "All my friends

346

think so. They hate to come to my house. He asks everybody hundreds of questions and makes them feel bad. Then he tells me my friends are no good and too old for me, and he forbids me to go to their houses or go to the movies with them or – "

"I'm sure he's just looking out for you, thinking of your best interests, honey," I said. "Usually when a girl your age pals around with kids much older, she gets into trouble. I'm sure he's worried about you and trying to do the right thing."

She looked from Jimmy to me and then covered her face with her hands. "He does bad things to me!" she blurted out.

"What?" Jimmy nearly jumped out of his seat. "What do you mean, does bad things? What sort of bad things?"

She shook her head and started to cry. I went to her quickly.

"Don't cry, honey," I soothed. "Tell us what you mean. We can't help you if you don't explain," I said. I put my arm around her. She buried her face in my shoulder.

"I can't," she mumbled. "It's too . . . nasty."

"Dawn!" Jimmy was on his feet.

I nodded, closing and opening my eyes so Jimmy would remain calm and let me question her more closely.

"You know now that Jimmy is your brother, honey. I'm his wife, but we grew up together, and I took care of you from the day you were born until we all split up."

"You did?" she said, straightening up.

"Uh-huh. You used to love when I sang to you. Momma became very ill, and I had to help out. I'll tell you all of it, how Jimmy and I thought we were brother and sister for years and years and how we discovered we weren't, yet we realized we were in love. We'll tell you all about your real mother and father."

"What happened to them?" she asked quickly.

"Momma's dead," Jimmy replied. "Daddy's okay, but he's remarried and has a new son, so you have another brother. His name is Gavin."

"Well, why didn't I live with my real father? Why did he give me away?" she cried, the tears still streaming down her face. I took out my handkerchief and wiped them off her tender cheeks.

"He didn't give you away; you were taken away by the courts. We're going to tell you all of it, honey, but you have to trust us, too, and tell us what you mean when you say Clayton does bad things to you. What sort of bad things? How long has this been happening?"

She swallowed hard, closed her eyes and sat back. Jimmy sat down again to listen.

"As long as I can remember, I guess," she began, her eyes closed. She wiped away her remaining tears and continued. "Clayton was the one who took care of me most of the time because Leslie was always busy with her paintings. Clayton often used to dress me and give me baths." She closed her eyes again and then opened them quickly and fixed her gaze on Jimmy. "He still does," she said.

Jimmy's face turned so crimson, I thought the top of his head would burst into flames.

"What?" he cried. "Still does?"

"You're old enough to give yourself baths," I said, my voice almost a whisper again.

"I know I can do it myself, but he always comes in on

348

me and tells me I don't wash myself properly. He says I miss the important places," she said. "And when I once tried to lock the door, he got furious and pounded and pounded on it until I had to get out of the tub and open it."

I swung my gaze to Jimmy. He was on the edge of his seat and looked as if he would leap off any moment and go charging out the hotel room door. Maybe even charge through it! His neck was taut, and his eyes were bulging.

"I knew when I first set eyes on that guy – "

"Jimmy, don't jump to any conclusions," I advised.

"Jump to any conclusions? Listen to her," he said, holding his hands out toward Fern.

I nodded and turned back to her.

"Do you know what you're telling us, dear, what you seem to be saying?" She nodded.

"Your father . . . Clayton . . . comes in on you when you're taking a bath and touches you?" She nodded again.

"He makes me stand up and turn away from him. I close my eyes because I can't stand it anymore," she said. "He takes the washcloth and starts down my back, but soon his hands come around and . . ."

She covered her face with her hands again and sobbed. I embraced her and pulled her to me, rocking her gently and stroking her hair.

"It's all right now. It's all right," I assured her.

"You're damn right it's all right now. She's finished with that," Jimmy swore. He stood up, pulling his shoulders back and throwing his chest out. "I want to go see this man immediately," he declared.

"Wait, Jimmy. Let's do this right so we don't make

349

things worse. Let me call Mr. Updike and get some legal advice, find out what we have to do," I begged. "If you go charging off, you might ruin it."

His face relaxed a bit, but he kept his posture stiff and his fists clenched.

"Go call him, then," he commanded.

"Why don't you go to the bathroom, honey, and wash your face?" I said to Fern.

"Okay," she said. "But I'm scared. He's going to be so mad I told you. He made me swear I would never tell anyone. You won't make me go back there to live, will you? Please don't make me," she begged, her mouth twisting with apprehension. She looked positively terrified.

"You're not going back there. Not now, not ever," Jimmy promised. "Don't you worry about that or about him," he added, nodding.

She smiled through her tears. I helped her up and directed her to the bathroom. Then I went to the phone. Jimmy stood by my side as I called Mr. Updike.

As soon as I explained where we were and what we had learned, Mr. Updike referred us to a New York attorney he knew, a Mr. Simington, who told us we would have to contact the child welfare agencies and ask for an investigation. He said that the seriousness of the situation would make it impossible for things to be done overnight.

"From what you told me," he said, "Mr. Osborne has already been in contact with his own attorney about you two. He and his wife do have rights they can expect will be protected. There will be legal maneuvers, court action."

350

"What happens to my husband's sister during all this?" I asked.

"The child welfare agency will keep her in one of their homes until the matter is resolved. I can tell you from observing similar cases from time to time that it is an ugly mess for everyone concerned, especially the child. Most likely she will have to testify in detail in an open court. Make sure she understands that, and be absolutely certain she's telling the truth.

"Kids say the most incredible things when they're unhappy with a punishment or frustrated by a parent's refusal to permit them to do something, things they don't really mean," he continued.

"Oh, she means it," I assured him. "She's very, very disturbed by it. If you took one look at her . . . but I just hate putting her through any more. She's suffered enough, and for years and years, it seems."

"Hmmm," he said. "Well, sometimes these things can be resolved quickly if the events are as the child describes. The parent who has abused her might not want to see this dragged out in open court. You might investigate that avenue first."

While I held on Mr. Simington looked up the appropriate government agency numbers for me and Jimmy to call.

"Call me at my office tomorrow if you need anything further," he said. I thanked him and cradled the receiver. Then I explained everything to Jimmy just the way Mr. Simington had explained it to me.

After washing her face and drinking a glass of water Fern sat down on the sofa again and thumbed through some of my fashion magazines while Jimmy and I conferred. I thought she looked amazingly relaxed for a little girl who had gone through so much. I whispered so to Jimmy.

"You know how kids are," Jimmy whispered back. "Just think about us when we were her age, what we went through and how we were able to bear it. Kids are made of rubber; you can stretch and twist them all sorts of ways, and they don't break."

"On the outside, Jimmy. On the inside they tear to pieces," I said.

"I know. That's why I want this ended tonight, not tomorrow, and certainly not after months and months of legal maneuvering in New York courts."

"What are we going to do?" I asked.

He thought for a moment. Then he turned to Fern. She looked up from the magazine when he went over to the sofa and sat down beside her.

"Do you think," he began softly, "that you can go back with us and confront Clayton just one more time?"

"What do you mean?" she asked. She looked from him to me and back to him. "Why?"

"Tell him to his face what you told us," Jimmy explained.

She bit down on her lower lip and dropped her eyes back to the magazine.

"You're going to have to do it eventually, dear," I told her.

"Why can't we just leave New York and go live in your hotel?" she cried.

"I told you," I said softly. "They are your legal parents."

"But Jimmy's my real brother! And you're his wife!" she exclaimed.

352

"That doesn't mean we have a legal right to take you away with us, Kelly," I said.

"I don't want to be called Kelly anymore. I want to be called by my real name: Fern. Fern!" she emphasized, her eyes burning with determination and anger.

Jimmy turned toward me, his face lit with satisfaction.

"And I want to go home with you. I want to be with my family, my real family, and not with them. I hate them," she repeated, pounding her knees with her fists. "I hate him for what he did to me."

"That's why we've got to go over there and tell him what we know and make him understand he has to let you go home with us or . . . or he'll go to jail," Jimmy said. "You don't have to be afraid," he emphasized, taking her hand into his. "I'll be right beside you, and if he should so much as threaten you – "

"And he can't make me stay there?"

"No, not after what you've told us," Jimmy said. "That's for sure."

Fern shifted her gaze to me to see if I agreed with what Jimmy was telling her.

"Okay," she said. "As long as I can leave with you right away."

"Good," Jimmy said, clapping his hands over his knees.

"Jimmy." My heart began to pound in anticipation.

"What?"

"We can't guarantee that she can come home with us right away," I said.

"Sure we can," he said, waving me off. "Don't worry, Fern," he said, running his hand over her hair, "you're going to be safe from now on. No one's going to do sick things like that to you again as long as I'm around."

Fern's face broke into a wide smile, and she threw her arms around his neck.

"Oh, Jimmy," she cried, "I'm so happy, so happy you finally found me." Jimmy beamed. He gazed at me over her shoulder, his eyes so full of happiness and pride, I couldn't resist smiling back at him. Only deep down inside, I had a feeling there was more to this . . . much, much more, and only time would tell if we were doing the right thing.

"Let's go," Jimmy said, standing and pulling Fern to her feet along with him. "Let's finish this off."

"How did you get to the hotel?" I asked Fern as the doorman hailed us a cab.

"I snuck out of the house and walked to the corner and waved and waved until I got a cab," she said. "I've done it before, by myself and with Melissa," she said proudly. "I have my own money. I took it all with me when I left," she added, and she opened her little pocketbook to show me. There was a pile of bills all crunched up inside.

"That looks like a lot of money, Fern. How much is in there?"

"More than five hundred dollars."

"Five hundred dollars? How did you get so much?" I asked.

"I saved it up from my allowance," she said quickly. "I just knew I would need it someday."

"Clayton must have given you a big allowance," I remarked.

"Oh, no. I saved it over a long, long time. Sometimes

he punishes me and doesn't give me any allowance for weeks and weeks and weeks. He says I don't deserve it. He tells me I should be paying him instead, for keeping me . . . for putting up with me," she added.

"Putting up with you, huh? That son of a – "

"Jimmy," I cried, swinging my eyes toward Fern. "Please. Watch your language."

"Oh, right."

We all got into the cab, and Jimmy gave the driver the Osbornes' address. Fern sat between us. I thought she would become more and more frightened as we drew closer and closer to Clayton and Leslie's townhouse, but she was filled with questions about Cutler's Cove and about Christie and the other members of what might soon be her new family. What a remarkable young girl to have such courage, I thought.

When we got out of the cab I grasped Jimmy's arm.

"You have to promise me you won't lose your temper and do something foolish, Jimmy. It would only make things worse," I warned.

"Don't worry," Jimmy assured me. "I can handle his sort." He locked his eyes tightly on the door. "Ready, Fern?" he asked, taking her hand. She looked up at him and nodded. "Remember," he said, "tell the truth and don't be afraid."

"Okay." She nodded and started forward, but to me she finally looked terrified.

"It will be all right, honey," I said, coming up beside her. I put my hand on her shoulder. Together the three of us climbed the stairs. Jimmy pushed the button for the doorbell, and just as before, Snoogles began to yap. The look of surprise on Clayton Osborne's face when he opened the door turned instantly to a look of anger when he saw Fern standing between us.

"What is the meaning of this?" he demanded. "Kelly Ann, where have you been? How dare you leave this house without permission?" He reached forward to seize her by the shoulder, but Jimmy grabbed his wrist in midair.

"Hold on," Jimmy snapped. "We have some things to discuss and Fern," he said, pronouncing the name sharply, "has to be present."

Clayton pulled his wrist out of Jimmy's hand.

"So you've gone and broken your agreement," he said, rubbing his wrist. "I should have known. Well, you can both just turn around and get out of here before I call the police."

"Actually, that's what we want you to do," Jimmy said. "If you don't, we will."

"What?" He scowled darkly.

"Clayton, what's wrong?" Leslie said, coming up behind him. "Kelly? What are you – "

"She sneaked out of the house and went to them," Clayton explained quickly. "Obviously they have told her who they are."

"Oh, no." Leslie grimaced. "Kelly, dear, you must not be upset. There are many children who have been adopted, and that doesn't mean their parents love them less."

"She's upset, all right," Jimmy said. "And it's not just because she's found out she was adopted." He turned and glared daggers at Clayton. "I think we had better discuss what's really upset her," he fired, his words forcing Clayton to retreat a step.

356

"Now see here," Clayton began. "If you think you can come here and threaten us with – "

"Let them come in, Clayton," Leslie said. "It's stupid to argue on the doorstep, and Kelly should be getting ready for bed. Did she have anything to eat?" she asked me.

"Food isn't our concern right now, Mrs. Osborne," I said, standing as firmly as a rooted tree.

"Oh, I see. Clayton, let's bring everyone inside. Please. There's no reason we can't behave in a civilized manner and settle any questions."

Reluctantly, Clayton backed away, and we all entered.

"Do you want to sit down?" Leslie asked when we entered the living room.

"I think we'll stand," I said. Clayton, as if to show his defiance, strolled past us and sat down. He glared at us and especially sent looks of fury toward Fern. She held on to Jimmy's hand as if for dear life and kept her body snugly against me.

"All right," Clayton said, his hands palms down on his legs, "what's this all about?"

"This is about the abuse of my sister," Jimmy said firmly.

"Abuse?" Clayton's lips moved into a grotesque mockery of a smile, the kind of cold smile that sent shivers down my spine. "No question we've abused her, especially if you call spending hundreds of dollars on piano lessons for her, only to find out she never practiced, abuse. Especially if you call spending hundreds of dollars on tutors to get her to do at least what is basic, only to discover she doesn't do her homework, abuse. Abuse?" he snapped, his eyes widening maddeningly. "Yes, especially if you consider how many expensive

357

summer camps she's attended and politely been asked to leave. Especially if you go up and look at the closets and closets full of expensive clothing, some of which she has never worn. Go look at the mountains of records, the cartons of dolls, the stereo, the radio . . . go on, go look at all the abuse!" Silence draped the room for a moment. Even Leslie looked astounded by Clayton's emotional outburst. He sucked in his breath and looked away, his face scarlet.

"We're not talking about those sort of things," Jimmy said calmly. "We know you've provided well for her."

"Then what the hell are you talking about?" Clayton shouted.

"We're talking about the sexual abuse," Jimmy pronounced, undaunted. For a moment it was as if thunder had clapped at the ceiling of the room. My ears rang with the deadly aftermath of Jimmy's accusation. Clayton Osborne's mouth opened and closed, but nothing came out. Leslie gasped and brought her hands to the base of her throat.

"What? What did you say?" Clayton finally asked.

"You heard me, and Fern is here to tell you to your face what she told us."

Clayton looked at Fern. I watched her reaction. She stood her ground, her eyes fixed, unblinking.

"What did you tell these people, Kelly?" Clayton demanded.

"I told them what you do to me in the bathtub," she said without hesitation.

"Bathtub?"

"Oh, my God," Leslie gasped. "Kelly, what are you saying? What bathtub? When?"

"She's saying that your husband does and has for

years sexually abused my sister when she takes a bath."

"That's not true; that can't be true. Why would you say such a terrible thing, Kelly?" Leslie asked. She stepped toward her, but Fern didn't flinch.

"I said it because it's true," Fern replied. She turned toward Clayton and narrowed her eyes. Confusion knitted his eyebrows together. Then he shook his head.

"I don't believe this," he said. "Did you two put her up to this?" he asked, raising his gaze toward Jimmy and me.

"Of course not," I said quickly. "She came to us, and only after a lot of persuasion did I get her to tell us what was really bothering her. She was quite hysterical and quite terrified. You obviously didn't know," I continued, turning my attention to Leslie, "that she has known the truth of her birth for some time now – years, in fact."

"Known?" Leslie shook her head and looked at Fern. "How?"

"She found her birth certificate and the adoption papers one day," I said. Fern looked more frightened by my revelation of her discovery than she did about accusing her adoptive father of sexual abuse. "But she was afraid your husband would punish her for looking at his private papers, so she never said a word."

"Is this true, Kelly?" Leslie asked softly.

"My name's not Kelly. It's Fern," Fern said defiantly. For the first time tears formed in Leslie Osborne's eyes. She pressed her hand over her mouth and shook her head.

Clayton Osborne stood up slowly and started toward Fern and us, his gaze focused only on her. He had his shoulders hoisted and looked like a buzzard about to pounce.

"So you found your name is really Fern and you're not our flesh and blood, huh? You like that? You like being Fern Longchamp and not Kelly Ann Osborne? You like having parents who were kidnappers?"

Fern looked up at us with surprise.

"It's not true," I said softly.

"It's true; it's true," Clayton said. "And after they showed up, you sneaked out of here to go to them and tell them this ridiculous fabrication in order to get their sympathy. You want to live with them and leave us? Is that what you want?"

"Yes," Fern answered quickly. "I do."

Clayton nodded, his eyes burning with exasperation and fury.

"All right, then. Go. Go live with them and see how you like it."

"*Noooo*," Leslie cried.

"Yes," Clayton responded. "Let her go." He turned back to Fern, glaring down at her. "Maybe then you will realize what you have here and finally appreciate it, only I might not take you back," he said. "Not after you've created this horrible lie about me.

"This is what comes of your hanging around with those older kids," he said, nodding. "They put these ideas into your head. You're right: You're not our daughter anymore."

"Clayton!" Leslie screamed. "What are you saying?"

"I'm saying I don't want her in this house, not until she apologizes to me for telling these lies," he said. He turned to Jimmy. "Take her out of here. Take whatever things of hers she needs and take her with you. Only when you realize how wrong you are and how mean she can be, don't come crawling back to me for help. You spend the money on psychiatrists and special teachers. Yes," he said, liking his idea. "She's your sister. Suffer with her. I'm going to my office," he said to Leslie. "Make sure they're all out of here within the hour," he added, and he stormed away.

"Clayton!" she called. His footsteps echoed. "Kelly," she said, turning back to Fern. "Go apologize to your father this very moment."

"I'm not apologizing," Fern said defiantly.

"But you know he would never do such things to you," she said, smiling through her tears. "You know that."

"He did! He did, and I don't care if he's mad anymore! He did do those things! Do you want me to show you where he touched me?" she screamed back at the woman who had tried to be her mother.

Leslie clapped her hands over her ears and shook her head.

"Just go upstairs and pack a few things, honey," I said softly. "You don't need much. We'll buy you whatever you need later."

"Okay," she sang, and she shot off toward the stairway. Leslie Osborne shook her head and backed herself against the sofa. She sat down hard and began to cry.

"I'm sorry, Mrs. Osborne," I said, going to her. "But if Fern has been and continues to be abused – "

"She's hasn't. Clayton's not that sort. He's firm with her, and he's worried about her, but he would never do anything to hurt her," she said.

"Maybe you just never knew," Jimmy said.

361

"I would know something like that," she replied. Jimmy shook his head.

"Not if you bury yourself in your art studio and even forget to make dinner or celebrate her birthday," he said.

"What? I never . . . Did she say that, too?" She looked toward the doorway and shook her head.

"My sister belongs with us," Jimmy said. "It's time she came back to her real family."

Leslie snapped her head around and stared at him. Her tears looked frozen in her eyes.

"*We* are her real family. *We* made a good home for her here," she said slowly. "We gave her everything she could ever want or need."

"Except real love," Jimmy replied. He was unmerciful. Even I winced for Leslie Osborne. She sat there dumbly, the tears streaming down her face.

Moments later we heard Fern bouncing down the stairs.

"I'm ready," she announced, a small suitcase in hand. To me it seemed as if she had already had it packed and waiting. She had returned that quickly.

Jimmy smiled.

"Then let's go."

They started away.

"Fern," I said.

"What?"

"Don't you want to say good-bye to Leslie, at least?"

She looked back at the woman who had been her mother. A tiny smile formed at Fern's lips.

"Sure. Good-bye, Leslie," she said, and then she turned and rushed forward to open the door.

Leslie Osborne shook her head hard to deny what she was seeing and hearing.

"I'm sorry, Mrs. Osborne," I said. "I really am, but this might be the best for everyone concerned."

She sobbed silently but didn't respond.

"Dawn," Jimmy called from the doorway.

I took one last look at her and then joined him. Fern was already at the bottom of the stairs.

"Jimmy," I said, "I hope we're doing the right thing."

"We are. How can it not be the right thing? We're bringing her back to her real family. It's what Momma would want, don't you think?"

"I guess," I said. "I hope so," I added.

"Listen," he said quietly, "if Clayton Osborne weren't guilty, would he be so willing to let us take Fern away without a fight? Obviously he was shocked at how we simply confronted him with the truth. All that anger is merely his way of covering up."

I nodded. What Jimmy said made sense. How could Clayton send Fern out so quickly and easily? After all, she had been his and Leslie's daughter, for better or worse, all these years.

We walked up to the corner to hail another cab. Fern was so eager to get away, she practically ran up the sidewalk, her suitcase swinging in her hand. Now that the traumatic event was apparently ended, we all confessed to being hungry. As soon as we returned to the hotel and put Fern's things in our suite we went down to dinner. At the table she talked a mile a minute, and whenever she did pause, Jimmy fired a question. It was as if both of them wanted to catch up on all the years in minutes. All night I kept watching her and waiting for

the reality of what was happening to sink in. I expected
her to break into tears when she realized she was leaving
the only home she could really remember and the only
people she could really have thought of as parents.
But she must have really been unhappy and suffered
terribly under Clayton Osborne's abuse, for she hardly
mentioned either of them.

I couldn't help but be nervous. My eyes continually
shifted to doorways, and every time someone new
entered I expected to see either Clayton himself coming
for Fern, or some police officer, but no one came. When
we returned to our suite to retire I anticipated finding a
message, but there wasn't any.

The sofa in the sitting room of our suite pulled out
into a bed. We had the hotel maid prepare it for Fern. I
felt certain that Fern would experience anxiety and fear
now that she had to go to sleep in a strange place with
people she barely knew, but she didn't cry or express
any reluctance. The only thing that upset her was that
she had forgotten to pack her toothbrush. I sent down
for one from the hotel shop.

While Jimmy prepared for bed in the other room, I
helped her slip into her nightgown. She showed me the
things she had packed.

She had a half dozen pairs of panties, another training
bra, socks, a pair of her favorite sneakers, some blouses
and skirts. Under the clothing she had some romance
magazines, her hairbrush and a tube of lipstick. She
confessed she would never put it on in the house, but
only after she had left for school. Clayton forbade it.

When I recalled myself at her age and my own little
well-used suitcase, I remembered how important it was
for me to be sure to pack my favorite doll. It was a rag

doll, so ragged that it had worn thin in the cheeks of the face, showing the cotton filling. Fern had no dolls, no loving mementos. Her suitcase was more expensive than any I would have dreamt of having, and she had more expensive clothing, but she had nothing to remind her of some cherished moment, some loving time. I truly felt sorry for her.

She joined me in the bathroom to watch me brush out my hair.

"I'm going to let my hair grow longer now," she said, "down to the middle of my back. Clayton hates long hair."

"You have to take good care of it when it's long," I pointed out.

"I will. But you have a beauty shop in the hotel, right? Jimmy said so."

"Yes, we do."

"Good. And there's a maid in the house, too, right?" she asked.

"We all still take care of our own things," I said. "The maid helps out, but she's no one's slave," I warned.

"Oh, I won't be sloppy, but I want to work at the hotel, too. Just like Jimmy said." Her excitement brought a smile to my face. How different from my arrival it was going to be for her when she first arrived at Cutler's Cove, I thought. She would come right into a house of love, a place where she was wanted.

"And I just can't wait to meet Christie and see the twins!" she exclaimed.

I couldn't help myself. I had to ask.

"Don't you have any regrets, feel any sadness at all about leaving the Osbornes, Fern?"

"Well . . ."

Here it comes, I thought. Finally.

"I'll miss my friends," she said, nodding, "especially Melissa. But," she added, brightening quickly again, "I'll make new ones, won't I?"

I stared down at her, thinking about each and every time I had been ripped out of one world and carried off to another. Not once did I overcome my sadness by thinking about the new friends I would make or the new places I would see. It was always so tragic and sad to leave people behind. Friendship, real friendship, was not something easily replaced. Each time I left somewhere, I left something of myself behind. I had begun to fear there would be nothing left to take away to a new place. You had just so much love and loyalty in you.

Apparently Fern had not given much of herself to anyone yet, not even the people she had once thought to be her real parents. Then again, I thought how horrible it must have been for her to grow up being sexually abused by the man she assumed was her father. That was enough to make anyone want to run off.

I smiled again. Jimmy was right. It was good she was coming home.

I tucked her into the sofa bed.

"Do you want me to leave this lamp on, honey?" I asked.

"No, that's all right. I've slept in a hotel many times before," she replied.

"Okay. We're close by if you need us. Good night."

"Good night," she said.

"How's she doing?" Jimmy asked when I got ready to crawl in beside him.

"Very well, but I don't know if the full impact of

what's happening has hit her yet," I said. Jimmy nodded and then smiled.

"Isn't it something, Dawn? We're taking care of little Fern again. Momma would be so happy, and Daddy's going to be ecstatic," he said. "I guess if you hope and pray enough, the right and good things can happen. Don't you think so, Dawn?" he asked.

"I want to think so, Jimmy," I said.

But I was afraid, still so afraid to be happy. I swallowed my fears the best I could and closed my eyes, still expecting a knock on the door. I even had nightmares about it, but it never came.

But I knew that didn't mean it never would.

Adjustments

It was as if sleep had interrupted Fern in the middle of a sentence. From the moment she awoke, she talked. The morning after had laid no harsh realities on her head. There were still no regrets, no signs of sadness. On the contrary, Jimmy and I were overwhelmed with her bountiful energy. Before we had risen she had washed and dressed herself. Chattering as happily as a little bird in the morning, she tagged behind me throughout the suite while I got myself ready to go down for breakfast. Without pausing for a breath she moved from one subject to another: the clothes her friends wore, their hairstyles, the singers she liked, the movies she loved. After I told her a little about our new house, she described the homes of her wealthy friends, homes she had slept in whenever Clayton had permitted it.

Listening to her stories, Jimmy and I understood that Clayton and Leslie Osborne really had taken her many places. She had been to London and the English countryside, as well as France and Spain and Italy. Every winter they had taken two Caribbean vacations as well. When we arrived at the airport for our trip home we could see that Fern was indeed a seasoned traveler. She strapped herself into her seat expertly and settled back for the trip without the least trepidation.

As the plane lifted and we flew into the clouds I gazed at Fern to see if there were signs of regret, but she had her eyes fixed excitedly on everything going on around her. She turned and smiled at me, and Jimmy winked. He couldn't have been more pleased.

The weather was perfect. Although it was mid-fall, it was still as warm as summer. Tourists continued to flock to the beaches and seaside resorts, so the airport in Virginia Beach was busy and crowded, and there was a heavy flow of traffic.

Julius was waiting for us at the gate. He wore an expression of surprise when he saw us approaching with Fern between us, holding both our hands, and his eyebrows rose when Jimmy introduced her as his sister. Fern shook his hand firmly and politely said, "Pleased to meet you."

Charmed by Fern's handshake and smile, Julius opened the door quickly for her, and she jumped into the limousine.

"See," Jimmy whispered, thinking about the way Clayton Osborne had treated her in our presence, "she doesn't have to be threatened to behave."

Fern raved about the scenery on the way to Cutler's Cove, and when we arrived in our seaside village she clapped her hands excitedly.

"I love it!" she exclaimed. "It's like a storybook village with the little sailboats and fishermen and small shops. I can't wait to explore everything!"

Jimmy beamed. His eyes had been so full of love and happiness all morning, I felt my heart would burst with joy for him. Every time Fern said something cute or surprised us with her worldly knowledge, he brightened with pride. And I was truly amazed at how quickly and completely she had taken to him and accepted him as her brother. It was as though all the years of separation had been more like minutes. She held his hand as much as she could and hugged and kissed him at every opportunity. Jimmy was elated by her flood of affection. Normally, having a precocious ten-year-old throw her arms around him and kiss him in public would bring the blood to his face and make him somewhat uncomfortable, but he put a tight lid on his modesty and welcomed her display of emotion, shifting his eyes to me every time to show me his pleasure.

When she first set her eyes on the hotel Fern seized Jimmy's hand.

"Oh, Jimmy, it's just the way I dreamed it would be," she exclaimed in a loud whisper.

"Dreamed?" I said.

"Yes. I fell asleep thinking about it last night, and I dreamed it would be high on a hill so you could stand on the front porch and see the ocean for miles and miles," she explained. Jimmy looked at me as if there was some spiritual meaning in a child's fantasies, as if it proved she had belonged here with us all along.

"Oh, how I wish you had come for me long ago," she said wistfully. It nearly brought us both to tears.

"We'll make up for it, Fern," Jimmy said. "I can promise you that," he added firmly.

"I know you will, Jimmy," she replied, and she hugged him again. I couldn't help wincing every time Jimmy made her a promise. Promises to a little girl were the stars in her dream sky. If they were broken, they left the world dark and lonely and made her distrustful of everything adults told her. I was afraid Jimmy would make a thousand promises because each time he made one, Fern's eyes grew more loving.

We didn't stop at the hotel; we had Julius take us directly to the house. By this time Christie was home from school. When we drove up she burst out on the porch with Mrs. Boston right behind her and charged down the steps, her two golden pigtails bouncing on her shoulders, to leap into Jimmy's arms. I gazed at Fern and saw her eyes grow narrow as her lips tightened into a small smile. Holding Christie in his arms, Jimmy turned toward her.

"Christie, I want you to meet my sister Fern. She's come to live with us," he said.

Mrs. Boston widened her eyes and tilted her head in surprise.

"Hi, Christie," Fern said. Christie stared at her suspiciously, obviously unsure of her own emotions. She was excited by the prospect of having another child in the house, but she was also threatened by the prospect of sharing Jimmy's love with anyone. "Can I give you a hello kiss?" Fern asked her. Christie shifted her gaze to me to see my reaction. I stood smiling, so she nodded softly.

Fern leaned forward and kissed Christie on the cheek. Christie fingered one of her pigtails and continued to stare in awe.

"This is Mrs. Boston, Fern," I said. "Our house-keeper and our dear friend," I emphasized.

"Hello," Fern said quickly.

"Welcome, honey," Mrs. Boston said. She and Julius exchanged quick glances of wonder as he carried our bags into the house.

371

"Fern's going to take the room next to Christie's," I explained. Mrs. Boston nodded.

"I'll see that the bed's freshened and the room's aired out well," she said, turning to get right to it.

"Why don't you show Fern our house, Christie?" I suggested when Jimmy lowered her to the walk. Christie looked up at Fern to see if she wanted that, and Fern nodded and brightened her eyes.

"Okay," Christie said. "Come on," she cried, and she shot up the stairs. Fern threw a smile back at Jimmy and then followed.

"Isn't this great? Isn't this just wonderful?" Jimmy said. I took his hand, and we entered the house behind the excited children.

Christie was truly fascinated with her new young aunt. She couldn't wait to show her all her toys and all her pretty clothes. After Fern had seen everything, including the gazebo and Christie's swing and slide set in the backyard, and after she had been settled in her room, we went to the hotel. Jimmy was eager to introduce her to everyone. She met Philip and Betty Ann immediately, and then Christie took her hand and rushed off with her to see the twins. I went to my office to catch up on what had occurred while we were gone. I saw from my messages that Mother had been calling all day.

"Why did you tell me you were off to New York to shop?" she demanded when I phoned. "I might very well have gone along. Or didn't you want me with you?" she whined.

When I explained what our real purpose was and what had happened, she was astounded. I was quite surprised by her sympathy for Fern, however, half expecting her to go on and on about how difficult it would be for me to have another child in my care.

"Poor thing," she said softly, and then she added, "I understand what it means to be sexually abused. Is she quite withdrawn?" she asked.

"No, Mother. On the contrary, she's a very outgoing, exuberant little girl."

"Really? I can only remember how I was after your . . . my father-in-law . . . took advantage of me," she said.

"Maybe it's because she's still a little girl at heart," I suggested. "As Jimmy says, children are more resilient. When I think about all he and I went through, I guess he's right," I added. Mother didn't want to hear any of that.

"Yes," Mother said. "Well, now, I'll have to have a dinner to celebrate all this. I'll call you as soon as I make all the arrangements."

"Mother," I warned, "make it a simple dinner. No mob scene."

"Really, Dawn, I don't have mob scenes," Mother protested.

"You know what I mean, Mother. We don't want to overwhelm Fern."

"I think I know how to make a proper family dinner," she bragged.

"All right, Mother. Thank you," I said, and I left it at that.

The next few days I was quite occupied with Fern. I took her shopping to get her more clothing and the things she would need to start school, most of which she had left behind in New York because of her abrupt

373

flight from the Osbornes. Jimmy assured me Clayton Osborne wouldn't forward a single thing.

"He won't bear the expense," Jimmy said.

However, I could see from the clothing Fern chose and her selections of shoes and other things that she was accustomed to buying the most expensive goods. She was quite familiar with brand names, especially designer names. Clayton Osborne obviously hadn't been any sort of Scrooge when it came to the things she needed and wanted, I thought. When I asked her about it, she snapped back quickly with, "He bought me whatever I wanted so I wouldn't tell anyone what he was doing."

"Why didn't he buy you the dollhouse you wanted that Christmas, then?" I inquired as we were leaving the department store in Virginia Beach.

She didn't answer for a long moment, and then she said, "Oh, he did, finally, after he came in to give me a bath again. Do I have to talk about that?" she asked quickly afterward.

"Of course not, honey," I said. "I was just curious."

She looked satisfied.

The next day I registered her in the Cutler's Cove School. The principal, Mr. Youngman, said he would have to contact the Marion Lewis School for Fern's records.

"We have to know where her strengths and weaknesses are in order to place her correctly. Do you play an instrument, Fern?" he asked her.

"No," she said quickly. She glanced at me and then added, "I wanted to play the flute, but my stepfather thought it was a waste of time."

"I see. Well, maybe we can start you on the flute here,

if you'd like. Your niece Christie is quite a little pianist already," he added, smiling.

I thought Fern might be excited about starting an instrument, but she didn't seem enthusiastic. In fact, when we left she was glum for the first time since her arrival. I imagined it was because of her nervousness at starting a new school. Goodness knows, I understood what that was like, having had to leave and start one new school after another. Each time was a major emotional crisis because new students were always the objects of close scrutiny. When I entered a school after it had already begun I was singled out and put under a magnifying glass. I knew other girls were inspecting my clothing and thinking about my hair. I knew boys were gawking at my figure and my face, and I knew teachers were wondering what sort of student they were getting now.

From what Fern had told us, she had been transferred to and from a number of schools and had gone through similar experiences.

"This is a very nice school system, Fern," I reassured her. "You'll like it here. Everyone is friendly and concerned. The teachers know their students well, and because it's a small community, they know the families well, too."

She didn't look relieved.

"You'll go to school every day in the limousine with Christie," I said, hoping that would cheer her up a bit, but she had a reaction opposite to what I expected.

"The other students will just hate me for being a little rich girl," she complained. She had a way of pulling the corners of her mouth up and clenching her teeth when something displeased her.

"Is that what happened to you before?"

"Sometimes," she said. "The teachers resent you, too, because you come from a rich family and you have so much more than they do."

"Oh, no, Fern. That won't happen to you here. Christie loves her teachers, and they adore her. I'm sure you'll adjust and everything will be fine," I said, but she still didn't look convinced.

Then she brightened and asked, "When can I start working in the hotel?"

I had to laugh. I wished we could always be children at heart and see work as fun.

"Right away, if you want. What would you like to do?"

"I want to work at the front desk," she replied excitedly.

"All right. I'll introduce you to Mrs. Bradly. She's in charge of the front desk," I explained.

"I thought you were in charge of everything," Fern replied, her mouth sinking at the corners.

"I am, but every department in the hotel has its own head who oversees it," I explained.

"But you can tell her what to do, right?" she insisted.

"Yes, Fern, but Mrs. Bradly's been here a lot longer than I have, and she knows exactly what has to be done. I don't have to tell her anything," I said, smiling.

Mrs. Bradly was a very pleasant, elegant-looking sixty-year-old woman who always had her silver-gray hair held in place with the prettiest shell hairpins. She had gentle green eyes with a perpetual friendly smile about them. She ran her department efficiently and was as much a fixture around the hotel as anyone or

376

anything. Guests looked forward to her greeting them on arrival.

Now a widow, she lived alone in a small Cape Cod home in the village. Her two daughters were married and living away, one in Washington, D.C., and one in Richmond. I didn't know a soul who had difficulty getting along with Mrs. Bradly, and that included children of all ages. She had three grandchildren of her own. So when I introduced Fern to her and told her how much Fern wanted to help out at the front desk, she beamed with pleasure and welcomed her with open arms.

"I've been looking for a qualified assistant," she said, smiling. Fern's smile was more of a smirk, I thought. She resembled a child who knew there was no such person as Santa Claus and resented being told children's stories.

"Okay, then," I said, "I'll leave you here with Mrs. Bradly, who will explain what you do, okay?"

Fern nodded. Without going into any detail, I took Mrs. Bradly aside and told her that Fern had been going through a very difficult time and needed a great deal of tender loving care.

"You just leave her with me, Dawn," she said. "I don't get a chance to practice being a grandmother enough."

"Thank you, Mrs. Bradly," I said, and I went back to work myself.

Fern amazed me again. She was very outgoing and made sure everyone knew she was Jimmy's sister. She was beside him every opportunity she had, even going outside to be with him for hours and hours when he was supervising ground maintenance. She loved eating dinner in the hotel dining room and sat proudly – almost arrogantly, I thought – at Jimmy's side. It didn't take her long to get to know all the waiters and busboys. In fact, she took so quickly to the routine at the hotel and settled in so easily and comfortably at the house, it was as if she had been there for years and years. When I mentioned it to Jimmy after dinner one night a little over a week later, he nodded.

"I see that myself," he said, and then he shrugged. "I suppose that comes from her being on her own so much. You know, not being able to depend on Leslie Osborne to do the things anyone would expect a mother to do, and . . . living with that pervert. She must have searched for opportunities to be alone and away from him."

"I suppose," I said. Then I laughed.

"What?"

"I was just recalling Fern as a baby. Remember how demanding she could be, how she would get absolutely hysterical until I took her in my arms and sang to her, or how she would cry the moment Daddy came into a room if he didn't come right to her? She wasn't born shy," I concluded. "There's no reason for her to be shy now."

Jimmy smiled.

"Daddy's working out his trip," he said. "When I told him we had Fern I could hear the tears in his voice. He'll call in a few days and tell me exactly when he, Edwina and Gavin can be here.

"Won't it be wonderful?" he added. "All of us together again."

"All but Momma," I said sadly. I didn't want to throw a pail of cold water on his warm smile, but I couldn't help thinking about her and wishing that somehow she could have been there, too.

Jimmy's eyes filled with tears, but he held them in and swallowed. Sorrow, like sour milk, always wanted to come back up.

In the evening, when we would all return from the hotel, Christie would immediately beg Fern to come to her room to play, but I wanted to be sure that Fern got herself off to a good start at the Cutler's Cove School.

"You have to let Fern do her schoolwork," I advised. "When she's finished she can go to see you."

Christie screwed her face into a tiny pout and went off to wait. Usually Fern would go to her and they would sit and do coloring books or play with some of Christie's dolls and toys. One evening when I was walking by Christie's room I heard Fern firmly instruct her to refer to her as "Aunt Fern." I paused at the doorway to listen.

"I'm Jimmy's real sister, which makes me your aunt, so you have to call me Aunt from now on, or I'll pretend I don't hear you. Do you understand?"

"Uh-huh," Christie said obediently.

"I'm really much older than you are, but I don't mind playing with you to teach you things," Fern continued in a very grown-up-sounding voice. The tone of it surprised even me. In fact, I thought she was doing a rather good imitation of Clayton Osborne.

"Now," she continued, "you can ask me any questions you want, questions about anything. Even," she said, lowering her voice a bit, "questions about boys. You know why boys are different, don't you?

"No, you don't," Fern added quickly. "You're nodding,

but I can see in your face that you don't. Well, I will tell you," she said.

I entered the room and cleared my throat to get her attention, but when Fern looked up at me I saw the oddest glint in her eyes. They were bright with frustration and anger. She looked just like an adult who was furious she had been interrupted. After a moment, though, the ire left her eyes, and her face softened into a smile.

"Hi, Dawn," she said.

"Fern, dear, may I speak with you a moment?" I said. I took her out in the corridor. She stared up at me, a look of innocence and confusion on her face. "I couldn't help but overhear some of the things you were saying to Christie as I was walking by," I said. Then I shook my head. "She's much too young to learn about the birds and the bees." I smiled. "She's not quite six yet."

"I knew all that stuff when I was her age," Fern snapped back. "Clayton made sure I did."

"Well, things are different here, Fern, dear. There is no Clayton. Christie has time to learn about sex. We've got to let her be a little girl first, okay? I know you want only to be a nice aunt to her, but – "

"Clayton used to do that, too," she said quickly, glaring at me.

"Do what, honey?"

"Spy on me whenever I had friends over," she said accusingly.

"I wasn't spying on you, Fern. I was just passing by and – "

"It's the same thing," she said. "If two people are having a private conversation in a room, another person

380

is not supposed to stand by the door and listen," she lectured. I felt myself grow crimson.

"I'm sorry if you felt spied upon, Fern, but Christie is my daughter, and I must be concerned about everything she does, sees and hears. Now please don't bring up that subject with her again, okay? When the time comes you can be a great help to her. You're a very mature young lady, and – "

"Okay," she said. "We'll just do baby talk. I'm tired anyway," she added. "I'm going to go to bed and read and go to sleep. Am I excused?"

"Yes, honey. Good night."

"Good night," she said, and she sauntered off.

"Where's Aunt Fern?" Christie cried when I looked in on her again.

"She was tired and went to bed, sweetheart. You should think about getting ready for bed, too."

"But we were playing a game . . . school. She was the teacher and I was the pupil," she protested.

"You can play again tomorrow."

Christie gave me one of her furious little looks and reluctantly marched to the bathroom to brush her teeth. Afterward, when I went downstairs, I told Jimmy what I had overheard Fern telling Christie and about my conversation with her. He was sitting in the big cushioned armchair and reading one of his car magazines.

"She was very put out that I chastised her," I added. He shook his head and lowered his magazine.

"Poor kid," he said. "All those years of abuse must have done some terrible damage."

"Maybe we should arrange for her to see someone,

Jimmy. Perhaps a child psychologist," I suggested.

"I don't think so," he said. "I think her just living in a normal world with people who love her and care about her will heal her. After a while all that other stuff will fade away, I'm sure."

"I don't know, Jimmy. According to what she tells us, she's suffered for years and years. That's not forgotten overnight or even after months. And I'm just afraid that Christie . . ."

"What?" he said, snapping the pages of his magazine. "Don't tell me you think my sister is going to corrupt Christie." Jimmy's eyes were the same bright coal color Fern's had been.

"I didn't say that, Jimmy. Of course she won't, but Fern hasn't been around a child this young, and especially not one who is so bright and quick. If you could just have a talk with her, too . . ." I suggested softly.

His face relaxed, and he sat back.

"Sure," he said. "I'll talk to her, but we've got to be understanding. She's been through hell. We don't want her to feel she's left one horror only to fall into another."

"I hardly think living here with us will ever resemble a horror, Jimmy," I said.

"No, no, of course not. Okay," he said, taking a deep breath. "I'll handle it. I'm sorry if I seemed abrupt. I just can't help getting furious about what happened to her."

"I understand, Jimmy," I said. I went over to him to plant a kiss on his cheek. He smiled and went back to reading his magazine, but I couldn't help feeling that the tiny crack in the veneer of our marriage had widened some.

And for reasons I didn't quite understand.

If Fern was unhappy about my chastising her the night before, she didn't show it the following morning. In fact, for the first time, when she and Christie were about to leave for school in the limousine, she stood waiting while Christie kissed me good-bye. Then she stepped forward.

"Good-bye, Dawn," she said. "I'll see you in the hotel after school," she promised, and she threw her arms around me the way she threw them around Jimmy and kissed me on the cheek. Before I could respond, she took Christie's hand and rushed out with her. When I turned, my hand on my cheek, I saw Jimmy smiling widely.

"She's like a flower that was kept imprisoned in a dark, dank basement and finally set free in the sun," he said. "Now she's blossoming. She's quite a little girl."

"I guess she is," I said, still amazed.

That afternoon, however, some of my optimism waned when the school principal, Mr. Youngman, phoned.

"I know you're very busy, Mrs. Longchamp," he began, "so I thought I would simply phone you rather than ask you to come down. Do you have a moment?"

"Yes, Mr. Youngman. What is it?" I asked, my heart beginning to flutter with anticipation.

"We received Fern's – I should say, Kelly Ann's – school records today from the Marion Lewis School. I'm afraid her past performance leaves much to be desired. Were you aware of how poorly she was doing in her academic subjects?"

"We did understand she was unhappy there," I began.

"She was failing everything," he said, and then he repeated "everything" for emphasis. "But not only that. Her old teachers are on record complaining about her behavior."

"I think a lot of that might have had to do with her unfortunate home life, Mr. Youngman," I said. "Perhaps my husband and I should stop by to see you. There are some special circumstances."

"Well, yes, I suppose, considering all this, that might be helpful," he said. "I'm sorry to pull you away."

"No, I'm sure Jimmy would want us to come. What time later today would be convenient for you?" I asked, and I made an appointment with him for Jimmy and myself.

When I told Jimmy, he was in complete agreement.

"We'll have to tell him all of it," he said. "Anyway, her teachers should be aware. It will help them be more understanding and tolerant."

Later, when we had our meeting with Mr. Youngman and he had heard all of it, he shook his head glumly and said he was very happy we had confided in him.

"It would explain most of this," he agreed. "I'm sure her rebellious behavior in school was her way of reaching out for help. Why, just her decision to give up the name Kelly Ann and take back her real name is testimony to how much she wants to forget. Poor little thing. Rest assured, I will handle this discreetly for you, Mr. and Mrs. Longchamp. We will do our very best to turn things around."

"Please don't hesitate to phone us should there be any problems," I told him.

384

"See?" Jimmy said after we left. "That's an intelligent, compassionate and understanding man. It's the way we have to be."

I nodded, but I couldn't help worrying that the problems might be a great deal bigger than Jimmy anticipated. And then, as if I were a gypsy and saw the future, something happened to fan the flames of my anxiety and concern.

Two days later Mrs. Bradly came to see me. She was very flustered and actually had tears running down her cheeks. I rose immediately from my chair and went to her.

"What is it, Mrs. Bradly? Something to do with your family?" I asked quickly. She shook her head. I helped her to the leather settee and poured her a glass of water.

"Thank you," she said, gulping it down. Then she sat back, took a deep breath and revealed the source of her misery. "We're missing nearly three hundred dollars from the petty cash fund," she said. "It's the first time this has ever happened since I've been working here, and you know, Dawn, that's a considerable number of years."

"Oh, Mrs. Bradly, are you sure it's missing?"

"Florence Eltz and I have gone over and over it. We have all our receipts to the penny, and there is no doubt the money is gone."

I sat down beside her. My heart began to pound. Mrs. Bradly was too polite to say the thing I feared her saying. She would wait for me to ask.

"What do you think might have happened, Mrs. Bradly? Could it have been misplaced, put into another account? A wrong deposit, perhaps?" I asked hopefully.

"Dawn, Florence and I checked all those possibilities out thoroughly before I decided I had to come see you. We forced poor Mrs. Avery to go over and over the week's deposits. You know that meant funds from the cocktail lounge as well as room deposits, but she didn't complain. She was as eager as we were to find the error.

"Only," she said, sighing, "there was no error. No, Dawn," she said, shaking her head. "There is no doubt in our minds now – the money was taken. The people who have been working in my department have been working with me for years and years. I'd swear by all of them . . . all except one," she added. Her final words fell like balls of lead. Numbly, I bowed my head.

"Did you ask her anything about it?" I wanted to know.

"She was there while we were all searching frantically. She knew we had discovered the funds missing, but she didn't say a word."

"And she had access to them?" I asked, lifting my head. It felt as if it had turned to lead itself. Mrs. Bradly bit down on her lower lip and nodded. She shook her head, her eyes filling with tears again.

"There's no other explanation, I'm afraid," she said. "As soon as she saw all the commotion, she said she had to leave. She told me she had to go home to do homework. I did ask if she knew anything about this, and she snapped a quick no and then ran off.

"I'm sorry to have to tell you all this," Mrs. Bradly added.

"Now, now, Mrs. Bradly, you did the right thing in coming to me," I said, patting her hand. "My husband

386

doesn't know anything about it, does he?" I asked her quickly.

"Oh, no, I've told no one a thing, and I've asked my people to keep their lips sealed about it. None of them will say a word. I can assure you of that."

"Very well. Let me look into it," I said. She looked as if she would break into tears again, so I hugged her and helped her to her feet. "Just go on and don't let it bother you at all, Mrs. Bradly. It's certainly no reflection on you."

"Thank you, Dawn. I'm sorry," she repeated, and she left.

I felt a cold chill come over me and embraced myself. I recalled when I had glanced into Fern's pocketbook that evening in New York as we left the hotel and had seen the pile of money. Could she have been lying about her allowance? Had she been stealing from Clayton?

I thought I would try to get to the bottom of it without involving Jimmy, if I could, so I left the office and quickly went to the house. Mrs. Boston greeted me in the entryway and told me Fern was up in her room. I hurried up the stairs and went to her door. It was slightly open, so I peered in and found her lying on her stomach on her bed, reading a romance magazine.

"I thought you came home to do your homework, Fern," I said, spinning her around. She gazed at me with that furious dark look in her eyes.

"It's not nice to sneak up on people," she responded.

"I'm not sneaking up on you. I've come to check up on you. You told Mrs. Bradly you were going home to do homework. Why aren't you doing it?"

She sat up quickly and closed her magazine.

"I just told her that because I was tired of staying

387

there. It's boring, a lot more boring than I thought it was going to be. I want to do a different job at the hotel. Maybe I can help the waiters and busboys," she suggested.

I stepped further into her room. She looked up at me suspiciously when I continued to stare at her, and then she shifted her eyes away, guiltily, I thought.

"Your wanting to leave the front desk wouldn't have anything to do with the money that's missing, would it?" I asked.

"I don't know where it is. Why, did Mrs. Bradly say I did?" she demanded, the fire returning to her eyes.

"No, but I was hoping you might be able to help us locate it."

"Well, I can't. I don't know anything about it. She must have lost it. Maybe one of those other women took it. They look poor and probably couldn't resist," she said.

"All those other women have been working here for years and years and are very trustworthy people."

"Well, so am I," she cried. "I don't steal!"

"No one's accusing you of stealing, Fern. All I want to know is whether you have any idea where it could be. Maybe it was put in a wrong drawer or a wrong envelope," I said.

"I never saw it," she insisted.

I stood there, staring at her. She kept her eyes fixed on the bed.

"If you didn't like helping at the front desk, why didn't you just come to tell me?" I asked.

"I was going to . . . tonight," she replied quickly.

"Well, that would be a lot better than telling lies. You don't have to do that anymore, Fern. There is no reason to lie to anyone, and if you ever need anything – "

"I didn't steal the money," she repeated, pounding her knees so hard with her fists, I had to shudder thinking of the pain.

"All right. Let's not talk about the money. Don't you have any homework to do?" I asked.

"I have time to do it," she whined.

"How long have you been reading those kinds of magazines?" I asked, gazing at the magazine on the bed. I remember she had packed them in her suitcase.

"I don't know," she said, shrugging. "They're not dirty, if that's what you mean."

"I didn't say they were dirty. I would have thought they were just too old for you," I said.

"Well, they're not. I like the stories. You're not going to take them away from me, are you? That's what Clayton used to do."

"No, I'm not taking them away, but – "

"You're being just as mean as he was," she cried, and she buried her face in her pillow. Her shoulders rose and fell with her sobs.

"Fern," I said, going to her, "I didn't say you couldn't have your magazines." I sat on the bed and put my hand on her shoulder, but she pulled away and jumped off the bed as if my touch was scalding.

"I didn't steal that money. I didn't!" she screamed, slapping her fists against the sides of her legs. "Mrs. Bradly is an old witch for telling you I did. She's an old witch, and you're terrible to believe her," she cried, running from the room.

"*Fern!*"

I got up and went after her, but she bounded down

the stairs and out the front door. Mrs. Boston came to the foot of the stairs and looked up.

"I'm afraid I didn't handle that too well, Mrs. Boston," I said.

She shook her head.

"It's not going to be easy for anyone to handle that one," she said prophetically, and then she returned to her work. I went back to the hotel. A short while later Jimmy came into my office, his eyes full of pain and anger. He sat down quietly and stared at me.

"What happened with Fern?" he asked, his throat constricted, his voice under tight harness. I could feel the tension in the air between us.

"Jimmy," I said softly, leaning toward him, "I think Fern took money from the petty cash fund."

Before he could respond, I told him everything Mrs. Bradly had told me. He listened and then shook his head.

"Why would she steal money, Dawn, and from us? She can have anything she wants. She doesn't need money," he said.

I told him about the money I had seen in her pocketbook when we were in New York.

"So?" he said. "That proves she wouldn't need money. She has more than she needs."

"But Jimmy, people sometimes steal for other reasons," I began.

"She wouldn't steal from us," he insisted firmly. "And I'm really surprised that you went and accused her."

"I didn't accuse her, Jimmy. I asked her if she knew anything about it, and she got hysterical on me," I said.

390

"That's my point," he fired. "You knew how sensitive and fragile she is because of all that's happened to her. Of all people, you should be more sympathetic, Dawn. She came running to me and was crying so hard, I thought I would never calm her down. My shirt is soaked with her tears," he added.

"I'm sorry, Jimmy. I was only trying to head off a bigger problem. I thought – "

"I promised her I would talk to you and that later you would apologize to her," he said.

I stared at him a moment. His words and anger left me numb. Tears flooded my eyes, but I held them back.

"I didn't do anything wrong, Jimmy," I said softly.

"It's not what you did, Dawn, it's how Fern feels. I thought you understood her yearning to be loved, her yearning for family."

"Okay, Jimmy," I said, swallowing my pride. "I'll apologize to her if you think that's the right thing to do."

"It is," he insisted. "And Dawn," he said, standing, "next time there's any sort of problem involving Fern, please come to me with it first."

My heart felt like a chunk of lead in my chest. I couldn't swallow, and one of my burning tears escaped from the corner of my eye, but Jimmy was already on his way out and didn't see it.

"Jimmy!" I cried when he reached the door. He turned back.

"What?"

"What do you suppose did happen to that money?" I asked him pointedly.

"I don't know, Dawn. Mrs. Bradly is getting along in years. It wouldn't surprise me if she found it stuck under some papers one day," he said, and he left.

And suddenly I realized that love could be wicked, too; it could beguile us like witchcraft and turn day into night, black into white and guilt into innocence.

Fern's True Colors

I didn't want to apologize to Fern because I thought it would be worse for her than for me if I did so. Despite the terrible thing that had happened to her, I saw that she was a spoiled little girl in so many ways. We weren't helping her mature and change for the better by catering to her like this, I thought, but Jimmy was so upset, I had no choice. When I returned to the house I found her up in her room. This time I knocked on her door, but she made me knock twice before she said "Come in."

"I'm doing my homework," she said as soon as I entered.

"I'm not here to check on that, Fern," I replied softly. She was sitting up in her bed, her books spread over her lap, but I caught sight of one of her romance magazines under her notebook. She lowered her eyes and played with her pencil. "You went to Jimmy and told him I accused you of stealing the money at the front desk," I said.

"Well, you did," she snapped.

I swallowed. I wasn't good at overlooking faults, but I had to do it now.

"I didn't mean to accuse you, Fern. If you thought I did, I'm sorry. Jimmy and I love you very much, and we only want you to be happy here," I told her.

"You don't love me," she retorted, her eyes fixed on me so intently, I nearly lost my breath. She had Daddy Longchamp's temper, all right. I had seen the fire in those black eyes before, especially after he had had too much to drink, and every time they had made my heart shudder.

"Of course I do."

"No, you don't," she accused. "As soon as you found out I wasn't really your sister, you stopped caring about me."

"That's not true, Fern. I always cared about you, worried about you and missed you a great deal, especially right after we were all separated. I told you, I used to be the one to take care of you most of the time." I smiled. "Do you know you said my name before you said anyone else's? It was practically the first word you uttered."

"I don't remember," she said, but her face softened some, and her eyes cooled down.

"You couldn't remember. You were too little. It's true we're not sisters, but we're sisters-in-law. Why don't you think of that?" I asked.

"Sisters-in-law?" The realization intrigued her.

"Yes. Since I'm married to your brother, you're my sister-in-law, and I want to think of you always as my sister. I do; I really do."

"Wives don't always like it when their husbands show their little sisters a lot of attention," she declared.

"What? Who told you that?" I asked, half smiling.

"I read it," she said sternly.

"Read it? Oh," I said, understanding. "In one of those romance magazines?"

"That doesn't mean it's not true," she replied.

"It's not true for me," I told her firmly. "Jimmy has enough love in him for all of us – you, me and Christie – everyone. And besides, I'm not that selfish. I see how happy he is since we found you."

"He *is* happy he found me," she asserted, swinging her shoulders. "And he doesn't like it when I'm sad," she added, only the way she turned her face and directed her eyes at me, it felt more like a threat.

"Well, I don't want you to be sad either, Fern."

"Good," she said quickly. "Can I work with the bus-boys and waiters and bellhops now?" she followed.

"I think it's more important you worry about your schoolwork than working in the hotel, honey," I told her, and her face darkened again.

"Jimmy said I could," she whined. "He promised."

I shook my head.

"I just knew you would say no," she spat out in frustration. "I knew it!"

"All right," I relented. "I'll speak to Robert Garwood. He's our chief bellhop. Maybe he can find errands for you to run for guests, okay? But if you don't do well in school . . ."

"I will," she pledged.

"Do you like school here?" I asked.

"It's all right. Can I start tomorrow? Can I?"

"Tomorrow. Oh, tomorrow Daddy Longchamp's arriving," I remembered. Once Jimmy had learned when Daddy could make the trip, he had sent him the money for plane fare. "You're going to want to spend all your spare time with him and your new brother."

She pulled the corners of her mouth up and clenched her teeth.

"I don't have to spend *all* my time with them, do I?" she moaned.

"Don't you want to?" I asked, surprised. "Daddy Longchamp is very excited about seeing you. Aren't you excited about seeing him? After all, he is your real father."

"He let them take me away and give me to the Osbornes, didn't he?" she flared.

"We explained all that to you, Fern. I thought you understood."

Jimmy and I had taken her aside one night and had told her everything, but instead of asking me questions about Daddy she had harped on my life in New York and Christie's birth. Her questions to me in front of Jimmy had begun to be embarrassing, so I had brought the discussion to an end. But she knew enough about her past now to appreciate what Daddy Longchamp's arrival meant.

"Can I at least work with the bellhops until they come?" she asked.

"All right," I said, relenting. "As soon as you come home from school, go see Robert Garwood. I'll speak to him tomorrow morning. But everyone's arriving shortly before dinnertime. We're going to have them eat here rather than in the dining room."

"Why? I like eating dinner in the dining room," she cried. "It's more fun."

"Don't you want to spend time privately with your real father?" I asked. "And your new brother?"

"I suppose," she said reluctantly. "How long are they going to stay?" she asked quickly.

"Just a few days. Daddy can't stay away from his work long," I emphasized.

396

"Good," she said, and she looked down at her books.

Good? I thought, staring down at her. How different it would have been for me if I had been told Daddy Longchamp was coming after I had been here a while. How I had yearned to see him, to hear his voice, to throw my arms around him and cling to him. They would have had to pry us apart when he left.

"Can I come in, too?" Christie asked. She stood in the doorway, one of her bigger dolls in her arms.

"Fern's doing her homework now, sweetheart," I said.

"She can come in," Fern allowed, "if she's quiet. You can sit right there and wait," Fern said, pointing to the chair by the small vanity table.

Christie smiled and hurried obediently to it before I could interfere. She sat down with her doll in her lap and folded her hands to show she would behave and be patient.

When I looked at Fern again she wore an expression of great self-satisfaction. Frustrated fury stirred around inside my stomach. Heat rose from my neck to my face. Quickly, so as not to let her see how she had disturbed me, I turned and left Fern's room.

Jimmy was waiting for a report downstairs. I told him how careless Fern was treating Daddy's arrival, but Jimmy didn't appear upset about that.

"I can understand why," he said. "It was only a short while ago that she learned she had another father. In her mind he's still a stranger."

"But Jimmy, shouldn't she be more curious and excited?" I asked.

He shook his head.

"Not that child, no," he said. "She's been hurt too much by people who supposedly loved and cared for her. She's cautious now. That's why I want us to work so hard at winning her love; it's the only way."

"It's a way of spoiling her, too, Jimmy," I insisted.

"Dawn, how can you even think that, considering what she's been through? Can you imagine what it must have been like for her every night, going to sleep after her father had done those things to her? Why, every time he approached her she would cringe inside," he said, grimacing. "He wouldn't kiss her good night without first fondling her under the blanket."

"How do you know all this, Jimmy?" I asked, aghast.

"She's been telling me more and more," he said, "now that she's learned to trust me, and now that she's convinced I care."

"She never wants to talk to me about it," I said. "The moment I bring up anything that even relates in a small way, she pleads not to discuss it."

"Dawn," he said, lowering his newspaper, "she thinks you don't like her. She thinks you resent her."

"But why?" I asked, arms out. "I took her shopping for the things she needed, bought her everything she wanted, got her set up in school, arranged for her to do what she wanted in the hotel – "

"It is just part of her mental and emotional condition, and this thing with the missing money only aggravated it. That's why I was so insistent you apologize to her. She's like a little bird who was kept tightly squeezed in a fist so it couldn't use its wings. Now every time someone comes near her and tries to show affection, she's wary. That's probably another reason why she's not showing a great deal of excitement over Daddy's arrival," Jimmy said. "Don't you think I'm right?" he asked. I could see he was waiting anxiously for my agreement.

"I suppose so," I finally said. He smiled.

"Daddy's coming tomorrow. Just think of that," he declared.

I thought about it all night. I lay in bed thinking about it. The last time I had seen Daddy Longchamp was in a police station. They were taking me out to bring me back to Cutler's Cove. The police had told me Daddy had kidnapped me; they had said he confessed to doing it. I couldn't believe what was happening. I didn't know where Jimmy was or where they had taken Fern, and I was terrified of being brought hundreds of miles to a family I had never known. Surely Daddy would do something to stop it, I thought. I was hoping that right up to the moment they were taking me out to the car, and then a door opened and I saw him sitting in a chair, his head down to his chest.

"Daddy!" I had screamed, and I ran toward the opened door. Daddy lifted his head and gazed out at me, his eyes vacant. It was as though he were hypnotized and didn't see me standing there. "Daddy, tell them this isn't true! Tell them it's all been a horrible mistake," I had pleaded. He began to speak and then shook his head and looked down in defeat instead.

I remember I kept screaming when I felt someone's hands on my shoulders trying to pull me away. I couldn't imagine why Daddy wasn't doing anything, why he didn't show his power and strength. They pulled me back out the door, and Daddy finally looked up and said, "I'm sorry, honey. I'm so sorry."

For a long time I had to live with that. Then I

discovered the truth: how he and Momma had done what they had believed was the right thing in taking me, and how Grandmother Cutler had connived and manipulated everyone.

But that nightmare had ended, and tomorrow I would see Daddy Longchamp again. I was so excited about it, I tossed and turned most of the night. The next day, from the moment I awoke, I kept myself as busy as a drone so I wouldn't dwell on Daddy's arrival. Every time I stopped and thought about it the sleeping butterflies in my stomach woke and flapped their paper-thin wings around my heart.

Late in the morning I saw Robert Garwood and told him about Fern. He didn't seem very happy about the idea.

"She's already been hanging around the busboys and waiters and some of my bellhops, Mrs. Longchamp. It's none of my business, but . . ."

"But what, Robert?" I asked.

"Well, she smokes," he revealed. "She follows the guys down to the basement where they hang out – you know, off the laundry room – and she begs cigarettes from them."

"She *what?*" I exclaimed in shock.

"I know she acts older, but I've got a sister not much younger than she is, and I don't imagine she would even think of doing that. If you'll pardon my saying so, Mrs. Longchamp, I don't think having her work alongside us – even just to run little errands – is such a good idea," he said. I could see from the way he was speaking that he had more to say. I was sorry now that Jimmy had made her another promise.

"I hate to ask you this, Robert, but let her do it for

400

a little while, and keep a close eye on her for me. The moment you see her doing something wrong, please tell me," I said. He nodded, but I saw he wasn't happy.

I was going to discuss it with Jimmy, but before I had an opportunity to be alone with him, Daddy Longchamp, his new wife Edwina and their son Gavin arrived. Julius had picked them up at the airport and brought them to the hotel. Jimmy found me in the tearoom and announced their arrival. With my heart pounding so hard I thought it would burst out of my chest, I grabbed his hand and hurried through the lobby with him. We stepped out and onto the porch as Daddy emerged from the limousine. Edwina was right beside him, holding Gavin's hand.

As soon as our eyes met, the years fell away like dried leaves fell from branches in autumn. Daddy was still tall, but he was much slimmer, and his face was a great deal leaner, so that his cheeks and chin were more bony and hard. His dark eyes were still very prominent, and although gray strands had invaded his temples and were spotted through his coal-black crown, he still had a thick, rich head of hair. He wore a dark blue jacket and slacks with black boots, and I saw he had a thick, wide belt with a silver buckle shaped like a horse's head. After all, Daddy was now a Texan, I thought.

Gavin gazed in awe. Jimmy and Fern's six-year-old half-brother was tall for his age. He looked adorable in his blue suit and bow tie. He had Daddy's black hair, but a round face with a lighter complexion. He had Edwina's brown eyes and soft, small mouth, but Daddy's straight, strong nose.

Edwina looked younger than she had in the pictures I had seen. She had a warm, gentle smile – a lot like

Momma Longchamp's smile, I thought – and I imagined that was one of the things that had attracted Daddy to her so quickly. She stood nearly as tall as he did, and she had a firm, sleek figure with long arms and legs and a narrow waist. She wore a dark blue wool coat and a dark blue dress. She had her brown hair brushed back and pinned with pearl combs, and she wore only a trace of rouge and some light red lipstick.

Jimmy rushed down the steps to shake Daddy's hand and hug Edwina. I could see how much she liked him. Then he lifted Gavin in his arms and turned as I approached.

Daddy stood there smiling and shaking his head. I drank up the special kind of virile, pantherlike handsomeness that was his.

"You've become a mighty pretty woman, Dawn. Mighty pretty," he said.

"Thank you, Daddy." The tears were streaming down my face, but I didn't notice or care. He held out his arms, and I ran to them, ran to his embrace. He held onto me tightly for a moment. In his strong embrace I felt all the frustration and sadness he had endured, and I understood that his pain had been just as sharp as mine, if not sharper. He kissed me on the forehead and then wiped my cheeks with the back of his long, thin hand.

"Now, now, no tears. We're gonna have a nice reunion here. No sadness, hear?"

"Okay, Daddy," I said, smiling.

"I want you to meet my Edwina," he said, turning.

Edwina extended her hand. It was warm and soft in mine. I could see she was a tender woman whose smile came right from the heart.

"How do you do?" she said. "I'm glad we're finally meeting."

"So am I. Welcome," I said.

"It's so beautiful here," she remarked, turning. "Jimmy wasn't exaggerating." The bright, warm late-autumn afternoon did much to add to the sparkle and charm of Cutler's Cove. Our lawns were still rich green, and the trees were full of color: yellows, browns and reds. Above us the sky had turned a dark blue, and the clouds were puffy and milk white.

"Thank you." My heart was doing flip-flops. I could barely catch my breath.

"And now meet Gavin," Daddy said.

"Hello, Gavin. I'm Dawn. Wait until you meet Christie," I told the wide-eyed little boy in Jimmy's arms.

"And Fern," Jimmy emphasized.

"Where is she?" Daddy asked, looking around.

"She's inside doing errands for the bellhops, Daddy," I said.

"Put her to work already, huh?" he said.

"She loves it, Daddy," Jimmy said. "She can't wait to come home from school and be in the hotel. Come on. Let's go inside. Julius will bring your suitcases to the house, but first we want to show you the hotel. Are you hungry?" he asked Edwina.

"No, we just ate on the plane," she answered.

"I'm hungry," Gavin quickly piped up. Everyone laughed.

"He's always hungry," Daddy said. "I think he's got two hollow legs."

We marched into the hotel, and Daddy and Edwina gaped around at everything.

"Bigger than I remember," Daddy remarked, nodding, his hands on his hips.

"Over there is the dining room," Jimmy said to Edwina, pointing, "and off left is what we call the card room or tearoom. There's a ballroom to the right where the guests see shows and dance at night. We'll take you out to see the pool and the tennis courts and – "

Jimmy stopped when Fern came running down the corridor to report to the bellhop desk. She never even saw us watching her.

"That's her, Daddy, little Fern," Jimmy said.

Daddy squinted as he gazed. Finally Fern turned our way, and Jimmy waved. She said something to Robert Garwood and then sauntered across the lobby slowly.

"Spitting image of Sally Jean," Daddy muttered.

"Fern," Jimmy began, "this is your father."

Fern looked up at him with cold scrutiny as Daddy smiled.

"Don't you want to give your father a hug, honey?" I asked.

She shrugged.

"Oh, it's gonna take some time," Daddy said understandingly. "But I guess we can shake hands, can't we?" he said, extending his. Fern looked at it as if it were diseased and then reluctantly placed hers in his. She pulled it back as quickly as she could.

"Hi," she said. "We don't look alike," she added quickly. Daddy threw his head back and roared. Fern looked away, but I saw her smirking.

"No," Daddy said. "You look more like your mother."

"This is Gavin," Jimmy said. Fern turned to him with

404

more interest. Gavin, shy, looked back intently, his dark brown eyes scanning her from head to toe.

"Hello, Gavin," Fern said. Then, surprisingly, she leaned forward to kiss him on the cheek. He looked just as surprised as the rest of us. "May I take him and show him around?" she asked. "I can take him to the ballroom where Christie's having her piano lesson."

"Gavin, you want to go with your sister?" Jimmy asked him. He looked at Jimmy and then at Daddy, who kept smiling widely. Gavin nodded, and Jimmy lowered him to the floor. Fern seized his hand and started away, Gavin trotting to keep up.

"Wait, Fern," I said. She turned back impatiently. "You haven't said hello to Edwina," I reminded her.

"Hello," Fern said quickly.

"Hi, Fern," Edwina said, smiling. Fern started away again.

"We'll meet right here in ten minutes or so," Jimmy called after her.

"Ain't she something?" Daddy said, shaking his head. "Gonna be a heartbreaker, that one," he added.

"I believe you're right, Daddy," Jimmy said. "Come on. Let us show you about. Sure you don't want something to eat or drink first?"

"I'm too excited," Edwina said. She threaded her arm through Daddy's. I decided they did look good together, and I could see from the way he looked at her that he loved her very much.

I never realized how proud I was of Cutler's Cove until we showed Daddy and Edwina around. They were so impressed with everything and Daddy kept saying things like, "I can't believe this is all yours, honey. Wouldn't Momma be just burstin' with joy?"

After we had shown them about the hotel and Daddy saw all the changes, we gathered Fern, Gavin and Christie together and walked over to the house, where Daddy and Edwina oohed and ahhed some more. Jimmy took Daddy around to show him some of the details of the construction while I paraded Edwina about the dining room and living room, showing her our furniture and artwork. Mrs. Boston put up some water for tea, and we sat around and talked some more. The children went upstairs with Fern so Christie could show Gavin all her toys. Fern had taken to the role of big sister rather quickly.

"I can't get over how mature Fern is for her age," Edwina said, shaking her head.

I knew that Jimmy had told Daddy everything about her, so I didn't have to go into Fern's tragic history. Instead, Edwina told me about herself, how she had been married before, but how her husband of only two years had been killed in a truck accident in Texas. Less than a year later she had met Daddy, and they had taken to each other quickly. We had a good talk while Jimmy and Daddy inspected the house and the grounds. I decided I liked Edwina a lot, and I could see how she would be a good stabilizing influence on Daddy. He and Jimmy came in on us while she was telling me how much Daddy's boss liked him.

"Nobody blows my horn better than she does," Daddy remarked. Edwina smiled up at him, and they kissed. Jimmy and I exchanged a quick glance, both of us happy to see Daddy so pleased with his life now. I thought Jimmy was right about him – he was a changed man, more settled, gentler, wiser.

When we looked in on Gavin, Fern and Christie we

406

found Gavin and Christie seated quietly on the floor with Fern standing above them, her arms folded across her chest. She looked like a stern schoolteacher. Christie and Gavin had toys and games all around them.

"Everything is fine," Fern told us. "Everyone is behaving," she said.

"Ain't she the little lady?" Daddy said.

"The whole world should get along as well as children do," Edwina said.

"Ain't that the truth," Daddy added.

We showed Daddy and Edwina to their room so they could shower and dress for dinner. Mrs. Boston had prepared a turkey and all the fixings. It was truly going to be a Thanksgiving.

Jimmy had talked me into permitting Christie and Fern to stay home from school the next day so they would have more time to spend with Gavin.

"Otherwise the poor guy will be bored to death all day," Jimmy said.

In the morning after breakfast Jimmy took Daddy Longchamp around with him to see the kinds of work he had to supervise. I knew the two of them would be happy off discussing boilers and motors. I had introduced Edwina and Daddy to Betty Ann and Philip. Edwina got along very well with Betty Ann, who took her to see the twins and their portion of the old section of the hotel while I tended to some business matters.

In the afternoon we all had lunch in the dining room. To my surprise and delight, Philip volunteered to take Edwina and Betty Ann into town to see some of the sights and shops. Daddy was content spending his time with Jimmy around the hotel. Fern, still acting the role of big sister, took Christie and Gavin back to the house. I returned to my office for a meeting with Mr. Dorfman. It ran longer than I had anticipated, and when I looked up at the clock I saw it was nearly four.

Wondering how the children were getting along, I decided to stop over at the house. Mrs. Boston was in the kitchen preparing a large roast beef. We were going to have Philip, Betty Ann and the twins over for dinner as well, since Daddy had to leave the next morning.

"I hope the children haven't been a problem for you, Mrs. Boston," I said when I paused in the kitchen.

"The children?" She thought a moment. "You know, Dawn, I completely forgot they were here. They've been so quiet up there."

"Oh? Well, that's very nice," I said. I imagined that Mrs. Boston was so involved with her dinner preparations that she wouldn't have heard them anyway. I went up the stairs quickly and was surprised to discover they weren't in Christie's room; they were in Fern's, and the door was shut.

I started to open it when I heard Fern say, "You can touch it, Christie. It's not going to bite you."

I hoped they hadn't brought a little garter snake into the house. Mrs. Boston would absolutely faint if she saw it, I thought, laughing to myself. But when I opened the door I was shocked to discover Christie and Gavin facing each other, both totally naked. Fern was standing with her back to me and apparently hadn't heard me enter.

"Mommy," Christie cried. Fern spun around, her face turning beet red.

"What in the world . . . what's going on here, Fern?" I demanded.

"Nothing," she said quickly. "I mean . . . I don't

know," she sputtered. She stepped away from the two of them.

"You don't know? Why are they undressed?"

"They did it themselves," she said quickly. "I was . . . downstairs, and when I came up I found them like this. It was Gavin's idea," she said, pointing accusingly at him. "He told Christie he would show her his if she would show him hers."

I looked at Gavin. He stood terrified, his eyes glazed with fear.

"Is that true, Christie?" I asked.

She started to shake her head, but her eyes caught Fern's furious look of warning. Then she started to cry.

"Get them dressed," I commanded. "Immediately."

"Come on, Gavin," Fern said, pulling him to the bed, where most of his clothing lay. She lifted him up and started dressing him while I helped Christie.

"I don't understand this, Christie. Why would you do such a thing? Don't you know it's not nice to undress yourself in front of boys?" She kept crying, but I was seething inside. I knew Fern was lying, and I wanted Christie to tell me so.

"I'm sorry, Momma," she bawled. "I'm sorry."

"And Gavin's momma and daddy will be very upset, too."

"Maybe you better not tell them," Fern said. "Daddy Longchamp looks mean enough to beat the skin off him."

"Fern!" I spun around on her. "You will have him absolutely terrified of his father."

She shrugged.

409

"Nothing happened. They just looked at each other. You don't have to tell," she insisted.

"We'll discuss it afterward," I said. "Finish dressing him."

As soon as the two of them were fully dressed I sent them out of the room and downstairs to wait while I spoke to Fern. She sat on her bed and stared down at the floor.

"How could you do such a thing with children that little?" I said, forgetting for the moment that I was speaking to a girl only a little more than ten herself.

"I told you," she said, glaring back hatefully, "I didn't do it."

"Stop lying. I heard you just before I opened the door."

She stared at me a moment, and then suddenly she burst into tears.

"Oh, you're going to go tell Jimmy now, and Daddy Longchamp, and everyone will hate me. That's just what you want," she cried.

"Fern, that's not so. I don't want anyone to hate you," I said, but she just cried harder and harder. "I'm not going to tell them," I said finally. "I'm not."

Her crying stopped instantly.

"You're not?" she asked, grinding the tears from her eyes.

"No. But it was a very naughty thing to do. Why did you do it?" I demanded.

She thought for a moment and then said, "They were playing with dolls, and Gavin wondered why the boy dolls didn't have what he had," she said. "Then Christie asked what that was, so I thought they should

410

both know the difference. It was just educational. Like science class," she explained.

"That's not the way to teach them, Fern, and I asked you once before not to talk about those things with Christie yet. She's too young," I said firmly.

"Okay," she said. "You're really not going to tell?"

"I said I wasn't, but that doesn't mean I'm not very upset. Nothing like this must ever happen again," I emphasized. She nodded.

And then she narrowed her eyes and said, "If you tell Jimmy after saying you won't, I'll hate you forever." My mouth gaped open. The force of her threat made my breath catch in my throat. For a moment I couldn't speak.

"It's not nice to threaten, Fern," I responded, but she didn't look away. She made her eyes blank and refused to speak. My heart pounding, I turned and left the room.

Maybe it was a mistake, but I didn't say anything to Jimmy about the incident. Everyone was enjoying Daddy and Edwina so much, I didn't want to spoil the day and the evening. Our meal was wonderful. Even Philip, who I feared would be snobby and condescending to Daddy, was charming and friendly. I assumed he was doing everything he could to continue to make up for the horrible way he had behaved when Jimmy was away. He kept looking at me to see if I was pleased with him.

Before the evening ended I played the piano and sang. I saw that it brought tears to Daddy's eyes. When I was finished he got up quickly and came to me to draw me into his embrace. He bowed his head into my hair, his breath stirring it as he spoke.

411

"If only Momma was here to see this," he said. We both cried, and then Betty Ann talked Christie into playing the piano, too. Little Gavin looked absolutely fascinated with her. He sat unmoving, his eyes fixed on her every move. Afterward, when we all applauded, I thought he clapped his little hands harder than any of us.

Betty Ann got the twins to perform a little dance when I played for them. Everyone loved the way the golden two-some hugged and turned each other and then clapped their hands for themselves. We all laughed.

Only Fern looked unhappy. She sat in a corner, away from everyone, a sour expression on her face unless Jimmy spoke to her or looked at her. Then she would smile widely, lovingly. Toward the end of the evening Daddy tried to talk to her, asking her questions about school, but she was very flippant and acted completely disinterested. Finally he laughed and gave up.

It was time for all the children to go to bed anyway. Betty Ann and Philip left with the twins, promising to meet Daddy and Edwina for breakfast in the dining room in the morning. After they left, Daddy, Edwina, Jimmy and I sat in the living room talking about Fern.

"I think you two did a wonderful thing rescuing her from that terrible life and bringing her here to live with you. She's certainly got a lot of advantages," Daddy said, shaking his head. "She's lucky now, growing up in a place like this."

"It doesn't bother you that she's not going back to live with you right now, Daddy?" Jimmy asked.

"Oh, no, Jimmy. I think she's better off here, now that I see her. She's a big girl already, and – well, to

412

tell you the truth, we're just making ends meet as it is, and we want to do as much as we can for Gavin," Daddy said.

Jimmy nodded, but when he gazed at me I saw the sadness in his eyes. I knew he was wishing Daddy had had these thoughts about him when he was Gavin's age, but that was a different time, almost a different world.

"Okay, Daddy," Jimmy said. "We'll do the best we can for Fern, and we'll keep in close touch with you."

"Oh, I know you two will do just fine by her, just fine," Daddy said. A silence dropped around us as Daddy gazed from Jimmy to me and then back to Jimmy. Jimmy and I glanced at each other. We knew what had to be going through Daddy's mind: He had known us only as his children, and now we were man and wife. He tried his best to hide it.

"Well," he said, "I guess Edwina and I should turn in. We got a big day of traveling tomorrow." He clapped his hands together and stood up. "Thank you for a wonderful dinner."

"You're more than welcome, Daddy," Jimmy said. Then Daddy stared at him, a slight smile on his lips.

"A sight better than the meals I used to provide."

"We made do with what we had, Daddy," Jimmy said.

"We had no choice," Daddy added. "But that's all behind us now. We gotta be happy, gotta try to be happy. Good night, son," he said, shaking Jimmy's hand.

"Good night, Daddy," Jimmy said, tears in his eyes.

"Good night, Jimmy," Edwina said, and she kissed him. Daddy stopped in front of me.

"Dawn. Thank you, honey. Thank you for making this old heart sing."

He kissed me and gathered me tightly in his arms again. I could barely speak. Then he turned and walked out quickly with Edwina. A melancholy such as I had never known clamped down over my heart.

Jimmy smiled at me, and I rushed into his arms so I could cry against his shoulder. His arm around me, Jimmy turned me toward the doorway, and we went upstairs to fall asleep securely in each other's arms, as we had done so many nights before.

Daddy and Edwina rose early in the morning to say their good-byes to Fern. I was hoping, as was Daddy, that she would finally relent and plant a kiss on his cheek; however, she would only shake his hand again. Edwina kissed her, but Fern looked uncomfortable in her arms and couldn't wait to squirm free. She did kiss Gavin good-bye. Daddy walked out with the children and me to watch them get into the limousine to go to school.

"Good-bye, Fern," he said. "I'll try to come back soon to see you again. Your mother would have been pleased as punch to see how well you've grown."

She barely glanced back at him before she got into the car. He waved as they pulled away, but Fern was looking out the other side.

"I guess her bad time with those people must've clamped her up tight like a clam," Daddy muttered as the limousine disappeared.

"I guess so, Daddy."

"Well, I guess I'm quite a sight for her, this old gent from down Texas way. Can't blame her for not sucking up to me," he added.

As soon as Edwina completed packing their things we went over to the hotel for breakfast. Betty Ann and Philip were already at our table. We all had a good chat, and then Julius, who had returned from taking the children to school, picked up Daddy and Edwina's things and waited for them in front of the hotel. Jimmy and I escorted them out to the car, where we said our good-byes.

"Thank you so much for your hospitality," Edwina said. "I really enjoyed our little holiday. Maybe some-day you can come see us."

"I hope so," I said. We kissed. Daddy shook Jimmy's hand for one last time, and Jimmy hugged Gavin. I hugged him, too, and then I stepped forward to kiss Daddy goodbye.

"One of these days," Daddy said, "I plan on visiting Sally Jean's grave, and when I do, I'm going to blabber like some old fool about you, I'm sure. She always knew you'd be something special, honey," he said.

"Oh, Daddy, I'm not anyone special. Circumstances just put me here," I said.

"Yeah, but you've lived up to your chores and then some, and that takes someone special," he insisted. "Bye, baby." He kissed me on the cheek. "Sorry I made such a mess of things," he said, and he began to get into the limousine.

"Daddy."

He turned.

"I love you," I said. He smiled, and for a moment I saw him young and strong again, that charming smile

415

on his face. I remembered him as he was to me when I was a very little girl – the strongest, handsomest man in the world.

Then he got into the limousine, and they were off. Jimmy and I remained on the steps watching them disappear down the street. When I looked at Jimmy I saw the tears in his eyes. The cool autumn breeze lifted the strands of hair from his forehead. It seemed to be growing colder and grayer with every passing moment.

"I've got to get back to work," he muttered, and he hurried off.

Jimmy was right – only work could keep us from thinking of the sorrow we had left behind. I went to my office and dived into book work, not thinking about anything else until the phone rang. The voice on the other end took me by surprise – it was Leslie Osborne.

"Clayton would be furious if he knew I had called you," she began, "but I couldn't help myself. How is she doing?"

"She's enjoying life at the hotel," I said, "and I think she's adjusting well to her new school, although I haven't seen any of her grades yet, nor spoken with any of her teachers."

"That's good," Leslie said, her voice growing smaller. "She was having a lot of trouble at the Marion Lewis School recently. I never told Clayton all of it."

"I know. Her records were forwarded. The principal believes she was acting out to get help," I told her.

"I'm sorry," she responded quickly, "but I can't believe any of what she told you about Clayton. I wish you would believe me, too. He's not that sort."

416

"Mrs. Osborne, I must tell you that there are problems with Fern. She does have emotional difficulties. Something happened to her; something went wrong," I insisted.

"She was a problem child right from the start. We even had trouble with her when she was in first grade. I don't know what to say," Leslie Osborne replied.

"Well, I hope she will change for the better," I said.

"It was nothing we did," Leslie maintained. "We tried to give her everything she could want."

"Maybe that was part of it, Mrs. Osborne. She does show signs of being spoiled. Giving a girl that young such a big allowance, for example . . ."

"Allowance? She never had a regular allowance. Clayton was against that. She was given money whenever she needed it for specific things, but he didn't believe in her getting a weekly amount to squander on silly things."

"No allowance? Well, somehow she managed to save hundreds of dollars," I told her. "I saw it myself, in her pocketbook."

There was a tiny cry from her end.

"What is it?" I asked.

"It's my money," she said. "She was taking it behind my back, I'm afraid. I couldn't imagine why I didn't have as much as I was supposed to in my pocketbook.

"I must tell you," she continued, "that she once took money from a friend who had slept overnight. I never told Clayton about that time because he gets so worked up over those things, but I should have realized. I don't know why she steals; she never lacked anything. She's

417

not still doing that sort of thing, is she?" she asked quickly.

"No," I lied.

"Good. Then maybe she will change for the better. Just do me one favor," she said.

"Of course. What is it?"

"When you can, when the moment allows, please tell her I still love her very much. Will you?" she begged.

"Yes," I said.

"I'll try to call you again real soon," she said, and then she said good-bye.

Later in the day I found Jimmy on his way down to the basement. I stopped him and told him about my telephone conversation with Leslie Osborne. His eyes narrowed, and he shook his head.

"It's just like the school principal said," he remarked when I told him of her stealing. "She was trying to reach out, to get someone to notice her and the terrible thing that was happening to her."

"But Jimmy, it's not happening to her here. Why should she still steal?"

"*If* she did," he emphasized. "*If* she did. I still think that money's been misplaced. Anyway, even if she did, it's just a bad habit now," he added. "She's going to grow out of it as she becomes more and more secure about us and herself. You'll see.

"Besides," he said, growing angry, "I wouldn't believe anything that woman said. Those two . . . How could she not know what her husband was doing? Next time she calls, don't speak to her," he commanded. "She was either blind or too selfish to see," he added, and he marched away.

Oh, Jimmy, I thought fearfully as I watched him turn the corner in the hallway, it's you who have become blind now.

And how will I ever get you to see?

Tarnished Images

Mother made good on her promise and held a dinner in Fern's honor. As usual, it was more of a banquet. Why she felt it was necessary to impress a ten-and-a-half-year-old girl, I'll never know, but there we were, seated at the long table: Mother in one of her elegant gowns, Bronson dressed impeccably as usual in a burgundy sports jacket and matching cravat, and servants flying all around us, pouring water and wine, mixing our salads, hovering nearby to lunge if one of us should so much as lean toward the butter dish. The one thing that Mother did to please me was not invite any other guests. There were only members of the family present: Jimmy and me and Christie, Philip, Betty Ann and the twins, and Fern, of course, who Mother insisted be permitted to sit at the head of the table.

"She is, after all, the guest of honor," Mother announced. "And quite a pretty one, if I might say so."

Fern looked as pleased as could be at the comment. Jimmy had asked me to take her to one of the finest department stores in Virginia Beach to buy her a new dress for the occasion. She had chosen an expensive blue velvet with a white lace collar and cuffs. The dress had a sash at the waist with a bow on the hip, too. Actually, it was more of a dress for a girl well into her teens, but with a few adjustments Fern could wear it well. She also talked me into buying her a padded bra, claiming all her new girlfriends at school were wearing them. I gathered that she was hanging around with older children, just as she had when she attended the Marion Lewis School in New York, but I didn't make an issue over it.

Naturally, I had to buy her shoes to match the dress, and when we walked past a jewelry store she eyed a gold-plated necklace and matching teardrop earrings so covetously, I just had to get the set for her. After she hugged me and thanked me profusely, I began to regret what I was doing.

Was I no better than Clayton and Leslie Osborne, trying to buy her affection and love?

I gave her permission to go to our hair salon in the hotel, and our top stylist, Elaine Diana, washed and styled Fern's hair in a much more mature look. Elaine, unbeknownst to me, made up Fern's face for her as well. When Fern emerged from her room, dressed in her new clothing, bedecked in her new jewelry, her hair redone, her cheeks brushed with rouge, her eyelids painted and her lips covered in a bright pink shade, she looked years older than she was. Jimmy stood gaping in astonishment.

"Is this my baby sister?" he cried, and then he drew her into his arms and hugged her. Her dark eyes brightened and shone like onyx. She flashed me one of her self-satisfied looks, and what I saw in her dark eyes startled me. It was as if she had been competing with me for Jimmy's romantic love and had won. She kissed him on the cheek.

"Thank you, Jimmy," she said.

"Don't thank me, honey. Thank Dawn. She's the one who bought you all this," he replied. Fern turned to hug me as well. As she did so, Jimmy beamed and nodded. I knew he thought he was right: Lavishing all this affection and raining down all this love on her was making her a better person.

She couldn't have been more polite or more delightful at Mother's. The Osbornes had taught her well when it came to dining etiquette. She didn't have to be told which fork and spoon to use, and she dazzled Bronson by referring to him as sir. When either he or Mother asked her a question she replied softly, with measured phrases, describing places she had visited, things she had seen, art and theater she had experienced. She sounded as sophisticated and experienced as a girl twice her age. I saw how impressed they were with her and how Jimmy radiated pride.

"What a delightful young lady she is," Mother told me at the end of the evening. "Obviously she's had good training."

I saw immediately that Jimmy didn't appreciate any praise being given to the Osbornes. His face darkened with displeasure.

"She's not a racehorse, Mother," I replied before he could voice his own objections. "She's a little girl. True, she was brought up in a well-to-do home, but believe me, she didn't have a happy life."

"Oh, I know, I know. I'm just delighted to see a child behave nowadays," she said, swinging her eyes from me to Jimmy. She sighed deeply. "Which reminds me," she added, placing her right palm over her heart as if she were close to a faint, "I have news concerning Clara Sue.

"She's living with that truck driver, Skipper, outside of Raleigh, North Carolina. We found out when she phoned to get Bronson to send her some money. She sits in his truck and travels around the country with him. Can you imagine? How she finds these people, I'll never know.

"Oh, what did I do, what did I do," she moaned, "to have that child become such a burden?"

"It's not what you did, Mother," I said, unable to keep the caustic tone out of my voice, "it's what you didn't do."

"Please, Dawn, don't start one of your famous lectures about Clara Sue – not tonight, after we've had such a special time celebrating the return of Jimmy's long-lost sister," she said, spinning around quickly to shine her charm on him.

He thanked her, and then we thanked Bronson and said our good nights. Mother complained that we were leaving too early, but I explained it was a school night. I felt certain Fern hadn't done all her homework. As it turned out, I was wrong: She hadn't done any of it. And for days and days.

Mr. Youngman phoned late the next morning to give me a summary of Fern's activities since we had enrolled her in the Cutler's Cove School.

"All of her teachers here have the same complaints," he explained. "She is erratic. Sometimes she will do her work and do it well, and then she won't do it at all, and for days at a time. She makes up all sorts of excuses. Blatant, obvious fabrications, I'm afraid.

"She has also been insubordinate on two occasions, one serious enough to have the teacher send her to me. I think our problems might be bigger than I first anticipated, Mrs. Longchamp. Tender loving care isn't all she needs right now; she needs some strict discipline as well."

"Thank you for the call, Mr. Youngman," I said. "I'll speak to my husband about it immediately, and we will speak to Fern."

"Thank you, Mrs. Longchamp," he said.

I went to see Jimmy as soon as I could and told him everything Mr. Youngman had said. His eyes shadowed, grew deep, dark, and he shook his head.

"I think he's right, Jimmy. We have to be firmer with her, too."

"I thought she was doing so well," he said.

"That's what she told us, Jimmy," I pointed out. "It's not the truth."

"All right," he said. "We'll speak with her."

That evening he and I had a meeting with Fern in her room. We laid down new rules.

"You are to go right to the house after school," Jimmy said, "and do your homework before you do anything else. When it's finished, bring it to Dawn to check. If it's done all right, you can do what you want in the hotel.

"But if we hear that you've been insubordinate to your teachers again, you won't be able to come to the hotel at all," he said. "You will be confined to your room. We know you've been through bad times, Fern, but you've got to do your work, and you've got to behave. If we don't make sure you do, we're being very bad guardians, and we have no right to keep you here. Do you understand?"

The whole time she kept her eyes down. She nodded without lifting her face toward us. I looked at Jimmy and saw how painful this was for him, but he knew he had to do it.

"Okay," he said, "let's see if we can start over and start on the right foot."

Fern said nothing, but as we turned to leave she finally lifted her head and looked my way. Her face was filled with rage: Her eyes were narrowed into black slits, her lips thinned and taut so that the bottoms of her clenched teeth gleamed in the light of the nearby lamp. Her hateful gaze made my blood run cold. I knew she was accusing me of turning Jimmy against her, but I was convinced more than ever that we had to get firmer with her before it was too late.

Instead of pouting and sulking, however, Fern turned over a new leaf. During the next few weeks she did just as we asked: concentrated on her homework and schoolwork and behaved well in her classes. I expected her to be belligerent toward me the first time she came to have me check her homework, but she was as sweet as could be. Afterward, instead of running off to be with the older boys and girls at the hotel, she volunteered to help Mrs. Boston with some of the household chores and spent time helping Christie with her schoolwork, too. Her improvement was so dramatic, in fact, that Mr. Youngman phoned me to express his pleasure and gratitude. I couldn't wait to tell Jimmy, and at dinner that night we let Fern know how happy we were with the changes she had made.

"Thank you," she said. "I suppose I was just being a brat."

Jimmy smiled at me, but before we finished dinner Fern turned to him to make a special request.

"I've been asked to go to a dance," she announced.

"Can I go? I can wear the dress and jewelry Dawn bought me for the dinner."

"A dance? In grade school?" Jimmy looked at me, but I shook my head. I knew nothing about it.

"Well, it's not in grade school; it's in the junior high school," she said.

"Junior high school? Who asked to take you?" Jimmy inquired.

"Just a boy. Can I go? Can I?" she begged, directing herself entirely toward Jimmy. He sputtered and stammered.

"I don't know . . . I . . . junior high . . ."

"I'm already in the sixth grade. I'm practically in junior high," she moaned.

"How old is the boy who asked you?" I inquired.

"What's the difference? It's just a dance," she complained.

"Are any other girls from your class going?" I pursued suspiciously.

"I don't know," she said quickly. "Most of them act like babies."

"How old is this boy, Fern?" I repeated. "Is he in the seventh grade, the eighth grade . . ."

"He's in the eleventh grade," she admitted.

"Eleventh grade? That's not junior high, that's senior high," I said, looking at Jimmy.

"Oh, it's all the same dance," Fern pointed out.

"Why would a boy that old ask you to a dance?" I said. "You're just going on eleven. I don't think a girl your age – "

"I knew you would say no," she cried. "I knew it!"

"Now just a minute, Fern," Jimmy began.

"She hates me; she hated me from the moment I

426

came here," she cried. "She couldn't wait to tell you bad things about me."

"Fern, that's enough!" Jimmy snapped.

She gazed at him and then looked down, real tears streaming down her face. Christie's eyes widened in shock at the scene before her.

"Dawn's right," Jimmy said. "A boy in eleventh grade shouldn't be interested in a girl your age. You're growing up too fast."

Her head snapped up, her eyes glazed with tears and pain.

"You two didn't wait to grow up," she charged.

Jimmy's face reddened.

"That's not fair, Fern," I said softly. "We lived in different times, under entirely different circumstances."

"I think you owe us an apology," Jimmy said. "I really do."

She looked down, her shoulders sagging.

"I'm sorry," she muttered. "May I go upstairs now?"

"You're not finished with your dinner," Jimmy said.

"I'm not hungry anymore."

"Fern, it's better that you listen to us this time. We're just trying to do the right things for you," I said.

"Okay," she said, wiping her cheeks with the napkin. "I just want to go upstairs and read."

"Go on, then," Jimmy said.

As soon as she left the room Christie turned to me.

"What's the matter with Aunt Fern?" she asked.

"She's growing up too fast," I said. Christie looked at me quizzically.

"Am I growing up too fast, Momma?" she asked.

"I hope not, sweetheart. I really hope not," I said. It

brought a smile back to Jimmy's face, but he couldn't help turning toward the door and looking after Fern, worry drawing dark shadows around his eyes. I reached across the table and touched his hand. "I'll speak to her, Jimmy," I promised.

Afterward I went upstairs and knocked softly on her door.

"Come in," she said. She was curled up on her bed, reading a library book.

"Fern," I began, "I think maybe you and I ought to have a heart-to-heart talk."

"You mean talk about sex?" she said, turning the corners of her mouth down.

"Yes. Apparently you are growing up very fast. Did Leslie ever sit down and discuss it with you?"

She laughed.

"Hardly," she said. Then she leaned toward me and said in a whisper, "I don't think she and Clayton even do anything together anymore. They have separate bedrooms, you know," she said, sitting back.

"That," she added, "is probably why he did what he did to me."

I was astounded. How could a girl this young be so sophisticated when it came to sex? And then I thought, maybe growing up in New York City did it. She was exposed to more and consequently learned faster.

"You seem to know a great deal more than I did when I was your age, Fern," I said. She shrugged. "Where did you learn it all, then, if Leslie didn't talk to you?"

"From friends at school and stuff," she said nonchalantly.

"What's 'stuff' mean?"

"Books and magazines and things. Just stuff," she said.

"I see. Well, may I tell you something, some wise things I have learned, then?"

"Sure," she said. She finally looked intrigued, interested in something I had to say.

"Your body is just turning into the body of a young woman. Things are changing in you – "

"I know. I'm getting a bosom. Boys notice, too," she added, pleased with herself.

"It's not just getting a bosom, Fern. Becoming a grown woman involves a lot more. You have different feelings. Suddenly things – things you never expect to happen – happen. You cry for apparently no reason; you long to feel things, touch things, hear and see things that didn't interest you very much before.

"And boys . . . boys can become fascinating. You notice things about them that you've never noticed before, and you want to be around them a lot more.

"Mostly," I continued, "you want them to think of you as a young woman now, and not as a little girl, right? That's why you like hanging around the older boys at the hotel, and that's why you beg cigarettes and smoke with them in the basement," I added.

Her eyes widened.

"Who told you that? Robert Garwood, I bet. He's an ogre. I don't even like him. He's lying!"

"I know you smoked cigarettes down in the basement, Fern," I repeated, "but I've never told Jimmy. You shouldn't think I want to turn him against you. I don't, but *you* will turn him against you if you don't take your time growing up.

"I know it might sound silly to you, but you've got

429

to be careful about your feelings. Sometimes they run away with you, and you do things you regret later."

"Like when you got pregnant with Christie?" she asked quickly.

"Yes, but I was lucky I had Jimmy to love me. Not everyone is so lucky, Fern. Instead of relying on being lucky, you should rely on being wise. If you throw yourself at older boys, they're going to think you're not wise, and they're going to take advantage of you. I think you understand what I'm saying, don't you?"

She nodded.

"It's just a dance," she muttered.

"Older boys don't think of it that way, and I think that this older boy saw something in you that gave him reason to believe you didn't, either. Otherwise he might not have asked you," I said.

"Why? I'm just as pretty as some of the girls in the ninth and tenth grades," she asserted.

"I'm sure you are – even prettier – but that's not the point, is it? Why didn't he ask one of those girls? All we're asking is that you take your time growing up. It will all come; you will have an army of boyfriends, I'm sure, and you won't miss a thing."

"Then when can I go to a dance?" she asked.

"Soon, I'm sure. And when the time is right, we won't stop you; we'll be happy for you." I patted her on the hand and got up.

"Jimmy's really mad at me, isn't he?" she asked quickly.

"No, he's not mad; he's worried. Why don't you go downstairs and talk to him?" I suggested.

"Okay," she said, sliding off the bed. Then she paused at the doorway and turned to me. I thought she was going to thank me for the little talk, but instead she asked, "Someday will you tell me how you let yourself fall in love and get pregnant at such a young age?"

"Someday," I said. She smiled and walked out quickly, leaving me struck nearly breathless by her request.

It had been a while since I had thought much about Michael Sutton. Occasionally, when Trisha would call or visit, she would bring me some tidbits about him and his career, things she had heard or read in the trade magazines. But Fern's request to tell her about my tragic love story seemed like some magical spell cast by a wicked witch, for less than a week later I received the most shocking phone call – a call from Michael himself.

"Hello, Dawn," he said, and I knew immediately that it was he. I would never forget that melodic, resonant voice, the voice that had called to me in dreams while I was living in New York and attending the Sarah Bernhardt School of Performing Arts. For a moment I couldn't respond. My heart lodged somewhere in my throat. It was as if all the time between us had been a dream. "It's Michael," he finally said.

"Michael?"

"Yes." He laughed. "I know you never expected to hear from me again, and you probably don't want to, but I couldn't stop myself from calling you. I'm in Virginia Beach."

"Virginia Beach!"

"Yes, only a few miles away. After all this time," he continued, "only a few miles away. How have you been?"

"How have I been?"

This was the man who had said he loved me and wanted me with him always, and when he found out I was pregnant he had told me he was happy about it; this was the same man who had deserted me and left me crying on a city street in a snowstorm.

"How have I been?" I repeated, as if I had to have him confirm he was actually asking such a question.

He laughed again, a nervous laugh. The great Michael Sutton, nervous? I thought. How unlike him; how especially unlike him to show it.

"I made some inquiries about you after I returned to the States and traveled to Virginia. From what I've been told, you've inherited quite a well-known resort, one frequented by well-to-do vacationers," he said.

"That's true, Michael," I replied in a voice so formal Grandmother Cutler would have been jealous. "I'm also happily married."

"I know, I know." He laughed again, a thin, weak laugh this time. "You married that soldier boy you thought was your brother, right?"

"Who has been a wonderful and loving father," I added pointedly. My words were as sharp and as pointed as darts, all falling on a bull's-eye.

"Really," he said. "Well, I'm glad about that. Anyway, I would like to see you."

"See me? What for, Michael?" I demanded. "Why would you want to see me now?" My voice dripped with anger and sarcasm.

"I know you have a right to be furious with me, Dawn," he said quickly. "But if you will give me a chance to explain – "

"Explain?" I started to laugh.

"And tell you things I couldn't tell you then," he added in a louder voice, "you will at least understand.

"Besides," he said in a softer, more solicitous tone, "I'd like to see our child."

"Our child? She's not our child anymore, Michael; she's mine and Jimmy's. We've gone through all the legal steps. Jimmy has formally adopted her."

"I understand," he said. "I just want to see her, just once, that's all."

"Why would you suddenly care about her now, Michael? Where have you been all these years?" I asked sharply.

"As I said, you will understand once we meet. It's not the sort of thing one can explain over a telephone. I'm staying in this nice hotel, the Dunes."

The two contradictory parts of myself began a desperate struggle. Everything good in me, everything mature and sensible told me to scream back at him, to tell him how despicable, insensitive and irresponsible I thought he was and then hang up on him, forbidding him ever to call again. But that softer part of me begged me to be compassionate and merciful. Why shouldn't he see his daughter, and she see him? Perhaps he had come to suffer remorse for his actions and wanted, sought, craved a way to make some sort of amends, at least to her. Who was I to deny him that? Also, I couldn't help being curious about him and his story. What could he possibly tell me that would justify what he had done to me?

But if Jimmy should find out, he would be furious with me, I thought. He would be more than furious – he would be deeply hurt. I couldn't decide.

"You don't have to tell her who I am," Michael

suggested, anticipating some of my hesitation. "We'll pretend I'm an old friend visiting. That way no one need know," he said, and he added, "No one knows who I am here. I'm not in town to do any performing; I'm just passing through."

"I don't know, Michael. I – "

"What's her name?" he asked quickly.

"Christie," I said, realizing how terribly sad and tragic it was that her father hadn't known her name until now.

"Beautiful name. Did we pick that out? I can't remember."

"No, Michael, we didn't."

"Anyway," he said, wisely changing the subject, "for me to be so close to you and Christie and not to see you . . . it would be a sin," he said.

"Don't talk to me of sins," I snapped back.

"Oh, I wouldn't be blaming you. No, no. I'd be blaming myself. It would be another sin added to those I have unfortunately accumulated. Dawn, just for a few minutes, even just ten minutes . . ."

"It would have to be late in the afternoon tomorrow, after Christie returns from school," I said, relenting.

"Fine, fine. We'll have some tea at my hotel. What time?"

"Four o'clock," I said, not believing I was agreeing to this.

"Perfect. I'll do nothing but wait all day. Thank you. Good-bye until then," he said, and he cradled the phone just as I had second thoughts.

"Michael, wait – "

The line was dead. Slowly I returned my receiver to its cradle and then sat back. I shouldn't do this without

434

telling Jimmy, I thought. He would never understand. And yet I knew if I did tell him, he would be furious. He might even go down to the hotel in Virginia Beach before I did and pound Michael through the floor or throw him through a window.

No, it was better I did it without his knowing, quickly, staying only a few minutes. I would do just as Michael suggested – I would tell Christie we were visiting some old friend. I'd pretend we just happened to meet him.

I couldn't believe how my body was shaking. Was I trembling because of fear, or was I trembling because of excitement? Michael's handsome face flashed before me. I had done so well keeping those memories locked and buried in the deepest chambers of my heart, but in a moment Michael had burst into my new life and torn open the black chest of remembrances, permitting them to escape into my conscious thoughts. Once again I heard the music, saw his impish glint, heard his laughter and felt myself being swept up in his arms. Falling in love with someone so debonair, sophisticated and handsome had been overwhelming for a girl my age. The power of those recollections was enormous. They could still bring a flush to my face and take my breath away.

Try as I would, I couldn't put my impending rendez-vous with Michael out of mind. Every moment of silence was filled with the sound of Michael's voice, the memory of his singing or his laughter. And if I stopped working, my mind drifted back quickly to some scene with him in New York, even just walking alongside him in the corridors of the school.

At dinner Jimmy noticed I was going in and out of daydreams, and finally he asked me if anything was wrong.

"You look so distracted at times," he said. "Are you worried about something new?" he asked, shifting his eyes toward Fern.

"Oh, no," I said quickly, realizing how guilty I looked. "I was just thinking about some of the suggestions Mr. Dorfman made concerning the hotel's expansion."

"I thought we were going to try to put the hotel behind us when we entered our sanctuary," Jimmy reminded me.

"You're right, Jimmy. I'm sorry," I said, and I immersed myself in the conversation he was having with Fern and Christie about school.

Later, when I went in to kiss Christie good night, I told her she and I were going to go shopping in Virginia Beach as soon as she returned home from school.

"Is Aunt Fern coming, too?" she asked.

"No, no, it's just us, honey. She has to do her schoolwork. In fact, you shouldn't tell her anything; it would just make her unhappy that she can't go," I said. I hated bringing Christie into this deception, but I still believed it was for the best.

"You mean like a secret," she said.

"Sort of. Yes. Think of it like that," I coached, and I kissed her. "Good night, sweetheart," I said, and I thought, Soon you will see your real father, and you won't even know it – not now, not for a long time. But at least you will have that memory when I do tell you, I reasoned, and I kissed her a second time.

"Sleep tight," I said.

I closed her door behind me and stood there in the hallway for a few moments. I couldn't help being a little terrified of meeting Michael again. How would

I react when I first saw him? What would come out of my mouth? Words of fury and anger, or words of sadness? Can you have been so in love with someone and then years later look at him and feel nothing at all? I wondered.

Tomorrow I would find out.

I was on pins and needles all day until Christie and Fern were brought back from school. I had already instructed Julius about taking Christie and me to Virginia Beach. When he pulled up in front of the hotel with her in the backseat I hurried down the steps and slipped into the vehicle as quickly as I could. I couldn't help feeling sneaky about it. I had told Jimmy I intended to do some shopping, claiming Christie needed some things. He didn't question me; I even asked him if there was anything he needed.

"No. I wish I could get away to go with you," he said, "but we have that problem with the oil burner in section four."

"That's all right, Jimmy. It's just a fast trip," I said, afraid that he might find a way to join me later.

Now, as I sat in the limousine and we drove off, all my fabrications came home to roost, and I felt just horrible.

"Aunt Fern wanted to know why I wasn't getting out of the car, Momma," Christie said.

"What? Oh . . . what did you say?"

"I told her I was going to the hotel. She looked at me funny," Christie added.

"It's all right, honey. It's better this way," I assured her.

"Where are we going?"

437

"Oh, just to do some shopping, and to stop by and see an old friend who's staying at a hotel in Virginia Beach," I added as casually as I could.

"Why didn't this old friend stay in our hotel?" Christie asked quickly. She was so sharp.

"He had business in Virginia Beach and is staying only one day," I replied. I'm sure I was imagining it, but she looked skeptical.

I had Julius drive us directly to the Dunes. My intention was to see Michael and get it over with immediately. Then I would take Christie to a department store and buy her some new underwear and stockings, as well as a new sweater. Winter was just around the corner. We had already had cold mornings with flurries, and the clouds that came rolling in from the northwest looked angrier and darker than ever. The period between the end of fall and the heart of winter always depressed me. Trees had lost their leaves and looked bare and still but had not yet taken on sleeves of snow over their branches. They looked most gloomy in the moonlight, until they had either snow or ice crystallized on them. Then they would twinkle and make me think of Christmas.

"Here we are," Julius announced. The doorman at the Dunes shot forward and opened our doors before Julius could. Christie stepped out, thanking him, and I followed, my heart beginning to pound against my chest like a sledgehammer. I had to stop to catch my breath. Christie looked up at me quizzically.

"We'll be no more than fifteen minutes, Julius," I said firmly.

"Very good, Mrs. Longchamp. I'll be right out here."

"Okay, Christie, honey." I took her hand and started

438

for the front door. My legs felt as if they had turned into rubber. I was positive I was wobbling and looked every which way to see if people were staring at me, but no one was looking. The doorman opened the door for us, and we entered the posh lobby.

For a long moment I didn't see him – or, more correctly, didn't recognize him – for he was seated on the sofa directly ahead of us, reading a newspaper. He lowered it and smiled. My heart stopped and then started again, the blood draining from my face so quickly, I thought I would embarrass all of us by falling into a faint.

But when Michael stood up my trepidation turned to surprise and curiosity. Approaching us was a man who looked years and years older than I remembered him. His dark, once-silky hair was dull and spotted with gray. He was still six feet tall, of course, but his shoulders turned in, and he didn't have that arrogant, confidant gait. He looked a great deal thinner, his face almost as lean as Daddy Longchamp's; and although he wore a dark blue sports jacket and slacks, I thought he looked seedy: the pants not pressed, the jacket stretched and out of shape. Even the knot in his tie looked clumsily made. This was not the immaculate, debonair man with whom I had fallen so quickly and so deeply in love. This man couldn't even sweep one of my chambermaids off her feet, I thought.

"Dawn," he said, extending his hand. Gone was the impressive gold pinky ring and the glittering gold watch. His fingers seemed to tremble in my grasp. "It's so good to see you after all these years." Although his face was ashen, his dark sapphire eyes still had that impish glint.

"Hello, Michael."

"And this," he said, stepping back and looking down, "must be Christie. I couldn't have missed you in a crowd of schoolgirls your age," he added. "She's beautiful," he said, lifting his eyes to me. "You've done a wonderful job. Hello, Christie." He offered her his hand, and she took it and shook it like a little lady. He laughed. "I bought you something," he told her, and he fished in his jacket pocket to produce a small box.

"Oh, Michael," I said.

"It's all right; it's nothing special," he said.

"Yes, but I'll have to explain it," I said.

"I'm sorry. I couldn't resist getting her something."

"What is it?" Christie asked. Michael winked at me.

"I'm a jewelry salesman," he said, "and I thought you might like a sample of what I sell."

She took the gift.

"What do you say, Christie?"

"Thank you. Can I open it? Can I?"

"Sure," Michael said. "Let's go right in here and have a cup of tea or something," he said, indicating the lounge.

"We can't stay long. I have my chauffeur outside," I told him.

"I know. We'll sit for just a few minutes and visit. Christie," he said, extending his hand. She took it, and he led her toward the lounge. I took a deep breath and followed. We sat in a booth, and Michael ordered Christie a Shirley Temple.

"Would you like tea, or something stronger?" he asked.

"Tea would be fine."

"Tea, and a scotch and soda for me," he said. He

smiled at me across the table. "Remember that first day when I took you for cappuccino?"

"I remember. But more important, I remember the day you weren't there," I said pointedly. Michael's aged and disheveled look diminished the magic I feared would blind me to the truth and cause me to overlook the effects his mean and cruel behavior had had on me and my life. Looking at him now, I saw him as only a man. He didn't walk in a spotlight; there was no music in the background. His face was no longer the face enshrined on magazine covers.

"Oh, look, Momma," Christie exclaimed after she opened the box. She had lifted a gold chain and a locket from it; the locket had a musical note on the outside.

"Oooh," Christie exclaimed with admiration as she dangled it before herself.

"I once gave a locket like that to someone I loved very much," Michael said, gazing at me.

I remembered; it was on a Thanksgiving, but I had left that behind with so many other things when I had been whisked off to The Meadows to give birth.

"The note looks like an A," Christie declared. Michael laughed.

"Don't tell me she's a musician, too."

"She's taking piano lessons," I said.

"I bet she's very good," he replied, nodding, his eyes small and intent, "considering her parents' genes. What grade are you in, Christie?"

"First grade," she replied proudly. "And I'm in the first group."

"First group?"

"She's being accelerated," I explained. "She does second grader's work."

"Oh, I see. That's very nice. She's absolutely the most precious little girl I've ever seen," he declared. "What I lost, huh?" he said. The waitress brought our drinks. I sipped my tea as Michael took a long gulp of his scotch and soda, as if to fortify himself.

"Yes, Michael," I finally said, "what you lost, what you turned away, discarded without so much as leaving a note behind. Do you have any idea what that was like for me?" I asked, my eyes burning with anger. His eyes turned softer, meeting and locking with mine as I went on. "Not to even give me a warning, a hint, a phone call." Tears flooded my eyes, but I kept them trapped. I was determined not to cry, not to give him the satisfaction.

"I was horrible, I know," he replied. He lowered his gaze to his glass and then looked up at me. "But I couldn't stop myself from falling in love with you, even though it was very wrong for me to do it."

"We were overcoming those things, Michael. We had real plans, and you knew I didn't care what people said, including my so-called family at the time. Our age difference wasn't important, and as far as your being my teacher and your risking your teaching career, you were a renowned performer. You didn't intend to remain a teacher."

"No, no, none of that is what I mean," he said. "It was wrong for other reasons." He shifted his eyes away.

"What other reasons, Michael?"

He bit down on his lip, inhaled deeply through his nose and sat back.

"I think," I said, "it's time I knew everything, don't you?" He nodded.

"When I met you in New York and we began seeing

442

each other and loving each other, I was already married," he confessed.

"What?" I exclaimed.

"I had been married for almost two years."

"I don't believe it. No one said anything, and the magazine stories about you never – "

"No one knew it," he said. "My public relations man made me keep it a secret. He warned that my announcing my marriage would hurt my career; it would stop young women from fantasizing about me."

"Where was your wife all this time?" I asked skeptically.

"She was back in London; she was an English girl I had met while I was working on a show. She was with the set designers. We fell in love quickly, almost as quickly as you and I had, and one day we just drove off to the country and got married in an old church. I was quite foolish and impulsive in those days, and as I said, my manager and publicity people were quite upset.

"My work and my traveling eventually diluted the love we had for each other. Actually, I had intended to tell her about you and ask her for a divorce, but before I could, I got word she was dying from a kidney ailment back in London, so I left to be with her and accepted a role in a London show. She hung on for months and months, and by the time it was all over, you were already gone. I did try to find you, but your whereabouts were secret.

"Disillusioned and lost, I returned to Europe to continue my career. Eventually I found out about your marriage and all."

"Why didn't you ever tell me about your wife?" I asked.

"I was afraid to; I was afraid you would leave me," he said.

"But why didn't you tell me at the end, or leave me a note?"

"I couldn't. I was weak, I know. I let my manager and publicity people take control of my life. They threatened to leave me; they told me I was destroying myself. What can I tell you?" he said, lifting his eyes toward me – eyes that seemed so full of tears now, they looked on the verge of releasing a flood of drops down his cheeks. "I had to choose between romantic bliss and my career, and I chose my career.

"I guess deep down I was married to the stage before I was married to anyone. That was my first love, and my strongest. Everything else weakened and paled beside it. I was younger, and very much infatuated with myself and my fame.

"Now that I look at you, and at beautiful Christie, I realize how great my loss has been.

"But it doesn't have to be," he added quickly. "I've come to my senses. Oh, admittedly years late, but still, I'm here."

"Michael, what are you saying? What are you proposing?" I asked, astounded.

"We had magic once, magic like no other two people had. When two people have such magic, they can get it back," he asserted.

It depressed me to hear the quaver in his voice. He seemed a small boy who was pleading for the impossible to happen.

"I couldn't be more happily married than I am now, Michael. Heaven and earth couldn't pull me away from Jimmy. What you and I had was magic, at least for a little while, but you destroyed it. I'm sorry for what happened to you, and I'm sorry you never told me these things when we were together. Nothing would have come between us then, but I'm a different person now. That star-struck young girl is long gone."

Michael nodded and gulped down his drink.

"I thought you would say something like that," he said, smiling. He looked down at Christie and smiled wider. She sipped the last of her Shirley Temple.

"We have to go, Michael. I'm taking Christie shopping."

"Oh. Of course." He signaled for the bill.

"What are you doing in Virginia Beach?" I asked.

"I'm just passing through on my way to New York City. I was in Atlanta."

"You're driving?"

"Yes. I have some time, and there are things I haven't seen, so I thought I would."

The waitress brought the bill, and Michael fumbled through his pocket for his wallet. He looked at the bill and then at the money in his billfold.

"Oh, I have to go to the main desk to cash a check," he said. "I don't have enough cash."

"That's all right. I'll pay for it," I said.

"Well, actually," Michael said, smiling and leaning forward, "that was another reason I wanted to see and speak with you."

"Oh?"

He kept his smile.

"Since you are doing so fabulously now, I thought you might be willing to lend me some money," he said.

"What?"

"I need to get back on my feet. Five thousand dollars would do fine."

"Five thousand dollars!"

"I'm sure it's not a great deal to someone who owns one of the country's most famous seaside resorts."

I stared in disbelief. This wasn't just another reason he wanted to see me and Christie; this was his main reason. Never did he look more dishonest and cheap to me.

"Michael, even if I wanted to give you the money, which I don't, I could never do it without drawing attention. All my business affairs are run by a comptroller."

"You must have some personal funds," he pursued.

"Jimmy and I have personal funds," I corrected.

"So?"

"You expect Jimmy to approve such a thing?" Was there no end to his gall? I wondered.

Michael shrugged.

"What he doesn't know won't hurt him," he said.

I pulled myself back into a stiff, firm position and glared at him.

"Jimmy and I don't keep secrets from each other. Our marriage is built on trust."

Michael stared at me, his eyes growing smaller, the impish glint turning into something harder, something sly and conniving.

"Did you tell him you were coming here to meet me today?" he asked.

"Of course not. He would be furious, and he wouldn't have permitted it."

"So?" Michael said, lifting his arms and smiling again. "You've lied to him before."

I shook my head.

"You're despicable, Michael. I came down here out of pity. I thought it was horrible that you had never seen Christie, and now you're turning it into something sordid. I've got to go," I said. "Come on, Christie."

I took some money out and threw it on the table for the bill. Then I stood up and helped Christie out of the booth.

"Wait a minute, Dawn," he said.

"No, Michael. There's no reason for me to stay here any longer."

"I need that money, Dawn," he said, his eyes fixed on me. "I need this second chance, and you are in a position to help me now."

"How can you ask me after what you did, no matter what your reasons were?" I said. I shook my head and started away.

"*Dawn!*" he called, but I didn't turn back.

"Momma, that man is calling," Christie said.

"Just walk, honey," I told her. She turned around, and I dragged her along, fleeing from what seemed to me to be the evil side of the man I had once loved.

Just Desserts

The phone was ringing in my office the moment I returned. Somehow I anticipated it would be Michael.

"Dawn, you had no right to run out on me like that," he declared angrily.

"I had no right to run out on you? You call that running out? How about the way you ran out on me?"

"I thought I explained all that," he said.

"Michael, there is nothing more to be said. We have to go on with our lives."

"That's exactly what I'm trying to do," he insisted, "and why I need the money."

"Michael, I can't – "

"I have some rights, you know," he said quickly.

"Rights?"

"To Christie. She's my daughter, too," he asserted. "I was nice enough to play your little game, pretending to be someone else for now, but if I come around again . . ."

I sat down slowly.

"Michael, are you trying to blackmail me?"

"I just need a miserable five thousand dollars for now," he contended.

"For now?"

"And you can continue to pretend Jimmy is Christie's father, if you like. I won't contest the adoption."

"Contest the adoption? Do you think you would have any chance? A man who deserted a pregnant teenager?" I said, amazed he would even suggest it.

"Maybe not, but the trial would certainly bring me much-needed notoriety. As my agent says, publicity is publicity. There is no such thing as bad publicity in my business. That's why performers don't really mind it when they find themselves written up in the tabloids.

"Besides, a good lawyer could easily paint a different picture – the picture of a man who was going to do right by you. It was you who disappeared and then went and married the man who had lived as your brother. Can you imagine what the tabloids would do with that?" he asked in a laughing tone.

"You're despicable," I said. "Even more despicable than I imagined."

"All I want is a little money," he whined. "It's a drop in the bucket for you, but for me it's a chance to get back on my feet."

"It's not a drop in the bucket," I snapped. "And it's not just the money. Jimmy would – "

"Would be very angry to know you've been lying to him and meeting me on the side," Michael said, his voice dripping with erotic suggestion.

"My God, there is no limit to how low you will go," I said.

"I'll give you two days. Bring the money to the hotel," he ordered. "I'll need it to pay my bill. Two days," he repeated, and he hung up.

I sat there with the dead phone in my hand, my face flushed, my heart pounding. What was I going to do? Jimmy would definitely be enraged and very disappointed in me. And yet I knew if I got Michael the five thousand dollars, it wouldn't end. He would be at me continually for more, always threatening, always promising to bring us great emotional pain. I wanted so to protect Christie from the sort of misery and turmoil I had experienced. She had a wonderful, happy life with all her needs well provided for; she lived in a world of love and security, protected, never exposed to the bleak, dark forces that dwelt outside our gates.

If I told Jimmy about all this, there could be a terrible scene, and Michael might do just what he threatened to do anyway. I heard the desperation and the determination in his voice; he had nothing to lose, and in a sick way, he was right – he could gain some fame. Lawyers could distort the truth and make it look like I was the evil one. Christie would be considered no better than a freak. She would grow up with people always whispering around her. I knew firsthand how cruel other girls could be, especially when she became a teenager. How could I permit such scandal to follow her all the days of her life?

What was I to do?

I buried my face in my hands and started to sob. Would it never end? Would the sins and indiscretions of my youth follow me and those I loved forever? I felt exhausted, overwhelmed, defeated, and I sank back in my chair.

My gaze drifted to the portrait of my father. His eyes seemed to be locked on me, his wry smile an expression of anticipation. It was as if he were waiting to see what I would do, how I would contend with this new and great crisis. Would I be strong and win, or would I be weak and lose? I was sitting in Grandmother Cutler's chair, working at what had been her desk, overseeing the business she had built so well.

This sort of crisis wouldn't throw her into a desperate panic, I thought. She wouldn't sit there weeping and feeling sorry for herself. I hated to model myself after such a hard, cold person, but apparently there was a place in this world for such people and such behavior. Events dictated it.

I suddenly realized that sometimes we had to put on masks and become people we despised as well as people we admired. The more responsibility we had, the more chance that would happen. I could almost appreciate and understand Grandmother Cutler right now, I thought.

It was as if I gathered this desperately needed strength and resolve from the very walls of the office Grandmother Cutler had inhabited for so long and so well. I wouldn't permit Michael to burst into my life and destroy the happiness I had finally found. But more important, I wouldn't permit him to hurt our daughter. If he wanted to be ruthless and selfish, fine, but he would discover he was no longer dealing with an innocent teenage girl infatuated with his fame and glamour.

I straightened up in my chair, my back as firm and as stiff as Grandmother Cutler's had been whenever she sat there. Then I picked up the phone and called Mr. Updike. He listened carefully as I described the events and what demands and threats Michael had made.

"I'm sorry to thrust you into yet another Cutler family crisis, Mr. Updike," I concluded, "but I do rely on your good judgment and legal advice."

"That's all right," he said. I didn't like the long pause that followed. "These child custody cases can get very ugly, very ugly indeed, as you almost learned years ago when you went to retrieve Christie."

"But does he have any real rights after what he did?" I asked, growing frantic.

"Real parents always have some recourse in the courts. It's true he deserted you and the baby, but the situation gets complicated when you insert the fact that you were sent into hiding to give birth. I'm sure he will claim that once he learned of your pregnancy he tried to make contact but was unable to locate you."

"But what about all the time since?"

"It doesn't show good intention, but it doesn't eradicate his parentage or preclude his parental rights, if the court sees fit to grant him any. And there are, it is true, some unpleasant circumstances that would almost certainly be exposed in a court proceeding. A person with any sort of celebrity would draw publicity. In short, we couldn't stop him from initiating a litigation, and I think I'm correct in saying that the emotional strain and all the unpleasantness surrounding it would be quite distasteful for all of you, not to mention the effect it might have on the hotel."

I swallowed hard. It felt as if a lead lump had gotten stuck in my chest.

"Then what do you suggest, Mr. Updike . . . that I give him the money?"

"No. Let me find out a little more about him and call you back."

I tried to keep myself occupied with other work, but my mind continually drifted back to my discussion with Mr. Updike, and I couldn't keep my heart from racing.

452

Whenever the phone rang I seized it instantly, hoping it was Mr. Updike. Finally it was he. He said he had an English friend who was a barrister in London, and he had finally gotten through to him to make some inquiries. Now he was calling me with his report.

"Michael Sutton's career," he began, "is going downhill. He was dismissed from one role after another during the past year because of his problem with alcohol."

"I suspected so."

"And as far as any sort of marriage and wife who died . . ."

"Nothing?" I asked.

"A complete fabrication, I'm afraid. If anything, he has a reputation for being something of a rake. His affairs with members of the casts and crews of his shows are infamous and have often been detrimental to the productions."

"What does all this mean?" I asked.

"Well, his lawyer would certainly have a difficult time presenting him as a reliable and responsible individual whose parental rights were abused. But there would still be the negative effects of a trial to contend with.

"No, I think our best course of action is to direct ourselves to this act of blackmail, for that is exactly what it is. I want you to meet with him again," Mr. Updike said. "By yourself," he added.

"Why?" I asked. "I can't stand the thought of it."

"I understand, but I want him to repeat his demands."

"But it's still his word against mine, isn't it, Mr. Updike?"

"No. I and one of my associates, a man I use as a private investigator, will be present, too. Unbeknownst to Mr. Sutton, of course," he said. "I intend to record what he says to you. Do you think you can do it?" he asked.

I hesitated. What if Michael saw through me and found out what we were up to? He would surely go ahead and make more trouble. I gazed at my father's portrait again. The wry smile was still there, but his expression was more pensive, even tense.

"Yes, Mr. Updike," I said, filling my voice with determination. "I can do it. How do we proceed?"

Mr. Updike said he would get back to me with the details after he had spoken to his associate. Needless to say, I was on pins and needles the rest of the day and all night. Fortunately, Jimmy was distracted with some mechanical problems at the hotel and didn't notice my nervousness.

Late the next morning Mr. Updike called.

"Arrange to meet him in the hotel restaurant again. We will be sitting in the booth behind you. I'll come to your office this afternoon and go over the things I want you to say in order to draw out his blackmail," Mr. Updike explained.

"I'd rather come to your office, Mr. Updike," I said quickly. He was silent a moment.

"You haven't told Jimmy about any of this?" he asked perceptively.

"No, I was hoping I could end it without involving him. He has a temper, and . . ."

"I understand," Mr. Updike said. We arranged to meet at two o'clock.

At Mr. Updike's office I met his associate, Mr. Simons, a stout, tall man in his late thirties. Mr. Updike explained that Mr. Simons had once been a policeman, but an injury had caused him to go on disability. He did his investigative work to supplement his income. He had a slight limp, but other than that he looked strong enough and big enough to be a nightclub bouncer.

After I went over the things Mr. Updike wanted me to say, Mr. Simons showed me the battery-operated tape recorder they would use to record Michael's threats.

"Don't worry about looking nervous to him," Mr. Simons said. "He'll probably think you're that way because of the situation. Just forget about us, if you can, and let the man do himself in. That's usually what happens in cases such as these," he assured me. He spoke with a quiet confidence that gave me reassurance.

When I returned to the hotel I phoned Michael and made arrangements to meet him in the restaurant at one o'clock.

"Will you bring the money?" he demanded.

"I'll see you at one, Michael," I said, and I hung up the phone quickly.

I arrived at the hotel a few minutes early. I saw Mr. Updike and Mr. Simons in the lobby. Mr. Updike nodded reassuringly. A few moments later Michael appeared. He looked more dapper and better dressed. He wore a light blue sports jacket and slacks with new loafers.

"How do I look?" he asked me instead of saying hello. "I bought this new outfit this morning in the hotel clothing store."

"You look very nice, Michael."

He smiled and gazed at me licentiously.

"Well," he said, "let's go have a cup of coffee

455

together." He held out his arm for me to take, but I walked ahead of him. Mr. Updike had already arranged for the two booths, so when the hostess saw me she smiled and led Michael and me to ours.

"Just coffee for me," I told the waitress.

"Just coffee?" Michael said, looking at the menu. "I'm feeling a bit hungry. I think I'll have the shrimp special, please, and a cup of coffee."

The waitress took our menus and left. Michael folded his hands on the table and smiled at me again.

"I hope you didn't bring it all in cash," he said.

"I can't believe you've come here to demand money from me, Michael," I began. He shrugged.

"You won't miss it."

"What if I don't give you this money?" I asked. His eyebrows lifted.

"You think I was kidding? I told you, I'll get a lawyer and start a legal action for custody of Christie," he said.

"You don't have a chance of winning."

"What is this? I told you, I don't care if I win. It's the publicity that will do the damage to you, but it'll help me."

"Don't you care what it would do to our daughter?" I asked.

"She'll get over it," he said. "Children forget."

"You don't know how wrong you are about that, Michael. She would hate you for what you'd done."

"What's the difference?" he said. "She doesn't know I exist. Look, Dawn, I'm not joking about this. This is the second time you've met me, and I'm sure you haven't told your husband." He smiled. "If I have to, I'll tell him, only . . . I'll add a few things." He winked. "Get my meaning?"

The waitress brought the coffee. I waited for her to leave.

"No, Michael, I don't," I said. He lost his smile.

"I don't care if you do or you don't. Do you have the five thousand dollars?"

I shook my head.

"No, Michael. I would never give you money like this. It would never end."

"I'm warning you . . ."

I got up.

"I hope you have enough money to pay for lunch," I said, and I pivoted quickly, leaving him with his mouth open.

When I looked back from the doorway of the restaurant I saw Michael start to rise as Mr. Simons and Mr. Updike slipped into the booth and sat across from him. Slowly Michael sank back into his seat and listened, his face growing pale as Mr. Simons and Mr. Updike began. Then Mr. Simons produced the tape recorder.

Michael turned sharply to look my way. I didn't look back. I turned my back and left him – forever, I hoped.

The moment I returned to Cutler's Cove and entered the lobby I sensed something was wrong. It was too quiet and too still. A number of staff members and a dozen or so guests were gathered in front of the reception desk speaking softly. Mrs. Bradly came out from behind the counter and hurried across the lobby to greet me. She wore a very troubled expression. My heart began to race in anticipation.

"What's happened, Mrs. Bradly?" I asked.

"Miss Clara Sue's been in a terrible truck accident

457

somewhere in Alabama," she said, shaking her head, her tears flowing.

"Where's Jimmy? Where's my husband?" I cried.

"I think he's in your office, Mrs. Longchamp," she said. "I'm so sorry."

I rushed toward my office, and when I entered I found Jimmy on the phone. He looked at me and shook his head. I dropped my coat on the settee and went to him.

"Dawn's just returned," he said into the phone. "We'll be right up." He cradled the receiver. "That was Philip. He and Betty Ann are up at the house. Where have you been?"

"What happened, Jimmy?" I cried, ignoring his question. I pressed my palm against my pounding heart.

"Tractor trailer jackknifed, turned over and crushed the cab."

"Oh, Jimmy, how awful," I said, falling back against the desk.

"I know. A death like that is too horrible, even for someone as miserable as Clara Sue," he said, shaking his head.

"How's my mother?" I asked.

"You can just imagine. All she's been asking for is you. Where were you?" he asked again.

"I had to see Mr. Updike about some new tax laws," I lied, looking down so Jimmy wouldn't see my eyes.

"I've already spoken to Mrs. Boston, so she'll look after Fern and Christie. We had better go up to Beulla Woods without delay," he said. "Philip just told me your mother's screaming for doctors and sedatives, and Bronson is beside himself."

Jimmy took my hand, and we hurried out to his

car. My heart was still pounding so hard and fast by the time we arrived that I thought I wouldn't be any good to anyone. Livingston opened the door for us as quickly as he could and stepped back, his normally gray face even more ashen. Philip and Betty Ann were in the sitting room having tea. They both rose when we entered. Betty Ann and I embraced.

"I'm afraid the news is rather gruesome," Philip said, his lips trembling. I saw the moisture in his eyes and the dry streaks where the tears had traveled down his cheeks. "It took hours for them to cut Clara Sue and her truck driver boyfriend out of the cab.

"We didn't get along well during these years," he said, turning to Jimmy as if Jimmy were some stranger, "but we used to when we were little. Most of the time we only had each other. Mother and Father were always very busy with one thing or another, and we would be left alone for hours at a time."

He smiled.

"We once made a pretend hotel in the storage building and had all the children of the hotel staff and even some guests playing along. I was the president of the hotel, and Clara Sue was . . . was Grandmother, I suppose. You should have seen her, with her hair in golden pigtails like Christie's, ordering everyone about. 'You sleep here; you clean up that corner.' She had all the guests' children working like little beavers.

"We were taking things out of the hotel and bringing them to our make-believe one. When Nussbaum finally discovered all the missing silverware and dishes he told Grandmother, and she came marching over. You should have seen the look on her face. For a moment she was speechless, and for Grandmother Cutler, that was something." He shook his head and looked dumb-founded. "Then everything began to change, and Clara Sue became a different sort of person.

"I suppose I should have spent more time with her." He looked at me hard. "Fate has a way of assuming control of your life when you fail to do so yourself."

"Where's Bronson?" I asked.

"He's upstairs with your mother," Betty Ann said. I hurried up. Jimmy remained below with Betty Ann and Philip. I knocked softly on the bedroom door, which was partially open. Bronson was sitting on the bed and holding Mother's hand. She had her right hand over her eyes and lay back against the large silk pillow. Her hair was loose and flowed every which way. The curtains and drapes were all drawn to prevent any sunlight from entering.

"Oh, Dawn," Bronson said, rising. Slowly Mother slid her hand off her eyes and gazed at me. "I'm glad you're here," Bronson began. "Maybe you can help put some sense in your mother's stubborn head. She insists that all this is somehow her fault."

"It is!" Mother cried, and she covered her eyes again. Her shoulders lifted and fell with her sobs.

"That is silly, Mother. How can you think it's your fault?" I said, approaching. "You didn't cause the truck to jackknife."

"She wouldn't have been in that truck with such a person if I had insisted she live here with us," Mother cried.

"Clara Sue wasn't the sort of young woman you could order about, Mother. We all knew that. She did what she wanted, when she wanted, no matter who thought what about it. If she hadn't met this truck driver, she would have met someone else and gone off anyway. She was rebelling," I added. Bronson nodded his agreement, but Mother shook her head.

"That's exactly it. She was rebelling, and I didn't care; I didn't mind as long as she was rebelling far away and no one knew. Now look at what's happened," she moaned.

"What were you going to do with her, Mother, chain her to the wall here? She would have gone no matter what you said."

"You always blamed me for how she was, Dawn," Mother accused, lowering her hand from her eyes again. "Don't deny it just to make me feel better now."

"I won't, Mother. What you should have done with Clara Sue, you should have done years and years ago, when she was first growing up. But that time passed, and she was her own person. For better or for worse, she was considered an adult. There's no point in blaming anyone else now. She did what she wanted, and what happened to her was horrible, but none of us wanted it to happen. There's no point in any of us making it any worse," I added firmly.

Mother stared at me a moment and then turned to Bronson.

"She's just like my mother-in-law now, Bronson. So strong, so logical and right all the time," she remarked, but her voice was filled with admiration. My face turned crimson. Mother turned back to me. "You're the strongest one of all of us now, Dawn. You are."

"That's not so, Mother," I said, lowering my eyes.

"No, no, it is, and I'm happy, happy to see you this way. You won't end up like me, sobbing in some bed and getting old before your time because of the things other people are able to do to you," she declared. She smiled and held out her arms. "I need you to comfort me, dear."

I gazed at Bronson, who looked on the verge of tears himself, and then I went to her and felt her embrace me with all her strength.

Soon afterward the doctor arrived to give Mother something to help her sleep. While he was upstairs with her we all gathered in the sitting room.

"I'll leave immediately for Alabama and make arrangements for Clara Sue to be brought back for burial," Philip said.

"Maybe I should go," Bronson interjected.

"No. You should probably stay with Mother. Don't you think so, Dawn?" Philip asked me.

"What? Oh, yes. I'll see to the arrangements here," I said.

As we were leaving Bronson pulled me aside.

"No one's ever told Philip that I was Clara Sue's true father, have they?" he asked.

"I didn't, and I doubt Mother did. Philip never mentioned it, so I assume Clara Sue wanted it kept secret. Some skeletons are better kept in the closet," I said. He nodded, a half smile on his face.

"Laura Sue is right about you, you know. You have become the strength in this family. You're practically the only one who can handle her these days," he confessed. "I can't be hard on her, even though I know she needs it from time to time. Poor Clara Sue," he added. "I hardly got to know her."

"I'm sorry, Bronson."

He kissed me on the cheek, and I joined Jimmy at the car.

When we returned to the hotel I found a message that Mr. Updike had phoned. Jimmy left to finish his work, and I went into the office.

"I just heard about Clara Sue," Mr. Updike said. "One crisis after another for you."

"Yes," I said.

"At least one is finished. Once we confronted him with the recording, he promised to leave you alone. I'll keep the tape in my safe just in case, though."

"Thank you, Mr. Updike. I've never told you this before," I said, "but I can appreciate now why you were so valuable to Grandmother Cutler."

"That's very nice of you to say, Dawn. I can't help believing that if the two of you would have known each other in the early days, things would have turned out quite differently."

"At this point, Mr. Updike, nothing would surprise me. Thanks again," I said.

For the next few days we were all occupied with the mourning period for Clara Sue and the arrangements for her funeral. As with Randolph, many old friends arrived, as well as people from the surrounding community. To her credit, Mother behaved properly. She didn't doll herself up; she was truly a bereaved parent. Philip and Bronson stood on each side of her and held her up at the site of Clara Sue's grave in the family section of the cemetery until the service was over. Afterward the mourners went to Beulla Woods to pay their respects. Mother remained in her room the entire time, unwilling to see anyone. Betty Ann and I hosted and greeted people. Jimmy spent most of his time with Fern and Christie and helped with the twins. For all practical purposes, the hotel itself shut down.

463

We were moving into the slow period anyway. Winter was practically on top of us. Most of our regular guests were traveling to warmer climates for their holidays. A number of staff had left to work in Florida. We had decided this was the time we would begin our expansion. The fewest possible people would be disrupted by the tradespeople, trucks and construction. For Jimmy it was going to be his busiest time, for he took on a major role as construction foreman. During the days immediately following Clara Sue's funeral I thought the work and responsibility were to blame for Jimmy's distraction and avoidance of me, but late one morning, while I was reviewing Mr. Dorfman's year-end reports, Jimmy came to my office, and I discovered his behavior was caused by something else.

He had a strange look in his eyes, one I had never seen before. His face was stern, angry, but he looked hurt, in some deep emotional pain. Without speaking he approached the desk.

"I just want straight, truthful answers," he said icily. The cold tones in his voice froze my heart. He put his hands on the desk and leaned toward me, his dark eyes as hard as stone.

"What is it, Jimmy?" I asked, and I held my breath.

"Last week, when you took Christie into Virginia Beach to shop for her clothing, who did you meet?" he demanded.

My heart sank. For a moment I couldn't speak, I couldn't swallow, I couldn't breathe. He fixed his eyes on me with such fury, I was afraid to utter a sound.

"The truth!" he cried, slapping his hand down on the desk. I jumped in my seat.

"Michael," I said. He nodded and turned.

"I was going to tell you, Jimmy. Honest. I just wanted more time to pass," I cried quickly.

"How could you go to him after what he had done to you?" Jimmy asked slowly. "How could you belittle yourself so?"

"Jimmy, I didn't want to go. He begged me on the phone. He said he wanted to see Christie once, at least, and I didn't think I had the right to say no. But when I got there I found he had different intentions."

"What sort of intentions?" Jimmy demanded, his eyes growing hot.

Quietly but quickly I told him everything. He sat down and listened when I got to the description of how Mr. Updike and Mr. Simons had handled it. Then he shook his head.

"You did all this and never told me what was happening?"

"I thought if I could end it quickly . . ."

He shook his head, his eyes filled with pain.

"But I'm your husband, Dawn, and Christie's father now. I was the one to come to, the one who should have protected you both. Instead, you lied to me."

"I thought you would do something terrible to him, Jimmy. I was going to tell you afterward. I tried a few times, but I couldn't do it, and then, when Clara Sue was killed . . ."

"You tried," he spat.

"I did, Jimmy. I couldn't stand the fact that I was lying to you. It's bothered me ever since," I swore.

"And you had Christie in on this deception," he said, shaking his head. "Telling her a jewelry salesman gave her a sample."

"It was better than telling her who he really was, Jimmy," I said. He stared at me so coldly I had to lower my eyes. "I'm so sorry I didn't tell you."

"And you wouldn't have, probably," Jimmy said. "I wouldn't have known anything about it if it weren't for Fern."

"Fern?" I looked up quickly.

"She asked Christie about that necklace and found out his name. She remembered who that was, and then she came to me and told me."

"Oh, Jimmy, she was just trying to hurt me, to hurt us. How horrible," I said.

"Sure, go and twist things around. Fern didn't lie, did she? Fern didn't conceal the truth, did she? She told me because she cares about me," he said, poking himself hard in the chest for emphasis. He stood up. "At least someone around here does!" he cried, and he marched out of the office, slamming the door behind him.

"Jimmy!" I screamed after him, but he did not come back.

I lowered my head to my arms on the desk and broke into uncontrollable sobs.

I had hurt the one person who loved me more than anyone in the world. How foolish and stupid I had been to have kept anything at all from him. I didn't deserve him. I made up my mind I would grovel at his feet, if I had to, in order to get him to forgive me.

I left the office to search for him and hurried outside to look for him somewhere on the grounds. I found some of our maintenance people working, but no one had seen Jimmy. Thinking he might have driven off, I went to where he parked his car and found it still there. Distraught and bewildered, I started back to the hotel.

As I was walking by the gazebo I happened to look at the rear of the main building and saw the doorway to what had once been Philip's and then Jimmy's hideaway. The door was open. My heart began to flutter.

It was in there, in that forgotten little place where Jimmy and I had first revealed that our affections for each other were more than brotherly and sisterly. It was in there that we had kissed each other romantically and touched each other with the passion of lovers. It brought tears to my eyes to realize that after I had hurt him so and he had felt betrayed, he had gone back there.

"Oh, Jimmy," I cried, and I ran over the lawn to the doorway of the hideaway. I paused at the top of the steps and looked in. The single uncovered light bulb was on, and it cast a pale yellow glow over the otherwise dark room. I walked down the steps slowly and gazed in. Jimmy was on his back on the old cot, his hands behind his head, staring up at the ceiling.

"Jimmy," I said softly. He turned slowly and then shook his head and turned away. I rushed across the old dirt and stone floor and knelt down at his side. Without speaking I buried my face in his chest.

"Oh, Jimmy," I cried. "I'm so sorry. I didn't mean to hurt you. Please don't hate me. Please," I begged through my tears.

"I don't hate you, Dawn. I'm just afraid you're becoming too much like the woman you once despised."

"No, Jimmy, I'm not."

He stared at me a moment.

"You know why I was so mad at you when I first heard you had gone to him?"

"Yes, because I didn't tell you."

467

"No," he said. "Because I was afraid I would lose you to him again."

"Really, Jimmy?" He nodded. "You will never lose me, Jimmy. Never, never, never. When you ran out of my office before, I thought I was going to lose *you*."

"I don't ever want to feel that way again, Dawn," he said. "We must promise never to lie to each other again. Will you promise?"

"Of course I will, Jimmy."

He looked around and smiled.

"I can remember every moment in here with you. I remember our first kiss, how long it took for me to bring my lips to yours."

"And then we pretended to be meeting each other for the first time," I said.

"We were, for the first time as boyfriend and girlfriend."

"And now we're here as husband and wife," I said.

He shook his head and smiled again, tenderly.

"What am I going to do with you? I guess I'll just have to keep a closer eye on you," he said.

"There's nothing I want more," I told him, and we kissed. He guided me up and moved over on the cot, coaxing me in beside him.

"Jimmy . . . here?" I said when he drew me to him.

"What could be more romantic than for us to make love where we had our first kiss?" he asked.

I answered with another kiss, a longer and more passionate one, and then I slipped in beside him and welcomed his caress.

Jimmy and I behaved like teenagers sneaking about as we came up the stone steps. We didn't want to have to answer anyone's questions. Jimmy peered out first to be sure no one was nearby.

"I'd better get back to work," Jimmy said, and we parted by the duck pond, him rushing off to join the construction team at the south end of the main building and me walking back to my office. The afternoon sunshine was weak, but still strong enough to feel like a warm caress on my cheeks and forehead. In the distance two enormous puffy clouds looked like mountains of white cotton rushing toward each other over a sea of blue. The winter wind made a burlap bag caught on the handle of a lawn mower flap like the flag of some unknown country.

Nature had a way of making me pensive and philosophical. How close I had come to losing Jimmy, I thought, and how lucky I was that he loved me so much. Would I eventually have told him about Michael? I wondered. Thinking about it reminded me of what Fern had done. Why did she dislike me so much? Why did she want to drive a wedge between Jimmy and me? How sad it made me feel to think that the little baby I had once loved and cared for almost as much as my very own child had grown into a spiteful and mean little girl. How much could we excuse because of what had happened to her? I wondered. And what damage were Jimmy and I doing by overlooking and forgiving?

Instead of going directly to the hotel I marched across the grounds to our house. Before dinner tonight I wanted to have a private conversation with Fern so she understood that what she had done was wrong. I wanted to impress upon her how deeply and completely Jimmy and I loved each other, and that nothing she could do would change that. She should be happy she is living in a house of love, I thought. Wasn't that what she wanted? Wasn't the absence of that what she despised?

When I arrived at the house I went directly upstairs, expecting to find Fern working on her homework as usual. I knocked on her closed door and waited, but I heard nothing. I knocked again and then opened the door. She wasn't there. Looking around the room, I realized she wasn't keeping it very neat these days. Some of her clothing was strewn about, draped over the backs of chairs, on the vanity table and on the poorly made bed. One half of a pair of sneakers was in front of the bed while its mate rested on its side near the closet, which was opened wide, the garments dangling precariously on hangers, some clothing already fallen.

My gaze moved to the pile of blouses and skirts on the closet floor and settled on a partially opened shoe box. Something in it caught my eye, and I walked forward slowly, knelt down and opened the box completely. Inside there was a pile of money. The missing petty cash? I wondered, and I began to count. After I went over eight hundred dollars I knew it must be so. I wasn't surprised. I wasn't sure what I should do. Surely she would claim this was the money she had brought with her, I thought, even though it was a great deal more than I had seen in her pocketbook in New York.

As I rose and turned to leave I noticed one of her older romance magazines opened on the bed. What made this particular one odd to me was the way Fern had underlined some passages. I turned the pages back to get to the beginning, and when I saw the title of the story my face flushed so from the blood that rushed into it, I was sure I was feverish. As if I needed to hear the words spoken to believe them, I read the title aloud.

" 'My Stepfather Raped Me, but I Had No One to Tell.' "

Slowly, my fingers trembling, I lifted the magazine and began to read.

For as long as I can remember, my mother was too busy to really look after me. She was a clothes designer and was always involved in her work. It was my stepfather who would look after me, dress me and even feed me. He did it so often and so casually, I never thought much about it until I was in fourth grade and happened to mention to a friend of mine that my stepfather usually came in while I was taking a bath to make sure I washed the "important places."

My friend looked at me strangely and asked, "What important places?"

I giggled and simply said, "You know. Your important places."

She still looked confused, so I pointed. Now she looked frightened and stopped talking to me about it, but I soon realized why she was uncomfortable. No one else's father did what my stepfather was doing.

I lowered the magazine to my lap. My heart was pounding, and I felt the beads of a cold sweat break out down the back of my neck. For a moment I couldn't move. I looked at the magazine again and shook my head. Then I went to the telephone quickly to call the hotel. I asked for Robert Garwood.

"Robert," I said frantically, "please go out and get Jimmy. Tell him I need him at the house immediately. Please."

"Right away, Mrs. Longchamp," he said. I hung up

and sat down to wait, and while I did, I read some more. The girl in the story talked about her mother forgetting her birthday. That line was underlined, too. Her stepfather's rape of her began with him coming in to kiss her good night, but staying to fondle her under the blanket. Finally one night he slipped in beside her.

Still reading, I heard the door slam downstairs.

"*Dawn!*" Jimmy cried.

"Upstairs, Jimmy." He pounded up the steps and stopped in our doorway, out of breath from running all the way.

"What's wrong?"

"It's Fern . . . it's this," I said, extending my arm, the magazine in my hand.

"Romance magazines?" He grimaced. "We always knew she read that stuff – "

"Look at the story and read the passages she underlined."

"Underlined?" He took the magazine from me and began to read. His face, red from his running, gradually turned more and more ashen. His dark eyes registered shock and grew cold with horror. "My God," he said, lowering the magazine, "she got it all out of here!"

"She's been living a romance-magazine fantasy, and we believed her and accused those people of horrible, horrible things," I said.

"But why didn't Clayton Osborne put up more of a fight," Jimmy wondered, "if it wasn't true?"

"He was probably afraid of what a scandal would do to his career, and he knew Fern wouldn't abandon her story.

"At the bottom of her closet," I continued, "there's

a shoe box full of money, some of which I am positive is the missing petty cash."

Jimmy lowered himself into a chair and stared dumbly down at the floor, shaking his head.

"What are we going to do?" he muttered.

"We have to confront her, Jimmy. She has to know we realize everything she's done," I said.

"Do we send her back?" he asked.

There was no question in my mind that Jimmy would do whatever I told him now. A part of me wanted to rid us of this evil child, this problem that, I now realized, would take much of our energy and attention to correct. I would be forever worried about Fern's influence on Christie, too.

But Fern was Jimmy's sister, and something stronger in me rejected the idea of sending away family. I had seen and lived through too much of that myself.

"I don't think her going back to the Osbornes is the answer, Jimmy. They are obviously not as mean and as evil as Fern had painted them to be, but they are two people who are overwhelmed by her and unwilling, perhaps, to make the sacrifices of time and energy required to give her the love and attention she needs to overcome her nasty ways.

"No, she should stay, but stay under a different set of rules and circumstances," I concluded. Jimmy nodded. Then we heard the door open and close downstairs. The children were home. Christie ran for the kitchen, where Mrs. Boston had her milk and cookies waiting, but Fern began a slow ascent to her room. We waited until she reached the second-floor landing, and then we both stepped out to greet her. She looked up with surprise.

473

"Why is everyone home already?" she asked, her eyes narrowing suspiciously at me.

"We want to talk to you, Fern," I said firmly. "In your room."

"What? Why?" she countered.

"Now," I commanded, and she hurried along. We followed her in. She dropped her books on her bed and flopped back on it, folding her arms defiantly over her chest.

"So?" she said. "You're mad because I told Jimmy about you seeing Michael Sutton, I suppose."

"I'm mad about that, yes – mad because of the way you went about it – but that's not why we want to speak to you right now," I said.

She lifted her eyes with new interest.

"Then what is it?" she asked.

"This," I said, holding out the magazine. As soon as she realized what was in my hand, her face blanched and her eyes filled with fear. She tried to cover it with anger.

"You went snooping in my things?" she cried.

"Dawn doesn't go snooping in anyone's things," Jimmy said sharply, stepping up beside me.

"That's not what's important here, Fern," I said. "It's what's in this magazine, what you read and memorized and pretended had happened to you."

"I didn't," she cried, real tears emerging.

"You did! You did!" I insisted, slapping the magazine over my open palm. It sounded like a gunshot, and her sobbing stopped instantly. "We're not going to pretend anymore, and you're going to tell the truth once and for all. And I warn you, Fern: If you lie to us just once – just once, mind you – we'll ship you out of here. If

474

the Osbornes don't want you, you'll go to a home for wayward girls."

I don't know where I garnered the strength and coldness to pronounce these words, but as I spoke them I saw flashes of Grandmother Cutler before me, her face stern, her shoulders hoisted, her fury fierce.

Fern cowered.

"I . . . I hated it there," she said.

"All you had to do was tell us the truth," Jimmy said.

"I knew you couldn't get me back, because I was legally theirs."

"So you made it all up, copied the ideas from this story?" I demanded. I had to have her confess it. She hesitated and then nodded. "What?" I said.

"I made it up. But please, please don't send me back to them. Clayton is cruel, he really is mean, and he doesn't love me, and Leslie doesn't help. He treats her like a child, too," she claimed.

"In that shoe box in your closet there is a lot of money," I said, nodding toward it. "How did you get it? All of it?"

"I stole it," she muttered.

"What?" Jimmy asked, wanting her to speak louder and own up to her crimes.

"I stole it," she shouted through her tears. "Some of it from Leslie and Clayton, and some of it from the front desk," she admitted.

"Why would you steal from us?" Jimmy asked. "We never denied you anything you needed or wanted."

"I thought you might ask me to leave someday, and I was going to run away if you did, so I needed money."

"You did a terrible thing, Fern," I said. "Not just the stealing of the money, but the attempt to steal our love and concern for you. You tried to win our love by turning us against the Osbornes. No matter what life was like with them, it was wrong to make such accusations about him."

The tears grew heavier, thicker down Fern's cheeks.

"Are you sending me back?" she asked, looking from me to Jimmy.

"That's up to Dawn," Jimmy said firmly. Fern's eyes widened, and then she looked at me, expecting the worst.

"We should," I began. "You said you came home with us because you wanted to be with a family where there was love in the home, but you have tried in all sorts of ways to hurt us." She looked down. "Jimmy and I love each other as much as two people can love each other in this world, and nothing can change that," I said. "But that doesn't mean we can't love other people very much, too. It's because we have such love for each other that we understand how important it is.

"You can't be selfish if you want people to love you, Fern. But more important," I said, "you can't love anyone if you love yourself more. Do you understand?"

She nodded, but I didn't think she understood nor wanted to just yet. She still had defiance in her eyes.

"Do I have to go back?" she repeated.

"No," I replied. "You can still stay with us."

She looked up, surprised.

"Because we want you to stay, we want you to be a better person, we want to love you and have you love us. But that will happen only if you don't lie and cheat and steal. It will happen only if you are honest and really care."

"You will be on probation here with us," Jimmy said sternly. "You understand that?"

"Yes, Jimmy."

"All right, then. First thing you do is take the money you stole and go over to the hotel and give it back to Mrs. Bradly, along with the best apology you can dream up," he commanded.

"I can't!" she cried.

"It takes a lot more courage to do right sometimes than it does to do wrong, but once you do it, you're gonna feel a lot better about yourself, honey," Jimmy said.

"Everyone's going to hate me and think horrible things about me," she moaned.

"For a while, perhaps," I said. "But if you want them to think better of you, you will have to earn it."

"Go on, Fern," Jimmy commanded.

Fern swallowed hard and slipped off the bed. She went to the shoe box and counted out the money she had stolen. She stuffed it into her pocket and left the room.

"Do you think she's going to change?" Jimmy asked.

"I don't know, Jimmy. You don't erase years and years of misbehavior, distrust and deceit overnight. But," I said sighing, "we'll give her the chance."

Jimmy put his arm around my shoulders.

"Did I ever tell you that you're just about the best reason for me to get up every morning?" he asked.

"Not for a couple of minutes, you haven't."

"Well, let me just do that. Better yet," he said, turning me toward our bedroom, "let me show you."

Winds of Change

A great many changes occurred in our lives that winter. Unfortunately, Fern's turning over a new leaf was not one of them. Despite her promises, her behavior at school continued to be a problem for us. On two occasions Jimmy had to leave work to have a meeting with the principal and Fern's teachers. She was still being insolent in class. We would punish her for a while, and for a while she would improve, but then she would do something to throw us all back to step one.

She continued to be selfish and inconsiderate, playing her rock-and-roll music so loud it vibrated through the walls, finding reasons not to help with household chores and breaking curfew after curfew. She would go into mood swings that took her from utter tragedy, where she would cry at the drop of a pin and peck at her food like a bird, to periods of ecstasy, when she would float through the house dreaming of a new boyfriend.

She did become a budding dark beauty. She let her hair grow long and sat at her vanity table brushing it for hours while Christie sat beside her on the floor jabbering away. Unfortunately, Fern continued to choose school friends much older than herself. Even so, we tried to be understanding and permitted her to go to her first school dance. She went with a boy three years older, and she marched into the house that night two hours after her curfew.

Jimmy was beside himself. He bawled her out, threatened, imposed new punishments, and did all that he could. Fern fell back on familiar excuses for her bad behavior. She used them so often, they became her anthem: "I had a horrible childhood. I was deserted by my real family. I'm trying."

As usual, in the end Jimmy felt bad and softened, and she was forgiven.

"I guess it's just going to take her a little longer," he said.

That spring Christie performed her first piano recital for our hotel guests. She wore a pink chiffon dress with crinoline under the skirt and had her long golden hair brushed down until it fell softly to the middle of her back. She melted hearts just marching into the room and curtsying. Then she sat down and played a piece of a Mozart concerto, as well as Brahms' Lullaby. Philip and Betty Ann's twins, Richard and Melanie, sat in the first row. They wore matching outfits and clapped vigorously, their little palms turning red. Afterward we served tea and cakes. Jimmy and I were so proud of Christie and the adorable way she accepted all the compliments, batted her eyelashes at the older gentlemen and permitted their wives to kiss her on the cheek.

"She works a party better than Mrs. Cutler used to," Mr. Updike remarked. "She's a natural hotel owner."

I laughed, but I thought I wanted better things for her. She was too special.

In late spring Daddy Longchamp, Edwina and Gavin made their second visit. Gavin was very excited about their return and about being with Christie and Fern and the twins, all of whom he considered family now. Daddy told us how he bragged about his brother's and stepsister's big hotel back east.

"He's been asking regularly to come back since the day after we returned from the first trip," Daddy said.

Fern didn't behave any more warmly toward Daddy Longchamp. If anything, I thought she was ashamed of him. She sat and answered his questions politely because we were watching her, but the moment she could, she excused herself and went off to talk on the phone to her new boyfriend.

"She's getting more and more beautiful," Daddy Longchamp said. "I know she's a handful for you, but you and Jimmy are doin' a great job with her, Dawn. I'm mighty proud how you all turned out," he added.

So many good things were happening to us, one after the other, that I kept looking around corners and waiting for that brisk, cold wind to come or the dark clouds to return. Jimmy scolded me about it.

"You've got to stop looking for trouble, Dawn," he lectured. "If there's trouble ahead, it doesn't need you to find it. It will find us, but until it does, let's be happy. Let's enjoy our lives.

"You still don't let yourself relax," he chastised. "Being uptight and nervous makes it harder for the good things to happen," he added. I knew what he meant. The doctor, on more than one occasion, had placed the blame for my not getting pregnant again on my emotional and mental attitudes.

"I'm trying, Jimmy," I said. "I am. I'm just . . . cautious," I said.

"Well, throw caution to the wind for a while, will you? You're working too hard anyway," he complained.

I couldn't deny that. Our expansion of the hotel had proven successful. We were serving an additional one hundred and twenty-five people, and that meant we had to increase the staff and everything that went along with it. Almost everyone's responsibilities grew, not just mine.

In late spring, right around the time Daddy Longchamp came with his family, we booked our first convention. It wasn't a very big one, but it made Mr. Dorfman very nervous nevertheless. It was the most dramatic change I had made at the hotel, because it was something Grandmother Cutler had fought doing for years and years. As Mr. Dorfman inspected and watched everything occur I could see the tension in his eyes. Every once in a while he would look behind his back, as if he expected Grandmother Cutler to come flying down a corridor and furiously chew him out for permitting such a thing.

But it proved successful, and Philip decided he would make conventions a major part of his responsibility. At our weekly meetings we were already talking about another expansion, this time building onto the ballroom so we could book larger and larger groups.

The only truly dark and depressing note in our lives these days came from Beulla Woods. Shortly after Clara Sue's death a dramatic change came over Mother. She began to keep more to herself. Her extravagant formal dinners diminished until she rarely held any, and she was hardly seen going anywhere with Bronson. There were physical changes in her as well. She stopped dyeing her hair and permitted the gray strands to appear. She ceased the multitudes of beauty treatments, the mud baths and facials, and the once-endless stream of beauty experts at Beulla Woods came to an end.

I was so busy these days that I didn't even notice how few times she phoned me and how long it had been since I had last seen her, but one day Bronson telephoned to beg me to visit and see if there was anything I could do to pull her out of the doldrums.

"She's back to being the emotional and psychological invalid she was when she lived at the hotel," he complained. "Some days I can't get her out of the bed, much less the room. And you wouldn't believe the weight she's gained."

"Mother? Gained weight?" Bronson was right: I couldn't believe she would have permitted herself to add an ounce. She had been terrified of having a double chin.

"She lies there and eats sweets all day," Bronson said. "She knows what's happening to her. A few days ago she asked the maid to put a sheet over the vanity-table mirror. She doesn't care to look at herself anymore.

"I know she went to extremes with these things before. I let her spend a fortune on new miracle products to stop aging, but I would much rather have her that way than the way she is now. For the past few days she's barely eaten. All she does is sleep and sleep. It's as if she wants to fade away," he added, his voice breaking.

"I'll be there tonight, Bronson," I promised.

"That's good. Actually, you're my last hope," he confessed. "She thinks so highly of you now. I bring home all the good news about the hotel and the children. I'm very proud of you myself," he concluded.

After I hung up I sat back and thought how ironic

482

it was that Mother depended on me. I couldn't find the hardness in my heart to refuse to help her. If the tragedies of my own life had taught me anything, it was to be more tolerant and sympathetic toward others. In one way or another we were all victims of a sort. Only Grandmother Cutler, whose spirit still haunted us somehow, remained unworthy of any sympathy, I thought.

When I arrived at Beulla Woods later in the day Mother was, as Bronson had described, cloistered in her room, lying listlessly in her great canopy bed. Seeing her without her makeup, unadorned by expensive jewelry, her face pale and her hair unbrushed left me speechless for a moment. It didn't seem to matter, for when I entered the suite she appeared to be in a daze herself, looking through me. Bronson, standing right beside me, whispered in my ear.

"She's worse than I told you," he confessed. "For the last few days she's barely uttered a word to anyone."

I stepped forward.

"Mother?" Her eyes blinked, and her head turned slowly toward me. I saw no note of recognition in her eyes. My heart began to flutter nervously. I looked at Bronson, who stared at her with concern.

"Laura Sue, it's Dawn. You asked about her, and here she is," he said.

Suddenly Mother laughed, but it was a strange, almost hideous peal of thin laughter. Then the mad and bizarre smile left her face, and she glared at me angrily.

"Who are you?" she demanded. "Another one of her nurses? Answer me. Who are you?"

"Oh, dear," Bronson said.

"Who am I? Mother, you don't know who I am?" I drew closer to the bed.

"*No!*" she cried, cringing. "Go away. Go away. It's not my fault. All of you," she said, turning to Bronson, too. "Leave me alone!" She began to wave her hand in the air as if she were chasing away flies.

"Laura Sue, what's come over you?" Bronson asked, rushing to her side. She seemed to shrivel up under the blanket, shaking her head, her eyes wide.

"I don't understand," Bronson said to me. "What's happening to her?"

"This hasn't happened before?" I asked.

"No. Up until now she's just been . . . withdrawn. Laura Sue, please," he cajoled.

She started to cry, grimacing like a child.

"I didn't mean it. It's not my fault, Daddy," she moaned.

"Daddy? Dear God, what's happening to her?" Bronson cried more frantically.

"Mother," I said, seizing her hand, "snap out of this. What's wrong with you?"

"They're all looking at me," she whispered, shifting her eyes to the side. "All of them, whenever I go downstairs. They know. They know it all. She told them; she's got them against me. She's spreading the lies, and they believe them." She grabbed my arm with her other hand and squeezed hard. "I want you to help me," she pleaded. "Make them understand it wasn't my fault."

"All right, Mother. I will," I said, deciding it was best to humor her.

"Good," she said, easing her grip. "Good." She turned toward Bronson. "Doctor, I need something stronger, something that will make me forget. Don't you have anything powerful enough? I can't sleep," she cried. "Every time I close my eyes I think it's going to happen again. And even if I do fall asleep, I wake up and hear his footsteps outside my door. I hear him breathing hard through the cracks. He's whispering my name, calling to me. I want another lock on the door," she demanded. "And no one is to come up here but the servants. No one, do you understand?" She turned to me, and I saw the fear in her eyes, the fear and the sadness, and I felt very sorry for her.

"She's reliving Old Man Cutler's attack on her," Bronson said.

"Mother," I said softly. "You're safe. No one will come into your room unless you want them to. I promise," I said.

She stared at me, and then her lips began to tremble more and more until she was crying again.

"One more time, please. Let me look at her one more time. I won't touch her," she said, seizing my arm. "I just want to look at her. I can say good-bye, can't I?"

She tilted her head and smiled.

"She won't know; she's too small to know. She won't remember, so it doesn't matter, does it? Please, one more time."

"She's talking about you, you know," Bronson said sadly.

"All right, Mother. All right. It's going to be all right."

She looked away, not at Bronson, not at me, but at something she saw in her own mind. Her eyes grew smaller, and she shook her head slowly.

"I'm saying good-bye again, aren't I? Another one's

been taken away from me. She had . . . such . . . golden . . . hair," Mother said, and she dropped back against the pillow, her eyes closing.

"Laura Sue," Bronson cried, taking her hand in his.

"I'm so tired," she muttered. "Just let me sleep a little while. And then I promise I'll get up and get dressed and look beautiful again." Her eyes popped open, and she smiled madly once more.

"I'll show her," she pledged. "I promise. I'll be beautiful. The more she hates me, the more beautiful I'll be. And while she grows older and older, I'll get younger and younger. Put out the lights, please," she said. "I need my beauty rest," she added, and she turned her head, her eyes tightly closed. In moments she was asleep.

Bronson looked at me, and I shook my head. I fixed the blankets around her. Bronson put out the light, and then the two of us left.

"I'm sorry," he said in the hallway, wiping his forehead with his handkerchief. "I didn't know it had gotten as bad as this."

"She needs treatment, Bronson. You might have to send her away."

"Oh, no," he said firmly. "Whatever she needs, it will be brought here. No one must know, either, except for the immediate family. She's going to get better," he said, his eyes small with determination. "She's going to recuperate and be the beautiful woman she once was. You'll see.

"This is only a temporary setback, an aftershock," he continued. "She's gone through a great deal of unhappiness in her life. Everyone thinks she's had it so soft, gotten everything she wanted, but we

486

know differently, don't we? It's understandable, this condition. Isn't it?"

"Yes, Bronson. I'm sure when you get her professional help she will begin to recuperate," I said, even though I wasn't as optimistic as he was. I saw he needed the encouragement.

"Right. And I'll get her the best doctors. You can be sure of that. I'll start right away. This very moment I'll go to the phone and make some calls. You'll come back often, won't you? And help?"

"Of course I will, Bronson."

"And bring the children. Always bring the children. Once she sees the sort of grandchildren she has, she won't be feeling so sorry for herself," he assured me, nodding his head for emphasis.

"Okay, Bronson, but first we'll have to explain things to them. They'll have to understand Grandmother's not feeling well," I said.

He bit down on his lower lip, the tears flowing freely from his eyes.

"We had a little bit of happiness together, at least," he said sadly.

"It will get better, Bronson. It will," I said more firmly. "You two have years and years of happiness ahead of you yet," I said.

"Yes, yes, of course we do," he replied, smiling again. He took a deep breath. "You wouldn't know how much she cared about you and Clara Sue. She was pulled by so many different forces. But at night recently I would wake up to find her screaming either your name or Clara Sue's.

"I guess," he concluded, "being a mother is not something a woman can ignore. She gives birth, and

487

her children are no longer inside her womb, but there's always a part of them inside her. She can try to deny it, but in the end she always hears her baby calling to her. Am I right?" he asked.

"Yes, Bronson. You couldn't be more right," I said, recalling how much I had longed for Christie after she had been taken from me.

We embraced each other, and then I took his hand and walked down with him to make his phone calls.

Early in the summer Bronson and the nurses managed to get Mother dressed and out so she would sit in the gazebo or on the patio. Some days were better than others. On those days she actually recognized us and enjoyed the children; on other days we were no different from complete strangers, or she saw us as people from her past. One of her nurses got her to do needlework, and that seemed to be the best therapy. She would sit for hours and hours working on a project and always seemed disappointed when it was finished.

Bronson never completely lost his optimism, but it waned considerably, and he began to accept the possibility that this was the way it would be forever. I felt very sorry for him and actually went up to Beulla Woods more for his sake than for Mother's, especially on her bad days, when she had no idea who I was or who he was. He had spent so much of his life caring for his invalid sister, and now he was burdened with another invalid of sorts.

It took its toll on him, too. He began to show his age, and that once-dapper look, that spring in his gait wilted. It was as if they had both tripped and fallen headlong into the autumn of their lives.

With the coming of a new summer resort season – one

promising to be bigger than any we had had before – we all became occupied with our duties. We still made time for Mother, but our visits had to be shorter and fewer. I thought nothing could take my attention away from my demanding work now. I was living and breathing the hotel.

One day, as I was rushing down a corridor to check on something in the kitchen, I caught a glimpse of myself in a wall mirror and stopped dead in my tracks. I backed up and gazed at my reflection.

It's no wonder Mother doesn't recognize me anymore, I thought. I barely recognized myself. Concern, worry and responsibility had deepened the lines in my forehead. I wore my hair brushed back more severely than ever, and I had taken to wearing cotton suits and blouses. Even though I was never one to wear a great deal of makeup, I did use lipstick and some eye shadow, but now I was going for long periods of time without a touch of color on my lips and eyes. This view of myself actually terrified me. It was as if Grandmother Cutler's spirit had begun to enter my body and change me.

But before I could think more about it, Fern came running to tell me there was a funny-talking man on the telephone demanding to speak to Lillian Cutler.

"Lillian Cutler? You know who that was. Did you tell him she's passed away?"

"Yes. I told him you were the boss now, too. Then he demanded to speak to you. He said you would know who he was for sure, for dang sure," she mimicked, and she grimaced.

"Dang sure? What's his name?"

"Luther somebody," she replied.

"Luther?" Luther, I thought. Luther, from The Meadows. But why was he calling?

I gazed once more at myself in the mirror and thought I saw the satisfied smirk of Grandmother Cutler coming back at me. Then I hurried off.

"It's Miss Emily," Luther said after I picked up the receiver, told him who I was and said hello.

"What about Miss Emily, Luther?" I asked.

"She's gone and died," he replied.

"Died?" I didn't think that cruel, hard woman was capable of dying. She was too mean and ugly for even death to touch her.

"Yep. I'm calling you from Nelson's General Store," he declared, as if that were the most important fact of all. Of course, I remembered they had no phone at The Meadows.

"What happened to her, Luther?" I asked.

"Her heart run out, I guess."

Heart? She didn't have a heart, I thought, just some chunk of meanness beating away under her breast.

"Charlotte come out to tell me Miss Emily didn't get up to make breakfast this morning, so I went up to her room and knocked on the door, but she didn't reply. I went in and found her sprawled on her back, her eyes and mouth wide open," Luther continued.

"Did you call a doctor?" I asked.

"Doctor? What for? She's dead as last Christmas. Ain't nothing a doctor gonna do for her now," he replied.

"You still have to call a doctor, Luther. She has to be declared legally dead, and you have to make arrangements for the burial," I said.

"No arrangements necessary. I'll dig a grave in

490

the family plot on the grounds and drop her in," he said.

"You can't do that without first calling a doctor, Luther," I stated, even though I didn't think that hateful woman deserved any better.

"I don't know where she kept her money for such things," he told me.

"Don't worry about money. I'll see to that. How's Charlotte?"

"She's all right. She's singing in the kitchen and making herself some eggs," he said, not hiding the joy in his voice.

I would have laughed, but I recalled the Spartan meals Miss Emily prescribed for all of us: that horrible oatmeal with the vinegar in it so we would taste bitterness and know hardship, that single apple for lunch, and those measured portions for dinner. Even the drinking water was rationed.

"But I guess you people got to come down here to see about things," he said.

"We people?" Yes, I thought. We do have to see about things, especially about poor Charlotte. "All right, Luther. We'll be there right away. But you call that doctor," I ordered.

"I'll do it, but it's good money thrown down a gopher hole," he remarked.

After I hung up I went to tell Jimmy and Philip. We decided that Jimmy and I would go to The Meadows. Philip wanted to remain at the hotel. He hadn't seen Aunt Emily or Aunt Charlotte for years and had little interest.

"Don't worry about Christie or Fern," Mrs. Boston told us. "I'll look after both of them and make sure

491

Miss America behaves herself or else," she promised, winking.

Jimmy and I smiled at each other. It was practically my only smile during this trip, for I couldn't help but recall the nightmare of my incarceration at The Meadows. Grandmother Cutler had sent me there to give birth to Christie in secret. Her sister Emily was a midwife, but more importantly, she was a religious fanatic who was determined to see me suffer for my sins.

I still had nightmares in which I saw her looking down at me with those steel-blue, icy eyes set in a narrow face. She had a pasty and sallow complexion with thin, colorless lips. She would hover over me like a bird of prey, hoisting her shoulders and spouting her threats of hell and damnation.

How could I ever forget that horrible little dark room she made me sleep in; the hard chores she forced me to perform; those weekly baths in water she had already used; and the overdose of laxatives she made me drink, trying to cause a miscarriage.

Grandmother Cutler must have known all this would happen when she sent me there, I thought. After all, she and Emily had conspired behind my back to give away Christie shortly after she was born. If it hadn't been for Jimmy's arriving to save me, I might have withered away there myself.

Now we were on our way back to that old plantation, which was a shadow of what it had once been. We made our travel arrangements as quickly as we could and set out, neither of us eager to make the trip. But I did feel sorry for Charlotte. She wasn't more than a little girl in mind and heart, yet she was a soft and gentle person who had been Emily's whipping post.

We rented a car at the airport when we arrived and drove out to Upland Station. I was surprised at how well I remembered the exact route. I guess that escape was implanted in my mind forever and ever. We bounced over the long and narrow cracked macadam road and turned down the dirt road where the property of The Meadows began, and once again the tips of the brick chimneys and the long, gabled roof of the great plantation house loomed over the treetops.

Nothing had changed. The marble fountains were still dry and broken, some leaning over precariously. The hedges were just as dead and scraggly, and the stone walks were still chipped and battered. In the dark shadows of the late afternoon sun the leafless vines that ran over the columns of the full-facade porch looked like rotting rope. After we got out and approached the porch I looked up at the roof that seemed to touch the clouds. The windows in the gabled dormers resembled dark eyes peering down angrily. This was still a cold, dark house.

Our footsteps echoed on the loose porch floor. We tried the brass knocker and waited. Moments later we heard the scurry of footsteps within, and then the door was thrust open and Charlotte gaped out at us, her blue eyes bright with curiosity. She wore her simple shift and her father's old slippers. Her gray hair was still tied in long braids. Aside from the fact that she looked even plumper, she seemed unchanged from when I had last seen her.

"Hello, Charlotte," I said. "Do you remember me?"

She nodded, but I didn't think she did.

"Emily's dead," she announced. "She's died and gone to heaven on a broom, Luther says."

"On a broom?" Jimmy asked. He smiled at me.

"I know what Luther's saying," I replied. "Has the doctor been here, Charlotte?"

She nodded.

"Where's Luther?" I asked.

"He's at the family plot digging a grave. He said it's the first time he's enjoyed digging," she added. Jimmy couldn't help but laugh.

"May we come in?" I asked her.

"Oh, yes. We can have mint tea."

"That will be fine," I said, stepping into what had been a house of horrors.

I couldn't help but shudder. The memories came rushing back the moment I entered that dark, dismal entryway and saw the oak chest, the hardwood benches too uncomfortable-looking to sit upon and the upholstered chairs that were great dust collectors. On the walls were portraits of ancestors – women with pinched faces dressed in dark clothes, their hair pinned back severely, and men, unsmiling and stern. There was no doubt Emily had been a descendant of these horrid people, I thought.

"Emily's still upstairs," Charlotte revealed. "She's still in her bed."

"Luther didn't call an undertaker?" I looked at Jimmy. He shrugged.

"I'll go upstairs and take a look," he said. We had decided on the way that I would spend most of my time going through papers and documents in what had been Emily's office.

"I'll go, too," Charlotte cried. "And then we'll have tea."

"Lead the way, please," Jimmy said. Charlotte shuffled toward the stairway. She still walked like a geisha girl, with her hands clasped to her body, her head down. Jimmy followed, and I went to the office.

The moment I entered, the grandfather clock in the corner bonged as if warning me to stay out. I lit the kerosene lamp on the desk quickly, and the flame threw a sheet of light up and over the giant picture of Mr. Booth. He looked as if he were frowning down at me. I found another kerosene lamp on a table and lit that one as well. In fact, I tried to light every kerosene lamp in sight, recalling how Emily had forced us to live in such darkness, hoarding the fuel and distributing it with a miserly hand.

I went behind the desk and began to sift through papers, most of which were common household bills.

"If you're lookin' for a will, you won't find one," Luther said, suddenly appearing in the doorway. The shadows on his face made him look leaner and older. As he approached I saw that he was otherwise unchanged. It was as if everything and everyone about this place were frozen in time, trapped forever and ever in one of my nightmares. The strands of his dirty brown hair were long and disheveled. As always, he needed a shave badly, his rough, gray-brown stubble growing in ugly patches over his otherwise pale white face.

He wiped his muddy hands on his overalls.

"She told me once that she had no will. She didn't care what happened after she passed," he explained.

"I see," I said, sitting back. "Then it will have to go

to probate. Didn't you call an undertaker to provide a coffin, Luther?" I asked.

"Got one made already," he said. Then, with his eyes small, he added, "I had it made and waiting in the barn a long time."

"Sit down, Luther," I said, nodding toward the leather chair by the desk. He looked at it as if it were some sort of trap. "Please, I want to talk to you. Neither of us has anything to fear from the other, especially now that Miss Emily's gone."

That pleased him, and he sat.

"If you hated her so much, why did you stay on and take her mean ways?" I asked.

"I told you once," he said. "This place was all I knew, all I had. She thought she owned it, but she didn't. She didn't know nothin' about it. You got to work a place to own it."

"She made you her slave because you made Charlotte pregnant a long time ago," I charged. "Isn't that so? She held it over your head." I remembered Charlotte telling me herself how Luther had done the "wigglies" on her, and how after that she had become pregnant.

"I got nothin' to be ashamed of," he said by way of an answer. He leaned forward. "Emily, she made out like she was God Almighty's personal messenger on earth. All the Booths except Mrs. Booth thought they were better than anyone else. Turned my pappy into a common slave and worked my momma into a hole, but I knew their sins," he added, smiling. "Even when I was just a little boy I knew, and besides, my momma, she told me everything that went on."

"What went on?" I asked. I was surprised he was so talkative now, but I assumed it was because the shadow of Emily Booth had been lifted from him.

"The old man, he was a good farmer, but he liked the ladies and imbibed often," he said.

"Imbibed?"

"Drank his good brandy like other people drank water," he explained. "Mrs. Booth, she was a nice lady; I always liked her. She was always kind to me, give me things whenever none of the others was lookin'. She was always sickly and weak. My momma used to say Mr. Booth drained Mrs. Booth like a rain barrel. Sucked her dry," he added.

"She got sick and died soon after she gave birth to Charlotte, right?" I asked, recalling the little about her I was able to learn when I was here.

He sat back, a strange self-satisfied smile on his face.

"She ain't never gave birth to Charlotte," he said. "Oh, she pretended she did, but my daddy and my momma, they knew the truth. Momma, she had to take care of her, you know, and," he added, leaning toward the desk, "see after Lillian."

"Lillian? Grandmother Cutler? What do you mean?" I asked. Jimmy appeared in the doorway but didn't come forward. He didn't want to interrupt.

"She's the one give birth to Charlotte," he said. "Lived in that little room, just like you did."

"Gave birth to Charlotte? You mean Charlotte wasn't really her and Emily's sister?" I asked. His smile widened.

"Oh, I guess you could say she was, sort of."

"I don't understand," I said, now turning to Jimmy, who had overheard it all. He started toward the desk.

"Her pappy," Luther began, and then he stopped.

"Fathered Charlotte?" I said, finishing the horrible sentence.

"It's what my momma told me," Luther said, and he looked up at Jimmy. "And my momma," he added, turning back to me, "she never told no lies about the rich people. Not never. They were the only ones who told lies about themselves.

"They made Mrs. Booth look and act pregnant to cover the shame, and then, after Charlotte was born, they treated her like some dumb animal," he said, showing anger for the first time. "She used to come to me to show me where they whipped her, and when they starved her, I would get her food," he added with vehemence.

And suddenly I realized that in his way Luther had loved Charlotte and probably still did.

But what a dreadful tale, I thought. This was truly a house of horror. Considering the age difference between Grandmother Cutler and Charlotte, I realized she couldn't have been much more than fourteen when this beastly thing had happened to her. I sat back, dazed. Jimmy and I gazed at each other, both thinking the same thing.

No wonder she had been the way she was.

Neither Jimmy nor I saw any reason to prolong Emily's burial. We knew no other people to inform, and from what I remembered and what Luther told us, she had no real friends. Luther gave me the name of the minister, and I had Jimmy drive me to Upland Station so I could phone him. His name was Carter, and he knew of Emily Booth. I explained our situation, and

498

he said he would come right out to perform a service at the grave site.

When we returned I told Luther the arrangements were complete. He hurried to bring the coffin upstairs and placed Emily's body within it. He pounded it shut, the clank of his hammer reverberating throughout the house as he hit the nails extra hard. Then he and Jimmy carried the coffin downstairs and put it on the back of Luther's truck.

I looked after Charlotte, now feeling sorrier for her than ever. She didn't have anything proper to keep her warm outside, and the sky was dismal gray. There were flurries, too, so I went into Miss Emily's room and found a dark blue wool coat. At first she was afraid to accept it.

"Everything that was Emily's is now yours, Charlotte," I explained. "She left it to you," I lied. Gingerly she took it from me and put it on.

Reverend Carter arrived with his wife, a small, birdlike woman. They were both dressed in black. His wife looked like a professional mourner. She never smiled, and her eyes were glassy and swollen, as if she had been crying for days.

Luther led us out to the family burial plot where the Booths lay side by side, going back as far as the beginning of the nineteenth century. When I looked at the fresh grave dug for Emily I thought Luther had gone far deeper than necessary. It was as if he wanted to be sure she would have pounds and pounds of dirt over her to keep her securely within.

As the minister read from the Bible Luther and Jimmy lowered the casket into the grave. I stood beside Charlotte and wondered if she really understood what was happening. She had a fine angelic smile on her lips.

The minister said a few words about Emily being happy now that she was where she deserved to be, and then we started away, leaving Luther to fill in the grave. He insisted he would do it all himself. When I turned back and saw how he shoveled the dirt, I thought he looked gleeful. He worked with a youthful vigor that seemed to straighten his back and rejuvenate him as he dropped the soil into the grave and heard it rumble onto Emily Booth's coffin. I was sure a lifetime of pain and suffering was being buried along with Emily.

I paid the minister something for his trouble, and then Jimmy and Charlotte and I did finally have that mint tea. Charlotte actually prepared it for us. As she moved about the kitchen I realized she was more capable than Emily had made her out to be. Free now of the chains and restrictions Emily had put on her, Charlotte seemed to take on more and more responsibility eagerly.

"Where do you want to go now, Charlotte?" I asked her.

"Go?" she said, looking up from her cup. She gazed around the kitchen. "No place. I gotta do some cleaning today," she said, "and work on my needlepoint."

"She does beautiful work," I told Jimmy. We heard the front door open and close.

"I put the marker up," Luther said, coming into the kitchen.

"What about a gravestone?" Jimmy asked.

"Almost got it done," Luther replied, sitting down at the table. "I've been working on it for years," he added. Jimmy flashed a smile at me.

"What do you want to do now, Luther?" I asked him.

"Do now?"

"Are you going to stay here?" I inquired.

"Until someone drags me off," he said. "Got no other place to go, and" – he turned toward Charlotte – "someone's got to look after Miss Charlotte."

I nodded, smiling.

"I think that would be very nice," I said. "When Jimmy and I return to Cutler's Cove I'll have our attorney see about the legal questions involving the property. No matter what happens, I don't see why you and Charlotte can't stay. That is, if you really think you can take care of her, Luther," I added.

He fixed those dark brown eyes on me hard, his face as serious as I had ever seen it.

"I've been taking care of her in one way or another ever since I can remember," he replied.

"I guess you have," I said.

"And here's your cup of mint tea," Charlotte said, placing it before him. Then she stepped back, her eyes glimmering with pride.

"Thank you, Charlotte," he said. She smiled down at him happily. Then she looked at me and clapped her hands together.

"I almost forgot," she said. "Tomorrow's my birthday."

I started to laugh, remembering how she would say that every day, but Luther looked up smiling.

"She's right," he said. "It really is!"

501

Epilogue

As Jimmy and I drove away from The Meadows that day I thought how right it was that the two people who were made to suffer most there could now live there happily. I had no doubt in my mind that in time some of the more dreary and dismal aspects of that sad house would be buried along with the memory of Miss Emily. The shadows she had kept stored in the deepest corners – shadows she had protected and fed with her insane insistence that the light be rationed – would surely follow her to the grave.

When we returned to Cutler's Cove I had a meeting with Mr. Updike concerning The Meadows, and he said he would see to it that Charlotte and Luther could live there for as long as they wanted. I told Philip about our trip, Emily's burial and what we had decided. He was glad not to have to have anything more to do with it.

"The one or two times I was there," he said, "I was terrified. Aunt Emily made me feel I was the devil's own."

In a way it was good for me to have attended Miss Emily's burial. Seeing Charlotte and Luther happy and knowing that the dour, evil woman was gone from their lives as well as my own put an end to my nightmares about The Meadows. Those days stopped haunting me.

I had much too much to do with my life now anyway. There was Christie's musical education to continue; there were things to do in our home and, of course, there was the hotel. Jimmy and I made plans to take our first vacation together after the summer. We decided to return to Cape Cod to finish our honeymoon.

It was the most romantic week of our marriage. We were able to pledge our love to each other again and again in dozens of little ways: Jimmy just touching my cheek and not saying anything, me resting my head against his shoulder as the sun went down, or the two of us waking up before dawn and rushing out to hold hands and walk on the beach as the sun rose.

When we returned to Cutler's Cove we discovered Bronson had made arrangements for all of us to have Thanksgiving at Beulla Woods. He thought it would do Mother inestimable good to be surrounded by family. We were all there: Philip and Betty Ann, the twins, Fern and Christie, Jimmy and me. Mother sat in bewilderment throughout most of the dinner, it seemed, but afterward, when Christie and I played a duet on the piano, I turned to see her smiling through tears.

At the end of the evening she permitted each of the children to kiss her good night. Bronson beamed. He hadn't looked as happy or as handsome in months.

"Thank you," he whispered in my ear when we embraced. "I think this was one of the happiest Thanksgivings I can recall."

I went to Mother and said my good night, hugging her and kissing her cheek. She seemed to hold on to me for dear life, and when I pulled away her eyes were wide but smiling.

"You've come back," she said.

"Yes, Mother. I've come back."

"Good, good." She appeared to want to hold onto my hand forever. Bronson stepped up beside her and put his arm around her shoulder.

"It's time they put the children to bed, Laura Sue," he said softly.

"Oh, yes. Good night. Good night, everyone," she called. The children ran out laughing, and we all left.

It snowed the next day, one of the heaviest snowfalls ever for Cutler's Cove at this time of the year, but everyone was happy about it because it made them all think of the impending Christmas holidays. There did seem to be a jingle in the air. Never were the seasonal decorations more colorful and wonderful to behold. In the afternoon the children went sleigh riding behind the hotel.

Just before I left the hotel to go home I received a phone call from Trisha.

"I wanted to wish you a happy holiday," she said. "I'm going on vacation with my family. I let Daddy talk me into it," she said, laughing.

She and I had spoken since Michael had come to Cutler's Cove, so she knew about it.

"I heard something about Michael," she told me toward the end of our conversation. "He's giving vocal lessons in Greenwich Village."

"I can't help but feel sorry for him," I said, "even though everything in me tells me not to, and even though Jimmy would be furious if he knew."

"He hasn't changed; he's still trying to have affairs with his prettier students."

I laughed.

"Nothing will change him; he's incorrigible. Have a

504

wonderful holiday, Trish, and call me when you return. I want to know all about your upcoming dance audition."

"I will. Are you all right? Is everything all right?" she asked with concern. "I hear a note in your voice."

"I'm just feeling a little sorry for myself these days."

"Oh, give up that hotel and go back to your singing," Trisha snapped.

"I might just do that one of these days. Wouldn't you be surprised?"

"Yes."

We laughed.

When I went home I sat by the piano and tinkered with notes until Jimmy arrived with Christie, both of them soaked to the skin from sleigh riding. I bawled them both out and sent them up to take hot baths.

Afterward, while I was drying Christie's hair, I felt a terrible wave of nausea come over me. It was so bad I had to sit down. It passed, but that night it woke me out of a deep sleep, and I had to go to the bathroom and vomit. I did it again in the morning, but I kept it from Jimmy. I knew how much it disturbed him when I got sick. When the feeling didn't leave me, I made a quick appointment with the doctor.

As always, though, Jimmy found out. The hotel had a hundred different sets of eyes and ears. It wasn't a good place to keep secrets, at least not for me. After my visit with the doctor I went right home. Jimmy found me in the sitting room at the piano again. Whenever anything happened to me I felt a need to retreat to music. When Jimmy came in I had my head down and my eyes closed.

I didn't even hear him enter, but I looked up when he touched my shoulder.

"What is it, honey? What's wrong?"

"James Gary Longchamp," I said.

"Yes?"

"You're going to be a father."

Jimmy's face exploded with happiness, and he hugged and kissed me, nearly squeezing me to death with excitement. I let him swing me about.

Through the window that faced the ocean I could see the sun slip in between two clouds. They grew farther and farther apart, permitting more and more of the sunlight to caress the ocean, turning the gray into a sparkling blue.

That night we held onto each other more closely and more dearly than ever, neither of us speaking for the longest time. I wondered if Jimmy was thinking about when we were both little, when we had been left alone and something had frightened us. We clung tightly to each other until Momma and Daddy finally arrived and made us feel safe again. Then, and only then, did Jimmy say good night to me, and I to him.

"Don't be afraid, Dawn," Jimmy finally whispered, drawing me out of my reverie. "Everything is going to be all right with the baby this time. You'll see. Be happy," he said.

"I'll try, Jimmy. And I won't be afraid, not as long as you're beside me."

" I always will be."

"Good night, Jimmy," I said, closing my eyes.

"Good night, Dawn."

I fell asleep, dreaming of our younger days. There was music; there was always music, and we were running over some beautiful green lawn, running toward the sun.